AF006021

The Ranger Gets His Girl

JANE POLLER

BOOKS

Vinci Books

vinci-books.com

Published by Vinci Books Ltd in 2026

1

Copyright © Jane Poller 2023

The author has asserted their moral right to be identified as the author of this work in accordance with the Copyright, Designs and Patents Act 1988. This work is a work of fiction. Names, characters, places and incidents are the product of the author's imagination or are used fictitiously. Any resemblance to actual persons, living or dead, places and incidents is entirely coincidental.
All rights reserved. No part of this publication may be copied, reproduced, distributed, stored in any retrieval system, or transmitted in any form or by any means, including photocopying, recording, or other electronic or mechanical methods, nor used as a source for any form of machine learning including AI datasets, without the prior written permission of the publisher.
The publisher and the author have made every effort to obtain permissions for any third party material used in this book and to comply with copyright law. Any queries in this respect should be brought to the attention of the publisher and any omissions will be corrected in future editions.
A CIP catalogue record for this book is available from the British Library.
Paperback ISBN: 9781036707989

By Jane Poller

Crimson Creek

The Soldier Gets His Girl
The Sheriff Gets His Girl
The Songwriter Gets His Girl
The Surgeon Gets His Girl
The Mechanic Gets His Girl
The Ranger Gets His Girl
The Cowboy Gets His Girl
The Convict Gets His Girl

Chapter One

September

Lucy stopped her little beat-up sedan in a cloud of dust and grabbed her garment bag and backpack. She rushed up the steps of the white church in Crimson Creek, continuing to the left hall and ignoring the crowd in the sanctuary. A closed door had deep voices on the other side, so she strode past. Instead, she made a beeline for the last door and pushed it open.

"Lucy, thank God! I thought you weren't going to make it," Nana Helen said as she smiled and held out her hands.

Lucy grabbed them, pulling her into a hug. "I know, I'm so sorry. My professor was late, and I had to take the final today to pass the class. I got here as fast as I could."

Helen turned back to the mirror where Katie continued putting the finishing touches to her makeup. They'd met at the planning meeting Helen had arranged last month right after Ray had proposed. They had it all planned so well they hadn't even needed a dress rehearsal last night.

She smiled at Nana's best friends, Vonda and Margarita. They wore the same peach colored gown and glowed as they chatted about their grandkids.

Lucy hung her garment bag on the back of the door and dropped her backpack, unzipping it as Vonda said, "You've got half an hour, Lucy. Think you can make it?"

Lucy nodded. "Yeah, I did my hair early this morning, so I just need to pin the curls back."

"Does your dress need to be steamed?" Margarita asked.

Lucy shook her head as she pulled it out of the bag. "I don't think so. I think it's fine. Thank you though."

The next few minutes flew by in a flurry of activity. Lucy chatted with Katie about the town. They'd run into each other a few times over the years. Although Lucy had moved to Denton in middle school with her parents, she'd spent all her summers here.

"I can't believe you're finally done. That's so exciting," Katie said.

Helen beamed. "I'm so proud of you, sweet pea. This has been a long time coming. And your mother, bless her heart... she'd be so proud of you too."

Lucy turned and waved to the back of her dress, her throat threatening to close. Katie zipped her up but didn't say anything. Some topics didn't need words.

Lucy pulled her heels out of her backpack and slipped them on. She grabbed some pins from the small table littered with hair accessories and makeup.

"Lucy, I know this isn't the right time to ask, but now that you're graduating—"

"Assuming I pass this class and finish my dissertation," Lucy said wryly.

Helen raised her brows. "Of course you will. You're my

clever little sweet pea. You've always been an excellent student."

Katie grabbed a pin and batted Lucy's hands away. "Once you graduate, what are your plans? I know you were doing nails in Denton to help pay for tuition. Are you going to stay there or move on home?"

Lucy met Helen's gaze in the mirror. "Did you put her up to this?"

Helen lifted her hands in an overly innocent gesture. "Me? Never."

Katie grinned. "So she put a bug in my ear. No big deal. I'm just saying, we need a nail tech at the salon. Our last girl moved away this summer with her new husband. You'd be the only one in town, so the demand is there."

Lucy smiled, her cheeks heating in a blush as she worked on her hair. "I could give it a try, sure. I was hoping to move back to town this semester anyway."

"I can get you set up as early as next week with appointments," Katie said.

Lucy's brows rose. "Wow, that's so soon!" Excitement rose, making her giddy. Bouncing on her toes, she clapped her hands. "Alright, let's do it! I'll have to talk to my roommate about moving out and find a place to stay, but I'm so excited now."

Katie laughed as she cleaned up the room from the hair supplies she'd brought. "Great, I'll text you, and we can work out the details. But for now…" and jerked her chin to Helen, who was wringing her hands, staring out the window unseeingly.

Lucy took her hands so she wouldn't mess up the nail job she'd done last weekend. "You sure you want to go through with this? I can still sneak you out the back, Nana."

Helen's far away gaze cleared as she smiled. "What? No,

it's just... the last time I was in this position was so long ago. It makes me think of your grandpa, that's all."

Lucy's eyes misted. "He's looking down with Mama right now. He's probably excited to see you finally so happy again, Nana."

"You don't think it's too soon?" she asked softly.

Lucy hugged her, the familiar scent of vanilla enveloping her. "You've been dating for months, Nana. Sure, it's not that long, but you've known him your whole life, right?"

Helen nodded and turned back to the mirror with a frown, fiddling with the lacy sleeves on her v-neck dress.

"But your aunts and uncle—"

"They can shove it," Lucy said, crossing her arms.

"Lucinda!"

"What? They can. If they can't feel happy for you, they shouldn't be here, so it doesn't matter that they're not."

Helen's face fell. Lucy's mom was gone, but she had two aunts and an uncle who could've been here for their mom. Well, one aunt was deployed, but the other two could be here if they'd only made the drive.

Lucy put her chin on Nana's shoulder and stared at her in the window's reflection. "Do you need them here to marry him? Or do you love him and are ready to be with him forever?"

Helen sighed. "Of course I'm ready, but between them and your grandpa, it's just—"

Vonda interrupted. "Helen, I swear to God, if you're pussyfooting around because you're comparing Ray to Jerry, let it go. They're like night and day."

Margarita nodded and stepped closer. "She's right, Helen. Jerry would want you to be happy, wouldn't he?"

Helen nodded, her eyes bright with tears. "I just wish the kids were happy for me too."

Vonda patted Helen's forearm. "Now, now, don't mess up the makeup."

A knock on the door interrupted them, and Vonda's granddaughter, Lola, opened the door. "Ready? The guys just went into the sanctuary."

Katie left with Lola to join the guests, and Vonda and Margarita followed to line up in the foyer. Lucy watched Helen, seeing her jaw firm and chin lift.

Lucy relaxed to see that excited, determined look cross Helen's face before she turned to the door and waved. "Well, let's get this show on the road."

Lucy chuckled and followed her nana down the hall to stand in line behind Margarita. Then Vonda was walking down the aisle with Margarita a few steps behind her. Lucy took a deep breath, pasted on a smile, notched her head up, and strode down the aisle to the beat of the soft music.

As the woman glided down the aisle, Mason's heart raced, and his palms grew clammy. The sheer sight of her beauty felt like a physical blow to his chest. Her long, flowing hair cascaded down her back in perfect curls, sparkling diamonds woven throughout catching the light and emitting a radiant glow. He stared at her delicate features—the curve of her jawline, the fullness of her lips, the sparkle in her eyes. She was like a goddess floating on air, and he couldn't believe she was real. Who was this woman and why had they never met before?

Her long-sleeved peach v-neck dress was the same as the much older ladies standing across the aisle from him. But on her, it clung to every curve. Those curves trapped his mind in possibilities. No, he couldn't go there. He refused to think of her like that.

He dove into his training, trying to cut off his emotions and make a professional assessment. She was average height, probably five-seven or five-eight. She was fit and toned, an athletic type, but with curves that made him salivate.

She had an elegant, swan-like throat that sparkled with the diamonds that caressed it. She was now close enough to see freckles dotting the bridge of her nose. Maybe she liked hiking or fishing. She had a body meant to be worshiped outdoors.

No, damn it, turn it off, Mason. Get it together.

She walked past the pews, smiling at each person on her right, but when she met his eyes, she stumbled a step before catching herself.

Her expression froze like a deer in the headlights. Then she stepped beside the other two bridesmaids and the music changed to the bridal march.

Mason blinked, and it seemed like the ceremony was over. He couldn't stop staring at the Maid of Honor and lost track of time.

Professionally speaking, she should've been average in every way. Brown hair and eyes, medium height, athletic build.

But there was something about her that pulled at him. She exuded this quiet energy that seemed to brighten the room. He kept waiting for her to hop away like a bird, the way she looked at him then away like she was hoping he didn't notice.

Music pulled him to the present and Helen and his grandpa, Ray, turned to face the now cheering crowd

The Ranger Gets His Girl

behind them. Ray tucked Helen's hand into the crook of his arm and beamed down at her. She smiled, her cheeks flushed, as they began to walk down the aisle as husband and wife.

Mason cleared his throat and offered his elbow to the peach vision. Her cheeks flushed too as she briefly met his eyes then looked away.

Hesitantly, she took his arm. His stomach flipped, and he felt like he'd won the lottery. He dragged his eyes off her and stared after his grandpa. Together, they walked down the aisle and followed them to the foyer.

The girl let go of his arm and hugged Helen. "It was beautiful. I'm so happy for you, Nana. Congratulations."

Nana? Oh. *Oh.* Of course, she was Helen's granddaughter. He'd seen pictures in Helen's house when he'd gone for dinner a few weeks ago. They didn't do her justice at all and must've been several years old.

In person, she was a vision. A vision that he couldn't afford to get involved with. He shook his grandpa's hand and slapped him on the back.

"Congrats, Pops."

Ray just nodded, a big grin on his face as he turned back to his bride. The girl stayed beside Helen, so he fell into line beside her. She skittered around him like a little bird, careful not to venture too far from mama bird. Or in this case, grandma bird.

The receiving line would funnel the crowd into the fellowship hall. The rest of the bridesmaids and groomsmen joined them, and the entire town stopped by to shake hands on their way to the reception.

The entire time they were taking pictures, he tried to ignore her. But the nature of being Best Man meant he stood beside her most of the time. She smelled like oranges, and more than once, he breathed deeply just to capture it.

When they finally approached the main table at the reception, he pulled out her chair. He half expected her to dance and flit away from him, but she sat. She barely glanced at him through her long lashes, but he took another breath and tried to distance himself.

He sat beside her as the food was served. Avoiding eye contact during the surrounding conversations made it awkward.

He turned to her and held out his hand as a server placed their plates on the table. "I'm Mason, Ray's grandson. You're Helen's granddaughter?"

She wiped her hands on her dress and pasted an overly bright smile on her face. Finally, she looked him in the eye. "Yes, I'm Lucy. It's nice to finally meet you."

"You too," he said, enveloping her long fingers in his big hand. He felt like a bear pawing at an orange. She was a delicious delicacy, and he was a big oaf.

"I guess we're family now, huh?" he asked, cutting into his chicken. She fiddled with her fork and squirmed on the chair, then nodded.

"I guess you can call me your stepcousin?"

She laughed and nodded, the sound enchanting him. "I've never had a stepcousin before. I have a few cousins on Nana's side, but I haven't seen any of them in years."

The sadness on her face made his chest ache, and he changed the subject to try to cheer her up. "I guess you have nice, quiet holidays with her then?"

Lucy nodded, but didn't say anything, so he continued. "We don't usually get together for Thanksgiving, but we do a little small get together for Christmas. Not sure that my brother will be here this year, but what kind of Christmas present would you like?"

She glanced at him through her lashes, "Oh I couldn't possibly think of anything right now. I have everything I need."

She bit into her chicken and shook her head as she chewed. She still seemed reserved and lost in her own thoughts as she looked at the newlyweds, almost sad still.

He angled his body closer to hers. "Oh, come on. You have to have something you want. Every girl I know has a list a mile long."

She shrugged. "Sure, I have a list, but I don't even know you, and if you get me something, I'll have to get you something, and it'll turn into this big thing. How do you and Ray normally do Christmas?"

He took a drink before answering. "We normally go to dinner either before or after Christmas. I'm usually working, so I'm not guaranteed holidays, but since I'm working Thanksgiving, I should have Christmas off."

"What do you do?" The fork slid into her mouth with a grace that held him captivated before her words penetrated his brain.

"I'm a Texas Ranger." He frowned, not sure how much longer that statement would be true. "What about you?"

She took another bite, and he waited for her to chew. "I'll be graduating college in December, but I work at a nail salon in Denton and teach yoga a few times a week. I might be moving to Crimson Creek soon though."

The excitement and joy on her face made him relax, and he stopped paying attention to his words. "Ah, that makes sense. I thought you were the athletic type," he said.

She frowned and her body tensed. "What's that supposed to mean?"

He froze, fork halfway to his mouth. Shit, what had he said? "Uh, you've got muscle definition. Not a lot of women do, that's all."

She leaned forward, her frown growing deeper. "What are you trying to say? That I'm not feminine enough?"

He frowned and turned his head to face her, feeling the collar on his button-down shirt grow tighter. "What? No, not at all."

"Uh huh, sure." She stabbed her chicken with the knife and cut it so hard the knife screeched on the plate.

He winced. This was why he needed to stay away from women and relationships. He could never say the right thing, and it always ended in disaster. He shifted on the chair and rubbed his back, trying to ease the constant pain that radiated down his leg.

"I'm sorry, but that's not what I meant. You've got curves in all the right places, trust me." He felt his ears burning. Damn it, he needed to shut up already.

She shifted on her chair uncomfortably, but before he could open his mouth and shove another foot in it, his grandpa stood and tapped the knife against his glass.

The crowd hushed. "I'm not one for speeches, but I appreciate everyone comin' out today to celebrate with us. This is one of the happiest days of my life. I didn't think I'd have a second chance at love, but here we are. To Helen. May God give her patience in the years to come."

The crowd both chuckled and cheered to Helen. Then the speeches were on. A flurry of activity and a flow of wine led to more laughter. He didn't have a chance to talk to Lucy again.

Dancing was impossible because of the small fellowship hall, but everyone was elated to shower the couple with flowers at the end of the night. They drove away with coke cans tied to the tailgate of Pop's old truck.

He lost sight of Lucy as the crowd dispersed. So he told his few friends goodbye and hopped in his own truck. He wasn't too drunk to require a designated driver, and Pop's house was just a few blocks away.

A beat-up car was already parked when he arrived. He frowned, seeing movement in the lit bedroom upstairs. He pulled out his phone and checked his app, verifying that Pops wasn't home. He was at Helen's house before heading to their honeymoon in Colorado.

He got out of his truck, careful not to slam the door closed, and grabbed his duffel bag. He checked the doors of the car and found them locked. He looked inside but it was spotless other than a backpack.

He frowned. If it was some teenager hoping that the wedding would lead to an easy score in the house... Mason sighed and pulled his gun out of his back holster, then he walked up the steps on silent feet and unlocked the door.

Chapter Two

Lucy stepped out of the shower and wrapped the towel around her body. The headache from the wine led her to the medicine cabinet, where she found some pain pills. She needed water though, so she opened the bathroom door.

Click. "Freeze, you're under arrest."

A gun was pointed at her head, and she shrieked. She threw the closed bottle of pain pills and fell to the ground, covering her head and curling into a ball.

"Lucy?"

She looked up at the behemoth and lowered her hands. "Mason?"

He lowered the gun to his side, and his brows rose as his gaze swept over her. "Uh," he stammered.

She looked down and gasped, quickly grabbing her towel and readjusting it. "What are you doing? Get out!"

He nodded, still staring, so she slammed the door with her foot. Her heart was hammering in her chest. Oh God, what had he seen? It's just her luck that the first guy to see her naked had been an accident.

"Lucy? Are you alright?" he called through the closed door.

She struggled to her feet and adjusted the towel, tucking the end into itself. She looked in the mirror and took a deep breath. Her hair hung wet and tangled around her pink face scrubbed almost clean of makeup. There was a zit on her chin and mascara leftovers smudged under her eyes.

"Lucy?"

She winced, tightening the towel as her heart still raced. "Yes, I'm fine. What are you doing here?"

"What am I doing here? This is my grandpa's house, remember? What are you doing here?"

Glancing around, she gathered her dress and underwear from the floor. "I had too much wine, so Ray offered his house for the night. They didn't say you'd be here too." She put on the dress, but damp skin made it cling to her. She reached behind her to struggle with the zipper.

"Yeah, well, they didn't tell me you'd be here either, but it's too late to drive back to Waco tonight. Look, are you sure you're okay?"

Her stomach flipped but she knew she had to face him. She couldn't stay in the bathroom all night or keep struggling with her dress. She wasn't a coward. She took a deep breath, held the towel and her underwear in front of her like a shield, and threw the door open.

He stood where she'd left him, but the gun was put away somewhere. His suit jacket was gone, and his white button-down shirt was rolled up at the sleeves with a gun harness over both shoulders. Arms crossed, his shirt looked ready to burst at the seams.

Standing face to face, he dwarfed her and filled the doorway. There was something about the way he looked at her so intently, the way she could feel his presence soaking into her soul that made her mouth salivate.

His black hair was cut short on the sides, gray at the temples matching the five o'clock shadow giving him a sexy man of the world vibe. His hair looked almost long enough on top to run her fingers through, and the silkiness called to her, making her hands itch to test the texture.

She held her hands tightly to the towel and watched him warily. "See? I'm fine. Now if you'll excuse me, I'd like to get more comfortable clothes now."

He stepped back and waved a hand. She bolted down the hall and to the door at the top of the stairs, slamming it behind her. She breathed a sigh of relief as her phone dinged.

She pulled her leggings and yoga tunic on then checked her phone to see a message from her former college roommate.

Are you coming back to Denton tonight?

No, I'm staying in town, apparently with my new stepcousin. (eyes wide open emoji)

What does that mean?

Ray's grandson.

You're babysitting?

No. (laughing emoji)
He's gotta be in his thirties or forties.

Oh, is he cute? Send pics.

Lucy gave a thumbs-up emoji and wanted to text Helen too but refused to intrude on her wedding night. She would just have to face Mason herself. Surely, they could share the house for the night without further incident.

She went through her memories to catalog what she knew of him. He was a Texas Ranger. Ray had two grandsons as his only family, and Mason was one of them. That was really all she knew.

She opened the door and ventured downstairs. He leaned against the counter with a glass of water in one hand, his biceps bulging, pulling his dress shirt tight.

Blue eyes captured hers as he watched her come to a stop and sit at the kitchen table.

He cleared his throat. "Sorry about earlier. I thought you were an intruder. If I'd known you were staying here tonight—"

She waved a hand and tried to relax in the chair. "Don't worry about it. Neither of us knew, so there's no use crying over spilled milk."

"Or spilled bottle of aspirin." He smirked, setting the pill bottle on the table along with a fresh glass of water. The tilt of his lips made her want to kiss him.

"Thanks," she said softly, looking away as she took the medicine. She'd never had this sort of reaction to someone this quickly before. Sure, she'd had crushes here and there over the years, but nothing this immediate or intense.

It made her stomach flip. She raised her phone and propped her elbows on the table, pretending to type as he rinsed out his glass in the sink. Then she took a picture and sent it to Taylor.

"You're welcome." He turned and leaned against the counter, staring at her with that intense gaze that sent shivers down her spine.

She smiled and tucked a wet strand of hair behind her ear. "Right, so I need to be up early tomorrow for a yoga class in Denton. I'll see you at Christmas?" She hopped up and avoided eye contact as she darted for the door.

"You never said what you wanted for Christmas," he said.

She put a hand on the door frame that separated the kitchen from the living room and stairs. His blue eyes swirled with emotions she couldn't read.

"We might be family, but there's no telling what Nana and Ray have planned for Christmas. Don't worry about me. It was nice to finally meet you, Mason."

And with that, she darted up the stairs and shut the bedroom door behind her. It was going to take a long time to go to sleep tonight. He was going to be right across the hall.

Her phone buzzed.

(wide-eyed emoji) Fuck, you need to go play the slots. You hit the jackpot with him.

He pulled a gun on me, Tay.
Thought I was an intruder.

A gun? WTF did he have a gun?? Are you safe??

Yeah, he's a TX Ranger.

(laughing emoji, wide-eyed emoji) That's the most action you've ever gotten.

Shut up.

You gonna hit that?

Hell no. I'd never!

Chicken.

If she were a bolder woman, she'd march down there and proposition him. If she were Taylor, she would've already seduced him by now. While Lucy had learned a lot from their friendship, she wouldn't ever have the courage to just ask a guy for a casual encounter.

No, she was more of a long-term relationship type of person. She'd had the same boyfriend for a year in high school, but that was the most she'd ever let herself connect. It had been a nightmare by the end. Then there was all that with her mom.

Her mind turned to the past and threatened to tug her under the tumultuous memories.

December

"Welcome back, Nana! How was your trip?" Lucy asked as she slid into the booth across from Helen and Ray. They both practically glowed with this settled, content look on their faces.

"It was great. I'm glad we timed it right for your graduation."

Lucy nodded, her leg bouncing under the table. "Me too. I know it'll probably be my last graduation, and it means a lot that you're here. Both of you," she said, nodding to Ray.

Ray grinned, his bushy white eyebrows shifting as his face widened. "Wouldn't miss it for the world, kiddo. Neither of the boys went to college, so this will be a real treat for me."

The server came and took their brunch order. Graduation was a couple of hours away, so they had time for the couple to tell her all about their adventures in Colorado. They'd loved their honeymoon so much they'd gone back for some of the Christmas markets.

"We were afraid we might not make it back, with that snowstorm that popped up," Ray said as he bit into his biscuit.

When the meal was over, Helen pulled an envelope out of her purse and slid it over the table.

"What's this?" Lucy asked as she opened it. Her eyes scanned the letter and ticket. "Oh my God, are you serious?"

Helen and Ray both beamed, but Helen leaned forward, her eyes shining. "Yes, absolutely. We won it on the cruise that brought us together this spring, and who better to use it than you? Consider it a graduation present, sweet pea."

She looked at the dates on the ticket. "This is—I mean, I don't know what to say."

"Say you'll go," Helen said softly, her eyes shining. "You deserve a break. You've worked so hard going straight from high school to college and to now get your master's. It's time to relax before starting the next chapter of your life."

Lucy felt her throat close up and tears threaten. "Thank you," she said, afraid to say anymore. She didn't get a lot of gifts but to get one as big as this was once-in-a-lifetime.

Ray rubbed the back of his neck uncomfortably. "Yes,

well, that's not the end of it either. You know how you've been staying at my house since the wedding?"

Lucy nodded, "Since I started working for Katie in town, it's been much easier than driving back to Denton every day. I appreciate it so much. Have you finally decided to sell the house?"

He grinned and shook his head. "Not quite. If you want to move out to Crimson Creek permanently, the house is yours for however long you want it."

Lucy's brows rose as she glanced from him to Helen and back again. "Are you serious?"

Helen laughed, "I hope you're more eloquent in that book you're writing."

Lucy's cheeks heated as she nodded. After all her hard work, her life was finally coming together.

Ray fiddled with his drink, so Helen patted his leg and said, "You don't have to pay rent, but you'll need to cover the utilities and cable or anything else you need. Please say yes. Having you back in Crimson Creek this semester has been… more important to me than I thought it'd be. If you move into the house, it'll make me feel like it's more of a permanent thing."

Lucy's eyes stung as she held her hand out over the table. The past semester, she'd been commuting to Denton for classes, having only needed one more in-person class to go along with her dissertation. She'd quickly gotten the job with Katie at the salon and had just in the past few weeks started teaching more yoga at the yoga studio under Holly.

Now that she was graduating, she'd have more time to spend writing her novel, something she'd always talked with Helen about. Since she'd been a child and had hung out at the library after school while her grandma worked the front desk, she'd been determined to publish her own books. It was a dream that Helen had whole-heartedly supported for years.

She squeezed Helen's hand. "I don't know what to say. I think I need to talk to Taylor first about the living arrangements."

"Holly will be looking for you to take over more classes, what with her being pregnant with the twins," Helen said, her face brightening with a grin.

Lucy nodded as the server came to cash out their meal. Ray insisted on treating them in honor of her graduation.

Thankfully, the graduation ceremony was indoors because there was a frigid chill to the wind that afternoon. When all was said and done, Lucy agreed to their Christmas plans for the following weekend before kissing them both goodbye.

When they were gone, Taylor dragged her out for a late-night post-graduation party on campus. They arrived at a house on the seedier side of town and tipped their driver.

"Two drinks, Tay. That's it. It's too cold to be out all night," Lucy said, flipping the hood of her jacket up.

"Oh, come on. Don't be a spoilsport. This is your last hurrah, Luce. Live a little before you grow up and adult for real." Taylor practically skipped up the porch steps and opened the door.

Loud music assailed them, but several people turned to see who was here.

"Hooray! Taylor's here," two guys said, clinking their beers together with a grin. Taylor threw her jacket off, revealing a too short skirt and a sweater with a v-neck cut down almost to her belly button.

"That's right, bitches. I have arrived," she waltzed into the crowd with a laugh, leaving Lucy to pick up her coat and shut the door. She looked around while she laid both jackets on a dining table immediately to the left of the door.

To the right was a large living room with two couches and a loveseat. A few couples were already making out where they sat. Behind one couch in the corner was a DJ with some complicated speaker system.

Lucy snorted to see the DJ wearing sunglasses inside. At night.

She'd lost count of how many parties Taylor had dragged her to over the past six years. Inevitably, she found herself in the kitchen pouring drinks. It was easier to be the drink girl and take care of everyone else than actually interact with people.

She didn't mind people. It was good book research to come to places like this and observe the human condition. It was fascinating to see. Sometimes she would make bets with herself on which person would slap someone first.

The longer she'd been in college with Taylor, the better she'd gotten at her game. She smiled and handed over a drink to a girl who was already swaying. Another guy walked up for a drink.

She set the vodka down and glanced up, a smile on her face. "What can I—oh. Oh no."

Her smile froze on her face. It was Mason, but not the Mason she'd met a few months ago. Instead of a neatly tailored suit, he now wore hipster jeans, pristine black shoes, and a black silky polo golf shirt. Her heart skipped a beat as he crossed his arms. Holy hell, those biceps were going to be the death of her.

His brow lifted in challenge. "Oh no indeed. What do we have here? Does your grandma know you're at a place like this?"

She frowned and shook her head. "No, does your grandpa?"

There was a shout behind them, then someone started yelling, "Dance, girl, dance!"

Mason looked back at the crowd and frowned.

Lucy narrowed her eyes. "You've dyed your hair. Trying to reclaim your youth, old man?"

Disappointment shot through her like an arrow. She'd thought he was older, a real adult. Real adults didn't go to frat parties looking for young college girls to hook up with. She'd misjudged him.

She thought she'd gotten better at identifying dirt bags, but apparently not.

His head spun to face her at her words, and his eyes narrowed. Some guy bumped into him and grabbed the tequila bottle. "Hey, watch it," the guy slurred as he poured the drink mostly into his solo cup.

Mason rolled his eyes and stepped around the island toward Lucy. She backed up, but he neatly boxed her into the corner with one hand on either side of the counter. He leaned in, the manly scent of him overwhelming her with his nearness. Her hands fluttered to his biceps. She was ready to push him away but was conflicted. Her body said bring him closer, but her head said run.

Their bodies were close, and she could smell his aftershave. Something musky, woodsy. It made her brain stop resisting, and she leaned into him.

"Don't move, little bird. Yes, I dyed my hair. Yes, I'm thirty-five and at a frat party, but it's not what you think. I'm here in a professional capacity, and I need you to not blow my cover, got it?"

She sucked in a breath, making her chest graze his.

Just then, Taylor came bounding up behind him. Her

eyes widened when they met Lucy's over Mason's shoulder. "Oh, thank God, I was thinking no one was going to pop that cherry. Do you need a condom? I've got a few in my bra."

She started to dig inside, but Lucy was afraid her boob would come out. "No, no, it's not like that."

"It might be like that," Mason growled into her ear. "Just play along."

He kissed the side of her neck, making her shiver and her eyes flutter. Holy mother of pearl. Mason was one hot mother fucker. She blushed as she heard her grandmother reprimanding her in her head for that language.

Taylor grinned. "Right," she drawled out. "I'll just leave this on the table, shall I? We really need to invest in a bowl of free condoms or something at these parties."

Lucy couldn't catch her breath with Mason so close. She squeezed his biceps as panic set in, but he pulled back and turned to smile at Taylor. "That's a good idea," he nodded his head.

Lucy could practically see Taylor swoon as she got a good look at him, and it was too early for her to be drunk. She snorted and poured another drink. This time, she chugged it herself.

Taylor hooted. "Hell yeah, now it's a party! Ready to dance, Luce? Lover boy here can drag you upstairs when we're done."

Lucy didn't have time to argue. Taylor grabbed her hand and dragged her into the other room. She looked over her shoulder in time to see Mason slide the condom off the table and into his pocket.

Chapter Three

Mason nursed his beer and followed the girls, nodding to Simon as they switched positions. He leaned against the wall by the stairs. While Simon covered the back door and kitchen area, he had the best view of those going up and down, the front door, and the living room crowd.

He was here to do a job, yet despite himself, his eyes kept straying to Lucy. She'd been pretty stiff when the dancing had started, but then she'd loosened up when that drink hit her system. How old was she? He frowned, shaking off the itch that came whenever he thought of someone breaking the law.

He knew she'd graduated today. His grandpa had invited him to the ceremony, since he'd texted he was in Fort Worth this week, but he was here to work.

The way she moved reminded him again of a beautiful bird flitting here and there, strong but delicate. He wanted to see her soar and ride his dick with those tits bouncing. Damn it, it'd been too long since he'd been with a woman.

She wasn't just some woman though. She was his stepcousin. Family, now, and off-limits.

He took another swig of his beer, and his smart watch vibrated, and he glanced down.

Incoming.

The message from Simon brought him out of his reverie. His senses heightened as he glanced around. He took a swig of his beer and tried his best to throw off a casual, don't give a fuck attitude.

A guy in slacks and an un-tucked oversized button-down shirt came through the kitchen door. He had a goofy grin on his face, but his clean-cut hair and demeanor screamed spoiled rich boy slumming it.

Mason watched with disgust as three scruffy men sauntered into the room behind their leader. Each one had a different girl on their arm, all of them too skinny and wearing revealing clothes. The girls laughed and flirted with the guys, leaning into their crude advances. Mason clenched his jaw, trying to contain his anger at the scene unfolding before him. How could those girls possibly enjoy being pawed at by these deadbeat losers?

Images of his ex flew through his mind, of her making that same damn giggle, of placing her hand on his chest just like they were doing. Bile rose in his throat, but he choked it down with another swig of his beer.

The ringleader circled the room, talking to nearly every person there. He stopped at Lucy and her dark-haired friend, his smile widening. Lucy seemed to stiffen even as she smiled and chatted. Her friend threw her arms around his neck, and he could hear her even over the noise of the music.

"Kevin, I didn't know you'd be here."

He grinned and slid his hands down her ass to squeeze. "Heard you were here, love. Where else would I go?"

Lucy's friend laughed and kissed him on the cheek. "Later. I'm celebrating my friend tonight."

He wiggled his eyebrows. "You know where to find me." He smacked her on the ass as he walked past to talk to the next person. Somehow, Mason wasn't able to catch any other conversations.

Eventually the man child approached him. Mason tipped his head up in the universal nod of hello, and the guy put his hands in his pockets and returned the nod. "Hey man, haven't seen you around before. Welcome."

Mason arched a brow and shrugged. "Heard this was the place to be after graduation, so here I am."

"Congrats on the grad, man. Enjoy yourself. Don't drink and drive, wrap it before you tap it, and all that shit."

His cronies laughed as the man grinned and turned to go upstairs, the others trailing after them. Mason drained his beer and walked back to the kitchen for another. He tossed the empty one in the trash and pulled out his phone to send a message.

Upstairs.

He opened the new beer and shot the cap into the trash like a basketball. A few other guys ribbed him for it, but he grinned and challenged at least two of them. His watch vibrated, and he looked down as the other two chugged and started a basketball competition.

Follow.

Mason nodded to a few of the other party goers as he exited the kitchen and walked casually through the living room to the stairs. He began to walk past the dancers, his eyes immediately finding Lucy as she shook her hips.

The red dress hugged every curve and flared at the hips, and when she shook, he could almost see her ass. He swallowed hard and pushed down the conflicted feelings. He didn't want to leave her down here, defenseless against the drunk boys who were obviously eying the girls dancing.

But he had a job to do, so he pushed past Lucy and her friend to get to the stairs. Suddenly, her friend swayed and knocked Lucy into him. His arms immediately went around her, and she spun in his arms with a gasp.

She looked up at him, her hands raised to his chest to push him away. Her plump lips were open and ruby red, ripe for the plucking. A ringing pulsed in his ears, drowning out everything around them and setting off alarm bells in his head.

"Mason," she breathed. The music changed to something more suitable to slow dancing, and someone pressed her into him. He didn't look up to see who, nor did he look up to see who took his beer from his hand.

He didn't care. His hands were now on her hips as they swayed closer and closer together. She was tall enough that he wouldn't need to bend his neck too much to kiss her.

She licked her lips, and her cheeks blushed. He soaked in the moment, the feel of her in his arms, the way she swayed against him, her curves molding to the rigid length of his body.

When his raging hard-on nestled in the v of her legs, she gasped at the feel of it and turned her head to the side, refusing to meet his eyes. Less than a minute had passed, but he still had a job to do. An idea blossomed fully developed, but it was probably a bad one. Still, he couldn't think of any other option with her in his arms.

Mason growled into her ear, "Sorry, I can't control it, but I need to go upstairs in search of a suspect. It might be more believable if you go with me…"

She tilted her head up as she whispered back. "You sure this isn't a ploy?"

Her hazel eyes, heavy with desire under those thick lashes, locked onto his and sent an electric current through his body. The heat radiated off of her as his arms tightened around her.

Mason smiled, his nature getting the better of him as he played with fire. "Little bird, when I ask you to my bed, you'll know it. Trust me."

She gasped, *"When?"*

A wave of possessiveness swept over him, and he kissed the side of her neck, unable to deny the truth of what he wanted. "Yes. When."

He felt her drag in a ragged breath that pressed her breasts into his chest. His dick leaped at the contact, more excited by her than it had a right to be.

"The—the suspect. Is he dangerous?"

He shook his head gently, trying to get back into the game and away from the distraction. "I'd never put you in danger, little bird."

She chuckled in his ear, and his eyes closed as he enjoyed the sound. "I think everything about you screams danger, Mason, but if you need my help, I'm probably the best candidate here."

He kissed her neck again. She smelled like oranges, but it didn't make sense why she tasted like it too. She was addicting, and while he wanted to turn this into something more, he knew it was a terrible idea. He couldn't afford to get close to anyone again. Not now, not ever.

The dose of reality washed over him like a bucket of cold water, and he pulled away slightly. "Come on. Just follow me and act like you're excited for us to find a room together, okay?"

She nodded imperceptibly, so he grabbed her hand and led her to the stairs. Her friend hooted on the dance floor, "Get it, girl! Finally!"

Mason refused to think about what those comments meant. His brain zeroed in on the assignment as he led her up the stairs.

The hallway was lined with doors, but his eyes were drawn to the one at the end. A burly man stood on one side of it, his arms crossed and expression stern. Across from him, the two cronies from earlier were locked in passionate embraces, oblivious to the world around them. Meanwhile, a couple and two men fidgeted impatiently in front of the closed door, waiting for their turn to enter.

Mason assessed the other doors and found two without socks on the knobs. He opened the closest free one and stepped inside, pulling Lucy behind him before almost shutting the door. He peered through the crack at the end of the hall as he pulled his phone out.

Room at the end of the hall.

He slid his phone into his back pocket as a creaking sound echoed through the room over the sound of the music below. He glanced back to see Lucy sitting on the edge of the bed, picking at the hem of her dress.

His watch buzzed.

Confirm the room before you move in.
Standing by.

He sighed and watched as the door at the end of the hall opened. A man just inside handed over a snack baggie of powder then took a wad of cash. The group turned and left, so Mason shut the door softly before they noticed.

He sent another message with the details of the group now carrying illegal substances downstairs, then turned to face Lucy. The dim interior was lit up by the streetlight outside. He knelt by the bed and boxed her knees in with a hand on either side of the bed.

"I'm going to stumble into the hallway and try to get the guys at the end to let me into the room. Stay in here, okay? You'll be safe here."

She looked at him but with the way the light was outside, he couldn't see her face. He saw her nod, so he stood and stepped away. She grabbed his hand, and he glanced down.

"Be careful," she whispered.

He caressed her cheek. "Are you worried about me, little bird?"

She snorted and leaned out of his touch, so he dropped his hand. "Ray would have my head if anything happened to you."

He grinned. "Noted." Then he turned back to the door, un-tucking his shirt as he went. With a yank, he pulled his boots off, then his socks, keeping one for the door.

He messed his hair up so it'd look like she'd run her fingers through it. He wished she had. He could almost feel her long fingers raking along his scalp.

Yep, that did it. His hard-on was now back, so he unbuttoned the top button of his jeans and threw the door open. Now it was show time.

Chapter Four

He stumbled out and slammed the door behind him, wrapping the sock around it.

With wide eyes, he swayed on his feet, then seemed to realize the guys at the end of the hall were there. One was watching him over his girl's head as she sucked on his ear.

He held one hand on the wall as he went closer to them. In a stage whisper, he asked, "Hey, do y'all have any condoms?"

The one who'd been watching him snorted. "Dude, why aren't you prepared?"

Mason shrugged and adjusted his dick, a pained look on his face. "I wasn't expecting to hook up. I just came for the vibe, man."

The guy sighed and rapped four times on the door. It swung open to reveal the other crony, who demanded, "What now?"

Mason shifted from foot to foot as if he was excited and wanted to jump back into his room. He looked over his shoulder for good measure and leaned forward. "I got a girl down the hall. Y'all got any extra condoms?"

The guy scowled and turned back into the room, leaving the door just barely open. Mason practically bounced back and forth as he took in the scene. A girl on the bed was making out with another girl, while the head honcho was sitting in the corner smoking a joint. On the dresser beside him was a row of white and green and a box of Ziploc baggies. A brick was sliced open, and someone was splitting it into several baggies for distribution.

None of it was surprising. Except for the naked, balding man on his hands and knees in front of the main suspect, acting as a stool for his propped-up feet.

The crony popped back in front of him, blocking the scene, and held up two condoms. "Here. Now get lost."

"Wait, is that hard stuff or you got weed in there too?"

The druggies by the door shifted imperceptibly, setting the girls to the side and stepping toward him. Mason held up his hands and took a step back. "Hey, I didn't see anything. Figured it didn't hurt to ask for a hit."

The guy in the door crossed his arms and scowled. "We don't hook up strangers."

Mason frowned and shrugged. "Seems like a terrible business outlook but whatever, man. Thanks for the condoms!"

Then he turned and practically ran back to the room, pushing it open and slamming it shut. His heart raced, but he immediately dropped the condoms and pulled out his phone.

He pressed the call button this time.

"Yeah, there's substance in there. Three males, two females. Did you get the other group as they left?"

"Yeah, we got 'em. Field testing it now, so give us a few

minutes. Keep watch on the door and let me know if anyone else leaves."

"Will do."

He hung up and opened the door a crack to watch. He felt Lucy touch his back and whisper, "What's going on?"

He turned his head to reply softly, "Drug bust."

She gasped. "Oh no. Are you going to arrest everyone here? I've never done anything like that. You have to believe me. If I'd known, I wouldn't have come."

He reached a hand back and linked their fingers, keeping his eye on the door at the end of the hall. "Sh, it's alright. I believe you. What about your friend downstairs?"

"Oh no, she'd never do anything more than weed, trust me. We've talked about it plenty over the years. She's my roommate."

"She seemed pretty familiar with the main suspect. They might want to question her."

Her hand trembled in his before she spun away and paced behind him. His watch vibrated.

At exactly 12:05.

He swiped to the time. "Three minutes," he whispered, glancing at the suspects at the end of the hall once more.

"What's going to happen?" Her voice was small with a hint of fear in it. The urge to protect her overrode his sense of duty to the job, and he shut the door.

He closed the distance and wrapped his arms around her. She melted into his embrace like she belonged there.

"It's going to be fine. You stay in here, yeah? No matter what you hear, don't leave. I'll come and get you when it's over."

She nodded against his shoulder and took a shaky

The Ranger Gets His Girl

breath. He kissed the top of her head and released her. He stepped back and ran his hands through his hair.

"They need to think we've been getting busy," he muttered, then took his shirt off and tossed it to the bed. He took off his gun holster and dropped it next to his boots. Then he slid the pistol into the waistband of his pants against his spine.

The cold steel made goosebumps spread on the back of his neck. This shit just got real, but it would be fine as long as she stayed in here.

It wouldn't go like his last girlfriend. The cold steel against his relatively still fresh scar was more of a wake-up call than anything else.

The dim light meant he still couldn't see her from this angle, but she had to have a pretty good view of him because she gasped. Her hand went to her lips, and she sat on the bed with a soft bounce.

"Oh shit," she whispered just barely loud enough to be heard.

He turned back to the door and opened it, slipping into the hallway and making sure his back never faced the druggies. He raked a hand down his face and fell against the opposite wall like he was drunk. He glanced at the goons at the end who both stared at him over their girls' heads now.

He grinned and waved like they were old friends. Then he looked over his shoulder down the stairs and turned back to them. With an exaggerated tiptoe, he went closer.

"Sh, she's passed out now. Where's the head in this joint?"

They pointed to the last door in the hallway that didn't have a sock on it. He turned to look and saw two of the team crest the stairs, weapons drawn.

"Hands where I can see 'em," one man barked. The two

goons tried to hide behind their girls who screamed and threw their hands up. Mason threw himself in a faux stumble against the door at the end of the hall.

It gave way, and he immediately took cover to one side, drawing his weapon and pointing it at the head dirtbag who was trying to escape through the window.

The two girls on the bed sat up and screamed, their mascara-streaked faces frozen in fear. Another guy crouched on the floor, whimpering and covering his head with his hands.

The guy at the dresser dropped the baggie of drugs and took a swing at Mason, but he lunged forward and landed a powerful blow to the stomach. The man fell to his knees, gasping for air.

Mason's heart raced as he lunged over the bed, reaching for the man trying to escape through the window. "Don't even think about it," Mason growled as they grappled with each other.

The drug dealer kicked and thrashed, sending them both tumbling to the floor with a loud thud. But Mason held on tight, determined not to let him get away. The rest of the team rushed in, shouting commands and joining in the struggle.

With a swift move, one of Mason's colleagues delivered a powerful blow to the intruder's head, knocking him unconscious. They quickly secured him with handcuffs, relieved that their mission was successful.

Mason lay on the floor as the team worked the room, breathing heavily. He was getting too old for this shit. He hadn't thought so before his injury, but now... Simon arrived and looked around as Mason groaned and sat up.

"You good, Novak?"

Mason nodded, holding his back as he slowly sat up. "I'm fine. Did we get them all?"

Simon inspected the dresser, opening drawer after drawer. He let out a loud whistle. "I'll say. Look at this. There must be a few kilos in each drawer. Looks like our lead panned out for a change."

Mason took the hand of one of the other agents and stood slowly. His back hadn't been healed enough for this. He'd argued with the physical therapists to go back in the field, but he wasn't supposed to get involved in the primary take down.

Pain shot down his leg as he tried to step. "Shit, shit, shit," he muttered, sinking into the chair in the corner.

Simon gave him the side eye. "I told you to give it a few months more, didn't I?"

Mason nodded and rubbed at his back. "I know, but if I can't be in the field, I'll be stuck behind a desk. That'd be hell, and you know it."

Simon hummed and turned back to the dresser as the forensics team came in. "Round up everyone downstairs and take them to the local station for questioning and drug tests. I want to know who knows where this all came from. We need to find the source. This might be the biggest score Denton's seen in a couple of years. It's gotta be coming up from Dallas. I just know it."

Mason stood once more and took a tentative step toward another agent who was going to do Simon's bidding. "There's a black-haired girl downstairs in a v-neck shirt and miniskirt. Bring her up here."

Simon looked at him curiously. Mason shrugged as he went slowly to the door. "There's a brunette down the hall who's her roommate. Black-haired girl might know something about our main suspect. I'll interview them."

Simon nodded and barked more orders as Mason shuffled down the hall. It took him so long that the agent was bringing the cuffed black-haired girl up the stairs. She was cussing like a sailor and struggling against her bonds until she saw him.

Her jaw clenched, and she practically bounded up the rest of the stairs. "You son of a bitch, where's Lucy? If you've hurt a hair on her head, I swear—"

Mason opened the door and turned on the light. Lucy stood up from the bed, her hands twisting together. The black-haired girl glanced inside, then raced to her friend.

Chapter Five

Lucy threw her arms around Taylor and sobbed. "Oh God, are you okay? Are you hurt?"

She pulled back and inspected her friend, who grumbled, glaring at the agent who stepped in the door behind Mason, "I'm fine, but what the hell's going on?"

When Lucy found the cuffs, she gasped and glared at Mason. "Let her go. She's done nothing wrong."

Mason nodded at the agent. "That's fine, you can uncuff her. Thanks. I'll call for backup if I need anything."

The other man uncuffed Taylor who rubbed her wrists and seethed. Lucy's attention latched onto Mason, who walked to where she'd nervously folded his shirt on the bed. He was moving stiffly and pulled it on with a groan. The shirt she'd not been sniffing after he left. The shirt she'd not held close to her chest trying to feel his comforting embrace.

She frowned. "Did you get hurt?"

He winced as he pulled his shirt down. "An old injury is acting up, that's all. I told my superior I'd ask some questions. If you'll both cooperate, we'll make this quick, and we can all go home and try to forget it."

She snorted, but it was Taylor who mouthed off, "Forget it? How the hell are we supposed to forget something like this? Six years. We've been going to school in this town and partying for *six years* and have never had anything like this happen before."

Mason grabbed his sock off the door and the other from the floor before sinking onto the bed with another groan.

"I saw you talking with a guy earlier. He came in with three goons, each with a girl on their arm. Taller, blond, preppy looking guy. Ring a bell?"

Taylor snorted and crossed her arms, cocking a hip and making her cleavage plunge. "Goons? What are you, like fifty?"

Lucy looked at Mason, but he didn't even glance down at her friend's boobs. He just sighed and pulled his boots on.

"My age doesn't matter. What can you tell me about him?"

Taylor frowned as she recounted their previous encounters.

Men and women in tactical gear walked back and forth in front of the door. She watched as each carried an armload of white coke bags. Lucy tuned out Taylor's words, the sight in the hall triggering flashbacks to her dad's episodes.

Her hands went clammy, and she sat on the bed once more to hold them still, a few feet from Mason. Dear God, she'd thought she'd escaped all this shit.

Maybe she should move to Crimson Creek, just to get away from all the druggies and crack heads once and for all. Surely the crime rate in the small town was way less than here.

By the time Taylor was done talking, Mason was sitting with a stunned look on his face.

Taylor frowned and put both hands on her hips. "What?"

He blinked. "Nothing, it's just. Not everyone gives so much detail. This is fantastic. Would you mind going with Simon to the station to record all that info?"

He stood and shuffled to the doorway still holding his back. "Simon? Someone get Simon for me."

"Hey now, you said we could go home. You didn't say anything about going to the station. Am I going to be booked or just give a statement?" Taylor demanded.

A guy who Lucy assumed was Simon stepped into the room and answered her. "Is there a reason to book you?"

Taylor frowned and crossed her arms. "Hell no. I'm not stupid. Those drugs you've been carrying downstairs have nothing to do with Lucy or I. I'm happy to do a drug test, if it'll make you happy. However, I draw the line at being booked because I've done nothing wrong."

Mason nodded to Taylor. "If you'll let us audio record your statement and give all your contact details, it'll be fine. No need to do a drug test."

Simon arched his brow. "Speak for yourself. That remains to be seen. If you'll follow me, miss, we'll be on our way."

Taylor looked at Lucy and frowned. "What about Lucy?"

Mason glanced at her, and Lucy felt her cheeks heat. "I'll take her home. She'll be fine."

Taylor frowned and opened her mouth to argue, but Lucy stood on shaky legs and nodded. "I'll be in bed before you, chica. Don't worry about me. Just watch your mouth around the cops, okay?"

Mason snorted. "We're not cops. I'm a Texas Ranger, and Simon's FBI. This was a joint raid."

Taylor's jaw dropped, making Lucy smirk. That shut her friend up. She followed Simon out the door, and Mason waved for Lucy to go ahead of him.

"Did you drive?"

She shook her head as she walked down the stairs. "No, we took a ride share." Her legs still felt shaky from all the adrenaline, but when she got to the bottom, Taylor was handing her the jacket from the pile still on the dining table.

They hugged, and Taylor whispered, "I'll try not to wake you when I come home, but for God's sake, make a move on that eye-candy!"

Lucy chuckled and released her friend. They all walked out the door and to separate vehicles. Mason held open the truck door for her, and she climbed in with a hesitant smile. As he rounded the cab and settled into the driver's seat, she nervously fiddled with the hem of her dress. The engine roared to life before settling into a smooth purr much like the desire that went through her anytime he was near. She tried to calm her racing heart as they made their way towards her campus apartment by giving him directions, but a part of her was rocked by doubt, fear, and shock from the events of the night.

"Your roommate seems nice," he said in the darkness as they backed up and got on the highway.

Lucy snorted and stared straight ahead. "Yeah, she's a handful, but we balance each other out really well. I wouldn't have survived all these years of college without her."

"Congratulations on graduation, by the way. I didn't get to tell you earlier."

"Thanks," she said, shifting on the seat.

"Pops invited me to it, but I had to work, as you found out tonight. What were you doing in a place like that, anyway?"

She sighed and leaned her head on the cold glass of the window. "She likes to party. A few times a year, there's a house party like that one. She says it's usually quieter and easier to handle than the packed clubs you have to pay at the door."

Silence fell between them as he pulled in front of her building. He turned the engine off and opened his door.

"Oh, you don't need to come up. This is fine."

He stared at her through the open door and narrowed his eyes. She couldn't see much in the dark street, but the interior light of the truck showed his frown. She wanted to see him laugh and smile like he'd done at the wedding reception.

"I insist. At least let me see you to the door," he said as he shut the door and walked around to the passenger side.

A small thrill went through her at his take-charge manner and the way he was holding the doors for her. She'd never been treated like this before, like a woman who was both wanted and respected.

That's assuming he wanted her. He'd acted like it at the party, but maybe that was just part of his cover with his job.

She led him up the stairs to the apartment and pulled her keys out of her pocket. Her hand was shaking, but she finally got the door opened.

She turned to him but couldn't bring herself to meet his gaze. "Do you want to come in for a cup of coffee?"

He put his hands in his pockets and shrugged. "Sure, but I can't have caffeine this late at night. It's already one, and I'll have a ton of paperwork to follow up on tomorrow."

He stepped inside and shut the door.

"But tomorrow is Sunday," she said as she kicked off her heels.

He nodded. "I know. My hours are inconsistent. Some days are super long, some days I don't even go home. Others are just an hour or two in the office, then I'm out."

"Sounds grueling. Why do you do it?" she asked as she opened the fridge and grabbed a bottle of water. She offered it to him, and their fingers grazed. His hands were warm, sending a jolt of awareness through her.

She'd done it. She'd invited a man into her apartment. This was major progress! Taylor would be so proud.

He opened the bottle and leaned against the wall next to the fridge. "I love helping people. I love that there's something different to do every day. It never gets boring. A lot of it's like a puzzle to be unraveled."

"I like puzzles," she murmured, walking to the couch with her own bottle of water and tucking her feet under her.

He nodded and continued as he settled on the other end of the couch, semi-facing her. "Me too. Plus, it's in my blood. Pops was the sheriff in Crimson Creek, you know. When I was growing up, I spent a lot of time in the summers in that building. I watched and learned and knew I wanted to put away bad guys just like him."

Lucy tilted her head and nodded. "I get that. Nana was an English teacher and librarian, and my degree is in English too. I used to love reading the summer away with her at her house and at the library."

"Are you going to teach like she did?" he asked before he took a drink.

She shook her head. "No, I'm actually working on a book at the moment. I'll probably continue to do nails and teach yoga while I write. It's a never-ending work in progress."

His brows rose. "Really? That's so creative. What's it about?"

She felt her cheeks heat as she looked away and shook her head. "I can't really say at this point. It's ran the gamut from action adventure to romance to cozy mystery. It's kind of all over the place."

He nodded and took another drink. "Well, you seem like a smart girl. You'll figure it out, I'm sure."

She preened under the praise. "Thanks, I appreciate the support."

He took another drink of his water and looked at his watch. "I'm going to take off now."

She felt her heart race, and she practically leaped to grab his arm. "No wait," she said.

His eyebrows rose in surprise, and she felt her face heat. "I—I mean, it's just that I'm so jittery from tonight. With all the yelling and busting in doors, I don't think I'll sleep a wink. I—I think it'll trigger some nightmares, and I don't really want to be alone right now, and Tay won't be back for a while probably, and—"

He leaned forward and placed a finger on her lips. "Sh, it's okay. It's a normal reaction. The shock is wearing off. Do you want to watch a movie or a show? I can stay."

Hope bloomed in her chest. "Are you sure?"

He nodded, his expression grave and determined. "I'm sure."

She breathed a sigh of relief and felt some of the tension leave her shoulders. She waved to the remote. "The center button is our streaming service. Pick whatever you like. As long as it's not gruesome. Sorry, I can't do Walking Dead or anything tonight."

He chuckled and turned the TV on, then scrolled. She stood up and walked to the door on the other side of the TV.

"I'm going to put some pajamas on, if that's okay." She didn't look back at him to see if it was. She just went into her room and shut the door. She leaned against it and breathed deeply.

She still felt on edge. Before he'd promised to stay, she'd had all kinds of flashbacks running through her head. Now she was just thinking about him. Kissing her neck. His finger on her lips. The scent of his aftershave.

It'd been a long time since she'd been this close to a guy. Years and years. God, that made her feel old, much older than twenty-three.

She went to her drawer and changed into some shorts and a tank top. Then she put her hair up in a messy bun and brushed her teeth. She wasn't planning on anything happening, but if it did, she was determined not to turn it down or push away.

It was damn time to ditch her celibacy and get some experience under her belt. She went back out to the living room and found an action movie on. But Mason already had his head back and mouth open as he snored softly.

She smiled and curled onto the other end of the couch. It just wasn't meant to happen, which was really for the best, considering she was probably going to see more of him from now on.

Maybe he'd be at their Christmas celebration next weekend. After tonight, she was more inclined to get him a gift, considering he was the hero of the day. She started to think of all she knew of him but wasn't sure what he'd want or use.

Chapter Six

Lucy was nervous as she parked in front of Nana's house the following weekend. When she'd woken up after the party, Taylor had been home, and Mason had been gone. She hadn't heard from him at all and didn't even know if he'd be showing up today.

But she'd done her best makeup and nails and had raided Taylor's closet for something sleek and sexy. It was hard to balance trying to impress him and not wanting her grandmother to find out what she was up to.

She bundled up and grabbed the huge Santa bag from the front seat. Then she opened the door and fought the cold air up to the front steps of the house. Helen had lived in this large farmhouse her entire life.

It was where Lucy's mom had grown up and where Lucy herself had come every summer. With all the chaos during her teenage years dealing with her dad, this house had always been home, her refuge from the world.

Especially her senior year of high school when her life

had gone to shit, and she'd moved in with Helen for the year. Being with Helen had been the light in the darkness.

She finally pushed the front door open and set her heavy bag down in the foyer. A staircase went straight up with a small bathroom built under it. Behind it was the living room that spanned the entire width of the house. To the right was the kitchen and the left was the dining room.

Ray sat in his recliner, hands behind his head as he watched a football game, the sound blasting loud.

Helen came out of the kitchen and wiped her hands on her apron. "There you are, dear. I was afraid the weather would keep you away."

Lucy smiled and hugged her, then kissed her cheek. "Nothing would keep me from seeing you, Nana. You know that."

Helen pulled back and eyed the bag on the floor. "Goodness, what'd you bring? The whole store?"

Lucy shrugged out of her coat and hung it on the rack by the door. "It's not just you this year, you know. I had to get Ray something too."

Helen's eyes lit up as she glanced into the living room and smiled. "True. I invited your aunts and uncle, but they can't make it."

Lucy clenched her teeth together and forced her smile to remain as she shrugged. "That's okay. More food for me, right? What can I help with?"

She knew dwelling on the missing family would just bring Helen down, and she didn't need that right now. Lucy did her best to chat and take her mind off it while they cooked.

A knock sounded from the door followed by a male voice saying, "Hello, hello, anyone home?"

Lucy's stomach dropped. She hadn't asked Helen if he

was coming but had hoped he would. He stepped into the kitchen and filled the doorway with his broad shoulders.

She stirred the gravy and stared. She couldn't help it. He just took her breath away with that black hair that was already starting to show gray again at the temples. His blue eyes pierced hers and a small smile hovered on his lips.

Helen bustled around Lucy and pulled him into a hug. "Mason, you made it! And just in time for dinner too."

He hugged her back and chuckled. "I wouldn't have missed your first Christmas with the family. Maybe next year you'll be rid of me, though."

Helen leaned back and slapped him playfully on the arm. "Oh, don't talk like that. I'm so glad you're here."

She stepped back and dabbed at her eyes. Mason frowned and stepped over to hug Lucy, whispering, "Why the tears?" She ignored the shivers up her spine at his touch and replied in his ear, "Tell you later."

He nodded and stepped back to remove his coat, going into the living room. She heard Ray greet him and Mason ask about the score before Helen called them all to the table. Lucy turned off the stove and carried the gravy over.

Helen had put out the fancy China, but Lucy's frustration with her aunts and uncle built as the gaping hole of their absence stared at her. Thankfully, Helen had taken a few leaves out of the table and removed the extra seats.

Lucy sat and Helen held her hands out. Mason was across from her, so she didn't need to be nervous about touching him.

"Ray, will you say grace, please?" Helen asked.

Ray nodded and bowed his head. "Thank you for this meal that we are about to receive. Thank you for the beautiful hands that prepared it. Thank you for nudging Helen to say yes to our marriage. And bless this food, fellowship, and family. Amen."

Lucy watched as Helen met Ray's gaze across the table and smiled. Then they started to pass the food around the table. They really were happily married, and it left a lump of emotion in her throat. Helen was practically glowing when she turned to Mason.

"Ray tells me you've been doing some work out of the Dallas field office. Any chance that'll become permanent and we can see you more?"

Lucy's eyes flew to his, watching to see if he'd say anything about last weekend. He just smiled at Helen and shook his head.

"I don't know what they'll do. I had to do some extra therapy sessions this week due to aggravating my back in a sting operation last weekend. There's talk of benching me for a few more months."

Ray grumbled as he speared a potato. "I told you it was coming, didn't I?"

Mason frowned and pushed the food around on his plate.

"What's coming?" Lucy asked, surprising herself but confusion driving her. Mason frowned, but Helen was the one who answered.

"Mason was shot this year and had a long recovery. He's just recently started field work again, but Ray's afraid they're going to stick him in an office somewhere."

Ray nodded, but Lucy watched Mason carefully. His shoulders seemed to hunch as he shoved a bite into his mouth and avoided the conversation.

"He's too young to retire, but Ray's trying to convince him to move to Crimson Creek and join the police force here."

Mason stared at Ray and almost growled, "I started here, but I'm not ready to move back, Pops. There's still a lot of fight left in me, and I can do the most good in the city."

Ray grunted, and Helen turned to Lucy and smiled. "Tell me what you've been up to this week, sweet pea. Did you have time to talk to your roommate about a permanent move or think about it at all?"

Lucy took a drink before answering. "Yeah, I actually did. We had a really good heart to heart this week, and we're both ready for some permanent changes, even if we're both scared about it. If it's alright with you, I'd like to take you up on the offer with the house."

The look of joy on Helen's face helped Lucy know this was the right decision. Since last weekend's fiasco, she'd been thinking more and more of moving to this little town. It felt safer, and it was time to move out of the campus apartments and live on her own. Being so close to Helen was comforting and felt right.

Ray pointed his fork at Mason and asked, "Are you staying the night too?"

"I cleaned Ray's house this week so both rooms have fresh bedding. Y'all can't stay here though because we painted all the spare rooms this week. It's still a bit too strong on the fumes," Helen chuckled.

Mason met her gaze across the table, his eyes twinkling. "So, we'll both stay the night at Pop's house again. Not a big deal. We made it work the night of the wedding."

Helen gasped and slapped a hand to her forehead. "Oh no, I forgot all about that. Ray, you didn't tell me Mason was staying the night."

"Of course he'd stay the night. No one would want to

drive all the way back to Waco. Even Dallas would've been too far to drive that night."

Helen frowned at them both. "I'm so sorry about double booking y'all. I didn't even think."

Lucy snorted and lifted her wine, hiding her smile behind her glass. She had to give it to her grandma. That was a stellar performance. If she didn't know better, she'd say she actually meant that little speech.

"Right," she drawled. "The wedding probably had you in a tizzy. It's fine, Nana."

Mason winked at her across the table, and she felt her cheeks heat as she took a drink. This was going to be a long night.

After dinner, they moved to the living room to open presents around the tree. Mason remembered a big tree growing up, but it'd been years since he'd celebrated like this.

Normally, Pops would put a small two-foot tree on the corner of the table, with one ornament for each of them, but Helen's tree was massive. He inspected it as Helen and Lucy passed out presents.

He smiled and pointed to an ornament. "Lucy, is this you?"

She stopped beside him, stared and winced. "Yeah, that was before I found my taming hair serum. It went all over the place, as you can see."

He chuckled, and she punched him in the bicep. He rubbed his arm and grinned at her. "What? I think you look cute with that poofy hair."

She rolled her eyes and walked away. "Yeah right. Liar, liar, pants on fire."

He grinned and looked around. "Where do I sit?"

Helen pointed to the couch. "Sit there, dear."

Lucy sat on one end with a neat stack of presents on the coffee table in front of her. Another stack was on the other end of the coffee table. Helen reigned in her rocking chair with her lap full of presents, and Ray was in his recliner, unable to take his eyes off Helen.

Ray nodded to the small present on top of her pile. "That one first, pearl."

Helen gave him the side eye as Mason sat, then tore open the wrapping, clearly too excited to argue. She held up a pearl and diamond necklace, and her eyes widened. "Oh Ray, it's beautiful."

He leaned onto the armrest. "Look closer at that center pearl."

She turned it to the light and lifted her glasses from the chain on her chest. She gasped when she saw it. "Oh, it's the ocean. Waves and flowers carved right onto it. It's so detailed. Thank you, Ray. It's perfect."

Ray leaned back in his recliner and smiled like the cat who ate the canary. "Only the best for you, pearl. Merry Christmas."

She held her hand out, and Ray took it, squeezing it as they stared into each other's eyes.

Mason grinned but said, "Geez, get a room already."

Helen and Ray laughed as Helen wiped tears from her eyes. "Okay everyone, now dig in and stop staring at me."

Mason opened his while trying to watch everyone else. Helen liked the cast iron skillet he got her, and Pops sniffed the box of cigars approvingly.

He opened his first two—a personalized coffee mug with his name on it and an envelope from Pops, which probably contained a steakhouse gift card. Before he could open the envelope, he saw Lucy reach for her last gift.

He'd put a lot of thought into it, but he didn't know her very well. Sure, he'd done some sleuthing in their database and online this week.

But she was squeaky clean with only two parking tickets in her entire short life. It still amazed him that she was a decade younger than him. She looked barely old enough to be in college much less graduated.

It made him feel ancient, and as much as he ached for her, he didn't want to be the creep in his thirties hitting onto a gorgeous woman ten years his junior. It would be too weird, wouldn't it?

She opened the gift and laughed, her eyes wide as she looked up at him with twinkling eyes.

"Do you like it?" he asked, shifting on the couch nervously. It suddenly seemed as if both their grandparents were staring at them.

She held up the bottle of whiskey and shook her head, but the grin on her face made him smile. "Writer's Tears?"

He nodded. "For when your book gets away from you. A shot of that will either make you forget your book entirely or help you tackle the next writer's block."

She dug into the box and held up a block of cheese. He'd printed a label at work especially for it. She laughed and said, "Writer's Block Cheese?"

He grinned and nodded. "It's supposed to pair really well with the whiskey."

She poked into the box and shook her head. "Post-it notes, a journal, and a fountain pen? Wow."

He shifted on the couch again and felt his heart stutter in his chest. "So, you like it?"

She laid her hand on his knee and leaned closer, her voice soft as she said, "It's perfect. Thank you."

He felt a knot in his throat as he nodded. It'd been a little thing that hopefully would make her think about him. Did he really want that, though?

He said roughly, "Maybe it'll help you finish your book."

Her eyes brightened with tears as she nodded. She looked away, then nudged him with her knee. "Open yours."

He looked down, realizing he still had one present to open. The handwriting on it had to be hers. It had swoops and was elegant and just fit her somehow. He tore the paper, careful to keep his name intact.

It was a green ammo box painted on one side. It had the Texas Rangers logo and his name. He traced the paint. He'd not even gotten something this nice when he'd hit ten years with the Rangers.

"Open it," she whispered.

He couldn't look at her. If he did, he might do something stupid like kiss her right there in front of their grandparents. He popped the lid and looked inside. A flask and two glasses were inside. The flask was engraved with his name, then it said: The man. The myth. The legend.

He grinned and held it up to show Ray who nodded approvingly. Then he pulled out the glasses. His brows rose, and it felt like a fishhook was in his mouth from grinning so wide.

One was a shot glass that said: Officer Off Duty. The other was a whiskey decanter that had three lines on it that said: Good Day. Bad Day. Don't Even Ask.

"Sweet. These are perfect."

He finally caught her eye, and he saw her shoulders relax as she smiled.

"Really?" Her voice was breathy as if she was waiting for him to say otherwise.

He nodded, unable to look away from her now. He was trapped in her spell and couldn't remember why this was a bad idea anymore. "Really," he said softly. "It's perfect, just like you."

Her mouth opened and closed but no sound came out. Her eyes widened in surprise.

Helen cleared her throat, and they glanced her way as she yawned. "Wow, look at the time, kids. I don't know about you, but I'm too old to stay up this late."

Lucy laughed, and the sound echoed in his soul. "It's barely eight o'clock, Nana."

Helen stood and stretched, then hugged Lucy. "I know, sweet pea, but you'll understand when you're older. You remember where the key to the house is, right?"

Lucy nodded and turned to hug Ray. Helen came to him next and wrapped her arms around him.

She whispered in his ear, "Merry Christmas, Mason. May this be the start of something beautiful, eh?"

She pulled back and winked at him, then gathered her presents to take them upstairs. Ray chuckled as he watched her go. Somehow it was only minutes later that Mason found himself and Lucy standing in the cold on the front porch holding their presents.

He looked at Lucy and chuckled. "I guess you can follow me to Ray's, since I'm parked behind you?"

She nodded and glanced away, fluttering her eyelashes as she walked carefully down the porch steps. "Sounds like a plan."

His stomach knotted even more as he got in his truck and backed out. What would this night hold for them? It was way too early to go to sleep, and he was wound tighter than a rooster in a hen house. Maybe Helen was right, and this would be the start of something beautiful.

No, he couldn't. With his job, relationships didn't mix well, and Lucy was relationship material.

Chapter Seven

Lucy followed Mason inside, rushing to bring her presents and overnight bag inside. Her cheeks felt half frozen by the time she stomped up the porch and through the front door he held open for her.

"Turned into a cold day, didn't it?" she said with a shiver.

He shut the door and nodded. "It's usually not this cold until January or February."

"I know, crazy, huh?" She felt her cheeks heat as she put her bag of presents on the kitchen table. God, he was going to think she was a nitwit, talking about the weather. She avoided his gaze and turned to take off her jacket, hooking it over the back of a kitchen chair.

"I'm going to work on my book now. You don't need to entertain me or anything. I'll stay out of your hair," she rushed, grabbing her overnight bag and racing up the stairs.

She shut the door to the spare room behind her and released a breath. She was such a spaz. Here was this hot guy downstairs with nothing to do, and she was hiding in her room?

She jerked her bag open angrily and pulled out her pajama pants and tank top. It was useless trying to write anyway. She was at a point in the story where she had to decide what was going to happen next, and she had no fucking experience to make that decision.

This might help her, actually. Her story was missing a strong male protagonist. The female was fine, if inexperienced, but the missing male was just something she hadn't been able to write. Every word she wrote got erased because it didn't feel real.

She was tired of sitting on the sidelines, watching people live their lives. If she was going to write believable characters, she needed to get out there herself. And that included getting some much overdue experience.

She paused and frowned. What if she *were* to go downstairs? They weren't tired like last weekend. She had been ready to let it happen then, so why was today any different?

It wasn't. It was actually a much better opportunity. She looked at the door. What would Taylor do?

She'd march downstairs—no, sashay downstairs—and cuddle up to him on the couch while watching a movie.

That didn't sound so scary. She could do that. She *would* do that.

Mind made up, she opened the door to find him standing on the other side, fist raised to knock.

His brows rose. "Um, I was going to see if you wanted to watch that movie we never got to last weekend."

She smiled, her cheeks heating, and nodded. "Sure, I don't know why I said I was going to write. I'm not in the right headspace."

He stepped back so she could walk ahead of him as he said, "Oh? What's on your mind?"

She almost tripped on the steps and was glad he was behind her, his hand grabbing her waist to steady her. She knew her face would've shown all her thoughts as she somehow didn't fall on her face on the stairs. What had he asked? Oh yes.

"Wondering how that whiskey and cheese tastes."

He chuckled. "I was hoping you'd say that. I just finished making popcorn and have a nice whiskey glass that's begging to be used."

You and me both, whiskey glass.

Good God, where had that thought come from? Her cheeks burned as she hit the bottom of the stairs and went into the kitchen.

He cleared his throat and grabbed the glasses while she found a plate and knife for the cheese. "Tell me more about this book you're writing."

They stepped into the living room before she replied. She set the whiskey and cheese on the coffee table while he brought the glasses and bowl of popcorn.

"It's a space fantasy with some romance sprinkled in. The girl moves to a new planet and stumbles on a dead body. There's a local cop who tries to keep her out of the investigation, but she's nosy and won't let it alone."

"Ahh, I see. And what made you decide on that type of book?"

She sank onto one end of the couch and poured a glass.

"Nana and I used to watch Murder She Wrote and Matlock all the time when I was a kid. That and Jeopardy. I play a mean game of trivia. Do you play?"

Mason scowled and shook his head as he sat, making her laugh.

She teased him. "Oh, come on. Who doesn't like trivia game night? Every bar these days has a trivia night."

He hunched his shoulders and crossed his arms. "I don't get out much. If I go to a bar, I'm probably undercover. I like to play pool or darts. I'm good with my hands and like to have easy access to something that can be used as a weapon."

She glanced at his hands, big and rough and—she blushed, pulling her gaze away. She had to take control of the conversation before she mouthed off something inappropriate. After six years, Taylor's loud mouth had seeped into her conscious.

"I like fun space movies too, like Star Wars, Star Trek, even Spaceballs and Hitchhiker's Guide to the Galaxy. I don't like the sad space movies where people die though. Not a fan of that emotional turmoil. I'd rather there be a problem to solve, you know?"

He continued after an awkward beat of silence. "I can understand that, but for the record, I don't think you're allowed to be a fan of both Star Wars and Star Trek. I think you have to pick a side and defend it as better."

She frowned at him, pouring him a drink and setting it on the coffee table in front of him. "Who says?"

He shrugged. "Everyone. Plus, Star Wars is clearly superior quality and story line."

She burst out laughing and punched him in the shoulder, making him smile. "I see which team you root for. Have you even read the books, though?"

He shrugged. "I like reading, but all I read are Star Wars canon and old western books like Louie L'Amour. I used to watch Walker, Texas Ranger with my Pops. And all the Lethal Weapon movies."

She nodded as he grabbed the remote and turned on

the streaming service. "I assumed you'd love that show, just based on your occupation. And you seem like a Lethal Weapon kind of guy."

He chuckled, low and deep, the sound vibrating through her body as she took a sip of the whiskey. It burned as it went down. Without a chaser, she relied on cheese and popcorn, and it was a tasty combination.

"What's that supposed to mean? A Lethal Weapon kind of guy." He hit play on the movie and kicked his boots off.

"I'm just saying, you've been in law enforcement your entire career. I'm guessing you're thirty-something, right? You would've been too young for Rambo or Top Gun, but the Lethal Weapon franchise made three more movies within ten years. Those would've been prime childhood absorption years."

When she glanced at him, he just stared at her blankly, blinking. He made her stomach flip with that intense blue gaze. Ignoring the intensity in them, she asked, "How old are you anyway?"

"Thirty-five," he said, his eyes narrowing.

Her brows lifted as she nodded. "I thought you were in your thirties."

"How old are you? I assumed you're over twenty-one, since you graduated."

She flushed and nodded. "Twenty-three, which is young to have earned a master's degree, but it's what I needed." He frowned but she waved to the movie and pasted on a forced smile. "It's been years since I've seen this. Not sure I've ever watched it all the way through. Did you try the cheese? It's wonderful."

He stared as she tucked her feet under her and moved the popcorn bowl between them on the couch. She had goosebumps on her arms, but she didn't want to talk about her past. She didn't know him well enough for that.

She tried to focus on the movie, but turned her body so she could see more of him out of the corner of her eye. He had a square jaw and high cheekbones covered in a dark five o'clock shadow. He had the hard, muscled body of a gym rat, but he wasn't like the other jocks on campus. He was a bear of a man, built like a linebacker, made to take a hit and keep going.

He watched, waited. Even at the party last weekend, she'd been able to feel his eyes on her. Just like now.

She turned her head slightly and caught his gaze. Tingles raced along her spine, and her body burned with lust. The raw power of her attraction to him disturbed her, made her wary of getting too close.

What would Taylor do? It was time to seize what she wanted, if only for tonight.

"Mason," she whispered, licking her lips. He glanced down at them and didn't look away.

"Yes, Lucy?"

"You're not watching the movie."

He shook his head.

"Why not?" She held her breath, because if he didn't want her then this entire idea was a moot point.

He slowly reached for the popcorn bucket and put it back on the coffee table along with his glass. She set her glass on the side table and looked back at him. He rested one hand on the armrest and the other along the back of the couch. His fingertips whispered along the skin on her shoulder, tracing the line of her tank top.

"I can't figure you out, little bird."

She shifted slightly, drawing closer to the web of desire he was spinning around her. "What's to figure out?"

"One minute you're ignoring me, and the next you're looking at me like you want me to kiss you."

She shuddered a breath, and her eyes widened. "Am I that obvious?" she held her cheeks with her hands and groaned.

He chuckled, his fingers sending shock waves of awareness down her body. Who knew shoulders could be so sensitive?

"Not obvious unless you're looking for the signs, and I definitely am."

She put her hands down and turned to face him, hope blooming in her chest. "You're looking for the signs? Why?"

He arched a brow. "Because I'm doing the same thing. I tell myself to ignore you, but I can't seem to take my eyes off you."

"You want me?"

He nodded, his face serious. "Yes."

She took a deep breath. This was it, her chance to finally live a little. "I—I want you too." She licked her lips, and his eyes darkened with desire. Her pulse raced. "This is a bad idea. We're going to see each other a lot, now that they're married."

He nodded, shifting closer and tracing his fingers up her neck. "I know, and I can't offer you a relationship, Lucy. With my job, it's too risky and unpredictable."

It was her turn to agree and slide along the couch. "I know. I've never had a one-night stand before, but I'm not opposed to it."

She could smell him now, the pine and cedar mixing with something that was uniquely him.

He grinned, and it made her core melt. "I'm not opposed to it either, but our grandparents can never know."

"Agreed," she said breathlessly. He was close enough to touch now, so she cautiously laid her hand on his thigh. His muscle tensed under her fingers, and he leaned in.

Chapter Eight

She leaned back, moving her hand to his chest as panic seized her. "Wait, one thing. It's been, um, well, I'm not that experienced. I hope you don't have any expectations. You'll have to give me clear instructions and—"

He leaned forward and nuzzled her neck with a chuckle. "Why don't we just go with the flow, hm?"

She shivered and nodded, his warmth, scent, and presence making her relax into him. She felt so safe with him. After analyzing the drug bust all freaking week, she'd somehow known that Mason would keep her safe; she'd mostly been afraid for Taylor.

When he nipped at her neck and his chin scratched her, she gasped, thoughts of the last time she'd seen him flying out of her mind.

"I've been thinking of kissing your neck since last weekend," he murmured, his lips moving up to her ear and across her cheek. He hovered over her lips, pausing as she felt her body melting in anticipation.

"And these lips. God, Lucy," he groaned.

She barely had time to suck in a quick breath before his lips met hers. She'd been kissed in middle school twice, and high school a few times. But this... this was a kiss.

Finally.

His tongue gently teased the seam of her lips, the rasp of his tongue making her stomach knot in anticipation. His kiss began softly, then built in intensity as she opened for him.

His stubble scratched her before he swept inside with the force of a blizzard.

Her bones tingled, and his hand on the back of her neck brought her closer. He cradled her head, and she felt his other hand tug on her knee.

Her mind was floating, narrowed in on the sensation of his mouth on hers. In the back of her head, she realized she was now straddling him, knees on either side of his hips. Hands kneaded her ass, making her groan and grind down on him.

He angled his mouth for a deeper kiss and squeezed her ass. This kiss had been a long time coming and was everything she'd hoped for. It sent licks of electricity through her veins, pooling in the center of her body where she pulsed with an ache so deep she hurt.

One last voice of reason in her mind made her hesitate. She broke the kiss with a gasp, her hands on either side of his face. His eyes were half-closed and without missing a beat, he leaned forward and began kissing along the exposed skin of her collarbone.

"Mason," she gasped. "What are we doing?"

He growled, "We're making out."

She nodded, closing her eyes as his chin raked along her sensitive flesh. "Oh God."

"You like that?" he murmured. She nodded and threw all her inhibitions to the wind.

She released his head and yanked down her tank top, exposing her breasts. The sudden cold air made her panic. She was torn between wanting to run away and stay in this moment forever. This was so unlike her, but the rush of excitement and desire still pumped through her veins. God, how could she be doing this?

When he groaned and pulled a taut nipple into his mouth, her eyes fluttered, her back arching. He sucked and teased, his fingers rolling the other as he hungrily devoured her. For the first time, she felt truly desired.

Why had it taken her this long to take a chance like this? If her high school boyfriend hadn't been such a letdown, maybe she could've been feeling like this much sooner than twenty-three.

She moaned, seeing stars as he bit and tugged gently. His hand slid around her to her ass again, and he pulled back, leaning his head against the back of the couch.

She panted in shallow breaths and looked down at him through lust-filled eyes.

He licked his lips as he gripped her ass hard and stared at her breasts. "I want to fuck you, Lucy, but it's your call. We can keep making out if you'd prefer. What are you feeling? What do you want?"

She bit her lip, pausing in this do or die moment. They said she'd regret more the things she didn't do than the things she did do in life. So far, she hadn't done anything to regret. There was no way she would ever regret him though, and she couldn't—wouldn't—back down now, not when she was so close to leaving her inexperience behind. She crawled off him and stood, quickly pulling her tank top over her head.

With a push down her hips, her pajama pants joined the tank top on the floor. She stood there, bold and unashamed even though she trembled with the fear of the unknown, fear of rejection... until she saw his eyes. They burned with desire for her. It was a heady, powerful moment and she breathed deeply, saying softly, "I'm all in, Mason. Are you?"

"Hell yeah." Grinning, Mason unzipped his jeans and stood, kicking them off and pulling his shirt over his head to toss it too.

She stared at him, her fingers on her lips. He was bigger than she thought, much bigger than her little toy back in her apartment. She glanced at his face, then back down at his dick.

He wrapped his fist around it and stroked up slowly. She gasped to see a bead of pre-cum on the tip. Past conversations with her roommate splintered through her mind, and she reached out a finger to spread it around.

He jumped at her touch, then she lifted her finger and sucked on it. Interesting. Salty but not too bad.

Mason groaned, then knelt to dig his wallet out of his pocket. He pulled out a condom and ripped it open. He slid it on with ease as he sat back down in the center of the couch.

She bit her lip, then straddled him again, pressing his dick against her clit and his stomach. She gasped as his hands settled on her ass again.

"That's it. Grind that clit on my dick, sunshine."

She lifted and came back down gently, his words lighting a fire in her for more. She was wet, had been wet since they'd first sat on the couch, but his hands dipped behind her, barely teasing her entrance.

She arched her back, moving forward to grind, his lips finding her nipple again.

"Oh God," she moaned, closing her eyes and moving faster on him. His hands moved to her ass and lifted her higher, lining up and teasing her even more with his dick. This was it, the moment she'd built up in her mind, and her breathing grew ragged.

He pushed slowly into the heated core of her body, releasing her nipple and leaning his head back. Time seemed to stand still as they both paused.

She froze, clenching wildly at the feeling of invasion with mouth open in surprise as she panted. Only half on his cock, she snapped her eyes open to meet his. The baby blues were deep and held secrets she wanted to explore, but the unknown didn't scare her.

This was just sex. What the hell had she been waiting for? It was time to finish this.

She took a deep breath and eased another inch inside. Gripping him like a vise, she tried to force herself to relax her inner muscles. She knew logically that he would fit, but the resistance was like a full-sized zucchini going through a penne pasta noodle. She winced, at the discomfort then took a deep breath.

She could do this.

"You... okay?" he choked out, his hands squeezing her ass but not pressing her to move.

She bit her lip and nodded, frowning as she finally met his eyes and breathed deep and slow. "Yeah, give me a minute. It's been a while."

Like seven fucking years, and even then, she wasn't sure it counted. Slowly, she sank down all the way, inch by inch until she took all of him. His cock seared her, burning like a brand. It was the most amazing, filling thing she'd ever felt.

"Take... your time," he gritted between clenched teeth, his nostrils flaring as his hands gripped her hips. Still, he didn't take control or move her, waiting for her to take the lead and set the pace. When he pulsed inside her, she gasped, her fingers on his shoulders digging into him.

She eased up, but this time when she sank down onto him, he flexed his hips up to meet her. Her mouth dropped as she moaned.

"Better... now?" he asked, pulsing again.

She nodded, whimpering. "Yeah but let me just feel you."

Several beats of silence settled between them, and he leaned forward and trailed kisses along her neck and collarbone. Eyes closed, she focused on the feel of him inside. He was so big, bigger than her tiny little dildo, which had never hurt. He filled her, stretching her wider than she'd ever thought possible.

Experimentally, she rocked her hips forward and gasped. She held him tight, her straddle taking him deeper until her clit hit his pubic bone, their bodies colliding in exactly the spot she needed him most.

He closed his eyes, took a deep breath, and settled his hands back on her ass with a groan. She lifted, then lowered herself onto him again, the friction making her dig her nails into his shoulders and gasp. Even though he was already all the way inside, the fullness intensified as he thrust, filling her completely until she gasped.

He shifted and sucked her other nipple, rolling his tongue around it as his hands lifted her ass, gently telling her to start the rhythm as old as time itself. She let him set the pace as he slowly pulled her back down on him. Her body trembled at his re-entry, and his deep, slow, sure strokes shook her. This man knew what he was doing, and her body was already humming in pleasure, the pain long forgotten.

She rode his cock, taking him deeper, wanting all of him. The tension built between her legs until she was lifting herself faster and faster. Wet and wild, a completely different side of her came out as he drove her closer and closer to orgasm, stretching her to the limit with each hard thrust.

He pistoned in and out, the slicking sound making her body arch into his. She grabbed the back of his head and twisted, wanting his mouth on her other nipple.

He hammered into her with a hot rush of pure need. Rough and gasping, she felt her entire body vibrate as her orgasm built. She teetered on the brink, then the storm swept her away.

She cried out and threw her head back as she came. Pleasure rocked through her in a soul-shattering orgasm that made white spots flicker behind her closed eyelids. Her toes curled as pleasure rippled through her.

He groaned beneath her, and she felt a heat spread with his pulsing inside. The fullness from before increased as he tensed, spilling inside like an avalanche.

She thrashed and moaned, lost in their combined climax to end all climaxes. Her bones went liquid, her soul shivering in contentment as she sank onto him. He stayed inside, letting her body milk him.

She wrapped her arms around his neck, letting them limply hang over the back of the couch. His hands wrapped around her in a hug as their breathing slowed and his hands caressed her ass slowly.

"Well, that was something else," he said breathlessly.

She hummed. "I'll say. If I'd known it could be like that, I wouldn't have waited so long."

He hugged her closer, his body relaxed under hers. "What do you mean?"

She shrugged and sighed, burrowing into the safety of his arms. "I've only done it once before, and it was nothing like this."

"Shit," he hissed, his arms squeezing her tighter. "If I'd known, I would've been gentler. Are you alright? Did I hurt you?"

She barely shook her head, too content to move. "I was worried you would, since I've never been stretched like that, but I'm good. More than good. I feel amazing."

His hands froze on her back. "Never? What exactly happened your one time before?"

She hummed again. "Hm, I'd rather not talk about it. But I have dildos too, and they don't stretch me like you did either. No matter what else happens, I'm damn glad we did this."

He chuckled, and he slipped out. "Me too."

She leaned back, suddenly aware that she was naked. She blushed, realizing that this was her first time naked with a man. She avoided his gaze and stood, gathering her pajamas.

"I'm—I'm going to go clean up."

He nodded and gathered his own. "Good idea, but you better run, or we'll have a repeat performance. I'm not sure I have any other condoms, so we'll have to be creative."

He wiggled his eyebrows, and she giggled, then ran up the stairs naked to her room. When she came back downstairs, he was asleep on the couch, his black basketball shorts higher on one leg and showing his blue boxer briefs.

She covered him with the throw blanket and went upstairs to her room. It was now almost ten. She was tired, sated, and sore, but she left the bedroom door open anyway, hopeful that he'd come upstairs and crawl into bed with her for a second round.

The next morning, she slept in. She hadn't slept that good in a long time. She stretched and hopped out of bed to find Mason.

He wasn't there. Instead, there was a note on the kitchen table.

Lucy,
Merry Christmas. I'd like to see you sometime, but my work schedule is crazy. Can I call you?
Mason

She frowned and looked around. He was gone? Her phone rang upstairs, so she went and grabbed it. Her heart was racing, hoping it was him.

She sighed as she read Taylor's name.

"Hey, chica," Lucy said, turning to throw on a sweater in the chill of the morning.

"How was your Christmas? Are you for sure moving back home? Do you have to work at the salon today?" Taylor demanded.

Lucy laughed and went back downstairs to clean up the snacks from last night. "I don't have to be there for another two hours. I'm just cleaning up the house now."

"What's to clean? Did you have a party and not invite me?" Taylor teased.

Lucy found some Ziploc bags to put the cheese in and tossed the popcorn in the trash. "Not exactly. It was just Mason and I."

"Mason? The best man from the wedding?"

Lucy nodded and put it on speaker so she could wash

the bowl hands free. "Yeah, do you remember the Ranger who took me home last weekend?"

"The hottie who I thought you were going to sleep with? Yeah, what about him?"

Lucy sighed, regretting not telling Taylor about all of it days ago. "Well, that was Mason. Nana's new step-grandson. The best man. My stepcousin."

Taylor gasped. "What? Shut the front door. No, he wasn't."

"He was." She'd wanted to keep him to herself and process the events of last weekend before talking about it, but she was no closer to understanding these feelings for him than she was then.

There was a beat of silence as she dried the bowl and found where it belonged.

"Wait a minute. You mean to tell me that after the wedding, you two stayed in the same house and nothing happened."

"Yep."

"Then he took you home last weekend and was asleep on the couch when I came in, so nothing happened *again*."

"Yep."

"And last night, the two of you were together for a private party." Taylor exaggerated the last words, but Lucy grinned as she repacked her presents into the Santa bag.

"Yep."

"I swear to God, Luce, if you say nothing happened a third night in a row, I am going to strangle you when you get home."

Lucy went into the living room and sat on the couch. It still smelled like him. She laid down and cuddled the blanket with a smile. "Okay, then I won't tell you nothing happened."

Somehow the pause of silence was louder than any words could've been, but Taylor couldn't stay quiet for long. "Wait, did something actually happen?"

"Well..." Lucy drawled.

Taylor must have slapped the table or something, then she almost yelled, "Lucinda Gail, you better tell me exactly what happened last night or so help me—"

Lucy laughed and started from opening presents at her grandma's house. Taylor squealed and oohed and ahhed while she talked, but otherwise didn't interrupt.

"And when I woke up, he was gone. Just a note that said Merry Christmas, and I'll call you."

Taylor was silent before she said quietly, "And how do you feel about it all? Are you upset he's gone?"

Lucy breathed and closed her eyes. "Do I wish he was still here? Sure, but it's honestly better this way. No awkward goodbyes. In theory, I'll see him at Easter, maybe Fourth of July, Thanksgiving, and Christmas. I can face him by Easter, surely."

Taylor snorted. "I can't believe you. Your first real dick in years, and it's to your new cousin."

Lucy wrinkled her nose. "Ew, don't call him that. I don't even know him."

"Only in the Biblical sense," Taylor chuckled.

"I wish you were here so I could throw a pillow at you. He's my stepcousin."

Taylor's chuckle turned into a full laugh. "Yeah, yeah. Go wash off all the cum and get ready for work and call me when you get out and are on your way home."

"Yes ma'am," Lucy said before hanging up. A wave of disappointment slivered into her post-sex high, since she still didn't know what Taylor was talking about with washing off all the cum. The condom had kept things pretty clean.

She tried not to think about it, but daydreaming and reliving it almost made her late to the salon. She had several appointments lined up from people who hadn't been able to get in before the holiday, but still wanted to feel confident for New Year's Eve next week. The weekend between holidays was always busy.

Chapter Nine

January

Mason stomped out of the doctor's office a few weeks later and tore his truck door open. "Stupid son of a bitch doesn't know what he's talking about. Neither of them."

He almost peeled out of the parking lot but needed to calm down before going back to the office. He wanted to burn the papers on the passenger seat, but it wasn't going to help.

He stopped for lunch, but he was still pissed when he stalked up the steps to the office. Several people waved and smiled, and normally he'd have no problem shooting the breeze with them.

But his career was on the line. He stopped by the secretary's desk and said, "Tell Johnson I need to talk to him."

She nodded but kept typing on her computer. She was a fierce woman, and he wasn't going to poke at her to hurry up. That would just make her take longer, so he went to his desk and sank into the uncomfortable chair. A stack of paperwork was in one corner, and he glared at it. They must have added at least three folders to the pile while he was gone to the doctor.

Simon started to walk past, then stopped. "Whoa, who pissed in your cereal today?"

Mason glared and crossed his arms. "Don't start."

Simon leaned against the desk and sipped his coffee. They'd been friends for years, which made being in the Dallas office the past few months tolerable without the field work he was used to down in Waco. He didn't say anything, just waited Mason out.

Finally, Mason sighed and raked a hand down his face. "The doctor wants me to have six more months of physical therapy and won't sign off on full-time field work. Today I got a second opinion, and that doctor said the same thing. Now I have to tell Johnson."

Simon nodded, his lips thinning. "He's going to bench you."

"Probably," Mason grumbled.

"You could take a sabbatical."

Mason narrowed his eyes on his friend. "Why the hell would I do that?"

Simon shrugged. "I saw your vacation request for next month on Johnson's desk, and I have an idea..." He trailed off and his gaze unfocused. Mason knew enough to let him puzzle out whatever was eating at him, but before Simon could say anything else, his desk phone buzzed.

"Hello?"

"Mason, I'm ready for you," Johnson said before hanging up. Mason sighed and stood, drawing Simon's attention.

Mason smiled ruefully. "Wish me luck."

Simon nodded absently and wandered away while

Mason strode to the hallway that led to his boss' office. Simon and a few other FBI agents worked out of their office, choosing to keep a skeleton crew at the actual FBI office. Simon said it was a matter of security. Mason secretly thought it was so the FBI would have their hands in the Rangers' pie and know more of the workings and dealings in the state.

Mason knocked on the door and peered into the office. Johnson sat behind his desk, an even larger stack of papers on the wooden surface. Actually, there were three piles. Mason sat in the chair across from the desk and waited for Johnson to look up from whatever report he was reading.

When he did, steely blue eyes met his own. "What can I help you with, son?"

Mason sighed and slid the two doctor's notes over. Johnson skimmed each with a frown. Then he looked up over the rim of his glasses. "More physical therapy? This is about that drug bust in Denton last month?"

Mason winced and sat up straighter even as he kicked his feet out and crossed the ankles. "Yes sir. I shouldn't have tackled the suspect, and it's put me back a bit in the recovery department. But we can still continue the plan, right? I can do range field work. Watch and observe from a distance instead of doing the hand-to-hand cases?"

Johnson rubbed his chin and leaned back in his chair. "I don't know, Mason. Do you think you can keep yourself out of the hand-to-hand work? Because I have my doubts. You like to be in the thick of it."

Johnson's frown made the hair on the back of his neck stand on end, and Mason shifted to bring his feet flat. He fought against bouncing his leg and leaned forward in the seat.

"I can do what needs to be done. If that means staying out of it and watching, then I will."

Johnson propped his elbow on the chair and rested his chin in his hand. "Hm, and if it means a suspect gets away or you stepping up to stop him? What then?"

Mason shifted in the seat, unable to answer. They both knew he'd do whatever it took to stop a perpetrator, whether he was signed off on the work or not.

"Exactly," Johnson sighed. "I can't have you following the rules while it's convenient only to throw them out the window in order to solve a case. I'll partner you with Taggert for the next six months. You'll work with him to dot all the I's and cross all the t's on the reports."

"But sir—"

"No buts," Johnson barked. "If you have even a hope of going back in the field, we need you in tiptop shape."

Mason leaned forward and dropped his voice. "You're trying to push me out, Johnson. I've been here over a decade, and the higher ups want younger guys that they can pay less. You know experience matters in this field. You need me out there."

Johnson stood and leaned on his hands on the desk, his eyes narrowing. "Exactly, so shut the fuck up and do your job. Keep your head down for the next six months and play ball. Then I'll work on getting you back in the field."

Simon knocked on the door and held up a file. "Actually, I have a better idea. How about sending him on sabbatical next month?"

Johnson stood and crossed his arms. "This doesn't concern you, Hargrave. Get lost."

Simon stepped aside and bowed mockingly. "Very well. Mason, come see me when you're done with Big Boss Man here. I've got a job for you."

Simon strode away while Johnson yelled, "He doesn't work for you, jackass."

Simon yelled back, "Not yet, asshole."

Johnson waited for the footsteps to recede then met Mason's gaze. "You could try, you know."

Mason frowned. "Try what?"

"Apply for the FBI again. It's been a few years since your application was updated, yeah? If the higher ups are trying to push you out, then you could move over to the FBI."

Mason wasn't so sure. If he physically wasn't capable of doing field work for the Rangers, what would make the FBI take a chance on him? Assuming he could even pass the academy training.

"Your vacation for three weeks in February was approved by the way. I just submitted all the paperwork." Johnson sat back down and asked, "Is there anything else you need?"

Mason shook his head and stood. "No, that's it. Thanks."

"No problem," Johnson said as Mason walked out. He really didn't want to do six months of paperwork. Day in and day out of the office. No fresh air, no change of scenery.

That was one of the biggest reasons he'd gone into this line of work. Working for Ray in Crimson Creek had been rather boring. With the Rangers, he had variety, especially when the FBI got involved.

He found Simon at the other end of the floor in his office. Simon grinned and waved him in.

"Shut the door and let's talk," he said.

Mason closed it and said, "Uh oh, this sounds serious. That can't be good."

Simon laughed and pushed a single folder across his pristine desk. Only a single laptop sat off to the side.

Mason took the folder and sat in the chair as he opened it.

"This is the preliminary report from the Denton drug bust last month?"

Simon nodded and leaned back in his chair. "This particular blend of heroin was laced with fentanyl and some other shit. It's a unique blend that we could actually trace."

"Shit, not more fentanyl," Mason grumbled.

Simon pursed his lips and nodded. "It's more powerful too, roughly fifty times more so than just straight heroin. Look at the second page. We followed up with some leads and found a pattern of cruise ships out of Cali. The Cali office busted one over New Year's and found the same blend. Page three shows their preliminary report too. Some cruises are going down to Mexico and Central America."

Mason flipped the page and frowned. "But this says Hawaii?"

Simon rocked his chair. "Right. We think it's coming up from South America through to Cali, then heading over to Hawaii before jumping planes for Guam, the Philippines, and Asia. Our Hawaii offices are aware, but they don't have the manpower to follow up on leads right now. Not after the incident last year."

Simon took a deep breath and rubbed his forehead, both of them thinking of the deadly encounter.

"This is where you come in," Simon said with a sigh.

Mason's brows rose as he glanced up from the file. "Me?"

Simon nodded. "Yeah, I saw your paperwork go through for a three-week vacation in Hawaii?"

Mason nodded. "Yeah, my grandpa gave me an all-inclusive for Christmas."

Simon put his elbows on the desk and linked his fingers together. "Hm, do you have an itinerary yet?"

Mason nodded and frowned. "Yeah, but what do you want me to do? The Rangers have no jurisdiction in Hawaii. We're strictly Texas, remember?"

Simon smirked. "Not if you put in for a sabbatical that starts first of February. Then I can hire you as a consultant for the FBI."

Mason shook his head. "And then what? That would just give the higher ups more reason to stick me on desk duty when I come back. I'm trying to get away from that, Simon."

"I know, I know, but if you have a successful mission in Hawaii as a consultant, you have your foot in the door. It makes a case for your application to move to the top of the pile. And with an internal recommendation from yours truly, plus you know Johnson will write you a glowing recommendation..."

Mason sat up, his pulse racing. "What are you saying?"

Simon smiled like the Cheshire cat. "Help us shut down this drug trafficking ring, and you're all but guaranteed a job with the FBI."

Mason's stomach flipped. This was his dream job, something he'd thought would never happen. He'd been afraid to even think about joining the FBI in the past few years, content with his work with the Rangers. They'd denied his application for years.

He sat back, his head spinning. Shit, he was serious. This was an opportunity he might not have again.

Wait, the doctors. He frowned and met Simon's

watchful gaze. "What about the doctor's notes about field work?"

Simon nodded, his gaze refocusing as he thought. "Keep doing what you're doing with the physical therapist for now. You'll want to be in tiptop shape by the time you go through academy, but that could take months to process and on board, then get an academy date. The doctors might sign off on it by then. Do you think you can handle the rigor of the academy?"

Mason's jaw clenched as he nodded. "Hell yeah, I can."

Simon grinned and stood, extending his hand. "That's what I thought. This is going to be great, Mason. I can't wait to bring you to the dark side."

Mason laughed and dropped the file back on the desk before shaking his hand. "Have you seen the new Star Wars show?"

Simon put his hands over his ears and shook his head. "No spoilers. Who has time to watch TV anymore?"

Mason grinned and walked to the door. "Don't worry. I won't spoil anything, but I do plan on catching up while on sabbatical in Hawaii next month." He turned and winked at Simon.

Simon picked up the file and said, "Don't forget to put in the paperwork for it."

Mason groaned, "Not more paperwork."

Simon chuckled as he left the office. At least the thought of this paperwork didn't make him want to grind his teeth. This was his shot, and he was going to take it and move to the big leagues. For the first time in months, he had hope for the future instead of dread. He'd done his time working up through the ranks, and soon the FBI would be his. Pops was going to be so proud and excited.

Chapter Ten

February

Lucy wrestled her bright pink checked rolling bag from the back of the hotel bus. It was already sweltering, but at least there was a soft breeze coming off the water. She joined the line that led up to the hotel lobby, pushing her giant bag. Another matching bag sat on top of it, and a third was slung over her shoulder.

Her pale pink summer dress fluttered around her knees. Thank God she'd remembered her sunglasses. The thirteen-hour travel time had dragged on, and although it was only four PM local time, she was exhausted. Her body felt more like nine PM and was ready for bed.

The hotel lobby was gorgeous at least. Open air without walls, big wooden pillars, and a thatched roof made her feel like she really was a world away from home.

She waited for her turn in the check in line and texted Helen while she waited.

Made it to the hotel.
Checking in now and about to get the key to the room.
Thanks again for this trip, Nana.

Almost immediately three little dots appeared, followed by her rather tech savvy grandmother's response.

I'm so incredibly proud of you, sweet pea.
You've worked non-stop for years to earn that master's degree.
(heart emoji, heart emoji, heart emoji)
Now time to relax and enjoy a few weeks of rest.

Lucy chuckled as she shuffled forward in line. She hoped to always make her grandmother proud. Heaven knew she'd disappointed her mother. Her grandmother had pulled her out of grief and supported her dream. She fired off a reply.

I'm not sure I remember how to relax.
The new jobs have taken some getting used to.
But thank you for the graduation present anyway.
I'm going to put it to good use and have fun.

"Excuse me, ma'am?"

Lucy looked up and smiled at the tall, gangly man behind the counter, his staff uniform crisp but slightly wrinkled. He had a frown on his face like he was perpetually worried. She smiled, trying to put him at ease.

"Yes, I'd like to check in please."

"Do you have your ID? I'll get you checked in and hand over your keys. We have golf carts that will take you to your room whenever you're ready."

He wiped the sweat off his forehead, and she opened

her big, bulky purse to find her passport. She handed it over and grabbed a map of the resort from the counter.

"Oh wonderful. You're in the ocean front bungalows labeled Peacock on the map. I see here your boyfriend already checked in. Here's your key. Please let me know if you have questions."

His voice droned on, but Lucy's brain had sputtered to a stop at the word boyfriend. She had no idea what he was talking about.

She held up a finger and tilted her head. "Pardon me, but did you say boyfriend?"

The man nodded, "Yes, a Mr. Mason Novak. You'll each have your own key, so here's yours. If you'll let me put this sticker on your bag, I'll get that taken to your room."

She shook her hand and swallowed hard. Oh God. Mason was here? How—oh. *Nana.* Dread filled her body. No, she wouldn't dare. Would she?

She grimaced and took the key. She definitely would. "Thank you very much. How many beds are in the bungalow?"

The man looked at her like she was crazy. "Just the one. Your confirmation from December said only one king bed. You also have the island-hopping tour. The concierge's desk is right over there if you have questions about your excursions or planned day trips. He can print out your itinerary."

Lucy felt her cheeks heat as her heart dropped to her stomach and turned to push her bag to the concierge. She absentmindedly had him print her itinerary while she processed what was happening.

Helen had given her the ticket for the resort to Hawaii at graduation in the beginning of December. Did Mason know she was here? Or was he going to be surprised like she was?

She took a deep breath, blowing out slowly through her mouth and reaching for the itinerary the concierge held out. A sense of dread settled in her stomach. She hadn't seen him since that night she'd finally lost her virginity for real.

This could be very awkward. Would he want to sleep with her again? A tiny thrill went up her spine at the idea.

She turned to the line of golf carts and a staff member took her bag while she sat down. After dropping her key and passport back into her bag, she pulled out her phone to see a text from Nana Helen.

I hope you do! (evil face emoji)

The emoji startled Lucy enough that she choked on her laughter. Her grandmother was on the church ladies' auxiliary committee and a woman of God. What in the world did she mean by that emoji?

She opened up the calling app.

"Did you get all checked in?" Helen didn't waste any time with hellos.

Lucy took another deep breath and calmly replied. "Yes, Nana, but there was a slight hiccup. It appears I'm rooming with Mason. You know anything about that?"

There was a significant pause on the line before her grandmother covered the speaker and mumbled to someone else. It wasn't enough to muffle the words, though. The staff member sat behind the steering wheel, and she showed him the number on her key before he started driving.

"Yes, she's asking about him. I told you this wouldn't work, you old coot. Now what do we do?"

Lucy rubbed her temple with her free hand then tilted her neck down and around to stretch the tension out.

"Nana? Tell me exactly what's going on here. You know I hate surprises."

Helen snorted. "That's an understatement. Okay, okay. You know how last year, all of us older folks at the church went on that cruise?"

Lucy nodded and held on while the driver turned a corner. "Yeah, that's why I'm here. You won the free trip while on board."

"Right, well, there was a little more to it than that. It was a trip for two, and technically Ray and I both won it in a strip poker match from a friend. It was the night we first started going steady, you see. And since the cruise was so life changing for us—we wouldn't have fallen in love otherwise—I wanted that opportunity for you too."

Lucy sighed, ignoring the love comment and the stinging pain it brought. "That still doesn't explain why *Mason's* here."

"He's had a hard time at work recently, and since the tickets and resort was a vacation for two, we decided he could use the time to get away and relax."

Lucy's lips pursed together before she huffed out, "Nana, don't play with me. You're matchmaking again."

A gruff voice came through the phone. "Mason's more law-abiding than the new sheriff and almost as strict. He won't take advantage of you if that's what you're worried about. He'll be a gentleman once he gets over the shock."

Lucy felt dread spread from her stomach through every cell of her body, leaving her cold and her feet tapping on the floor of the cart.

She licked her lips. "The shock? You mean, he's not expecting me either? Shit."

"Lucinda Gail McEntire, watch your mouth. You may be twenty-three, but you're still a lady."

She winced. "Yes, Nana."

"That's better. Now, you're going to march into your room and relax, maybe finish that book you keep nitpicking over, you hear?"

Lucy chuckled, unable to resist her grandma. "Yes, Nana."

"That's more like it. Now, once you find Mason, you call me back, ok? I want to hear all about it and make sure the dust settles."

The gruff voice of Ray came over the phone. "This is gonna be a good story, mark my words, Helen."

They hung up the phone as Lucy's cart rolled to a stop. Her expectations for this trip had just been tipped sideways, and she felt like she was on a slippery slope, about to plunge into the ocean beneath her.

She stepped out of the cart and stared. To her left was a line of bungalows, low houses with thatched roof that mimicked the main lobby. Behind the long, low bungalow was an equally long lap pool that she barely saw before getting out of the cart.

In the front, each house had four doors and looked more like four separate units, each with a view out the back of the ocean. On her right, miles and miles of endless clear blue ocean settled some of her nerves. She glanced to the edge about one hundred yards from the back of the bungalows.

The staff member pulled her bag out of the back and waved to the cliff. "Please stay away from the cliff. This is an adults only resort, so we don't have to worry about kids falling to the rocks below. We do, however, have to caution you against getting drunk and wandering too close."

She snorted and followed him to the bungalow. "Is that what the waiver was for when I got the key?"

The man grinned and nodded. "Of course. We will not be held responsible for accidents or stupidity."

Lucy chuckled as she handed him the key. He pushed the door open, and she followed him inside.

There was a small kitchenette right by the door with a small counter, a sink, and a tiny fridge. She inspected the counter and sighed, grateful to see coffee. The foyer opened on her left to a large bedroom with sliding glass doors that took up the entire wall.

She walked to the back glass door and grinned at the hot tub tucked into the corner of the patio, built into the floor. The hot tub had privacy from the other bungalow neighboring units, but they had to share the lap pool. Either way, she looked forward to lounging and staring across the ocean as she worked on her novel. The view was amazing, and she looked forward to waking up to that view.

She frowned, wondering if Mason would want to sleep in the bed. She turned to take in the room. There was a couch in the left corner along one wall that faced the bed. A door beside it was open to the bathroom, and a small computer desk sat in the opposite corner.

The staff member rolled her bag to the space by the computer desk and turned with a smile. "Will there be anything else, miss? The folder on the desk has good recommendations for dinner if you're hungry. Room service is open until ten as well."

She smiled and dug in her bag for the tip. "This is fine. Thank you so much." He left, so she sat her bag on the bed and dug out her phone. She took a picture of the view and sent it to Taylor.

So apparently, I'm rooming with Mason.

The silver walls of the bedroom were comforting to her anxious heart. They complemented the dark carpet, and a long dresser stood opposite the bed with a large flat-screen TV above it.

Three dots appeared. She practiced her yoga breathing techniques as she opened the door to the little back porch. A four- or five-foot wall separated the patio from the others that shared the bungalow. Unless her neighbors were in the pool, they wouldn't be able to see into her room.

Their room. Her phone buzzed.

Eek. This could be good or bad.

How could this possibly be good? I slept with him and haven't seen or heard from him in weeks.
It's going to be awkward as hell.

Oh, stop being so dramatic. You were going to have to see him eventually.

Lucy rolled her eyes and fired off one last text as her lids grew heavy.

I thought I'd have a few more months.
He doesn't know I'm here yet either.
He's probably going to be mad about it.

Lucy sat her phone on her lap and waited for the reply. She'd just close her eyes while she waited. Just for a few seconds because Taylor always texted back.

Chapter Eleven

Mason walked through the lobby with a headache. The woman he'd met with for coffee had been a surf instructor with a faux bright, peppy demeanor, but Simon had said she was his contact with the FBI on this mission. She'd shown him a travel binder and scooted close to flirt. Inside, however, had been details on the mission.

He'd promised his grandpa that he'd go on this fucking vacation, but the extent of his work here was already shaping up to be a full-time adventure. He carried the binder to the golf carts and asked a bellman to take him to his room.

He rubbed his temple. He was hungry and tired, as he'd gone straight from the plane to his room to town for the info drop. It might be a room service night, then early to bed. Sleep was the best way to reset his sleep schedule and shift to a different time zone. Then he'd be able to dive into the binder and begin poking around tomorrow.

Yes, room service on the patio sounded divine. The sun and ocean breeze were calling his name. Or maybe that was the seagulls overhead. The cart stopped, and he dragged himself out, tipping the driver before he drove away.

Mason opened his door and walked through the living room. It was a good-sized room with plenty of space.

He set the folder on the desk and went to the closet opposite of the bathroom. He tossed his clothes onto the floor and slid on his swim trunks. The sun would feel good on his scars, he knew, what little sun remained in the day.

He turned back to the room and walked slowly towards the sliding glass door, his steps muffled by the plush carpet beneath his feet. As he reached for the handle, he stumbled to a stop and pressed his hand against the cool glass and furrowed his brow as he peered outside. A wave of confusion washed over him as he frowned and stared at the sight before him.

A woman, her chest rising and falling in peaceful slumber, was curled up on the reclining chair just beyond the clear glass. Curiosity getting the better of him, he slid open the door and took a few steps closer, straining to get a better look at her. Her hair spilled out in waves across the cushion and her features were cast in soft shadows from the late afternoon sun. A sense of tranquility washed over him as he watched her breathe, lost in the beauty of this unexpected moment.

He stepped around the chair on silent feet and froze, his breath even freezing in his chest as his heart raced.

Fuck a duck, it was Lucy!

What was she doing here? He stared at her. Tall and willowy, her arms toned and bare in her spaghetti strapped pale pink dress, his fingers itched to explore every inch of exposed skin. It'd been weeks since he'd seen her, since he'd slept with her.

A stab of guilt ate at him over sneaking out and never

calling, but they'd agreed, hadn't they? So why was she here?

Bright pink sandals with sparkles matched her wide belt and hoop earrings. His eyes soaked her in, from the muscular calves to the tight waist to her graceful neck, perfect for biting.

His mouth salivated. The memory of the taste of her skin called to him, and his cock took notice. The woman was a walking cotton candy confection, and he wanted to eat her up. He didn't get to do that last time.

It was all he could think about at the moment. He knelt beside her and brushed a piece of hair off her face. Her long eyelashes fluttered.

When her eyes finally focused on him, her thick lips formed a perfectly kissable O of surprise. He couldn't resist.

He leaned in and kissed her. Her lips were plump, and he wasted no time in sweeping his tongue inside. He savored her, kissing her slowly with a dreamlike intensity. He liked the feel of her tongue tentatively tangling with his.

He slanted his lips and placed his hands on the chair, probing deeper with his mouth as if he'd find all the answers within her. He wanted all of her with a desire that slammed into him like a tidal wave.

The depth of his need for her made his heart race in panic. No, she couldn't be here. He was on a mission, and she could be caught in the crossfire. No, she was already too close, too important to him.

It would never work. Visions of his ex-girlfriend made the kiss turn from heaven to ash on his tongue, and he pulled away.

She blinked up at him, the dazed wonder on her face sending a pang to his chest. He was afraid of this slip of a woman. She jeopardized the entire assignment, and he wasn't just thinking of the mission. She was a weakness he couldn't afford.

"What are you doing here?" his voice was harsher than he intended. Pain lanced up his back from the crouched position, drawing a grunt. He shifted and sat on the other reclining chair, leaning back with a sigh.

She moved onto her side to face him as she yawned. "Nana and Ray set us up. They're matchmaking. I didn't know you'd be here until I checked in. They gave me this trip as a graduation present before Christmas."

He closed his eyes and groaned. "I should've guessed. He gave me the printout of the reservation confirmation as part of my Christmas present but didn't say anything that night we opened presents. It wasn't until I opened the envelope and called him the next day that he explained the gift."

"What'd he say? Nana said something about work being rough on you?"

He sighed and nodded, crossing his arms. "Yeah, I'm on sabbatical while my back heals."

Silence descended between them, then she said, "What happened with your injury? You were pretty stiff in December."

He smirked, "I'll say."

She grinned and blushed, ignoring his comment and looking down. "All I know is what Google showed me and what Nana mentioned. Something went down last summer, and the article said—"

"That's not open for debate." He winced at his tone of voice, but kept his eyes closed and reached for his phone. "Hold on, I'm calling Pops."

He sighed while listening to it ring. He saw her sit up and cross her legs to sit crisscross on the chair, making her dress ride up her thighs. His dick liked that, so he closed his eyes. He had to stay impartial. He couldn't get too close.

He certainly didn't need any more of that particular temptation.

The phone rang, then a gruff voice called, "Yeah?"

"What the hell is going on?" Mason growled.

Ray chuckled, surprising him. "Found your roommate, did ya?"

Mason swallowed hard past the lump in his throat and glanced at Lucy. "Sure did. Why is she here, Pops?"

"The girl graduated. She's there to celebrate her success, I reckon."

Mason rubbed his head. "Is that why you pushed for me to take the sabbatical? So you can throw us together? This is low, Pops. I didn't take you for the matchmaking type."

Lucy's brow rose as she shifted on the chair, pushing her tits up in the dress and showing some too nice cleavage. She was beautiful in the winter when she was all bundled up, but with this tropical weather, she was simply glowing.

He frowned as Pops continued, trying to steel his resolve against her.

"I pushed for you to take the trip so you could get some distance from what happened, so you'd take it easy and finish healing. It's been months, and you still haven't come to terms with it."

"I know, Pops, because I have to work—"

"You and I both know once this sabbatical is over, you'll be put out to pasture with the Rangers. They'll stick you in some desk job and trust me. It's not worth it. You need to figure out where to go next."

Mason sighed and looked up, catching Lucy's gaze. He might as well tell them both the truth. She was here, and he needed her to be aware of the danger.

"Pops, I didn't tell you, but the FBI wants me to do some snooping down here. Because I'm on sabbatical, they gave me a contract, and if all goes well, there's a job waiting for me when I get back."

Ray paused, and Mason just breathed heavily while Lucy's eyes widened. His back ached from the all-day travel, and he reached to rub at the spot.

Ray's voice dropped quieter. "Well, I didn't know that, did I? I thought maybe you'd move back to Crimson Creek. Even if I'm not the sheriff anymore, they'll welcome you back to the force."

He sighed and squeezed the back of his neck. "I don't think that's in the cards for me yet, Pops. I'd love to live close to you, and I see myself going back to the Crimson Creek police department eventually. But I've still got a lot of good years left in me, and if the FBI is calling, I want to take it."

A pause on the other line left time for him to arch his back. "I can understand that, son. Trust me. I didn't like when that heart attack put me to pasture, but I sure am loving life now. I just want the same for you."

Mason smiled absently at the ocean. "I love life, Pops."

"But there's no love *in* your life, Mason. Don't you see? That's where it all starts to balance out."

Mason's stomach dropped. They were definitely matchmaking, but he couldn't afford a relationship. Even if he could trust her, there'd always be some part of him that felt guilty going to work. His last girlfriend had shown him that, right before she'd been caught in the crossfire.

He hadn't seen it coming. His instincts were off, which meant he couldn't trust himself to do right by Lucy or any other girl. Lucy was picking at her bright pink sparkly nails.

She was bright, vivacious, and so innocent. She deserved more than he could offer her.

He sighed and stood, leaning one arm on the half wall that separated their patio from the neighbors. "I hear you, Pops. But it's not going to end how you want it to."

"Mason, it's time to get back on the horse."

His jaw clenched, and he closed his eyes against the memories. "No, Pops. I don't mind hanging out with Lucy. She's a great girl, but I'm here for a job, and I'm going to do it well. Without Lucy."

The pause on the other end of the line spoke volumes. He'd been by Mason's side throughout the chaos of last summer. The pause behind him said more though. He was afraid to turn around and see the hurt on her face.

"Just spend the next two weeks getting to know her, will ya?"

He sighed and rubbed his back again. "There's not really anything else I can do, is there? But I have work to do, so I'm not sure how much time we'll spend together."

"Just try, Mason. That's all I'm asking."

"Fine, but I'm not going to mix business and pleasure. Not again, Pops." He tried to clear his throat from the lump that threatened to choke him. "I'm going to go now. Gotta figure this shit out. Bye, Pops."

They hung up, and he glanced over his shoulder. Lucy stood up and propped a hand on one cocked hip. Her eyes were wide with curiosity and slightly sad, but she only asked, "So? What'd he say?"

Mason swallowed hard, the memories still at the forefront of his mind. "I guess we're here together for the next two weeks, but I do have to work, Lucy. Do you understand?"

She nodded. "I need to work on my book too, so that's

fine." She stared at him with those big brown eyes that seemed to see into his soul, and for one moment, he wished he could just relax with her for the next two weeks.

He glanced away and marched back inside to the built-in phone on the desk. He flipped through a binder, looking for the number.

"I'm starving. Are you hungry?"

She came inside and fiddled with her phone. "I am, but what are we going to do about the bed?"

He paused and looked at her as she plopped onto the couch, laying along the length of it and making her dress ride up again. Shit. How could he have forgotten about the bed? He groaned and sat in the computer chair with a sigh.

"I can ask if there's another room, if you're uncomfortable."

Just because they slept together at Christmas didn't mean they were automatically going to do so again. But if they shared the bed, the odds of more sex increased a thousand percent.

She shrugged and tucked her hands behind her head as her cheeks turned pink. "I asked about a room with two beds, but Nana specifically requested one bed when she confirmed the booking in December."

Mason snorted. "Of course she did. Your grandmother is something else."

She met his gaze with an arched brow. "Your grandfather isn't any better."

He grinned. "You've got me there."

Her blush deepened, and her eyes grew brighter. She lowered her arms and sat up, pulling the hem of her dress down and smoothing the edges nervously. "You don't have to ask for another room if you don't want to."

His pulse raced as his chest tightened. "Are you saying you want me to stay here with you? Share the bed?"

She shrugged. "I wouldn't be opposed to it."

He smiled at the words, reminding him of their night at Christmas. "I wouldn't be opposed to it either."

His words were too soft, but he didn't want her to get the wrong impression. He opened his mouth to clarify, but she spoke first.

She took a deep breath and blurted out, "We could share the bed. The couch isn't going to be comfortable with your injury. The bed's a king, plenty big enough for the two of us."

He stared at her and felt his body heat. "Lucy, if we share the bed, things might happen."

She shrugged, avoiding his gaze. His brain raced to find an excuse to keep her away.

"I didn't bring any condoms," he said, then winced. That wasn't the best reason, but it'd have to do.

Her cheeks flushed all the way down her chest. "Actually, I'm on the birth control shot, so that's covered."

His vision went white on the edges before everything hyper focused on her. It was like his ex-girlfriend all over again. That coy look, that blush.

But Lucy's not Amanda.

He knew that. Somewhere in his mind, he knew that. But he struggled to push past the memories while still keeping her from getting too close. He had to change the subject before he did something or said something dumb.

He cleared his throat and turned back to the hotel's amenities book, keeping her in his peripheral vision. "I'm not here for a fling and can't babysit you or entertain you. I have work to do, and it could be dangerous, so we can't go out and about on the island."

Her spine straightened as she scowled up at him. "I don't need a fucking babysitter, Mason, but just so we're clear. You don't have a girlfriend or wife tucked away somewhere, do you?"

He pursed his lips and shook his head. "Hell no."

Not anymore.

She frowned. "Rather opinionated about that, aren't you?"

He leaned forward, hands on his knees. "Lucy, I told you before that I can't be in a relationship. I'm not looking for one, I don't want one, and this is going nowhere. Do you understand?"

He felt like a parrot, repeatedly asking if she understood, but he had to be clear. Communication ruined so many missions. Her brown eyes narrowed, but she nodded before standing up and walking to her bag by the kitchenette.

How had he missed seeing that earlier? He was trained to notice fine details, but she'd snuck up on his soul, burrowed under his skin, and made herself at home. He scratched his arms and watched her.

She sniffed as she said, "That's fine with me. We can share the bed and if more happens, cool. If not, whatever. As long as some other girl doesn't come after me in a jealous fit, it'll be fine. I don't have time for a boyfriend anyway. I'm here for some fun experiences that I can use in my book, and that's it."

He flipped through the menu as a tightness pressed on his chest. He refused to analyze why as he rubbed the spot. He opened his mouth, but she kept talking as she unpacked her suitcase, opening and slamming drawers.

"I'm not so concerned about your work coming after me. This is a big island, and it's not like I have Taylor to drag me to a seedier part of town. I'll be safe and no one but this resort will know we're here together. Well, not together together, but you know."

He sighed and rubbed his forehead, his headache not letting up. Food would help, he knew. "Did you want something to eat? We can order now and take a swim while we wait. My back is dying to try the hot tub."

She gave him an order for a burger as she unpacked her bag, so he called it in. This was going to be a long vacation if he tried to keep her at arm's length, but he had no choice. At the very least, he had to keep this a casual fling. The more he was around her, the more his gut instinct told him he wouldn't be able to keep her out of his life. Just the thought of it made his head and chest hurt even more.

Chapter Twelve

Lucy finished unpacking and pulled out her makeup and accessory bags, hanging them up and untangling some necklaces.

She glanced around the bathroom, which actually had two doors. The first led to the small room with double sinks and the toilet. Then another door led to the jetted tub with a frosted window and a large shower with a bench seat.

She glanced at the tub, excitement coursing through her as she pictured a long bubble bath. Goosebumps raced along her spine to think that he might just be two doors away when she took that bath. Naked. Ooh, or maybe he could join her in the bath. It looked big enough for the two of them.

Lucy pulled her bikini on in the bathroom, her stomach in knots. This was a lot of stress and nerves to be a relaxing vacation.

Maybe it was the jet lag and the surprise of it all. He'd smelled of coconut sunscreen when he'd kissed her awake. And that kiss...

She stepped out of the bathroom, and her stomach flipped as she walked to the glass door to join him in the pool.

It was like every kiss was better than the one before. She'd thought she'd built up their Christmas encounter as some kind of amazing thing in her head. She'd spent weeks convincing herself that it really wasn't as great as she remembered.

And now, he was sitting on the side of the pool in those bright blue swim trunks, his thighs as thick as—as...well, tree trunks.

She chuckled at herself. This was highly irregular, as she was normally so good with words. She'd spent her entire college life in the library, talking with professors. None of it was with kids her own age and her vocabulary showed that. Normally. Around everyone but him.

Another message from Taylor appeared.

Well? Did you find him yet?

Lucy sighed and replied.

> *Yeah, he's going to stay here with me.*
> *But he's not after a relationship.*
> *Not even sure if anything else will happen.*

I call bullshit on that.
Of course, things are going to happen.
You're a gorgeous boss babe. He's not a moron, is he?

Lucy chuckled, sent a shrugging emoji, and tossed her phone on the bed. That remained to be seen, but so far,

The Ranger Gets His Girl

he'd been an overall nice guy. Sure, he'd pulled a gun on her, and then there'd been the drug bust...

She frowned and stared at his profile. He was one of the most handsome men she'd ever met in real life, but his job really was chaotic and dangerous. It was a good thing they weren't in a relationship, because she would worry about him all the time.

She opened the door, and he turned to watch her walk to the pool. Goosebumps spattered her skin, but she lifted her chin and refused to let him see how much he affected her.

How much she hoped for a repeat performance from Christmas. How much she wanted to confirm that it wasn't a fluke, and it was really that good.

She stepped foot on the first stair into the pool and looked away from him.

"The hotel doesn't have any double bedrooms or any roll-away beds." He ran a hand through his hair, causing some to fall onto his forehead with an Elvis cowlick.

Her stomach dropped. He didn't really want to sleep in the bed with her after all. Of course he didn't. She wasn't the kind of girl guys jumped at the chance to be with. Her shoulders hunched as she took another step into the water. Her hand snaked around her waist to hide the curves.

His blue eyes met hers, chilling the fire coursing through her veins. She took a steadying breath and stepped further into the warm water. She had to fake it and act chill.

"Guess you're stuck with me," she said before launching herself into a breaststroke. She was proud of herself for her steady voice and carefree tone. She would not let him see how much that statement hurt her. It wasn't his fault she was built like this after all.

A few strokes and she reached the opposite end of the

pool. He hopped off the edge into the water and swam toward her. She pushed off toward him. Neither of them talked until they met in the middle of the pool. Like two ships passing in the night, they both slowed to look at the other, but kept swimming as they passed.

"I don't mind being stuck with you. I just don't want to wake you up if I'm out on a stakeout or come back at odd hours," he said before he cut through the water to the opposite end behind her.

She kept pushing back to the stairs, and the burning in her lungs grew deeper. She hit the wall, turned to look at him, then pushed off to meet him in the middle again.

Taylor was right. She was a boss babe and didn't need him to have fun. She met him in the middle again and said, "That's okay. I'll probably be out dancing or partying or something. There's a whole island to explore."

She kicked away and kept swimming. Who was she kidding? She would last maybe half a day before she came back to the room, overwhelmed by peopleing.

They met in the middle again, and he growled, surprising her.

"Just don't go to parties at some random shady house, and you should be fine."

She rolled her eyes and swam away with renewed vigor. When they met in the middle again, she said, "Fine but don't go tackling anymore suspects either. Your back is already hurting, isn't it? Probably from a day of traveling and sitting in one position."

She kicked away. God, she was harping on him like she had a right to! She had no right to act like this. So what if this idea of him digging into some case while here made her nervous? It was his life, and he could do what he wanted. He was a big boy.

She flushed as she remembered just how big. They met in the middle again.

"Damn straight it hurts. I'm going to the hot tub. You're welcome to join me," his voice trailed off as he turned toward the stairs.

Of course, she wanted to join him, but she didn't want to appear too eager, so she waited until he was stepping out of the pool. Damn, that ass was fine.

She followed him to the built-in hot tub directly in front of their back patio. The lights in one of their neighbors' rooms turned on, but she didn't even bother to look. Instead, she followed Mason and stepped into the steaming water.

"You're going to write and work on your book?" he asked as he pushed the button to turn on the jets. His tone was no longer belligerent, but simply curious. Between his change in tone and the warm water, she sighed and leaned back against the edge.

"I am. Hopefully, I can push past this mental fog and get in the zone."

"Did you bring the Writer's Block or Writer's Tears?" His eyes twinkled, drawing her sharp gaze.

She smiled and slid back against the jet. "Nope, those are long gone. Enjoyed the hell out of them too, so thank you."

He nodded and pretended to tip his hat. "Anytime, little lady."

She chuckled and looked up at the sky. It was growing dark now, and the sun was setting over the horizon.

Ray's house was small but functional. Two stories with only two bedrooms and a shared bathroom upstairs, it was the perfect size for her. Living alone for the first time these past few weeks had given her the peace she needed to really tackle her novel.

Only she hadn't expected it to be so lonely. Her book had invariably turned into some sort of cozy mystery romance. She'd completely changed the setting too, making it more align with the sub-genre.

She had the mechanics down, had read enough to know how it was supposed to work, but when she wrote some scenes, it was all clinical with no feelings. The scenes she'd written before the Christmas incident with Mason had a rather lackluster view on sex. She knew it was because of her limited experience.

Now, every time she went to write, she kept daydreaming different ways Mason would act. What moves he'd make. How he'd make her feel. But that's all they were. Dreams—unless she could convince him to educate her while on this little vacation.

She bit her lip as the sun sank below the horizon. The feel of Mason's foot brushing against her calf had her breath catching in her throat. The man was a mystery. One minute, he was telling her no relationship. The next, he was asking about her book and playing footsie.

Before this vacation was over, she intended to unravel as many layers of him as possible. And finish her damn book.

A head peaked around the edge of the building, and Lucy frowned. The staff worker came around the corner carrying a paper bag with a receipt on the front. "Room service for 362?"

Mason looked over his shoulder and waved. "That's us."

He hauled himself up onto the edge of the hot tub before standing. Mason thanked him and took the bag to the two reclining chairs, moving the side table to be between them.

Lucy followed him as the staff member left. She shivered as the night breeze off the ocean hit her wet skin. Mason asked, "Do you want a towel? Hold on."

He darted inside, then returned with two towels. He tossed one to her, and it hit her in the face. She blinked, not expecting it, and snorted a laugh.

He chuckled and sat down. "You okay?"

She nodded and wrapped it around her. "Yeah, just wasn't ready, I guess."

"Sorry, I'll try to warn you next time," he said, his eyes twinkling in the twilight.

"I just haven't had a lot of experience with people throwing things at my head."

"You didn't play any sports in school?" he asked as he dug into the bag and divided up the food.

She shrugged and grabbed a fry, not really wanting to get into her past. "I was more of the hide in the library than the play sports kind of kid. What about you?"

He nodded. "I played baseball and football, but I really loved the drama club. It was my way of escaping the monotony of small-town life. I was more of a nerd than anything."

She chuckled and looked around. "I can understand that. Do we have any drinks in here?"

He nodded and stood. "Yeah, just a sec." He went back into the room and left the sliding glass door open this time. He held up a handful of mini bottles of alcohol from the fridge and two sodas.

She smiled and pointed to the table. "Don't throw them."

He chuckled and set them down, then she grabbed a vodka and chugged it. It probably wasn't the best idea with jet lag, but when in Rome. Or Hawaii.

She popped the top on the soda as she said, "Did you grow up in Crimson Creek?"

He nodded. "Yeah, with my parents and my little brother."

"Ray is quite the character. He used to be the sheriff, didn't he? How was that growing up?"

Mason nodded, his hair falling over his forehead. Her fingers ached to run through his dark hair. It would be so soft and silky. He'd let the gray hair grow in, and his temples and five o'clock shadow glowed in the pale light from inside.

"I never could get away with anything in high school, so I didn't even try. My little brother, though. He was a troublemaker," Mason chuckled and shook his head. "I joined the Army right out of high school as an MP, then went through the police academy at twenty-one when my four years were up. That's when I started working for Pops."

He was so young to have served in the Army and then joined the police. And she thought she'd done great things by getting her master's degree by twenty-three? Not compared to Mason. He was amazing.

She bit into her burger, trying to find the flaws. She couldn't get too close. It would be too easy to fall in love with him, but that was the road to heartbreak city.

"Was it hard working with him as your boss? He seems like a rough around the edges kind of guy, although he shows a different side around Nana."

Seeing the two at Christmas had been bittersweet. When he had given Helen her Christmas present, he'd looked at her like she hung the moon. He talked gruff, but underneath he was a sweetheart whose heart beat just for Helen.

She wondered if Mason was like his grandpa.

"It was hard because I had to prove myself to him and

everyone in town that I had actually earned that spot, that it wasn't just given to me because he was my Pops."

She nodded, taking another bite. "I bet you took all the hard jobs, didn't you?"

He grinned and his eyes twinkled. It made her heart skip a beat to see him playful.

"Sure did, but it paid off in the end when the Texas Rangers accepted my application. What about you?"

She shook her head, trying to brush off whatever spell he had on her. "What about me?"

"What was college like?"

Lucy picked at the cold fries. "Kind of lonely and boring, to be honest. I spent a lot of time in the library, never went to parties or bars like all the other kids. Unless my roommate dragged me, which she did a few times a year, usually around graduations or holidays."

"Why not?"

She shrugged. "I had goals and going out with the others wouldn't help me reach them. I had scholarships but had to work for more than half of it. That's why I became a nail tech. It paid the bills while I was in school. Toward the end, I got certifications in yoga, and that helped pay for my master's degree."

His brows rose, and he leaned back. "A master's? Wow, I thought it was just a bachelor's degree."

She felt her cheeks heat, and she glanced away with a soft nod. It felt weird to be praised, and she tried to wave it off. "Not that big a deal. Didn't have anything else to do."

He reached forward and put his hand on her knee. "Lucy?"

She looked up and met his blue crystal gaze. His eyes spoke of secret promises that she was afraid to believe in.

"Hm?" she asked.

"Take the praise."

She flushed and took another big bite into her burger. She was full but didn't know how to respond.

His hand fell away as he took a bite of his own food. "Why yoga?" he asked.

She saw his hands stroke the side of his tiny bottle of liquor, playing with the label. It was almost like he was touching her. She could almost feel his fingers sliding up and down her thighs just like that. Her knee still tingled where he'd touched it.

She cleared her throat and looked away. "It settled me. When the stress of finals came, yoga was the only thing that helped me clear my head."

"The only thing? Not drugs or alcohol like the other college kids?"

She scowled and shook her head, taking a drink, setting her food aside. "I won't touch drugs, and alcohol is fine in moderation, but going overboard and getting drunk just isn't worth the hangover."

His voice grew deeper. "What about sex? I hear that's a great stress reliever."

Her head shot up, and she met his gaze. "I—I didn't have any while I was in school."

He nodded slowly. "Yes, but why not?"

She felt her cheeks flame in embarrassment, but his eyes were just curious.

Chapter Thirteen

Mason frowned and took a drink as he thought. She nodded and looked away, pulling her towel around her body. He could see faint goosebumps on her arms as she squirmed on the chair.

"Sorry, I don't mean to pry. You don't have to talk about it if you don't want to."

She sucked in a deep breath and looked out over the now dark ocean. "No, it's fine. I—I had a boyfriend in high school. We fooled around, and it wasn't a good experience. I've avoided any opportunity since then."

"Until me," he said softly.

She looked up, her brown eyes hooded and vulnerable. She nodded and bit her lip. He wanted to take care of her. He wanted to protect her from bastards that would put that hurt look on her face.

But all he could do was show her that he wouldn't treat her like her ex. He had to make the next few weeks as pleasurable for her as possible. Without getting too close.

He gathered up their food and put it back into the bag while her big eyes followed him. He nodded to the drinks. "Bring those in, will you?"

He went inside and tossed the bag in the trash. She set the drinks on the computer desk, and he closed the sliding glass door before walking closer to her.

He faced her and ran his hands up her arms. "You're cold. How about a shower to warm up?"

She tilted her head back, and her pouty lips drew his gaze. "That's a great idea. Care to join me?" She blinked, her brows raised as if she'd surprised herself. Then she smiled.

He had to smile too. He liked her smile. He traced her lips with his thumb and said, "I'd love to."

He stepped past her and pushed open the bathroom door, going straight through to the shower and turning it on. It had a bench along one side, which was perfect for his plans. When he came out, he found her in the bedroom, rifling through a drawer of clothes stark naked.

She was one of the most beautiful things he'd ever seen. Tall with curves in all the right places. Toned and hot as fuck. She took his breath away.

"Shower's ready." His voice was deep and raspy. Her breasts were full, the perfect size for his big hands. He hadn't spent nearly enough time with them at Christmas. His mouth watered.

Her head snapped up, and she gasped, "Ah, Mason!" She grabbed for the discarded towel on the floor to cover up. "I thought you were getting in the shower."

He shook his head and stepped forward, not realizing he was moving until he was right in front of her. His brain had short-circuited at seeing her standing there. He couldn't stop his finger from reaching out to push the towel down slowly, exposing inch by delicious inch.

"No, I was getting it ready for you. Don't want you to catch a cold while on vacation, now do we?"

She sucked in a breath and let the towel drop, pink staining her cheeks and trailing down her chest to cover her breasts. Her hands wrapped around her stomach. Her nipples were a dusky rose, and he bent at the waist and flicked one with his tongue.

She gasped, and her hands waved to her sides. It was cute, like she didn't know whether she wanted to pull him closer or push him away. He straightened and stepped to the side.

"Your shower, Luce."

When he watched her walk to the shower, her ass swaying, his mouth went dry. This woman held a tether to him. He felt helpless as he followed her into the shower and stood in the doorway while she reached up and took the ponytail holder out of her hair.

The movement brought her breasts up more. Fuck. She'd hinted that sex was on the table for the duration of their vacation, and in this moment, it was all he could think about.

He shoved his wet shorts down and stepped forward slowly, giving her time to step away. She watched him warily as she finished her messy bun, and he pulled one nipple into his mouth, teasingly sucking. She arched her back, gasping his name and settling her hand on the back of his head.

He slid around her to back into the shower and sit on the shower bench. She came with him, her nipple still in his mouth, and he ran his hands up the outside of her thighs. Her skin was smooth as silk. He released her and looked up into her shining eyes.

"Tell me what you want, Luce." He wanted to make this good for her. He *needed* to.

She bit her lip as her eyes widened. Then she spread her legs further apart and blushed deeper.

"I—I want to feel your hands. All over. But especially there." His hands trailed over her ass and gave it a squeeze before sliding to the front. Her neatly waxed short mound of hair was unlike anything he'd ever seen before, shaped like a heart with the bottom tip pointing straight to her pussy.

He grazed his fingers down the short, cropped patch and cupped her. Her hands settled on his shoulders as she ground onto his hand. Her mouth dropped open on a silent gasp, and her eyes fluttered. She was so responsive, and he easily dipped a finger into her slick folds.

He watched her facial expressions shift with every touch until he found the spot that made her moan and bite her lip. Then he pressed into it, slowly at first, over and over until she threw her head back, the water cascading over her hair and down her back.

Steam filled the room, but he never took his eyes off her. She moaned softly, her eyes closed as she rode his hand. He flicked her clit with his thumb, two fingers inside, and she splintered in his arms.

She shook, her knees giving way, and he pulled her forward. He held her with one arm and felt her pulsing around his fingers. He was rock hard, but the beauty in his arms had him captivated.

"God, Lucy, do you know how beautiful you are? When you come like that, your little moans, the way you pulse around my fingers. It makes me want to turn you around and slide home."

She moaned and swayed in his arms. She squeezed his fingers tighter, and he curled them, making her gasp.

"Then do it," she demanded, raking her nails on his biceps where she hung on tight. "Fuck me, Mason."

He kissed her hard, their lips molding and his tongue diving inside. It wasn't gentle. No, this was raw and desperate. He needed her so much it scared him.

He broke the kiss and stood, spinning her around. Her hands landed on the bench, and she wiggled her ass at him. He grabbed his dick and at the first touch of her entrance, he groaned.

"Fuck, Lucy. Tell me what you want."

She glanced over her shoulder, her eyes half-closed with desire as she spread her legs wider. "Fuck me already."

His vision swam as he pushed just the tip in. She clenched, and he grabbed her hip with the other hand. "How do you want it? Hard and fast? Slow and steady?"

He wanted to give her exactly what she needed.

She dipped her head and faced forward again, breaking eye contact. "Nice and slow at first while I get used to you."

He gritted his teeth and eased in. She stretched and melted around him. Every gasp made him jump inside her. He pulled out almost all the way, then eased in deeper, one slow inch at a time.

She arched her back and lowered her head to her hands on the bench. The angle changed, and he went all the way to the hilt. He groaned and pulled out a little, then drove back in and paused.

He held still, hoping he hadn't cracked a tooth from clenching his teeth and trying desperately to keep it slow and steady the way she wanted. Then she squeezed him.

"Holy hell," he whispered. He set up a slow rhythm,

plunging into the wet heat that gripped him so tight. When he bottomed out, he paused for a heartbeat before pulling out slowly.

He started slamming in harder, holding still, then easing out. Over and over, he rode her. His strokes were slow, sure, and possessive.

Hands on hips, he dug into her skin, clasping her hips hard against him. His relentless thrusts rammed into her, too slow but oh so deep.

Finally, she threw her head back and gasped, "Faster."

It was like all hell broke loose. Hips bucking, shaft throbbing, he set up a brutal pace with her welcoming, wet body. She faced away, and he was bare inside her. The physical sensations were overwhelming, but it was more than just sex. He felt connected to her on a soul level in a way he'd never felt before. He was solely focused on her pleasure, keeping that goal in his mind's eye despite the pleasure that washed through him and made his eyes roll back into his skull.

When she pushed against him, meeting him thrust for thrust, he pistoned harder. She moaned, and the sound of her pleasure sent a shiver through him until he lost himself completely in her wet warmth.

Gritting his teeth, he hissed, "So fucking tight. That's it. Slam back on that cock, sunshine."

She clenched and pushed her hips to meet him, stroke for stroke as the pressure mounted.

"That's it. Come for me, Luce. Come all over that cock like a good little bird."

She moaned, and her entire body shuddered. Her pussy clenched around his cock and spasmed as her orgasm ripped through her. He fought his own release, but the need built in him with every squeeze. His balls tightened in response.

He pounded home with a groan and felt the tingle at the base of his spine. He clasped her hips, pulling her hard into a final deep thrust. He grunted as the pure animal satisfaction of his release swept over him, satisfaction that *he* made her explode, *he* brought her that mind-numbing pleasure. His body tensed as he spilled himself into her, internally crowing in triumph.

His pulsing cock gushed, and her body milked him of every drop. A fireball of pure bliss raged inside him until he was spent. Their bodies shuddered together, each fueling the other's climax. He melted into her heat, and it left him gasping as she continued to squeeze his cock until he slipped out.

She sank to the floor of the shower, leaning her back against the stone bench.

He stood under the water and felt the tightness in his back. She looked up at him through wet lashes with a content look on her face. Pride shot through him, knowing that he'd put that look on her face.

"What—what happens now?" Her voice was breathy and hesitant. He wanted her to look up at him with just that expression while she sucked on his dick.

But she wasn't ready for that yet. He held out a hand and helped her stand on wobbly legs.

"Do you need to wash your hair or anything? Now that you're warmed up, I'll put you to bed."

Her head shot up and her brows rose. "Put me to bed? I'm not a child."

He chuckled and cupped her cheek, kissing her softly. "I never said you were."

Her bottom lip stuck out. "Then why do you call me little bird?"

He drew her flush against his body and wrapped his arms around her. She gasped, and her hands fluttered to settle on his hips.

He smiled and kissed her again. Her lips just drew him in like a drug. If the world could market her kisses, it'd be just as addicting, but hopefully not as deadly as the drugs he tried to stop.

It was a sobering thought, so he pulled back and smiled. "Pops always said to be gentle around the little girls and animals. You remind me of both, so innocent and happy and flitting around from here to there."

She frowned but didn't say anything as she thought. "Innocent? I'm not a little kid."

He laughed. "Hell no. You're all woman, Lucy."

She glanced away and then laid her head on his chest.

"Lucy? What is it?"

She sighed and reached for her ponytail holder, avoiding his gaze. She shook her head and smiled as she lathered her hair, but he knew it was fake. "Nothing. I just don't feel like a woman sometimes, that's all."

He kissed her cheek then her jaw. She was so sensitive, and her insecurities had to have played a part in how few partners she'd had thus far. "You're definitely a woman. And not just any woman, but one of the most gorgeous, sensitive, brilliant women I know."

She blushed, and her smile turned real as she started to scrub her hair. He stepped out of the shower with a slap on her ass.

She yelped and looked at him with her wide eyes open in surprise.

He winked. "Don't take all day in there. The best thing for jet lag is sleep, and we're both beat."

He set a clean towel out for her, then dried off and tied it around his waist. He closed the door behind him and stepped to the sink. Funny. The mirror showed he was the same old man with graying hair.

But there was a lightness around his eyes that hadn't been there before. He reached for his toothbrush and pushed down thoughts on why.

Chapter Fourteen

Mason sat at the little cafe just before lunch the next day, his back to the corner with a clear view of the entrance door. He needed to see potential threats coming at him, and the woman who just walked through the door in a skintight white and pink striped dress was definitely a threat. That dress was meant to slay, with a deep v showing off her cleavage.

She wore pink heels but definitely matched the picture in his binder back in his room. She was the suspected ring leader's mistress, and he'd been tasked with watching her to gather what information he could.

They'd tracked her phone because someone at the FBI last week had put a mirroring code on it. He knew she was heading to this cafe when she'd put it into her GPS.

The waitress called his order, so he hopped up to pick it up from the counter. The target tapped away on her phone, not even looking at him. He sat down to eat his sub sandwich, his eyes and ears open as she placed her order.

She stepped to the side to wait as her phone rang.

Mason opened the mirroring app on his burner phone and held it to his ear to listen.

"Dollface, where are you?"

"The cafe on 7th, the one with the good smoothie. Why? Do you want me to bring you something?" She looked at her nails and turned to walk down the hall to the bathroom.

Now he was doubly glad he'd opened the mirroring app.

"Yeah, grab me a tuna salad sandwich and bring it back. This is gonna take a while."

"Are you still roughing him up? God, don't make a mess again. I'm getting tired of that shit."

The man's voice hardened on the other end. "You watch your tone with me, or I'll make a mess of you, babe."

The woman chuckled. "Promises, promises. Need I remind you not to bite the hand that feeds you?"

The man grumbled. "Whatever."

"Hm, maybe you're just hungry. I'll bring you back some food and set everything to rights, okay? Be there soon."

She hung up but was still in the bathroom. Mason set his phone down to see if she sent any texts as he ate, but nothing more came through. Then she was back and placing the second order.

Mason made a mental note in his head of the conversation, thinking through the meaning of it all. He'd need to follow her because they might have a prisoner or might be torturing someone.

He glanced down as he saw her send a text.

We're on for the Gala tonight.

No one replied, but he was done eating now. He slid the phone into his cargo pants pocket and cleaned up the table.

He walked out and down the street, dipping into a souvenir shop that looked over the door of the cafe.

He pulled out his burner phone and opened the secure app to send a message to the contact he met yesterday. He watched the door while he waited for a reply.

Yes, we have a ticket for you for the gala. Car will pick you up at 8. Keep following for now.

He watched as the woman exited and got behind the wheel of a red convertible. She peeled out, and he strolled to his rental car. He opened the tracking app and followed, not even catching up to see her car until she was turning into a high-rise hotel for valet parking.

He drove down the street and went around the block. When he came back to the front of the hotel, she was nowhere to be seen and the valet was taking her car to the garage. He pulled in and gave the other valet his keys with a tip, then went inside.

He glanced around the ritzy interior. Gold and mirrors seemingly everywhere, front desk straight ahead, lounge area to the right with a bar, and to the left was a large hallway that said Conference on a sign.

People mingled in the hallway, but the blond in white and pink stood out. She walked down the hallway with the to-go bag. Bathrooms were halfway down the hall, so he aimed straight for them, weaving between the thin crowd. He slowed his pace to see her push open a staff entrance door toward the end.

Dipping into the bathroom, he kept the door propped open to keep watch. She didn't come back, so he glanced into the hallway. No one was watching from the lobby, as everyone seemed to be focused on the conference.

He could hear guest speakers in the ballrooms on either side as he walked to the service door. It swung open, and a hotel staff member came out with a tray of hors d'oeuvres.

Mason stopped to let the man pass, but he was in too big a hurry to look back. With a smile at his good fortune, he slipped into the kitchen. He looked around, but no one paid him any attention. Kitchen jackets hung on a hook along the wall, and an office was open with a staff member on the phone.

Mason grabbed a jacket and pulled it on over his plain blue t-shirt. His cargo shorts stood out and obviously weren't part of the uniform, but no one seemed to even glance at him.

He spied a blond head disappearing through a door on the opposite side of the kitchen, so he walked through as if he belonged there. The door had a porthole, and he looked inside.

A smaller hallway led to the blond stepping onto a service elevator. He waited for the elevator to close, then looked behind him. A plate of pasta sat on a counter. He grabbed it and pushed through the door to see what floor she stopped on.

He stood there, watching the numbers light up. A door opened down the hall, and a security guard came walking toward him. His eyes narrowed on Mason's shorts and sneakers.

Mason's heart raced. He didn't know who was in the drug lord's pocket. He couldn't trust anyone.

He smiled and shifted the pasta. "Afternoon. Smells great, doesn't it?"

The security guard tucked his thumbs into his belt loops and frowned. "Sonny, I don't know what you're trying to pull, but you clearly don't work here. Are you going to tell me what you're up to or am I going to hold you until the police get here."

Mason widened his eyes and acted his heart out, pretending to be a dumb horny guy. "What? No, come on, man. I just saw the most gorgeous woman, and I'm trying to make my move. She'll think it's cute, right? I bring food. Every girl loves food."

The security guard rolled his eyes and shook his head. "You've got to be kidding me. Can't you just ask for her number like a normal person?"

Mason shrugged and glanced up to see the elevator light stop on the eleventh floor. "I could, but if I'm going to score with this blond bombshell, I have to stand out."

The security guard looked up at the light and back down at Mason. "Blond you say? I'm afraid you're out of luck with that one, sonny. She's taken."

Mason let his shoulders slump and his hopeful expression fall. "Of course she is. All the good ones are."

The security guard snorted and waved to the kitchen behind him. "I wouldn't exactly call her a good one. Consider yourself lucky you escaped her clutches. Trust me. Now come on. I'm going to escort you out of here. Unless you'd like to revisit that police situation?"

Mason shook his head and shuffled back toward the kitchen. "No, no, I'll go. Sorry, man. You know how it is."

The security guard clapped him roughly on the back, giving him no choice but to go back into the kitchen. "I remember, but you're not going to find a decent girl by stalking those types. You'll find the good girls in decent places like the grocery store or the beach shops."

Mason set the plate back down on the counter and winked at the guard with a grin. "Ah, but I don't want the good girls. I want the dirty ones."

The security guard laughed but didn't remove his hand from Mason's back as they walked through the kitchen. A few more staff watched them but didn't stop in their food prep to say anything. "You dodged a bullet with that one then. She's the dirtiest on the island, but not in the way you're thinking. Now, return the jacket."

They stopped briefly by the manager's office, who was still turned away on the phone. Mason took the jacket off and put it back on the hook as the security guard asked him if he was a guest at the hotel or attending the conference.

Mason shook his head since he had no conference badge or a room key to prove a lie. Then the security guard escorted him through the thickening crowd to the front lobby.

He smiled a hard, firm smile and crossed his arms as Mason stepped through the glass doors. "Now you have a great day, but don't try coming back in here, sonny. Not unless you're a guest, and even then, I'll be watching you."

Mason grinned and winked again as the valet brought his car around. "Don't worry about me, sir. I'm going to go hit up the beach and see what hotties are just waiting for me."

The security guard shook his head in disappointment even though his lips twitched. Mason got into his car and drove down the street. He circled the hotel in widening blocks and looked around.

Finally, he pulled into a parking lot and called the office.

"Yeah, it's Novak. She went to the 11th floor."

"Shit, that's the penthouse. We don't have any eyes up there. Our guy working at the hotel hasn't been assigned to clean that floor."

Mason looked up and squinted. "Do you have any surveillance equipment?"

"Like what?"

"Small drone with a camera or a long-range camera?"

"Yeah, why do you ask?"

"I'm two blocks away, and this old apartment building might offer a good view to the 11th floor."

Some papers rattled on the other side before she answered. "Yeah, I'll see what I can do. Meet me in an hour at the Costco gas station."

Chapter Fifteen

Lucy felt self-conscious in her tight floral print dress and pink heels, but she wasn't going to pass up her free ticket to the art event. She'd gone to the art museum today and won. Everyone who worked there had been jealous and had offered to buy her ticket, but she was curious. She'd never been to a fancy art auction and dinner before.

She'd gone all out with the dress, heels, and makeup. She'd even done her brown eyes with sultry evening makeup the way Taylor had taught her.

When she arrived at the estate, she followed the crowd up the stairs and into a large ballroom. People mingled as waiters brought appetizers and wine. She smiled and nodded but couldn't bring herself to just jump into a group.

She settled on the edge of the room where tables were set up. The silent auction had started with people walking around, bidding on items on the tables. She was enjoying herself when a hand settled on her shoulder.

She turned around and gasped, her heart skipping a beat in excitement. "Mason, what are you doing here?"

He frowned, looking down at her with a thunderous expression. "I'm working. What are *you* doing here?"

She shrugged. "I won a ticket at the art museum today. I'm glad you're here because I was feeling out of place with all these people. How was your day?"

Mason looked over his shoulder and ground out through clenched teeth, "Lucy, I said I'm *working*. You need to leave."

Her eyes widened. He was watching someone, spying for the FBI. She looked around slowly, not seeing anything out of place or even who he might be watching.

"Why? I don't see anything dangerous or unsafe. People are having a good time. I'm not going to pry into your business—I don't need to know—but if it's okay for everyone else to be here, then surely it's okay for me too?"

He shoved his hands in his pockets and smiled a tight smile. He nodded as someone passed them, but she could still see the tension around his mouth.

"I just don't want to see you get hurt," he said gruffly.

Her heart skipped a beat at his words, but his expression said he was reluctant. Was he frustrated because he cared for her? Or did he feel responsible because of their grandparents putting them in this situation?

She wasn't sure which one she wanted to be true. Did she actually want a relationship with him?

The lights flickered and people began to sit at the tables in the center of the ballroom. She frowned but Mason sighed.

"Damn it, stay close to me, alright? If anyone asks, I work for the Crimson Creek police force, and we're here on our honeymoon."

Lucy's eyes widened as he led them to a table on the opposite side of the room. Two older couples were already seated, and Mason introduced them.

Lucy shook the hand of the lady next to her as Mason pulled her chair out. "It's a pleasure to meet you. I absolutely love your dress."

They chit chatted as their food was placed in front of each of them. Lucy had already taken a few bites when a short, petite blond in a long flowing maxi dress joined them with her boyfriend.

Her blond wasn't natural. Lucy had worked enough in salons to know that kind of color took high maintenance. She also had her doubts about the naturalness of her breasts.

Her boyfriend was shorter but built like a gym rat. With his black hair slicked back and slitted eyes, the hair on her neck stood on end. There was something off about him. Perhaps it was the cold, empty expression in his eyes as he looked at her and nodded a greeting.

Lucy pasted a smile on her face and nodded at them both, forcing herself to swallow the bite that had turned bitter.

The woman smiled with bright pink lips and sat next to Mason. He turned stiffly and nodded hello as he chewed his food.

"Sorry we're late, Aunt Edna," the woman said to the older woman next to Lucy.

Edna patted her lips with her napkin. "That's alright, dear. I know traffic this time of night can be hectic. I'm just glad you made it in one piece."

The blond smiled and turned her piercing blue eyes on Lucy. "How do you do? I'm Malia, and this is Lee. Did we miss the auction?"

Edna shook her head. "It'll close when they bring dessert out. I expect a larger purchase this year with your new job."

The blond smiled and dipped her head. "Yes, Aunt Edna. Of course."

Lucy's nerves got the best of her as she grabbed her wine. "Congratulations on the new job."

Malia smiled, her face lighting up. "Thank you. It's been amazing so far. I never thought I'd be a CEO's assistant, but here I am."

Lee patted her on the hand and smiled. "And you're rocking it, babe."

She smiled at him. "Thanks. So what brings you to the islands?"

Mason cleared his throat and wiped his mouth, then he took Lucy's hand and kissed the back of it. "It's our honeymoon," he said simply.

The older couple at the table awwed, but Malia asked, "But where's your rings?"

Lucy saw Mason's eyes widen in panic. She looked at Malia and arched a brow. "Can you believe we've already lost them in the ocean? We've been here one day. One day! And poof, they just slipped off."

Mason latched onto her story and sighed, releasing her hand and turning back to his food. "I'll buy new ones, don't worry, dear. Do you know any good jewelers around here? Ones who won't take advantage of tourists?"

Lee chuckled. "I do actually. Let me write it down for you." He pulled out a business card and scribbled on the back, then handed it across Malia to Mason.

Mason took it and nodded at it before slipping it into his coat pocket. "Much appreciated. Gotta keep the missus happy, you know."

Edna pursed her lips and glared at Lee. "Glad to see some people starting a relationship on the right foot."

Malia leaned over Mason to whisper to Lucy. "Don't

mind her. She's just bent up over the fact Lee is still married to his harpy of a wife."

Lucy blinked. "Uh, I see. Well, you seem like a lovely couple."

Malia beamed. "Thank you, I think so too. So what do you do for work back on the mainland?"

They continued to chat as they ate, the conversation eventually turning to art and different places worth visiting on the island.

Malia said, "Do you have plans later this week? There's a Chinese New Year festival in a few days near Waikiki. You should check it out."

Lucy smiled, feeling more relaxed than she had before dinner. She'd misjudged them, and guilt crept up her spine. "I'd love that. I'm a sucker for a good festival."

Lee leaned back as someone took the stage and tapped the microphone. "That jeweler is on Waikiki too."

Mason nodded as everyone turned to the front and listened to the art director's speech about donations and sponsors. Lucy excused herself to go to the bathroom.

She stepped out of the stall as the door opened, and Malia entered. Lucy smiled and washed her hands, "Did you get to place your bids before they closed?"

Malia stepped up to the mirror and opened her bag to dig for her lipstick. "Yeah, I got them done. Aunt Edna will be happy."

Lucy pulled paper towels and said, "Good. There are some really beautiful pieces here. I hope I get the handmade coasters. My grandma would love those."

She felt the weight of Malia's gaze and looked up. Malia's eyes were narrowed and her face pinched tight around her lips, but when she saw Lucy looking at her, she smiled and relaxed her face.

"If you thought those were nice, just wait until you get to Waikiki. The vendors at the festival have some of the best goods around. Of course, they're overpriced. but tourists rarely realize that."

Lucy nodded and adjusted her dress as she stared in the mirror. "Thanks for the tip. I'll work on my haggling skills."

Malia chuckled and turned back to Lucy with a hand open wide. "Hey, I have a great idea. Let's meet up for lunch the day of the festival. I can take you around and make sure they don't take advantage of your wallet."

Lucy smiled. "Really? That'd be amazing. Where do you want to do lunch?" They walked out of the bathroom with smiles. Lucy had made a friend and wouldn't be alone. At least, not the entire time she was in Hawaii.

When they left the event, Mason ushered her into a car and closed the door behind them. They drove in silence, and Lucy felt more than tired. She felt this distance between them, like he was disappointed in her for being there tonight.

They arrived at the hotel and decided to walk along the paths back to their room.

Lucy sighed, "Okay enough with the silent treatment. What's wrong?"

Mason shook his head, barely visible in the dark through the solar lights beside the path. "Nothing."

Lucy snorted. "Don't insult my intelligence, Mason. You're mad that I was there and ruined your night spying on whoever, aren't you?"

Mason sighed and raked a hand through his hair. "Can you blame me? You weren't supposed to be there, Lucy. You were supposed to be safe back here."

"This is the frat house all over again. You tucked me away in that room to keep me safe from the shit show too, which I was fine with. But here? We're in a tropical island with so much to explore, and I'm not going to be hidden away in our room, lovely though it is, when I could be out here, living life, getting some experience."

They were silent for a few minutes before she sighed and added, "I am sorry I ruined your work tonight though."

She didn't know what else to say. She was just so frustrated by him being the strong, silent type. She'd seen a different side of him back in December.

The silence stretched until Mason growled, "You didn't."

She frowned. "What?"

"You didn't ruin it," he said. "You're distracting as hell, Lucy, but I can still do the job."

Lucy's stomach tightened and twisted. "Well, sorry for existing."

He grimaced. "Come on, don't talk like that. That's not what I meant."

"Well, what the hell am I supposed to think, Mason? You got all angry that I was there, you're giving me the silent treatment tonight."

She took a deep breath, trying to calm her racing heart. She finally pinpointed why her stomach was in knots anytime he mentioned his work. She had no idea what kind of work he was doing here, and the fear of the unknown ate at her.

"I didn't even know where you went today, for fuck's sake. Are you going to be in danger?"

Mason shook his head. "No, I'm just gathering evidence. Taking pictures, that sort of thing."

So he should keep his distance and be safe. Some of the tension eased in her stomach. They walked in silence for a few more steps, then she said, "Were you working all day?"

"Yes, I had to pick up some supplies from the field office, then trailed the target for a while."

Lucy reminded herself that this wasn't a relationship. He didn't need to check in with her or tell her where he was going. If she said something, she'd sound like a crazy bitch.

She couldn't just let this nagging idea fester in her head though. They were approaching their bungalow, and she needed to know where she stood before they went inside.

She had to know what she could expect from him. Lucy's stomach twisted again, but this time in nerves.

"You were gone when I came out of the bathroom this morning and when I came back to the room tonight to change. Are you avoiding me?"

Mason unlocked their door and followed her inside. His voice was distracted when he replied, "Of course not, Lucy. I just needed to work."

He went to the computer desk and opened a binder. Lucy felt a tightness press on her chest. He was obviously still thinking about work. He probably didn't even know she was there.

She was tired, but her mind was too wired to sleep. She slipped into the bathroom and put on her now dry swimsuit. Then she walked quietly past him to the sliding glass doors. Maybe she could quiet her mind with some laps in the pool.

Chapter Sixteen

Mason rubbed his temples and glanced at his watch. They'd came back to the room over a half hour ago, but he'd gotten sucked into the file. Some things Malia and Lee had let slip at dinner didn't make sense. The puzzle pieces called to him, and he needed to find out how they fit together.

He looked up. Where was Lucy?

A breeze blew in from the open sliding glass door. He stood and stretched, feeling the stab of pain on his lower back. He saw her reach the edge and push back in a backstroke. A dip in the pool sounded perfect.

By the time he changed and joined her, she was floating on her back and looking up at the dark sky. There were two guys in the hot tub at the other end of their bungalow, but the rest of the back patios were empty.

He did a cannonball almost on top of her. He heard her squeal even from under water, and he grinned as he broke the surface and pulled her to him. The feel of her near naked body against his own made his ears ring.

She gasped, and the sound went straight to his cock.

"Mason, what the hell was that? You scared the bejeezus out of me."

He grinned, "Oh yeah? Well, you scare me."

"What—what are you talking about?" He lifted her by the ass, and she wrapped her legs around him, making him groan. Her arms snaked around his back to hold him tight.

He walked forward, the water barely five feet and just cresting her shoulders. When her back hit the wall of the pool, he slid a thigh between her legs, making her moan.

He kissed down the side of her neck, saying softly, "I'm trying to look out for you, and you keep ending up in situations that I can't control."

"But—but you can tail criminals and tackle suspects?"

He frowned and nuzzled the hollow of her neck. "It's my job."

Her voice was thready. "You can deliberately put yourself in dangerous situations that you can't control, but if I do by accident, it's suddenly not okay? That doesn't make any sense."

He reached his hands down and cupped her ass, grinding his dick against her hot center. His fingers played with the ruffled hem of her bikini bottoms, sliding under to hold her bare ass in his hands.

"Mason." Her gasp of his name made him press into her, and she gripped his arms. Her long nails dug into his flesh.

"Lucy," he mimicked, kissing his way along her jaw to her mouth. When he reached the pillowy perfect lips, he leaned forward to kiss her.

But she pulled back, nearly leaning her head on the concrete pool edge. Her eyes closed, and he couldn't read her expression, but her sigh was as big as Texas.

"Mason, you—you don't regret last night, do you?"

He released a breath he didn't realize he was holding. When they were together, his head stopped processing at top speed. He could stop thinking about work because she took up all the space in his head.

He ground into her. "Does this feel like I regret it?"

She frowned and shook her wet head. "No, but you were gone this morning. We didn't talk at all today."

It was his turn to pull back. He released her and turned to lean against the back of the pool. Both of them stared out over the black ocean, stars visible to their right but not their left as clouds moved in.

He sighed. "I love my job, Lucy. I love doing new things every day, keeping the streets safe. I—I had a girlfriend. She hated my job. Begged me to move to a desk job. I put in applications with every agency out there to make her happy."

Silence fell as lightning flickered in the distance. Finally, her soft hand found his in the water, and she linked their fingers.

"What happened?"

He blinked, trying to push back the memories. His throat closed up, and he physically couldn't tell her. Not all of it, anyway. "It didn't work out. What I'm trying to say is yes, my job can be dangerous, but I'm not going to stop doing it."

She squeezed his hand. "I'm not asking you to. I just want to talk with you. Didn't we promise our grandparents we'd get to know each other?"

He nodded. "Yeah, I guess we can exchange numbers. That way we can talk."

"And you can tell me your work schedule? I had a lot of fun today at the art museum, but it was lonely by myself. If you have free time, I'd love to spend it with you."

Her voice was soft, hesitant and vulnerable. He turned and pressed their bodies together, gathering her into a hug.

His heart felt like it was beating out of his chest, and he kissed her cheek, his hands flexing on her ass. "I think I can make that happen, little bird."

She shuddered a breath, her nails digging into his biceps and making him want so much more.

"So you don't regret it? You aren't avoiding me?"

His chest hurt to hear the broken little voice coming out of this strong, capable woman. He buried his head in her neck.

"I could never regret knowing you, Lucy. And last night... I can't stop thinking about it, about all the things I want to do with you, to you."

Her breath shuddered. "Like—like what?"

He growled. Did his Lucy like dirty talk? His dick jumped at the idea. "I want to fuck you until you scream my name."

Her breath caught, so he continued. "I want to eat you until your legs are shaking around my head. I want to see and feel your pouty lips wrapped around my cock as I face fuck you."

"Oh God," she whispered, her nails biting into his arms again.

His lips hovered over hers, and she shifted, grinding onto his thigh and making his fingers dig into her ass.

She whimpered, "You—you want me?"

He swallowed past the lump in his throat, trying to clear his head from the haze of desire and register the note of pain in her voice.

"Hell yeah I do. You're every man's fucking dream, all tits and ass." God, he sounded like a pig. He ground her onto his leg, making her gasp. "No, wait. That didn't come out right. You're way more than gorgeous, sunshine. You're caring, kind, and scare the hell out of me."

She frowned and chuckled at the same time. She opened her mouth to ask how, but he didn't want to admit just how easy it would be to fall in love with her. He couldn't fall for her. He wouldn't.

It'd be so much easier to just focus on their physical relationship, but he'd promised his grandpa he'd try to get to know her.

He spoke up before she could ask. "I don't just want to fuck you, Lucy. I wanted to spend the day with you today. I want to get to know you."

Her lips brushed his tentatively. "Then what are we waiting for? Stop thinking and just—"

He didn't know who moved first, her or him. But their lips molded together, their tongues dancing as rain started to fall on his shoulders. Thunder boomed and the guys in the hot tub laughed.

"Hey, get out of the pool! There's lightning!"

Mason broke the kiss and glanced around, noticing the steady rain and distant flashes of light. He growled, lifted her by the ass and set her on the edge of the pool in front of him. Her legs naturally spread, and he licked his lips as he glanced down at her soaked core, covered by just a thin layer of pale pink fabric.

Next time.

Her eyes met his, and she tugged on his biceps. "Come on, we have to leave. This is dangerous."

"You're dangerous," he ground out, stepping to the side and hauling himself up and out of the pool. She didn't hear him and thank God for that. He wasn't sure he could explain why. He only knew that she threatened everything he thought he'd known.

She spun around and took the few steps to their section of the patio, once more secluded from others in their own little world.

They each took a towel from the chairs and dried off in silence. He wasn't cold from being wet, quite the opposite. Being near her, having touched her and held her so close—he was radiating heat.

He could feel the tension between them as he followed her inside and closed the glass door. She started to walk around the bed, but he pushed her against the wall and crushed his mouth to hers.

She smelled of sunscreen and tasted of oranges. Her towel fell to the floor as she wrapped her arms around his shoulders and tipped her head back to deepen the kiss.

He never wanted to stop kissing her. She was more addicting than any drug. Fear raced along his spine, but he couldn't stop kissing her any more than he could stop a tsunami.

Chapter Seventeen

Lucy's mind splintered as their kiss deepened. The back-and-forth swish of his tongue mimicked his hips, but it was his fingers on her ass that drove her crazy. He held her against the wall as if she weighed nothing.

She broke the kiss with a gasp, tugging on his hair. He growled and nipped down her neck, biting and kissing and making her core clench.

"Oh God," she moaned as his fingers dove inside the band of her swimsuit. His long fingers barely teased her wet open slit, but it left her begging. She dug her nails into his scalp and back. "Mason, please."

"What does my little bird want?" he whispered.

"Fuck me already," she moaned. Her mind was hazy with desire. Her pulse raced, and she felt like she was going to hyperventilate.

He spun around and laid her on the bed, ripping her bikini bottoms down as he stepped away.

"The top," he growled, clearly beyond sentences already.

She felt a thrill down her spine as she hurried to comply. She had driven him to that wild look in his eyes as he pushed his wet trunks down and stroked himself.

She licked her lips, wondering what he'd taste like. She sat up and reached for him, but he grabbed her hips first, pulling her to the edge of the bed and dropping to his knees.

His lips traced soft kisses from the inside of her knee up to her wet pussy. She squirmed, trying to find somewhere for her feet to rest. He reached up and wrapped her legs around his head, her thighs on his wide shoulders.

She lifted on her elbows to look at him, barely visible with the faint patio lights outside. His piercing blue eyes met hers right as his lips latched onto her clit.

She moaned, falling back on the bed as he sucked as if his life depended on it. His mouth worked its magic on her, alternating between the almost painful sucking and some soothing motion with his tongue.

She saw stars. She liked the feel of his lips, tongue, the way he drove her to distraction. Then he added a finger inside. She clenched on it, feeling her heart race toward a cliff. She was going to go over the edge any minute—

He added another finger, and her entire body was on fire with pleasure. Compulsive waves gripped her as she spasmed around him, her orgasm hitting full force. It robbed her of her senses. All she knew was the curl of his fingers, the hum of his mouth on her clit.

Her shaking slowed. She savored the little licks until he rose to his feet. He teased her entrance with his big dick.

"This what you want, little bird?"

She whimpered, unable to hold it and unwilling to try. "God, yes."

"Then tell me," he demanded.

She gasped, "Fuck me with that big dick. Fuck me. Fuck me now."

He groaned and slammed in to the hilt. She stretched on a silent scream as her muscles clamped down on him and held him prisoner. He slid out, and she whimpered.

"That's it. Take that dick, little bird." He thrust into her, the tendons on his neck standing out in the faint light. His hands slid under her knees, and he held her legs wide, holding still and deep within her. "Are you ready for a good fucking, sunshine?"

Her thighs burned, and she gasped, gripping the blanket beneath her hands. "Yes, yes, for fuck's sake, yes." The last sound stretched to a moan as he pulled out before plunging in deep once more. She arched her hips, meeting him thrust for thrust as he set up a steady rhythm.

"I want you to come on that dick. That's it, squeeze me tight. That's a good girl," his murmurings were soft. Every word out of his mouth made her moan and squeeze him tighter. She moved under him as he filled her. His thrusts were relentless, and she gloried in it.

Her body ached, demanding more, begging to be filled completely. Still he slammed into her, leaving her gasping for air.

"Touch yourself, sunshine." His command compelled her. She bit back a whimper as she cupped her breasts and lifted them up. "Oh yes, that's it. Pinch those nipples, baby."

She pinched and rolled them between her fingers. It triggered her pussy to clench on him, and she felt the pressure building once more.

His fingers bit into her thighs as he held her open. "That's it. Come for me, sunshine. Take this dick and come all over me."

The tension doubled at his words as her body chased

the orgasm. Her mind splintered, and she erupted. No more thinking. No more worries. Just the shock waves ripping through her as she cried out and threw her head back.

"Oh God yes," he moaned, thrusting deep twice more before he came with a growl. His dick swelled inside, making her pulse around him as he exploded. It was violent and virile, making them both gasp.

He stayed inside, letting her body milk him as his back bowed with his own spasms. He was all hard, sweaty muscles glistening in the soft light. She had put that open-mouthed slack jawed look of awe on his face. Pride swirled inside as she gazed up at him.

His eyes opened and met hers. She reached up and placed a palm on his chest. The moment seemed to last forever as they just soaked up each other's presence, staring into each other's eyes and basking in the vulnerability echoed within the other. Finally, he licked his lips and took a deep breath.

"I don't know what it is about you, Lucy, but you're one of a kind." He lowered her legs and stepped back, slipping free with a pop. "Come on, let's get you cleaned up in the shower."

Her mind was still too fractured to think as he tugged on her hand. She stood and, fingers laced, walked to the bathroom with him.

He turned the water on, and she stepped behind him, wrapping her arms around his waist. They just stood there as she felt his breathing even. His hands covered hers on his chest, then he reached out and tested the water.

"Come on, little bird. In you go," he murmured softly. She pulled her eyes open and followed him into the water. He sat on the bench and pulled her onto his lap, draping her legs to one side.

She leaned her head back against the wall. Her entire body felt boneless and satiated. He grabbed the loofa on the shelf next to him and lathered up her legs. She hummed with pleasure.

"You don't have to do that. I can wash myself."

The loofa swished back and forth over her stomach as he replied. "I know, but I want to. I like taking care of you, little bird. It makes me feel needed, and it's been a while since I've felt like this."

She smiled, her eyes still shut. "Me too. Actually, I've never felt like this. My ex in high school was a dick, but didn't do much *with* his dick, if you know what I mean."

Mason snorted as he ran his hands and the loofa over her breasts. "I'm sorry but also not sorry. Now I get to show you all kinds of things."

She grinned and opened her eyes as his hand dove between her legs. "Oh yeah? What do you want to show me?"

He pressed her legs apart, setting one foot on the floor of the shower with the other still across his lap. She saw his dick was half-hard again as he dipped his fingers in and around her, gently cleaning her up.

His blue eyes darkened with desire as he played with her slowly. "I want to show you the world."

She giggled and broke into song. "Shining, shimmering, splendid."

His eyes widened and he arched a brow. "You want me to call you princess from now on?"

She laughed. "Do you want me to call you street rat?"

He grinned and flicked her clit, making her gasp and her laughter fade. "I want you to call me master."

He slid a finger inside, and her eyes fluttered. "I—I can do that. But why?"

He pressed another inside, stretching her and making her tremble. "I want to master your body like a puppet on a string, pulling every orgasm out of you. I want to make you scream as you come. I know you got your master's degree, but I want to master your body, your mind, your soul. Do you like that idea, little bird?"

She looked at him through heavy-lidded eyes as her breathing grew shorter. She was too sensitive, and his fingers were distracting her. Was it a deal? Did that mean their relationship would continue after this two-weeks was over?

"Maybe," she said. "I guess we'll take each day one at a time and see how it goes. At least for this trip."

He nodded and paused, then his thumb circled her clit. "Are you ready for bed, little bird?"

She hummed, then sat up. "Yeah, but first there's something I want to try. If you're up for it." She crawled onto her knees in front of him, the warm water falling over her skin and soothing her as his fingers left her body.

His hands settled on either side of her face, and he leaned forward and kissed her. It was tender, gentle, and somehow more meaningful than any of their sexual encounters so far. It was full of gratefulness, of awe, of promises she was scared to question. When he pulled back and smiled, she knew it was only a matter of time before she fell in love with him. She probably wouldn't survive the two weeks.

"What did you have in mind?" he asked, his voice deep and dark.

She licked her lips and looked down at his dick. "It's just, I've not spent any amount of time with a dick before. My ex... it was a lot of heavy petting and in the dark. I—I wasn't, well, he said I wasn't that attractive and didn't want to take our clothes off. Anyway, I was hoping you'd let me, um, will you teach me how to give a blow job? I don't know what all the fuss is about, and I—"

His lips crashed to hers again, and she grabbed his thighs as he drew her closer. His tongue dove inside, twirling and twisting, making her gasp and try to take him deeper.

"God, yes. Lucy, little bird, my sunshine, you never have to ask," he chuckled, releasing her face and leaning back against the shower wall. "I wasn't sure how much you wanted to explore sexually, and I never want to push you into things. But yes, feel free to explore to your heart's content."

She looked down, hesitant as she slowly drew her hands up his thick thighs and traced her fingers along his cock. "If you're going to be master, does that make me your padawan?"

His eyes widened. "Hell yeah. Do you finally agree Star Wars is superior?"

She wanted to roll her eyes but was mesmerized by his dick. "We'll see."

He hissed a breath, and she glanced up then back down at him. It curved up toward his stomach now, and the head was darker than the rest. She followed the thick vein on the underside to the tip, then wrapped her hand around it.

Her fingers didn't connect all the way around, but she leaned down and licked the tip. It was salty but not overwhelmingly so like the ocean. She wrapped her other hand around it and slid them both up and down. It was hard as metal but soft as silk.

His hand settled on her cheek and pushed her hair back. He wrapped his hand around it like a ponytail, but he didn't force her head down. She looked up at him through heavy lashes then wrapped her mouth around the tip.

His breath caught in his throat, and his eyes grew

darker. It was like he was waiting on the precipice. She had all the control, and it was a heady sensation. She wouldn't mind having this control over him, making him so blind with desire that he could do nothing on his own. She had him in the palm of her hand. He wanted to be the master, but in this moment, she was.

She slowly took him deeper.

"God yes, Lucy. Just like that. Choke on that dick like a good little girl."

Lucy's own breathing went ragged to hear him talk dirty. It made her pussy pulse with desire.

"Wrap the other hand around my balls. Tug on them like this." He took her hand and showed her how he liked it. Her other hand still on his shaft, she set up a steady motion.

He threw his head back and closed his eyes with a groan. "God, yes, just like that. Fucking hell, little bird, suck that dick. I want to cum in your mouth."

She moaned and rocked forward, taking him deeper. Her gag reflex triggered, and she jerked herself up, gasping for air.

"That's it. I love it when you gag on me, bird. I just want to grab your head and slam your little mouth down on my cock."

She moaned and did it herself. His hand holding her hair nudged her, but he didn't force her. No, he was talking her through it, using his words to get exactly what he wanted. She gagged as she slammed her own mouth down so hard she choked.

And she loved it. It made her feel powerful but also at his mercy. She wanted to please him, but in doing so, she was more turned on than she'd ever been.

His hips began to thrust as he growled. Her tongue glided over his shaft in deep strokes as she sucked. She tugged on his balls, and his back bowed as his balls tightened.

He roared and came in a rush of hot cream. It surprised her as it hit the back of her throat. He flooded her mouth, each spurt sending more into her mouth until she choked and pushed herself off.

She fell to the floor of the shower as he grabbed his cock. He jerked his hand. White still spewed out of the tip, and she watched, fascinated as it landed on her chest and legs before the water washed it away.

She panted, looking up at him through hooded eyes, her body too weak to move. He sat back heavily on the bench and reached out a hand to cup the back of her head. She nuzzled into his hand and just sat in the silence, breathing in the orange blossom shampoo and the scent of their love making.

"Is that what you wanted?" His voice was harsh, but when she looked into his face, his eyes were dark and spoke volumes. Hot with promises, his black lashes flickering as he swept his gaze down her body.

She swallowed past the lump in her throat and nodded. "Yes, it was exactly what I wanted. Did I—do it right?"

He nodded, satisfaction settling over his face as he brushed the hair out of her eyes. "Baby, it was perfect. I think you're a pro already. Such a good girl," he chuckled, making her grin. "Are you done in here or do you need to do more washing?"

"I'm done." She yawned, and he helped her to her feet. He stood, turned off the water, and rubbed the towel up and down her body hard enough to make her giggle. Then he scooped her into his arms.

He settled her onto the bed with a sigh and tucked her under the covers. The rain still pelted the doors to the balcony and flashes of lightning cast shadows over his angular features before he stepped away from the bed.

Sleepily, she snuggled into the sheets. He came back a few minutes later, and she smelled minty toothpaste as she curled into his chest. His voice was soft as he brushed his hand along her arm softly.

"For the record, your ex has to be the stupidest man alive, to not want you naked. You're a goddess, Lucy. A fucking goddess."

She smiled, too sleepy to respond as the warmth of his words soothed some deep-rooted hurt within her soul. She definitely wasn't going to last the full two weeks before falling for him if he kept saying things like that. Curiously, she wasn't that afraid of love anymore though.

Chapter Eighteen

Lucy drank her coffee on the patio, looking over the ocean. Her mind kept picturing Mason's naked chest and all she wanted to do to him. She channeled all the desire and hope into her story and typed furiously on her phone.

Her main character flirted with the cop in charge of the murder investigation. They had just discovered a new clue when Mason sat down beside her. She looked up, blinking as she was pulled out of the story.

"Morning." His voice was gruff but his eyes were clear and open.

Her brows rose in surprise. "You're still here."

He nodded and sank onto the other patio chair, careful not to spill his own coffee. "I told you we'd do better about talking today. I'm going to head to work, but I don't have your number."

She opened the create contact on her phone and passed it to him. "What time will you finish working today?"

"Hoping for early afternoon."

"Great. Text me when you're done, and we'll meet up.

I'm going to write on the balcony and stare at the ocean for a few hours, then I might wander to the beach for some suntanning."

He handed her phone back, and she glanced down. She choked on her coffee, making some drip down onto her yoga shirt.

He grinned mischievously. "You okay, sunshine?"

She narrowed her eyes at him and took a drink to soothe her throat. He winked, making her blush. "Master?"

He shrugged. "Why not? I like teasing you and seeing that blush creep up your neck. How far down—"

Her phone alarm went off. "Ah, it's time for a writing sprint."

He stood and stretched. "I have to get to work anyway. I'll see you later?"

She nodded and Mason disappeared inside. When he came out, he was dressed in jeans and sneakers and a plain blue t-shirt.

He smiled and put his sunglasses on his nose, then leaned over to kiss her cheek. She felt a spike of nerves in her stomach. It was such an adorable, domesticated thing to do, kissing her goodbye before he left for work.

Her body had other ideas though, automatically turning her lips to meet his.

She gasped and opened her mouth as he groaned, then his hands wrapped around her head. The duel was on.

There was no other word for it. It was like their tongues were fighting or dancing. She was swept up in the kiss, the taste of him flooding her senses. Her knees went weak, but he took the kiss deeper, like always.

It set off a wild need within her. Where he touched, her body came alive as if from hibernation, as if she hadn't had mind blowing orgasms last night. This was what she'd been missing for so long. This feverish need made her lose all thoughts and inhibitions. It was better than getting drunk, better than chocolate and a bubble bath.

A sound bounced through her mind, but it wasn't until he broke the kiss and nibbled her lower lip that she registered her second phone alarm.

He pulled back and sighed, brushing her hair away from her face with a smile. "Have a great day, sunshine."

Her breath was ragged as she said, "You too, master."

He opened the door and looked over his shoulder with a grin. "Good girl. I like the sound of that on your lips."

She grinned. "Maybe master will like something else on my lips later."

His eyebrows rose as he chuckled, "Oh, definitely."

He shut the door behind him. Her heart rate eventually slowed, then she turned back to her book, typing away as a rush of inspiration hit.

Her phone alarm went off hours later, and she stretched. She'd made good progress on her book, but her stomach was growling now. She got up, changed, and headed for the front building to find the lunch buffet.

When her phone rang, she smiled. "Taylor! It's so good to hear your voice."

"Hey babe, tell me all the things. How's hunky roommate man?"

Lucy kept up a steady stream of chatter with Taylor on the phone, filling her in on all that'd happened on her trip so far. She walked through the jungle, following the golf cart trail to the main resort building.

She was determined to enjoy the island and relax. She told her friend bye and pulled up her phone itinerary. There were so many places she planned on exploring.

She smiled at the hostess and gave her drink order, then

grabbed a plate and hit the buffet. She had just sat down and taken two bites when Mason sat across from her with a heaping plate.

She blinked. "Oh, did you get off work early? I wasn't expecting you back for another few hours."

The waitress brought him coffee. Before he took a bite, he nodded. "Yeah, I was relieved of my shift. I didn't argue with them, as I wanted to get back to you as quickly as possible. What's on our agenda for today?"

His words melted her heart, and she grinned and leaned forward. "Do you want to stay here at the resort in our room or go out and explore?"

He looked at her under heavy lidded eyes as he chewed a bite of lunch. When he swallowed, he arched a brow. "You wanted to explore, right? As long as we're safely away from the area I've been surveilling, we should be fine. Although…"

"Although?" she asked, her hands pausing on her fork.

He grinned and wiggled his eyebrows. "Let's make sure the schedule has plenty of time to explore our room when we get back."

She laughed and rubbed her hands together. "It's a deal then. Today, I was going to Pearl Harbor then to the pineapple plantation. Is that okay with you?"

He shrugged. "Sounds fun. I like military history and have always wanted to see Pearl Harbor."

They hopped in his rented car and took off on an adventure. As far as adventures go though, it was rather boring. They spent a few hours at Pearl Harbor, got lost in the maze at the plantation, ate at a little restaurant for dinner, then began the drive back to the resort.

Mason kept looking in his rear-view mirror and frowning, which led her to looking in her side mirror. An old green car followed them for miles. Had it been there since they'd left the restaurant?

Eventually he pulled onto a small dirt road that opened to a dirt parking lot.

She looked around, sitting up in the seat. "Everything okay? I thought we were going back to the resort?"

"Yeah, give me a few minutes." His voice made it clear that he was distracted, and his body was definitely tense. He looked in the rear-view mirror as the green car drove past the turn off.

She couldn't see into the car, but Mason seemed to relax after they left. He smiled and reached behind him to pull out a backpack.

"How do you feel about hiking? The sign says there's a trail head here to the cliffs."

She shrugged and opened her door. "Sure, I'm all for seeing new things."

He opened his and joined her at the front of the car, pulling out a sunscreen from his backpack. "It's one of the things I appreciate about you, Lucy. Your sense of adventure makes me very nervous, but I'm glad I'm here with you today."

She turned her back to him and sighed at his hands on her back. "Me too, Mason."

They lathered up the sunscreen. He was so gentle, but his hands made her spine tingle with awareness. He leaned over and placed a soft kiss on the top of her shoulder.

The more time she spent with him today, the more relaxed she became. They walked hand in hand, and Mason carried the backpack. He must've planned this, and it made Lucy feel warm and loved to know he'd put effort into making their day enjoyable.

They stopped along the path to read different signs on

the history and significance of the area, but when they reached the western most tip over an hour later, she was breathless.

A Hawaiian couple stood on one side, the man's arms wrapped around the woman's pregnant stomach as they gazed to the sea. Lucy and Mason stood several yards away, hand in hand as they listened to the ocean crashing on the rocks below.

Neither of them spoke, but she wasn't sure if he felt what she did. It was magical here. She felt a sense of peace wash over her.

The couple approached, and the woman held out a seashell. "For you."

Lucy nodded. "Thank you."

The man kept a wary eye on them but asked, "You're tourists?"

Mason nodded, his hand protectively sliding to Lucy's back as she took the seashell and held it in her palm. It shone opalescent purples and blues in the bright sun.

The woman nodded to the water. "You toss the shell into the ocean. This is the leaping point to the spirit world. The shell will help ensure safe passage for your loved one to the afterlife."

The woman's words hit Lucy like a wave, causing her to gasp for air. She could feel the weight of the shell in her hand, heavy and burdened with memories. As she looked out at the vast ocean before her, she couldn't help but wonder if it truly was the gateway to the afterlife.

"These are sacred grounds," the man said.

Mason angled his body slightly in front of Lucy and said, "We're sorry. We didn't mean to intrude. Apologies."

Mason's stiff response only added to her inner turmoil. How could he not understand the gravity of this moment?

The pregnant woman put her hand on her boyfriend's arm and smiled. "It's fine. This is a public park, after all, and you're here for a reason. Perhaps it's time to let them go."

Lucy frowned, stiffening. "Let who go?" It was a rhetorical question, but she asked anyway.

The woman smiled and rubbed her stomach. "Only you know that answer. You can find more shells over there if you need them. Enjoy Hawaii. Aloha."

The pregnant woman's comforting touch brought a bittersweet smile to Lucy's face, reminding her that life goes on even in the midst of grief. As they walked away, Lucy clutched onto the shell tightly, unsure if she was truly ready to say goodbye.

She looked over the water. "Do you think she's right?"

Mason shrugged, still looking at the couple as they walked away. "About what?"

Lucy sighed, her memories swirling. "When my mom died, I dove into schoolwork. I still miss her a lot, but maybe I do need to let her go."

Her voice trailed off, and they stood in silence for a few minutes.

Finally she nodded. "I'll do it. I'll throw the shell. Now that I've graduated and moved out on my own... well, I've been doing a lot of thinking the past few weeks. About mom. About dad. About all of it."

"What have you been thinking?" he asked softly, now taking a bottle of water out of his bag and passing it to her.

She drank and thought. "Mom was amazing. Well, when she wasn't drinking. She did her best, but I'm not a kid in school anymore. I have to grow up. That means letting her go, doesn't it?"

Mason didn't say anything, so Lucy closed her eyes and

sighed. She felt the breeze off the ocean blow her messy bun. The sun beat down on her face.

Mason stepped away as Lucy opened her eyes, but Lucy didn't look away from the sea as she felt the heavy weight of the shell in her palm. With a deep breath, she tossed the shell into the water, letting go of all her pain and sorrow.

"Fly safe, Mama," she whispered. Aloha indeed. As the shell sank into the crashing waves below, a weight seemed to lift from Lucy's shoulders.

Minutes later, Mason stepped up beside her, his hands in his pockets.

"I'm going to let someone go too," he said quietly.

Her heart ached at that rigid set to his jaw. "Your parents?" she asked.

He shook his head, not looking at her or moving. She reached into the bag at their feet and found the sunscreen, reapplying where she could reach. She turned her back to him and handed the sunscreen over.

His hands were colder than she thought, but were they shaking slightly?

"Last summer, I had a girlfriend," he said in a rush. Her spine straightened, but she didn't turn around as he finished with the sunscreen.

"The one who wanted you to take a desk job?" she asked as he handed the bottle back to her. She knelt to put it back in the bag as he continued.

"Yeah. We were about to move in together, even though we'd been fighting about my job. I was on a stakeout one night after a heavy yelling match. She surprised me with dinner. She shouldn't have been anywhere near that area, but she was trying to apologize about our fight."

He stared at the ocean, as solid as a rock.

She slipped her hand into the crook of his arm and

leaned her head on his bicep. The pressure on her chest increased at his pain. "What happened?"

"She was caught up in the crossfire. We were eating in the car, and she—some associates of the guys I was watching drove by, firing on us."

He took his hands out of his pockets and snapped with one hand. Then he stared at the shell in his other palm. "When you were at that drug bust in December, I was so worried you'd be caught in the crossfire too. Our grandparents would be livid, and I wouldn't have been able to live with myself if anything happened to you."

His voice went gravelly, then he cut himself off, closing his empty fist and clenching his teeth.

She put her hand on his arm and leaned her head on his shoulder. "It's not your fault. You can't control what anyone else does. You had no idea I'd be there or your ex or the guys who shot at you."

He took a deep, ragged breath and nodded. "My head knows that. When they opened fire, I dove on top of her, trying to protect her. I was shot in the back, but it was too late. She'd already been hit. The look on her face..."

He rubbed his eyes with the other hand and his spine straightened. He stepped away from her and threw the shell into the ocean so hard, she thought he'd tear a muscle.

His hands fisted at his sides and his face clouded with guilt.

"Oh Mason, it's okay. It's okay to live, to let her go..." *To love.* She left it unsaid, but perhaps he sensed it. He turned his stormy gaze on hers, but she didn't look away. Her heart raced with possibilities as he let her into the dark recesses of his heart.

"I'm letting her go. It's still going to take time, but I'll tell you this, Luce, I won't let anyone else get hurt."

She wrapped her arms around his waist and laid her head on his chest. "Mason, you can't control life. If there's one thing I've learned, it's that our control is tenuous at best. You'll have to balance that need to protect everyone with accepting that sometimes things happen. There's nothing we can do to stop them."

Mason squeezed her tight and growled, "We'll see about that."

She smiled and shook her head as they stood there, holding on tight to her hopes and dreams of the future. She was starting to wonder if they were actually going to go their separate ways after this vacation or not. Sure, they'd only been here a few days.

But was it so wrong to hope for a love like her grandparents? Theirs had lasted decades, compared to her parents whose relationship hadn't even lasted until she'd grown up. She stared at the ocean, his arms around her making it hard to stay closed off. If history repeated itself, was she going to end up like her grandparents or her worse, like her parents?

Chapter Nineteen

When Mason woke, the sun was shining through the balcony doors. The clock said it was barely six in the morning, but Lucy was still on the terrace doing yoga in a little sports bra and shorts. He watched as she bent at the waist, her ass up as she flattened her hands on the ground.

He shifted off the bed and pushed open the balcony door. She looked behind her legs but didn't move. He eased behind her, holding her hips and pressing his dick to her ass, making her tense at the touch and gasp.

"You alright?" he asked.

She let out a shaky breath, but still didn't move as he palmed her ass in her skintight shorts. "Yeah, just doing yoga."

"If you like working out in the mornings, I can help with that." He pressed his hips forward, and she groaned as she pressed back against him.

Then she stood up and turned around with a smile. "Tempting, but I think I want some real food first."

He picked up her hand and kissed the back of it, just

because he could. She blushed, and he felt pride that he had that effect on her. He turned to walk back inside. "I'm going to hop in the shower, then we can head to breakfast. Give me five minutes."

He stripped in the bathroom and stepped into the shower, needing the cold one to take his mind off the woman who'd been infecting his dreams for so long now. He wasn't about to proposition her for anything, not after the incident last year. He didn't deserve her.

But his skin crawled with need. Tension between his shoulders left him feeling stiff. After they'd come back from their drive last night, they'd both fallen into a deep sleep, both emotionally exhausted. Now it was like he was going through Lucy withdraws. It'd been too long since he'd fucked her.

The cold water cascaded down his head, chilling his body but not the fire racing through his veins. Sleeping next to her, the scent of oranges tickling his nose and her hair tickling his chin, he'd woken up rock hard. He gripped himself, sliding his hand up slowly.

He gasped, leaning his head to the cold tile, picturing her kneeling in the shower and taking him into her juicy lips. God, those lips.

Her mouth was begging to be plundered, and he wanted to make her gasp and moan, bite that lower lip and hear her cry his name as he pounded away in her tightness.

He gasped, exploding in his hand and coating the shower wall. His stomach rippled with aftershocks, and his spine tingled.

After a few minutes of cleaning both himself and the shower, he shut off the water and stepped out with the towel wrapped around his hips. Lucy was leaning against the kitchen counter, wearing a little pink and yellow sundress and drinking a bottle of water. She choked when she saw him, shirtless and still slightly wet, and he checked that the towel was safely tucked in at his waist.

Her eyes widened, then roamed up and down his body. Pink tinged her cheeks as her gaze settled on the shaft pressing clearly against the towel.

Damn it, the shower had taken the edge off but around her, he was ready to go again. He imagined that same shade of pink on her cheeks was down below. He'd spread her juicy lips and lick up the center until she screamed.

"I—I'm going to walk to the breakfast buffet. I'll meet you there," she gulped, set her water on the counter, and backed up to the door.

He reached for her hand. "Not yet, I have a breakfast sausage right here, sunshine."

She giggled and shook her head. "I'll take a rain check. I really am hungry, hot shot."

She grabbed her big shoulder bag—pink, of course, with bright tropical flowers on it—and spun so fast, he saw a glimpse of pink lace underwear.

The door clicked shut behind her, and it took several minutes of arguing to convince himself to not follow her and drag her back to their room. She needed time, was probably sore and needed to recover. As inexperienced as she was, he couldn't push her too much. And he certainly couldn't keep her locked up in this room naked their entire trip.

He had a job to do, and he needed to let her go. He was nothing but trouble for her.

But still... he could eat a nice breakfast with her before going to work. The sooner he did his surveillance, the sooner he could come back to her beautiful face.

He raked a hand down his face and tossed the towel aside, swiftly throwing on shorts and a blue t-shirt.

Later that day, Mason came back from watching Malia and found Lucy at the big, main pool at the resort.

She was lying on her stomach on a lounger, her tablet on the ground in the shade of her chair as she typed. Her pink bikini made her ass look amazing, but his emotions were too chaotic at the moment.

He stood over her, blocking the sun until she looked up and smiled at him.

"Oh hey there, handsome," she said breathily. Her body was built for that bikini, the curves making his mouth water.

He looked her up and down. "I thought you wanted to do more sightseeing this afternoon, but if you'd rather stay here, I can think of a few things we can do in our room."

She grinned and grabbed her fruity cocktail from the poolside table. She sucked on her straw, and his dick twitched at the memory of her lips. He'd thought the more they slept together, the less he'd ache for her. So far, it had just made him crave her more.

"We didn't see the other side of the island yesterday. Do you want to take a drive then end up at the Polynesian Cultural Center for a luau later?"

"You know it, sunshine. Do you need to go change first?"

She grinned and shook her head as she sat up, gathering her pool bag and drink as she stood to face him. "You just want to get me naked again."

He shrugged and stepped closer. "Nothing wrong with that, is there?"

She danced away from him and put the pool bag on the table, thrusting her drink at him. "Nope, but if we're going to do all the things I have planned this afternoon, we need to get going."

He took it, tasting as she pulled her sundress out of her bag and slipped it over her head.

"Such a shame," he sighed as she covered her body. "Contrary to popular belief, I'm not such a horn dog that I *only* want to get you naked again. As long as I get to spend the afternoon with you, we can do whatever you want."

She slipped on her sandals. "Watch it. If you're not careful, I'll come to expect this kind of attention."

He kissed the side of her head and took her bag so he could link their fingers, setting the now empty drink on the table. "You should expect it. You're a brilliant, beautiful girl. Why you didn't date before is a mystery to me."

He knew she rolled her eyes again, but a smile hovered on her lips as she replied, "I told you. No time for guys. Now that I've graduated and have my own place, I hope to change that."

At her words, the fruit taste turned to ash in his mouth. "Oh yeah? What's your plan? Date all the eligible men in Crimson Creek?"

She shrugged, and they turned to walk to the parking lot. "I might as well. I do want a family someday, after all. Do you?"

He let go of her hand and shoved his in his pockets with a frown. "The car's this way. As for kids? I don't know. Amanda and I had talked about it, before she—well, you know. And by talk, I mean argue," he chuckled, trying to keep the mood light as they walked.

Lucy linked their fingers together, and some of the pressure on his chest softened at the touch. He didn't feel the emotions choking him anymore, either. Perhaps there was some truth to letting her go yesterday on the cliff.

He took a deep breath and let the vulnerability come. "We'd talked about having big families, but I wasn't sure about it with my job. I didn't want something to happen to me, and she be left with a big brood of rugrats. She was a secretary for a big law firm and wanted to be a stay-at-home mom."

They rounded the corner to the parking lot, and his voice lowered. "She should've dated one of those fancy lawyers she worked with. It would've been safer, and she could've had her dream."

Lucy didn't say anything until they were backing out of the parking lot. "Maybe you were her dream," she said softly, staring out the window.

He gripped the steering wheel harder and clenched his teeth. "Definitely not. As much as she wanted to be a stay-at-home mom, she was a workaholic and loved her job."

Silence descended as he drove, and he needed to change the subject before he grew too maudlin. "What time is the luau? Do you just want to drive around the island and get there when we get there or is there a timeline?"

She shrugged. "Just drive. There's a special road. Hold on, let me look it up."

The drive was nice and peaceful. They didn't talk much. Instead, they rolled down the windows and opened the sunroof. The salty breeze filled their senses, and every time he looked over at her, a small smile was on her lips.

It made him stay relaxed and in the moment. They stopped at a random food truck and a much less crowded beach for a smoothie. Lucy had wanted to dip her toes in the water, but she didn't want to miss the luau tonight.

It was perhaps one of the most relaxing afternoons he'd

ever had. No rush to get anywhere, as she made sure they had plenty of time before the next thing to see. Yes, the luau had a time, but other than that, there were no demands on them. No expectations other than to just enjoy the scenery, day, and company.

He reached for her hand and linked their fingers as they drove, content for the first time in a long time.

Chapter Twenty

The gentle breeze wafted off the ocean as the sun set. They joined the line for the buffet at the cultural center, filled their plates, and found a few seats with a good view of the stage. Soft ukulele music played in the background, and the soft murmur of voices rose around them.

They sat at a little table for four. She liked that they were side by side instead of staring at each other across the flower centerpiece. It was less intimidating talking with him like this, without being face-to-face.

She sipped her water and ate slowly, her eyes wandering and people watching. She glanced at Mason under her lashes as he shoveled food into his mouth. Lunch had been hours ago, but he hadn't complained.

The day had been a revelation, but he'd said some things earlier that made her wonder if his views regarding their relationship had changed. He was so attentive today, holding her hand, opening her door, touching the small of her back as they walked.

He'd scolded her for trying to pay for their smoothie

and again tonight for the dinner at the luau, which had made her smile. She wanted him to understand where she was coming from, though.

She didn't like surprises. Surely it was better to talk and get it all out in the open? She honestly didn't know, and not for the first time scolded herself for never having had a relationship before.

The idea of talking about her feelings made her shift nervously on the seat. She took a drink and cleared her throat.

She avoided looking him in the eyes as she said, "So Mason, about the paying for things. I appreciate you being a gentleman and all, but it's unnecessary."

He scowled at her and swallowed his food. "I think it is necessary. It's part of my job to take care of you, remember?"

She frowned, hope and confusion warring in her chest. "I get that, but it doesn't extend to money. My parents fought a lot about money. My mom tried to use it to control my dad so he wouldn't buy more drugs. It didn't work, but it was still a contentious issue with us all. I got a job as soon as I could in high school so I wouldn't ever have to ask my parents for money. I've been independent for a long time."

He put his hand over hers on the table, stilling her nervous twisting of the fork. "I'm not trying to take your independence, Luce."

"No? What about with that whole master thing?"

He arched a brow. "If you don't find it fun and something you want to explore, then we won't do it. What you call me has no bearing on whether I take care of you. I'll take care of you the same whether you call me master or moron. I simply want to show you how much I value you."

"By buying me?" her voice rose an octave, but he shook his head and leaned back in the chair.

"Never. It's not about the money, but about spending time with you, doing little gestures to show how much I'm thinking about you."

She frowned and shook her head. "But why? Is this going somewhere?"

His eyes turned guarded, and his hand slid away. "This?"

She nodded, putting her hands in her lap and picking at her nails. "Yeah, I don't want to get used to you doing all this. It's what a boyfriend would do, yeah? But we're not dating, are we?"

Her nerves left her hands shaking. She felt his heated stare but wouldn't look up. Couldn't look up. God, why had she mentioned it? They'd barely been on the island a few days, and she was asking where this relationship was going?

"No," he said, drawing out the syllable as if he were thinking about it. "No, we're not dating exactly. I'm still too raw from losing Amanda. She always said I didn't spend enough time with her, that she needed more than holding hands to know how much she meant to me."

Lucy's heart broke. She'd never take the place of his dead love. Her voice was soft when she replied, "I'm not Amanda."

He looked up. His eyes were shining bright with emotion, his lips pursed, nostrils slightly flared.

He swallowed, then said, "I know you're not. Back when we slept together a few months ago? I felt guilty, like I'd cheated on her. That's why I disappeared the next day and didn't even have the courtesy to text you." His tight, tense words were full of pain and emotion.

She took a deep breath. She'd disappointed him because

she wasn't Amanda. Did he regret sleeping with her? Maybe all this attention was his way of trying to make it up to Amanda. Maybe taking care of her would make him feel less guilty about Amanda's death.

She wasn't sure how she felt about that, but she had to get the facts straight. "Do you still feel guilty being with me?"

He glanced away, unable to meet her gaze, and he didn't need to say anything else. That look was enough, and it gutted her to her core. Yet he still said, "Not really, but I can tell you that I am definitely not ready for another relationship."

She chugged her fruity cocktail, hoping the alcohol would numb her to the emotional rejection. "That's good to know now, before I got too attached to how well you're taking care of me."

An awkward silent passed between them, then she blurted, "So, what's our plan moving forward? Regarding us," she said, putting her fork down. "You're not ready for a relationship, but we're stuck here with each other for another week. What do you want to do?"

His teeth clenched, and his spine straightened. "What do *you* want to do?"

She shook her head and laughed. "Oh no you don't. You don't get to play the master and then turn this around on me. Fess up, dude."

He chuckled and his shoulders relaxed slightly. "Fine, I'd like to continue the way we've been. We'll keep dating, being boyfriend girlfriend, or hell—we can even keep pretending we're married—but only while we're here. When we go back to Texas, we go our separate ways."

She tilted her head, trying to keep the pain in her chest from showing on her face. "And what about when we're both hanging out with our grandparents? The holidays?"

He shrugged, picking up his fork to take another bite. "We'll cross that bridge when we get there, I reckon. Is that okay with you?"

She pursed her lips and nodded. He'd asked what she wanted to do, but she didn't really have a choice. He was still grieving his dead girlfriend. It wasn't like she could rush that process, no matter how much she wanted to try a real relationship with him.

She took a deep breath and nodded. "This will work great, actually. I've never had much experience, as you know. But you can teach me all kinds of things in the next week, right?"

His eyes sharpened, turning dark with desire. "What things?"

She blushed and tapped her plate with her fork. "This is delicious. What did you get?"

He grinned and arched a brow, so she widened her eyes and lifted her brows in an innocent expression. "What?"

He chuckled, but the sound grew until he threw his head back and laughed loud enough to draw stares from around them. She blushed harder as he eventually replied, "Nice save, but I'm onto you, sunshine. I'll let it go for now. Something tells me this is a conversation best had in private."

He grinned, and her breath caught in her throat. Her heart raced in anticipation. Then he picked up his fork and said, "It's barbecue. Not Texas barbecue, but it's good. You should try it."

He took a bite, the soft light playing through his dark hair. She felt desire bubble up, threatening to explode. She needed a minute to process this heavy conversation and all the things she wanted, both physical and not physical.

Abruptly, she set her fork down and stood up. "Excuse me. I'll be right back."

"Bathroom?" he asked before he took another bite.

She slid her purse over her should cross body style and shook her head as she pushed in her chair. "No, just need some air."

He frowned as she walked away, but she heard him call out, "This is an outdoor restaurant. It's all air."

She strode past the bathrooms and down the path to the beach as the last sliver of the sun sank on the horizon. The plants had all smelled crisp after the rain last night, but now the flowers were cloyingly sweet. She just needed to escape, maybe walk along the beach.

If she got too close to him, she'd fall in love, and that was the path to heartbreak.

There were tiki torches along the beach, already lit even though it wasn't dark yet. She kicked her shoes off and shoved them into her large shoulder bag. Then she took her ponytail out and ran her hands through her hair, massaging the temples.

She wouldn't continue seeing him after this next week. Was she upset about that? Didn't she already kind of think that was going to happen?

She snorted. It was pointless to be upset by it. Being upset wouldn't change it. Kinda like her dad being a deadbeat druggie. She couldn't do anything about that either.

She felt helpless, powerless, even more so than when she was in that drug bust back in December. She shivered, then turned to walk to the waterline. The first wave lapped at her feet, and she gasped at the cold, wiggling her toes into the sand.

Peace settled over her as she closed her eyes and breathed in, just listening to the sound of the waves as it washed over her feet. She tilted her head up and looked at the stars, so bright as darkness settled around them. The music from the restaurant changed as the show began, and she sighed.

She didn't want to go back yet. Her brain was still confused on how to handle this temporary boyfriend situation. She rubbed her forehead and turned, knowing she had to face the music.

She sighed as she walked back to the path, but when she looked up, her heart raced as she froze with one foot raised. Mason stood maybe twenty yards away, near the entrance to the path. One of the torches cast his face half in light and half in shadow where he just stood there and watched her.

As still as a statue, hands in his shorts, frown on his face, he finally asked, "You okay now?"

She nodded and swallowed. Maybe it wasn't her brain that was confused. Maybe it was her heart. He was everything she'd ever hoped for in a man, mainly because he was an honorable gentleman, the exact opposite as her dad, although they were both rough around the edges.

She nodded and found her feet bringing her closer to him. She couldn't help being drawn to him like a moth to flame. When she reached him, she felt an overwhelming need to touch him.

It would just complicate things once they went back home. She had to treat him like a friend with benefits situation, not a boyfriend. Not that she had any experience in either.

She pulled out her sandals and slipped them on, balancing on one leg with an arm waving. Quickly, he reached out to grab her elbow and steady her. She jerked her arm away and put her foot down, but it landed on the edge of the path and gave way to the sandy ground below. She tumbled backwards, her dress flying up around her waist as she landed with a thud.

Mason scrambled to kneel beside her, his hands gently checking for any injuries. She lay there in surprise, her mouth agape, as he continued to assess her with worried hands.

"Son of a bitch, Lucy, are you alright? Are you hurt? Your—"

She started to chuckle, then it turned into a full body laugh the more he talked. It was the least elegant laugh she'd ever had, loud and boisterous. She might've even snorted when she saw his scowl.

His hands flattened on the sand beside her, and he glared. "It isn't funny, little bird. You could've gotten hurt."

She slapped her knee to clean off the sand and wiped a tear out of her eye. "I know, I know. I could've twisted an ankle or something."

She rolled her eyes as she got to her knees to stand, then felt his hands on her waist and elbow, helping her up.

"I'm fine, I'm fine. Tis just a flesh wound." She shrugged him off and stepped back onto the sand, needing more space as his touch sent that same fire through her veins. She had to rein herself in. He wanted to protect her so much but the one thing he couldn't protect was her heart. He couldn't protect her from him.

He snorted and crossed his arms. "There you go again, brushing it off like it's nothing."

"It literally is nothing, Mason." Her tone was exasperated, but she wouldn't keep arguing with him.

She sat on the path and put her sandals on, taking deep breaths to try to recenter her mind and emotions.

"Are you sure?" His voice was soft near her ear, and she realized he'd squatted behind her. She was cradled between his legs, and she felt his dick pressing against her back.

Her spine straightened and her nipples hardened with awareness. She felt his body heat behind her, and his hands raked up her bare arms to her shoulders. One hand gently swept her hair to the front, exposing the sensitive part of her neck to him.

Then he dipped his head and kissed it softly. Her breath caught in her throat. He was touching her, and it made the overwhelming need skyrocket.

Damn it, she wanted more. More of him. More of his time. His heart. His everything. Tears pricked behind her eyes, and she closed them and leaned back into his arms.

Chapter Twenty-One

Lust burned in Mason's brain at just that small kiss to her shoulder, and he shook his head to clear it. Lucy tilted her head back, her beautiful brunette hair shining in the tiki lights, making him think of an island goddess full of passion and spitfire.

She turned in his arms and looked up at him with a raised brow.

"Mason, I'm going to say this one more time. You do not need to protect me from everything. I tripped. Things happen, and that's okay. You have to let go of this need to control."

He frowned, standing up and gently pulling her to her feet. His hands hovered on her elbows to make sure she didn't fall again.

"It's not about control," he growled. Amanda had called him on that too, but that wasn't what was going on here, was it?

She waved her hands to the side, and his dropped limply.

"Isn't it? You're acting like a dad with a little kid, trying to make sure your little girl doesn't get a scrape on her knee. I don't need a fucking babysitter, Mason. You want to keep pretending we're together this week, that's fine, but I need you to treat me like an equal, not like a fragile little girl who needs to be put in a bubble of safety."

He frowned. "I'm not—"

She rolled her eyes, crossed her arms, and cocked a hip. Her look was the epitome of 'Ya think?'

He chuckled and shoved his hands in his pockets to keep from reaching for her. "Fine, fine. I'll try to ease up, but no promises."

She snorted. "Look, if you see me as a child who needs looking after, fine. I can't stop you from feeling that way, but we're not going to have much fun if we keep fighting about it for the next week."

His eyes raked down her body and back to her gorgeous eyes, thinking about all the fun he wanted to have with her. God help him, but he was more than aware of her as a woman. He felt it with every cell in his body anytime she was near.

She tried to step around him again, but his hand shot out to grab her wrist. She couldn't just walk away. His chest tightened.

"No, wait. I know you're not a kid, but to be perfectly honest, I like treating you like one."

Her hands waved wildly, and she raised her voice. "What the fuck does that mean?"

He pulled her flush, making her gasp when her breasts contacted his chest. "It means I want to kiss every booboo on your body. I want to spank you when you get mouthy, and I want to punish you when you run out of the room without telling me where you're going."

Her eyes widened, and he wondered if he'd gone too far. Then she licked her lips and looked at his. "What—you want to do what?"

Her voice was almost a whisper.

He took a deep breath and dove in. If he was only going to have her for a week, he wanted to explore *everything* with her. "I want to fuck you until you're incoherent."

She gasped and shifted her legs together, so he continued. "I wasn't lying when I said I wanted to master your body. I have so many ideas, so many things I want to try with you. If you're up for it. If you're serious about learning all you can while we're together."

She took a shaky breath and nodded eagerly. "Hell yeah, I'm serious." She bit her lip and glanced away nervously. "If you're serious about wanting me, that is."

He slid his hands up and down her back. "How could I not want you? You're everything, Lucy. Everything."

Words were meaningless. He was generally so good with words, including dirty talk, but suddenly in this moment, nothing was good enough for what he was feeling.

There was only one solution. He ducked his head and kissed her. He cupped her head and kissed her tenderly, trying to say everything he couldn't say aloud.

It rocked his world, turning his need into a burning inferno that might never fade. It was bone-tingling, and it turned hard, then soft, then hard again as his need increased.

He teased, then deepened the kiss, consuming her until they were both panting. Their tongues fought a silent battle, and he pulled back. Reluctantly, he broke the kiss. He touched his forehead against hers as his thumbs stroked her cheeks.

Together, they came back from the intensity of the

hunger that wouldn't be sated. Heat simmered in his groin, and he knew he would have her again.

She licked her lips and then pulled back. Her eyes were wide, her pupils dilated. "I—okay, now I'm curious. What else can you teach me?"

He grinned and wiggled his brows. "You'll just have to wait and see, won't you, sunshine?"

She sighed and nodded, her eyes still wide with desire. Then she turned and walked up the path, her hips swaying under the soft light of the tiki torches.

His eyes trailed down her body, then frowned. She only had one shoe on. He glanced down and saw the other lying in the sand. With a chuckle, he picked it up and carried it back to their table.

He walked slowly after her as his brain rushed to catch up with their conversation. At the restaurant just off the beach, the luau dancers were on stage, and Lucy was sitting at their table near the edge. Her arms were crossed, making her cleavage deeper.

He was drawn to her like a magnet. He made a beeline for their table, his eyes scanning the crowd but always coming back to Lucy.

Until he saw a particular shade of blond, a woman in a bright pink dress sitting at a table on the edge of the room. He kept walking, trying not to look at the woman as his heart raced.

It couldn't be Malia. Not this far out of the main city. The woman turned away from her companion to face the stage, and he breathed a sigh of relief. It wasn't her.

He'd thought he'd seen Lee following them yesterday as they drove, but when the car had kept going, he'd second guessed his instincts. This job was making him jumpier than normal. He shook his head and continued to Lucy.

After weaving through the crowd, he sat in the seat next to her and reached under the tablecloth to find her legs. She sat up with a jerk at his touch, but she refused to take her eyes off the stage or uncross her arms.

Slowly, he slid his hand down across her delicate knee, lifted her calf, and put her foot in his lap. Her leg was crossed, and he stroked her foot softly, twice. Then his hand just settled on her leg, his thumb sliding back and forth over her silky skin as they watched the stage.

Her foot wiggled, and her eyes swerved to meet his in surprise as her foot connected with his dick. Hard as it'd ever been, he ached for her more now than he did when he first met her months ago.

He wanted to whisper in her ear, but he just grinned and winked. She blushed and turned to face the stage.

He couldn't tell anyone what the performance was about or how long it took, but when it was over, he slipped her sandal on, and they both stood to clap loudly with the crowd. Her cheeks were flushed as they followed the crowd to the parking lot. When they stopped beside the car, he spun her around and pressed her against the side of it.

She gasped, and his lips crushed to hers again. There was nothing tender about this one. He was ravenous for her. His body hummed as her hand wrapped around the back of his head and crushed him closer.

He couldn't get close enough to her. She gasped and pulled away. He trailed his lips down her neck and said, "I'm going to take you back to the hotel and eat you alive, little bird."

She moaned and pulled his hair, making his dick jump. "God yes."

He jerked back, staring at her under the parking lot

lights. He blinked, excitement running through his veins. "Fuck," he whispered.

She grinned and slid to the side, reaching for her door handle. "That's the plan, hot shot."

He opened her door before she could and held it open like the gentleman he was trained to be.

When he sat next to her, he took her hand again and held it the entire drive back to the resort. The soft music of the radio washed over them, but they remained silent as the sexual tension rose.

His body was fascinated by the feel of her hand in his, so natural. It felt like a piece of him had been missing, and he'd finally found it.

Chapter Twenty-Two

They walked hand in hand to their room, and he unlocked the door. He ushered her in ahead of him then pinned her to the wall before the door even fully shut.

She gasped, and he reveled in the sound. The leash on his control was shredding by the second. He wanted to please her, pleasure her, make her smile all day and scream his name all night.

He nipped at her lips and growled, "I can't keep my hands off you. You make my mouth water. I've craved the taste of you all day."

He kissed her softly, dragging his lips atop hers as her breathing grew faster. "But it's more than just physical, little bird."

His teeth raked down her neck.

She gasped and pulled his hair. "It is?"

He sucked softly on the sensitive spot on her neck, and she twisted in his arms. "If I'm not with you, I'm worried about you. You haunt my dreams, and when I'm awake, I can't stop thinking about you."

He kissed her again, needing to stop the flow of his words before he said something he wasn't ready to commit to. His tongue swirled a little deeper, teasing her into a moan.

His tongue swept in and twirled around hers twice before breaking the kiss again. "You've cast a spell on me with your smile, your mind, your heart. I'm not sure if I want to run away from you or run closer."

She tipped her head back against the wall in frustration, her nails digging into his arms. "Run closer, Mason. Please. Run with me."

He peppered kisses along her jaw. "But where are we running to, Luce?"

"No fucking clue, Mason."

He chuckled into her ear and felt her shiver in his arms. "Fair enough. Are you agreeable to a few more orgasms along the way?"

"Hell yeah."

It felt like his chest was going to explode if he didn't kiss her properly, so he did.

Her mouth was warm and welcoming. He'd built up the kiss so much that now she was clawing at his arms and sucking on his tongue. He groaned, feeling his already hard cock swell as she imitated the movement he wanted below.

But this wasn't about him. It was about her, showing her how much he wanted her. He pulled her closer, deepening the kiss. His hands settled on her hips, then bent down to run his hands up the sides of her thighs. He drank in her gasp as he slid his hands over her waist and down her ass, sliding her panties off.

She kicked them away, along with her sandals. He toed off his own shoes, causing the kiss to break. She clawed at his shirt, and he pulled it up and over his head.

Then she attacked his mouth, nearly leaping into his arms. He grabbed her and lifted her up, pushing her against the wall. She wrapped her legs around him, and his fingers dug under her ass into the wet core beneath.

They both groaned, and he broke the kiss, digging his mouth into her shoulder as he fought himself for control.

"I'm not going to fuck you against the wall."

"Why not?" she gasped.

God, she was so adventurous, it drove him crazy. He bit her shoulder again, then brushed his lips softly across the bite. He picked her up and carried her bridal style to the bed. She leaned back, spreading her legs and setting her feet on the edge. Darkness enveloped them as he eased back and tugged on her dress.

"This comes off. Zipper?"

She sat up and pulled it up and over her head before laying back down. He froze, seeing her naked on the bed. When had she taken her swimsuit off? How long had she been naked underneath?

His mouth went dry, and he groaned, sinking to his knees. She gasped as his fingers trailed back and forth over her little clit. The scent swarmed his senses, making him sway with desire.

He bent and kissed her raised knee, making her twitch and moan. "Mason."

God, he loved when she said his name. Who needed a nickname when she sounded like an angel, his name a prayer on her lips?

"Yes, little bird?"

His mouth trailed down the inside of her thigh, and he pressed her legs further apart. His breath tickled her core, making her shiver as he breathed deep of her sweet-smelling nectar. His mouth watered for a taste, but he delayed both their pleasure.

"Mason, please."

He grinned. "Say it again, little bird. Beg me."

She gasped, "Master, damn it, please."

The name sent a thrill down his spine, and his hands gripped her flesh tighter. He hadn't realized how much he needed to hear her say it. It soothed his soul like nothing else.

His mouth descended over her clit, and she screamed, bucking her hips to meet him, but he held her tight and still. He licked and sucked, alternating until he learned what she liked. His teeth scraped her, and her hands settled on his head. There it was.

His mouth worked its magic on her, her tormented groan begging him to continue. He sucked and added a finger. She was so tight, wet and ready. He teased her folds, coating himself in her wetness. Emboldened by her panting moans, he added another finger.

She bore down on his hand, and he sucked on her clit. Like a tidal wave, her back arched as she came. Her entire body vibrated and jerked before melting into the bed. She writhed around him, clenching his fingers as she shook. Even with her thighs locked tight against his head, he heard her scream.

Raw, wild need shot through him, making his dick achingly heavy. He wanted—no, he needed—to feel her orgasm on his cock.

Her hands tugged on his hair, and he slowed his mouth, licking the nectar that ran down his hand and pulling his fingers out against the faint aftershocks that squeezed him. Small kisses trailed along her inner thighs, and he pushed them wide to hang over the side of the bed.

He kissed his way up her stomach and rested his elbows on either side of her body, caging her in. He licked first one nipple, then the other. Small nipples hard as pebbles, he felt a thrill as her back arched once more. Her breasts were heavy in his hand, filling first one, then the other as he tweaked the nipples and learned what made her gasp.

"God, Lucy, you taste divine. I can't wait to thrust inside you and see these tits bounce. You're a goddess, and I want to destroy you in the wickedest way possible."

"Oh fuck, master, yes. God yes," she panted, her hands sliding up his biceps and gripping his hair once more. She tugged, and he trailed kisses up her neck to seize her lips.

With one hand, he lined up with her dripping slit. He teased her folds, coating himself in her wetness as she arched her back, trying to get him closer.

He teased them both, over and over, just sliding the tip across her clit and down again. Never penetrating.

She broke the kiss with a gasp and demanded, "Damn it, master. If you don't—"

Then thrust, parting her with one bold, deep stroke that had her screaming his name.

He groaned, closing his eyes against the overwhelming feeling of being fully sheathed inside her. It was like a dive off a cliff into the cold ocean below. It jolted his system, paralyzing him with shock on how good it felt.

Except it wasn't cold.

This was hot, hotter than hell. If this was what hell felt like, he never wanted to leave.

She squeezed and pulsed around him with the aftershocks of her previous orgasm, making him groan. The need to move, to ride her, to claim her filled him until he could do nothing else.

He pulled out almost to the tip, then plunged deep, the

slick channel gripping his throbbing cock. Everything else faded away, and it was only the two of them and their need to be together.

He set a relentless pace, taking her with a pounding need and driving hunger. Together they ran to the cliff's edge, the tension building. Her legs quivered, and he hooked her knees over his forearms. She was gripping his biceps, arching her back and taking him deeper.

Her head began to thrash, and he was so close. He bit his tongue, trying to hold back, yet he still wanted to torture them both.

He ground out, "Touch yourself, Luce. Show me what you like. Let me feel you come around this dick, sunshine."

Her hand eased between them to her clit. At the first touch combined with the pressure of his hips, he felt her orgasm hit full force. She screamed with a bone-tingling orgasm that reverberated through every cell in his body.

He fought his own release, trying to savor the feel of her spasming around him. It caught him like a gale force wind, and he blew into her like a hurricane. He melted into her heat, his blood pumping hot and body tense as he spilled inside. It was the most violent and virile orgasm he'd ever had, and it left him gasping at the intensity of it all.

He stayed inside, letting her body milk him even as his arms shook. Eventually he eased her legs off his arms and slipped out. He fell on the bed beside her, panting, spent shaft still twitching.

She reached out a hand and linked their fingers together. He leaned back, other arm under his head as his breathing slowed. Peace settled over him and slumber called. Perhaps showing Lucy how much he wanted her wouldn't be such a bad thing. His half-lidded eyes slid closed as he breathed her name. "Lucy."

She took a deep breath and sighed, "Yeah, Mason?"

What could he say that would explain how earth shattering, mind-boggling, this was?

"I know you don't have a lot of experience, but you need to know... It's never been this good."

His eyes didn't open as he felt the bed dip, then she curled into his side with a sigh. He savored the nearness of her, and without shame or regret, he held her close as they both drifted to sleep.

Chapter Twenty-Three

"Lucy, I don't know about this." Mason said as they rode across the water in the speed boat.

Mason had worked this morning like usual, then he'd taken her exploring after lunch. The geyser had been fun, even when she'd almost slipped a few times. Mason had almost had a panic attack when she'd done that.

But then she'd wanted to go parasailing.

He still couldn't believe he was doing it with her. She had a way of making him relax and take risks, and he wasn't sure if that was a good thing or not.

But he did know that she wanted to have adventures, and he wanted to give her the world.

She nodded as the staff member slowed the boat. "I'm sure. We can't do this in Texas and should seize the moment. Have you changed your mind?"

He shook his head. "No, if you go, I go."

"Are you sure? What about your injury? Is this going to hurt you? You've been moving pretty stiffly."

He wiggled his brows. "I'll give you a stiffy later."

She giggled and it set some of his unease aside.

He kissed her softly on the lips, a lingering kiss that held promise. "Personally, the marathon sex sessions have been my favorite activity."

She blushed and laughed. "Mine too, but that doesn't answer my question. What about your back? I haven't pried into your scar or the way you hold it when it bothers you, but you haven't opened up about it either. I'm not sure if this is something you should be doing."

He swallowed and looked away, his stomach twisting. The staff member waved to them, and they hopped up to put on their harnesses. The man checked the straps and adjusted them. "I told you about being injured, how I was shot in the back."

She sighed, her voice soft. "I know, but there's more to it than that, isn't there?"

He pursed his lips, and she waited, giving him time. The staff member was checking other harnesses, so there was no rush. Finally, he sighed. He had nothing to hide from her, but he would keep it light and succinct.

He held her, just breathing in the salty sea breeze and the oranges in her hair. "I was in the hospital for a few weeks, then in physical therapy for months. They weren't certain how much mobility I'd have post surgeries. They thought it was a career ender."

She caressed her hands up and down his back. "It was almost a life ender, hot shot. You're incredibly blessed."

He smiled, leaning back to kiss her softly on the lips before replying, "That I am, little bird."

The instructor called for attention, and they listened as he gave directions and went over the itinerary. Soon they were soaring through the water on a boat with three other couples. One of the other couples went first.

Lucy watched the other couple with rapt attention. She grinned when the woman squealed and was lifted in the air. Seeing her legs bounce, feeling her hand on his thigh as they sat side by side on the boat, the wind blowing wispy hairs out of her braid...

He felt like this was the life, but a stab of guilt gnawed on him. Amanda would never get to experience any of this. She wouldn't be able to feel the sun on her face or enjoy a fun boat ride or even go on adventures like tandem parasailing.

The driver slowed as the instructor reeled the parasail in, lowering the couple to the back of the boat. They were laughing and talking as the boat stopped and bobbed on the water.

Lucy's eyes were hidden by the sunglasses, but her grin was wide as she squeezed his leg. "We're next. Oh my God, I can't believe I'm actually doing this. I've always wanted to, but never thought I'd—"

She choked back her words, pursing her lips and swallowing hard. He cupped her cheek, but she looked up at him and smiled.

"Thank you, Mason. This vacation has been everything I've always dreamed of."

His chest felt tight as she hopped up and swayed to the back of the boat for their turn. He followed her, unable to deny her and delighted that he had made her so happy.

He wasn't sure that he'd ever made Amanda this happy. She had been a very career minded businesswoman, strong and no-nonsense. They'd butted heads repeatedly.

Lucy was different, but still strong and resilient. She brought out all his protective qualities, but somehow, they could talk through their issues in a way that he and Amanda never had.

He half-paid attention as they received last minute instructions and were hooked into the parasail side by side. Lucy grabbed his hand as the instructor moved to the hydraulic winch and hit a button. Then the boat engines roared.

His jaw dropped open as they were launched into the air, but no sound came out. Lucy, on the other hand, screamed and squeezed his hand so hard he thought she'd break a bone.

"Oh my God, Mason. Oh my God, oh my God, oh my God," she panted.

He looked over at her and frowned. "Lucy, breathe deeper."

She shook her head, grinning and looking around. "It's amazing, isn't it?"

The rope jerked and the parasail swooped to one side. Lucy screamed and squeezed his hand, but Mason was distracted by trying to right them. He tugged on the strap to redirect them like the instructor had said.

They evened out, and he looked over at Lucy. He frowned, letting go of the strap and reaching across his body to pat at her cheek. Her head lolled to one side, her fingers no longer gripping his hand but hanging loose in his.

Panic speared him, and he went into fix-it mode. He made a signal to the instructor and felt the rope pulling them closer to the boat. He let go of the steering cord and reached for her, checking her pulse before patting her face lightly.

"Damn it, Lucy. Come on. Wake up, sunshine. Come on. You can't land like this, or you'll break a leg. Why did you insist on doing this crazy stunt?" His heart raced with each second she was out.

They were halfway back to the boat when she lifted her

head and said, "Wha—" She looked around and gasped, twisting and jerking the parasail.

"Sh, it's ok. I've got you. Look at me, Lucy."

She turned her head, and he squeezed her hand still in his. "That's right. I won't let you go, sunshine. Stay with me."

She groaned and grabbed for her side's steering cord. "Shit, shit, shit. Did I pass out?"

He nodded, gripping her inside hand tight and grabbing his own steering cord. "Yeah, are you alright? Are you afraid of heights? Why—"

She shook her head as she looked around. "Why now? I wasn't panicking, I was excited, and now I've ruined it."

She sniffed and his heart ached to do something to fix this.

He rubbed his thumb on the back of her hand and shook his head. "No, you didn't. Look around. You're doing it, right now. Nothing's ruined. You're fine, right?"

He ignored the desperate note on the last word, hoped that she wouldn't hear it. It was his job to keep her safe and reassure her that all was well, which it would be once they were safely back on the boat.

"Yeah, I'm fine. I just pass out sometimes when I panic. I can't catch my breath and pass out."

He frowned, not letting her hand go. "How long have you been doing that? Maybe you can see a doctor."

She shook her head. "No, there's nothing they can do. It started when I was in middle school. Oh my God, look, Mason! Are those whales?"

They glanced to the left, far from the boat that tugged them slowly back in. Neither of them said a word as they watched the majesty of it all. Mason let go of her hand and wrapped his arm around her back, grabbing onto a strap on her life vest. He took her left hand in his left hand as they approached the boat.

They landed with a jarring thud, and he clenched his teeth as he tried to hold her upright. Her knees wobbled, then they both fell. He grunted, trying to roll so she was on top of him. The instructor worked quickly to unlatch them from the parasail.

"What happened? Are you alright, miss?" the instructor asked.

Lucy nodded, "Yeah, I'm fine. That was fun! Thank you so much!"

The instructor looked confused and frowned, looking to Mason, but Mason just sat up and pushed to his feet. It felt like someone was poking his back with a spear.

"We're good," he grunted, coming to his feet. He shuffled back to their seat, following Lucy as she sat down. The next couple stepped up to take their turn.

Mason grabbed his backpack and pulled a bottle of water out for each of them, groaning as he leaned over.

"Are you alright?" she asked tentatively.

He growled, "No, my back hurts, but more than that, we never should've done this. You fucking passed out, Luce, and that's not cool. Scared me to death. Do you know how that makes me feel?"

She shook her head silently, and he continued.

"It's like Amanda dying all over again. I'm helpless and can't do anything to stop it or protect you from yourself. It's hell on earth, and I won't do it again. Do you hear me, little bird?"

She hunched her shoulders and nodded, turning her head away and drinking her water. His chest tightened at her defeated look, and he gritted his teeth. Their conversation at the luau shot through his mind, and he breathed deeply to calm himself. He didn't want to chew her out like a worried dad, but damn it, he cared for her. He *had* been worried!

His stomach lurched as the boat gained speed and the other couple shot into the air with a squeal. They finished the boat ride in silence, but his anger and frustration ebbed with the tide.

When they got back to the car, he felt more guilt claw at him as he gripped the steering wheel and drove back to the resort.

She looked around as he searched for a parking spot and said softly, "I'm going to the hotel bar for a few hours. I need to people watch and work on my manuscript."

He nodded. "I'm going to go take the night shift on the surveillance mission."

They walked silently to the room to change. When he came out of the bathroom, she was already gone. He stopped by the hotel bar to make sure she was there. She typed on her tablet and might not have even known he saw her.

He rubbed his temples and drove back to the old apartment building to watch Malia and Lee. While he drove, he called home.

"Hello?"

"Howdy son, how's the trip turned out?" Pops asked.

Mason nodded and turned into the parking lot. "Fine, we went parasailing today, and Lucy passed out. I might have said some words in the heat of the moment that I shouldn't have."

"She passed out? Is she okay?"

"Yeah, she's fine. She does that when she has a panic attack sometimes."

"That's not right, son."

Mason snorted, his hands tightening on the steering wheel. "Tell me about it."

"What did you say?"

He sighed and leaned his head back, closing his eyes for a moment. "I said something about how much I hate when she passes out and that she puts herself in situations that will lead to it. If she'd just stay safe and sound on the ground instead of pushing these boundaries, it wouldn't be a problem."

It was Ray's turn to snort. "You can't tell a woman what to do, Mason. Haven't you learned that by now?"

He grinned. "I guess not. She's giving me the silent treatment now."

"Sounds like you need to make it up to her. What can you do to apologize?"

Mason tilted his head back and forth. "I can think of a few things. She's working on her book now, and I'm not going to interrupt her. I think we both need some time apart, so I'm going to do some surveillance tonight."

"You have a few days left. Make them count. Focus on what's important, and I don't mean work."

Mason's chest tightened at the words, but he parked the car and nodded. "I will."

They said their goodbyes and hung up. Mason went upstairs to the room they'd rented and sent the other guy home for the night.

He had to finish their vacation on good terms. He couldn't let the silent treatment continue for too long. He had to know that she wasn't mad or hurt. Apologies were needed, yes, but actions spoke louder than words.

Chapter Twenty-Four

Lucy woke up to Mason spooning her. The light was just starting to change on the horizon as she slid out of bed. She did her morning yoga, trying to ease the heaviness on her chest.

Hearing him yell at her on the boat had given her so many flashbacks of her dad. It was hard to handle, coming right after waking up dangling over the ocean.

But now that she'd had a few hours to ignore the problem, she found her mind circling back to it, trying to puzzle it out. There wasn't anything she could do about it. She couldn't control his words or actions. She couldn't make him stop acting like her dad.

It wasn't even worth mentioning, really. They were going home in a few days and who knew how long it'd be before she saw him again? No, she'd pretend like nothing had happened when she saw him today. That is, if she saw him. He might go back to work and ignoring her like when they first got here.

It didn't really matter. Today was the festival, and she

had made plans that didn't involve Mason. She got ready for the day as silently as she could and left him a note.

Mason,
I think we need some space today. I'm going to the festival in Wakiki and plan to be gone all day. Good luck at work.
Lucy

She bit her lip. Would he catch her sardonic tone? She tossed it on his closed binder on the table and went out the door to call a rideshare. She grabbed a quick breakfast at the main building while she waited, then she was off on an adventure by herself.

The past few days of going around in the afternoons with Mason had been eye opening, but they'd mostly had fun. More importantly, he'd started to open up with her. Her heart was conflicted. The closer they became, the harder it would be to say goodbye.

When she arrived at Wakiki, she bit her lip in nerves. She didn't realize it would be so crowded already. She hated crowds. She walked down the street window shopping until she saw a bookstore. When she ducked in, she looked around in awe.

It was two stories, but there were no books on the ground level. It was probably too close to the beach. She spent hours in there and ended up racing through the crowd to get to her lunch date.

She saw Malia sitting at a bistro table outside the cafe and joined her. She was in a soft pink and white shirt with loose cotton shorts. Lucy smiled as she stood and leaned in for a hug.

"You made it," Malia said. "Gorgeous dress."

"Thanks. Have you ordered yet?"

Malia shook her blond ponytail. "Only a drink. Sit, sit. Let's chat, then I'll take you to the best shopping vendors."

The conversation flowed from talk of their grandparents and nosy family members to horrible bosses and finally to the men in their lives.

"So tell me how you two met," Malia said as she bit into her salad.

Lucy took a drink before answering, trying to think of what to tell her. Mason had said to follow his lead the night of the art auction. She wasn't sure why he'd lied to their table about being married, but it had to have something to do with his job.

She sipped her drink, watching Malia. She was just a nice girl helping out a tourist on vacation. There was no reason for her to take time out of her day to take Lucy around to the good vendors. She smiled and set her cup down, deciding to keep as close to the truth as possible.

"I walked down the aisle at our grandparents' wedding. I was the maid of honor. He was the best man. It was love at first sight."

She kept waiting for her hands to sweat and her heart to race as the lie rolled off her tongue, but her smile never even wavered. Maybe she was a better actor than she thought.

Or maybe she was already in love with him. She felt her cheeks heat and took a bite of her chicken wrap as Malia sighed.

"Oh, that's lovely. I'm surprised he let you go off to lunch on your own. I mean, this *is* your honeymoon, after all."

Lucy's blush deepened. She could see it spreading to her chest. She mumbled, "Well, you know how it is."

Malia laughed, "No, no I don't. Tell me about it."

A shadow fell over Lucy and a deep voice said behind her, "She's a little sore today, and I just can't keep my hands off her, but we both needed a few hours' break."

Lucy looked up over her shoulder, but Mason wasn't visible with the sun behind him. He leaned down and kissed her cheek before pulling up a seat to their table.

"Break's over, sunshine." His hand settled on her knee, and she realized they were sitting incredibly close. His hand was almost squeezing her knee too hard. She looked at him through her lashes, but his face was relaxed as he stared at her with a loving expression.

Malia laughed again, her grin coy. "Now that's what I call a good honeymoon. Well, in that case, let's hit those shops so you two love birds can go hump like bunnies."

Malia waved the waiter over, and Mason grinned. They left, and Malia took them around to various shops. They laughed and chatted about little things. Mason couldn't keep his hands off her, which left Lucy flustered.

When Malia asked the vendor about the price, Mason wrapped his hands around her waist from behind and whispered, "Just a little longer, and then I'm going to spank your ass so hard."

She gasped and turned her head to whisper, "What? Why?"

He kissed her hard, their teeth tapping as his tongue thrust inside. His hands squeezed her waist, and tingles raced along her spine. It was deep and ravishing. Desire shot through her, taking her from zero to one hundred in three seconds flat.

Malia chuckled, and they broke the kiss to look at her. She wiggled her eyebrows, her package hanging from her hand. "Alright, enough of that. I can only handle so much in one day. I'll see you two lovebirds around. Tootles!"

She squeezed Lucy's hand and turned into the crowd. She disappeared faster than Lucy thought possible, but her heart was still racing from that kiss. Mason's hands tightened on her waist as he stared intently after her.

Lucy's phone alarm sounded, and she shrugged him off to pull it out, swiping with a grin as she pulled up the itinerary.

"I'm going to the Ted Talk on the history of Hawaii and the festival. Are you free for the afternoon?" She bit her lip, unsure if he was still upset with her from yesterday's parasailing incident or not. "We can do something else if you'd like."

He scanned the street and took her elbow with a tight smile. "I'm free for now. I need to talk to you, though."

She looked at her watch and then the map. "Do you want to talk as we walk? It's about two blocks away."

His hand stroked down her arm to take her hand in his. Her heart raced at his silky touch. "Sounds good. Lead the way. While we walk, tell me everything that Malia talked about."

Her brow furrowed. "Malia?"

He wanted to talk about Malia? Oh. Oh, of course. She was a blond curvy knockout woman. Of course, he'd want to talk about her. Lucy's chest tightened but she told him about their conversations.

"Did you invite her to lunch, or did she invite you?"

"She invited me the night of the art auction when we went to the bathroom. Why?"

Mason shrugged and looked around. His face was relaxed as he smiled down at her, but she could see the tightness around his lips and in the way he held his shoulders as they walked.

"Nothing, sunshine. Is this it?"

He waved to the sign outside a glass building, and she nodded. He opened the door, and they went inside. When they took their seats, he crossed his arms and leaned his head back. She tried to pay attention to the speaker, as the topic was fascinating for her knowledge loving brain.

After the speaker had talked for about five minutes, Mason put away his phone and shifted so his arm was draped over the back of her chair. His fingers played with the exposed skin of her shoulder, drawing circles. It sent a stab of awareness through her. She imagined that light touch all over her body.

Would he want to explore more together? The sex had been amazing so far, but it'd also been hot and heavy. She wanted to touch him, feel those muscles move under her hand.

His coconut sunscreen wrapped her in a cocoon of happy scent. Or maybe it was an aftershave or lotion. Her mind wandered to seeing him step out of the pool, dripping wet. He was broad, and she'd never seen a man in real life with muscles like that. She'd thought the movies were grossly exaggerating, but not anymore.

Now she knew exactly what her smutty books meant by getting all hot and bothered.

This was ridiculous. She'd gone her whole life without being distracted in class, daydreaming about some boy she had a crush on, only to succumb to it now when she was on vacation? That was not who she was, and she didn't like it.

It was too much change at once. Frustration mounted, but she didn't want to take it out on him. Her dad had done that, and she wouldn't fall into the same pattern.

One glance at Mason, and she suddenly understood how her mom felt all those years. She'd always stayed by Dad's side, never questioned his excuses no matter how many times Lucy told her he was lying. Her mom never stopped hoping for the best.

And Lucy was doing the same with Mason. She wanted more time with him, more attention from him. She blinked, still staring at him even as her heart began to race in panic. She couldn't let history repeat itself.

It might be too late for that. One of the bricks around her heart crumbled as she stared at him. He was asleep, head leaning back against the wall, ankles and arms crossed.

The poor man, he'd been out until after midnight gathering whatever evidence he needed for the FBI. Between working half the day and taking her on all their adventures, he was probably exhausted.

He wore a plain t-shirt and jean pants over his boots. Who wore boots to the beach? Yet somehow, he didn't look uncomfortable in them. He looked open and relaxed. She wanted to stroke his face and lay on his chest.

She felt the energy threaten to explode. She reached out a hand to shake him awake but closed her fingers before she could touch him.

Her head hurt, but whether from thinking about Mason all morning, she wasn't sure. It was probably all the sun and crowds. Thankfully, the presentation was inside with dim lights. She tried to breathe deeply and regulate her breathing, but it just got shorter and shorter.

She looked around, looking for a way out, but the presenter stopped speaking and the crowd clapped. She'd completely blanked through most of the presentation. She winced at the sound and automatically reached out to Mason like a lifeline.

Chapter Twenty-Five

The lights came back on, and applause rippled through the audience, driving her heart rate up as she startled. She squeezed his thigh, but he grabbed her hand tight and twisted.

She gasped, and his eyes opened, unfocused. She tugged on her hand, and he blinked, glancing down and realizing what he was doing. He released her and sat up straight, looking around the crowd with a frown.

"Sorry about that. Side effects of the job. Are you okay?"

She rubbed her wrist and stood, grabbing her purse and shopping bags on shaky legs. First the panic at turning into her parents and then his weird wrist thing. He took the shopping bags and cleared his throat.

"Lucy?" his voice was soft and vulnerable.

She stood, his gentle hand on her elbow and his brow furrowed in worry. She nodded, glancing away. She had to get out of here. Swiftly, she passed the crowd out the door, leaving Mason to follow.

He cleared his throat. "What's next on the to-do list, sunshine?"

She breathed deeper at the topic change. She didn't want to talk about why she was feeling so overwhelmed. It was festival day, and she was determined to enjoy it.

Her body had other ideas. Dizziness washed over her. There were too many people, too many thoughts, too many emotions.

She stepped between two buildings and the crowd on the sidewalk. She leaned her head back and breathed deeply, closing her eyes.

"Luce? You okay? What's wrong? Talk to me."

She shook her head. "Nothing. Just need a moment, that's all."

She felt heat on either side of her head and opened her eyes. He was leaning his forearms on the wall next to her head, caging her in with his body. He wasn't touching her but was close enough to smell.

She raised a hand and placed it on his chest. She didn't know if it was to push him away or pull him closer. He didn't say anything else, and she just stared at her hand on his chest as it rose and fell with his breathing.

Somehow her breathing started to mimic his and the dizziness passed. She took a deep breath and looked up at him. His blue eyes stared at her, assessing and worried.

"You had a panic attack but didn't pass out." His matter-of-fact tone was assessing and clinical, but she nodded anyway.

"I needed some air."

He blinked, understanding dawning. "Like at the luau. That wasn't an excuse to get away from me. You really did need some air."

Her other hand cupped his cheek, and she raised on

tiptoes and kissed him softly. It was a gentle kiss, full of promise and hope. It made her long for a more lasting relationship with him.

But she couldn't do that. She wouldn't be like her mom, hanging her entire identity and all her hopes and dreams on one man.

She broke the kiss and sighed, leaning back with a smile. "I'd never want to get away from you, hot shot."

He stepped back too, his face smoothing as the worry faded. "If you're sure…"

"I'm sure. Thanks for helping me get back to normal," she said softly, pulling her phone out of her pocket. "Now, how about lei making on the beach, followed by ukulele lessons. You up for it?"

His eyes flared, and he growled, "Around you, I'm always up for it."

She giggled, and he picked up the bags from the ground and followed her out to the street.

Energy buzzed through her veins. Mostly because this big, gruff man took her hand and laced their fingers again. His body language was no longer mad or on edge like it'd been when he'd found her earlier at lunch. Instead, he protected her from the crowd, kept his hand in hers as they reached the beach. It was surreal how much he seemed to care—or he'd just been raised to be a gentleman, which was entirely possible.

If someone told her six months ago that she'd be walking on a beach in paradise with a handsome hunk, she'd have laughed in their face. Now, he laughed as he picked up the tissue paper and tried to follow the instructor's directions for the lei lesson.

She had never been a crafty sort of person. Why had she chosen this kind of activity? It was insanity. Her fingers just wouldn't follow her brain's directions. They stood at the table and threaded the flowers through, her big sunglasses in the way and frustrating her even more. She ripped the tissue paper and huffed a breath, making her hair fall in her eyes.

"No, you twist the end, like this."

He stepped behind her and wrapped his arms on either side of hers, cocooning her body and making her freeze. His fingers ran along the backs of her hands, then took the bundle of tissue paper and gently pulled the edges in opposite directions, opening it up into a faux flower.

"See?" His breath tickled her ear as he whispered. "You have to be gentle to get the flower to open up to you. It's a finesse game, Luce."

Shivers raced up her spine, making goosebumps pop on her skin. His lips moved down under her ear and kissed gently.

She gasped, "Wha—what are you doing?"

"Helping with your lei, of course."

"I—I think I've got it."

"So, you don't need help to get laid?"

"I—well, I'm not going to say no to you, if that's what you're asking."

"That's a good girl." He kissed the spot where her neck met her shoulder, and she groaned.

"I—oh God. Do you know what that does to me?"

He paused behind her, and her brain registered what she'd just admitted as he pulled away and went back to his own lei. "I have an idea," he smirked.

While his hands were huge, he was very good with them. She blushed as she remembered how good.

In the end, his lei looked way better than hers, but she couldn't help how her hands shook every time he brushed against her or touched the small of her back as he leaned across the table.

As her frustration mounted with her failure to excel, she blamed it on the sexual tension. For the first time, she understood Taylor's obsession with getting laid. It was highly addictive. The more they did it, the more she wanted to do it.

The instructor came by to help them finish their projects. Soon, they were walking to the ukulele lesson set between two buildings in a well-decorated alley. His hand on her lower back burned a hole through her defenses.

He pressed her against the alleyway wall, his head dipping as he ground on her. She gasped at the sudden movement, but when she looked up at him, his head was turned, staring at the crowd of people on the street.

"Sh, it's ok. I thought I saw someone, but I was wrong." His voice was low and finally his eyes turned back to hers. He looked down and smiled tightly. "But now that we're here..."

His voice trailed off as his lips met hers. The kiss was quick and deep, leaving her wanting more.

When they broke the kiss, he took her hand and led her to the ukelele lesson at the end of the alley. Chairs were set up at the mouth of the alley where it met another street, and they sat. An assistant came and processed their payment before handing over two instruments.

Once again, Mason surprised her. He was apparently a very good guitar player, making the instructor slightly annoyed when he started playing softly against the wall beside her.

She turned to him. "I didn't know you could play. Can you show me how?"

He was patient while showing her three chords. Some of

her frustration eased to have his full attention. They ignored the instructor and whispered in their own little world.

At the end of the lesson, when everyone else was walking away and the instructor was tapping his foot waiting to gather their ukuleles, she played *You Are My Sunshine* with him.

"Did you hear that? I only stumbled once when I went to that G!" She handed her instrument off and grabbed Mason's arm. He grinned, catching her off guard and making her heart race.

"You did great. Such a good girl."

She squeezed his arm, her grin widening as he looked at her with that calculating blue stare. She felt her face heat and she looked away, squirming on her seat.

He cupped her face with his palm, forcing her to look back up at him with his gentle touch. "I love your smile," he said. "So beautiful, so innocent. It makes me want to corrupt you a little."

She grinned. "I think you already have."

He grinned and kissed her on the cheek. She'd never been treated so well by anyone before, not man or woman. It made her dizzy but in a giddy, let's do it more kind of way.

He grabbed her shopping bags and said, "Ready when you are."

She pulled her phone out of her pocket to check the next event as they stood. He cleared his throat as they walked out of the alley, his hand once again taking hers and linking their fingers.

He looked around as they stepped onto the street, his eyes scanning the crowd as he asked, "So where to next?"

"Scavenger hunt. In about five minutes, the first clue will be texted to my phone, and it'll officially begin. First one to bring the correct secret code to the Event Coordinator at the festival's entrance gets a prize."

He let her hand go and popped his knuckles. "Oh, it is on. Let's do this."

She laughed, and they walked along the beach while they waited for the text. The silence was comfortable, but a random thought crossed her mind.

"Why did you say I was going to get a spanking earlier?"

He stiffened beside her and adjusted the bags. He looked around as they walked through the sand, weaving through the crowd. "I'll tell you later. It's not safe enough to talk about it now."

She frowned, but before she could ask more questions, her phone dinged. She sighed and read out the first word puzzle.

For the next hour, she laughed more and more at Mason's competitive attitude. They began to see other couples both ahead of them when they would find a clue and racing after them when they left to go to the next clue. One wife was dragging her clearly reluctant husband around while she harped on him.

Mason and Lucy kept giving each other side eyes and chuckling every time they heard her yell at him. But they just made him more competitive. The more competitive he became, the funnier it was. It got to where she was pretty sure he was doing it just to make her smile.

An hour later, they finally raced up to the Event Coordinator at the festival entrance booth.

Lucy was breathless as she asked, "Has anyone won the scavenger hunt yet?"

The woman shook her head, and Lucy blurted out the completed secret clues they'd gathered. "Under Lokahi, we learn the value of teamwork. No cliff is so tall it cannot be climbed. Dare to dance, for love gives life within. With Imi ola, we seek our best life together, and say Mahalo for all we have learned."

The coordinator grinned and clapped. "Congratulations, you're the first to collect all five clues and arrange them in the right order. Your prize is any excursion to Hilo, redeemable anytime this year, and includes lunch and dinner."

Lucy clapped as Mason pumped his arm in the air and yelled, "Yes."

She laughed and threw herself into Mason's arms. His meaty hands immediately settled on her waist as she gasped, "We won. We did it."

He picked her up and spun her around as he chuckled. "I know, Luce, I know."

She squeezed his biceps and pulled back as he set her back onto the ground. She looked up into his blue eyes. They made her melt inside, and she needed to press her knees together as need flooded her. She started to release him, but he growled again, glanced at her lips, and then dipped his head.

Before they could kiss, the coordinator cleared her throat. The couple with the annoying wife stood a few feet away as she said, "I'm sorry, but this couple just beat you to it."

Mason grinned and gave the couple finger guns. "Yeah, suckers. We won."

Lucy elbowed him, and he hunched his shoulders sheepishly, his grin not even slipping. The wife smacked her husband on the arm and began to berate him as they walked away.

The coordinator cleared her throat. "Sir? Ma'am? I need your phone number and details to make sure we get the Hilo excursion information correct."

Mason's voice rumbled as he gave their information to the woman, the sound vibrating through his chest to where her cheek lay.

"Mr. and Mrs. Mason Novak..." His voice continued to rattle off details, but Lucy's brain stuttered at his words. She didn't correct him, but her stomach twisted.

Why was he still telling people they were married? Did it have something to do with his work? Confusion and hope warred within her.

She sucked in a breath, and the coordinator walked back to her booth a few steps away. Lucy pulled away and patted her dress to make sure it was settled correctly. Then he held out a hand, palm up.

"How about an early dinner, and then we'll head back to the hotel? Brunch was hours ago, and that scavenger hunt worked up an appetite."

She slid her hand into his. "But there's supposed to be fireworks tonight and a parade. I want to watch it."

He frowned but nodded. They wandered the street and found a little beach front restaurant and took seats on the sand. Damn this tingling sensation. It happened when their hands were locked together, when he grazed her back as he pulled her chair out.

The waiter arrived as the sun dipped in the sky. Lucy smiled at the menu.

She nodded, causing her wavy brown hair to shake around her shoulders, finally coming out of her ponytail. "It all looks so delicious. I'd love something new. I want to be adventurous and try everything. This is a vacation, after all."

The waiter suggested something, and Lucy actually was excited to try the new fish. Then he turned to Mason. "And for you, sir? Or do you want your daughter to choose your appetizers for you?"

Mason blinked, his arms falling to the chair arms while Lucy burst out laughing.

"Do you want some fish too, big daddy?" she asked coyly, her laugh continuing around the words.

His eyes flared in warning, but he just said, "I do love fish tacos, but I think I'll have the steak tacos tonight."

The waiter nodded. "Certainly. And would either of you like to hear our drink specials?"

Lucy's lips quirked to hide a grin at the somewhat pout on Mason's lips as he gave a sharp nod. She looked at the waiter and tapped the menu. "What is this cotton candy wine?"

The waiter's grin widened. "Oh, it's delicious. You'll love it. And for you, sir?"

"I'll have an Old Fashioned."

Lucy's eyes misted and her smile slipped. Her dad used to order that.

Chapter Twenty-Six

Mason crossed his arms as the waiter walked away, staring across the beach and casing it for suspects or suspicious activity. He'd deliberately chosen a table with a seat against the wall of the restaurant so no one could sneak up on him.

Some things had just become habit after so many years, and that was one of them. His eyes took in Lucy as he turned his head to watch the area, then stopped. He frowned. "Are you alright?"

She rubbed her nose and avoided his gaze. "Yeah, I'm fine. Just thinking about my dad."

"Want to talk about it?" He genuinely wanted to know, and not just because she'd mentioned he'd been on drugs before.

"My dad used to yell at me when I passed out. It's jarring to wake up disoriented and have someone yelling in your face. I know he was just scared, especially when it first started, but I didn't like it."

"Then when we landed on the boat, I lit into you like

your dad?" His voice was soft, and a knot settled in his chest. He didn't want to remind her of bad memories.

His hand touched hers, squeezing softly before releasing it. "I'm so sorry, little bird. I didn't mean to hurt you. I just got so caught up in my fear of something happening to you while we were hanging up there, you passed out which was a shock, and me not being able to do anything..."

She smiled self-deprecatingly. "I'm sorry too, for putting you in that position. For making you feel so helpless. I should've warned you it could happen." The moment stretched between them, then she cleared her throat. "Anyway, my dad liked an Old Fashioned too. It's what made me think of him."

Mason nodded. "It's a good drink. Strong and manly."

She laughed, and the tension in his shoulders seemed to ease a little. "Of course that's why you drink it."

He shrugged. "Is there any other reason to drink?"

Her eyes twinkled as she took her sunglasses off the top of her head, and the waiter brought their drinks. She thanked him with a smile. When they were alone once more, she held up her wine glass.

"This is a reason to drink. Look at the cotton candy on top. Isn't it so cute?"

He snorted. "I don't pick a drink based on its looks. If anything, a drink should be based on taste."

She sniffed the glass then took a sip. Her eyes widened. "Oh, that's delicious. The cotton candy dissolves when it hits the wine. Normally, cotton candy wine is all I drink at home. I've never had any with actual cotton candy in it, though."

He leaned back in the chair and smiled. "Why cotton candy wine? It's a bit foo foo, isn't it?"

She snorted a laugh, nearly choking on her drink. "Foo

foo? Kind of a silly word for a big, strong, manly man like you, isn't it?"

He grinned, enjoying this flirty side of her. He just waited though as she took a drink and the waiter brought their food.

She cut into her fish and furrowed her brow. "Cotton candy reminds me of the Texas fair. We went there and to Six Flags once a year, normally six months apart. Those were happy days with lots of laughter. No worries or responsibilities."

Her voice trailed off as she ate, her face turning introspective and sad. He ate his tacos and glanced around the beach and restaurant, ever vigilant especially after seeing Malia earlier. She could still be in the area, although someone else was tailing her now. Mention of the fair led him to thoughts of his own childhood though.

"Pops used to take my little brother and I to the big rodeo in Fort Worth every year. Will would run off, I'd chase after him and drag him back, hoping to get back before Pops found out we were gone."

She took another sip of her wine. "How old were you? My parents never let me run around by myself."

He shrugged. "Maybe seven and nine? I don't remember exactly. Pops always scolded us and told us to stop worrying him because we were going to give him a heart attack if we ever did that again."

Lucy tilted her head, but he didn't meet her eyes. "But you kept running off?"

He squirmed in his seat and frowned. "Will was a troublemaker, a rough around the edges kind of kid. He took dad's car accident the hardest, I think. He was too young to really form solid memories."

She kept eating and didn't interrupt him, just gave him

time to remember and think. He appreciated her all the more for it, but it was like the emotions that had been bottled up his whole life were breaking into pieces. He couldn't hold things back from her if he tried.

"I was seven when he died." His throat closed up, so he took a sip of his drink.

"What happened?" Her voice was quiet, but she didn't stare at him or put pressure on him. The normal tone of voice made it easier to talk about somehow.

He cleared his throat and sat up straighter. "He was rushing after work to get to my baseball game. Someone ran a stop sign and t-boned him. They say it was instant, which is good, I guess."

He felt her hand on his knee, and he suddenly realized it was bouncing. Her hand made it calm, and he rolled his shoulders as he took a deep breath.

"It still hurts, though. Losing a parent," she said softly.

He nodded, and the waiter brought them the check. Lucy reached for her purse, but Mason beat her to it and handed over his card. She frowned at him, and he arched a brow. When the waiter walked away, he asked, "Sorry, sunshine, but I can't let you pay for dinner or even go dutch."

She shrugged and tugged on her dress. "I'm not really comfortable with you paying for stuff."

He tilted his head and sighed. "Is it something you're willing to work on though or is it a hard limit?"

He waited for her answer, fascinated by the play of emotions across her face. She was so expressive, and he loved it.

"I—I can work on it… while we're here at least."

The heavy silence made his chest ache with what

remained unsaid. When they returned to Texas, they wouldn't be a couple for her to work on it.

He sighed and tried to look at it objectively. "While we're here, we're married, but if we were truly married, it wouldn't matter which of us would pay because it'd come from our joint account."

She blushed and looked away. "Joint accounts are nothing but trouble. My parents taught me that." That vulnerable expression blew him away, made him want to rescue her, sweep her into his arms and kiss away the heartache.

Except he couldn't. She'd end up hurt, or worse, like Amanda. He stabbed at the last bite of steak and chewed.

The waiter brought the receipt and card back, and Mason signed. "So what next, sunshine? What time is the parade and fireworks?"

Lucy pulled out her phone and hummed as she tapped away. "In an hour, and it's two blocks away. It looks like there's a rooftop bar on the parade route. I bet it would be less crowded than the street and would be a decent place to hang out while we wait."

He tucked his wallet away and picked up her shopping bags. "Then lead the way, sunshine."

He reached for her hand with his free one and linked their fingers. There was something about holding her hand that settled his nerves. All day long, he'd felt like he was being watched. He was probably being a little paranoid, but he couldn't help but question why Malia had met up with Lucy at lunch. Did Malia see him tailing her before the auction dinner? Or this morning as she ran errands?

He tried to push aside the knot of worry in his stomach. It was highly unlikely. He knew how to do the job, and there were very little opportunities for her to see him.

Malia had seemed so open and genuine at the auction and at lunch today. His head told him to let it go, but his gut twisted in a warning that was rarely wrong.

Yet it'd been wrong last year, hadn't it? Could he even trust it anymore?

They reached the bar and went upstairs. It had a cool vibe with a live band and dance floor, a bar along the wall by the stairs, and chairs and tables near the roof's edge that looked out over the moonlit water. They went to the bar, and Mason opened a tab and ordered a drink. He turned back to Lucy to ask what she wanted, and his body froze, his heart racing.

Lucy hugged Malia. Son of a bitch, what was she doing here? He hadn't checked on her location on his phone since before dinner when he'd gone to the bathroom, but his gut was going haywire at the sight of her. This wasn't a coincidence, was it?

He forced his face into an easy smile and stepped over to them. "Malia, what a surprise. I was just ordering drinks. Would you like one?"

Malia bobbed her blond head. "What a gentleman. That'd be lovely. Thank you. I'll take a Hawaiian Mai Tai."

He didn't know her well enough to judge the look in her eye, but he knew he didn't like it. The hair on the back of his neck stood on end as she smiled.

Lucy nodded, "That sounds great. I'll have the same. Thanks, love." She took the shopping bags from him absently.

Mason's eyes cut to hers, but she was already turning back to Malia and chatting as they walked to a seating area in the corner. He kept his eyes on them as he stepped back to the bar and ordered their drinks.

His stomach roiled at Lucy's term for him. First big

daddy, then love? They'd joked around about the nickname thing, but when she'd said both, he'd felt more than a thrill.

It'd made him want to haul her over his shoulder and run back to the hotel. It'd made him want to see her lips wrapped around him as she stared up at him with those innocent eyes.

It made him want to master her and have her begging.

God, he was an old dog perving on the most beautiful woman he'd ever met, and she was barely twenty-three. She was trouble even without getting wrapped up in the drug case. He wiped his eyes and groaned.

The bartender slid the drinks to him and tilted his head. "You alright there, hoss?"

Mason nodded and took the drinks. "Yeah, sun's got to me, that's all."

The bartender nodded and turned to the next customer, so Mason carried the drinks over to the girls. He watched them in animated conversation. Every step that took him closer made the hair stand up even more in warning.

He felt like he was walking into a trap, but he didn't know how to get them both out.

Just what the hell was Malia up to? He wanted to pull out his burner phone, but it was in his boot. He sat the drinks on the small table between them and leaned over to kiss Lucy on the top of the head.

She blushed, and he asked, "Fancy seeing you here, Malia."

Lucy shrugged and sipped her drink. "Not so much, Mason. She was telling me earlier about how great this place was. I knew I had to check it out."

Malia nodded and smiled like a cat who ate the canary. "And I was right, wasn't I? It's a great vibe. And the view of the fireworks is amazing. Just wait."

Lucy smiled and sat back in the chair, so Mason sat beside her and sipped his own drink, trying to relax and observe those around him. The way the girls had sat had his back to the crowd, bar, and stage. He didn't like it. Anyone could sneak up on him, and he'd never know.

The girls chatted some more as the moon rose higher. That sense of doom never left, only grew stronger the longer they sat here. He felt like a sitting duck.

The band got louder, and the girls wanted a refill on their drinks. He hopped up and went to the bar to order.

While he waited, he pulled out the burner phone under the guise of straightening his pants and entered the password to the secure site to message his contact about his suspicions. Then he cleared his history and swiped to close the app.

There was definitely something fishy going on here, and he was going to get to the bottom of it. He grabbed their drinks and walked back toward the girls. He had to protect Lucy and get her out of there as soon as the fireworks were over. Hopefully, he'd hear from his contact soon on what to do.

Chapter Twenty-Seven

"I see you two lovebirds haven't made it back to your room yet, if you're still lugging around the shopping bags," Malia said with a grin as she nodded to the bags at their feet.

Lucy felt her cheeks heat as a few stars appeared overhead. "Unfortunately not, and the damn man has been teasing me all day long."

Malia laughed and nodded to the dance floor. "I don't recommend taking him to the dance floor then, not unless you want to end up getting fucked in the bathroom, which sadly they frown upon here."

Lucy glanced at the dancers and winced. "I wouldn't call most of that dancing. More like grinding."

Malia wiggled her eyebrows. "Exactly, babe. Exactly."

Lucy grinned as Mason returned with their drinks and set them on the little side table between them. He moved the chair so his back was to the half-wall edge of the roof and took his seat again, kicking his feet out in front of him, crossing the ankles as he looked around.

"Where's Lee tonight?" he asked.

Malia waved her hand absently. "Oh, he's around here somewhere, I'm sure. Can't go too far from him, you know. We're still in that honeymoon phase of our relationship. I'm sure you understand." She winked, and Lucy sipped her drink, glancing down with a flush. Lee was probably with his *wife*.

"Hm, we sure do, don't we, sunshine?" Mason's voice had darkened. She glanced at him through her eyelashes as she sipped her drink, not sure what he was agreeing to. She'd already forgotten what Malia had said. He arched a brow in a sexual challenge that had her blushing and heart racing.

Malia's laugh rolled over them. "Oh my God, you two are so in love, I don't know whether to slug you or clap in admiration. You know, there's a little coat closet downstairs. They don't like people fucking in the bathrooms, but they haven't found out about the little closet yet."

She wiggled her brows, and Lucy felt heat spread from her face to her chest.

Mason just grinned at Lucy. "You don't say? Well, there's an adventure for you, Luce. You did say you wanted to try new things while here, didn't you?"

Lucy glared at him. "Mason!"

He chuckled and took a sip of his drink. His eyebrows quirked, then he pulled out his phone and frowned at it. He looked at her with an expression she couldn't read. "I need to take this. Will you be okay for a few minutes?"

Lucy nodded, touched that he thought of her. Then he leaned over and kissed her cheek before putting his drink down, hopping up, and going down the stairs.

"Man, he is one fine cowboy. Seems like he knows what he's doing in the bedroom if he has you blushing like that all day. He's clearly in love with you."

She opened her mouth to deny it but caught herself from arguing. She'd almost forgotten that they were pretending to be married.

Instead, she sipped her drink and then laughed awkwardly. "That's good, since I'm in love with him too."

Lucy's heart raced hard and fast. Was she lying or was it the truth? Her mind was fuzzy from the drinks already, not too bad, just nice, slow, and relaxed. She didn't want to analyze her response, didn't want to question it or find the hidden meaning in everything.

A waiter came over and whispered in Malia's ear, then she sent him away. They chatted about the music and the parade, which Malia should start any minute now. When the band stopped playing, Malia's face brightened.

"Oh, there it is. Can you hear the drums of the parade now?" Malia asked as she stood up and went to the railing a few steps away. Lucy drained her drink and joined her.

Malia pointed out different parade floats and explained some of the cultural references. The waiter returned with two new drinks, so Lucy sipped as they talked and watched the parade.

She wished Mason was here too and pulled her phone out of her pocket. She typed but her fingers were clumsy. She frowned and fixed the spelling mistakes, working slowly and methodically as her vision blurred.

Where are you? You're missing the parade.

She checked that it was on vibrate and nearly dropped it in her pocket. As she sipped her drink and stared at the swirling lights and dancing people below, laughing at the antics and oohing over different costumes and floats, she grew worried about Mason's absence.

When the parade disappeared down the street, the rooftop band began playing again. Malia half turned and leaned her elbows on the railing with a smile.

"The parade will continue for maybe half an hour or an hour down the street. Then the fireworks will go off. This place is almost the beginning of the parade route."

Lucy nodded and sipped her drink, still looking at the street below. It was fascinating to people watch. She could learn a lot from it but being removed from the action also made her feel somewhat safe.

Malia threw her drink back, chugging it. Then she said, "Come on. Finish that up, and let's go dance while we wait for lover boy and the fireworks."

Lucy turned and looked around the bar for Mason. He'd been gone too long, but she didn't want to just sit around moping that he'd left her. He hadn't left her alone, after all. She was here with Malia now.

She nodded and went back to her seat. "Sure, let me finish this and text him right quick. But—um—I don't think I can dance and hold all my bags."

Malia laughed and lifted her hand. The waiter from earlier arrived almost immediately, and she said, "Take Lucy's things and hold them behind the bar. Keep them safe, will you?"

The man nodded and swooped her bags and purse in one hand.

"Wow, that's some fast service," Lucy said groggily.

Malia laughed too brightly. "Perks of owning the bar, dear. Ready to dance?"

Lucy barely registered her words as the cocktails made her mind swirl and her gut ache. She'd need water soon, but she thought it was partly due to worry for Mason too. She frowned and texted him again.

Are you alright? Where are you?

She slipped her phone back into the pocket of her dress and chugged her drink before setting it on the side table.

Malia grinned and stood. "That's the spirit. Come on, Lucy, let's show them how to have fun, instead of all that grinding shit."

Lucy grinned and followed Malia through the now crowded terrace. The lights were low, and the music was pumping. Lucy had no idea what the song was, probably because she hadn't kept up with current trends while in college.

She and Malia bounced from dance partner to dance partner. Some were cute, some were not. Those that weren't, Malia would make a gagging face behind their back before spinning her away, both giggling.

It reminded her of some of the harmless fun she'd had over the years with Taylor and definitely helped her relax and enjoy her buzz. She definitely wasn't worrying about Mason anymore.

She frowned, realizing that she'd thought the same phrase back-to-back. Too many definitelys meant she was more buzzed than she thought. Hm, how did one spell definitelys? Was it with an -ies?

She shook her head, trying to ditch her nerdy side and enjoy the vibe and atmosphere around her, but that was a bad choice too because it just made her dizzy.

Lucy swayed to her feet, holding onto Malia and patting her on the shoulder. "I need a break."

Malia nodded, leading them both over to the bar. "Fair enough. You okay?"

Lucy nodded and the bartender set a round of shots and cocktails in front of them.

Lucy waved her hand. "Oh no, thank you. I can't possibly—"

Malia wrapped an arm around her waist and pushed a shot into her hand. "Oh, come on. We only live once, right? Let's enjoy it."

Malia grabbed the other shot and clinked Lucy's shot glass before tossing it back. Lucy looked at her shot and frowned. She didn't want to be rude.

She took the shot and chased it with half the fruity drink before she stopped to take a breath. Lucy checked her phone. Still no reply from him.

She was getting angry at herself. This was exactly what her dad would do with her mom. Mom would be worried about him not coming home when he should've. Dad would never call ahead or warn her he'd be out late, where he was going. Mom ended up pacing in the living room, waiting up until the wee hours of the morning...

Only for him to stumble onto the porch smelling of cheap booze with bloodshot eyes and a wobbly smile. Mom would rant at him, then he'd get frustrated and yell at her. It was a vicious cycle.

The memories threatened to bring her down, and her eyes teared up. She wiped her nose and refused to be sucked in. This was why she didn't get drunk often; it always led to thinking of her parents and the sadness was too heavy. She had to sober up and focus. She flagged the bartender for a water while she planned. She'd watch the fireworks and then find Mason if he still hadn't shown up.

She was guzzling her water when a cute sandy haired boy came up beside her, pressing close to say over the music, "Let me buy you a drink."

Lucy leaned back and smiled tightly. He was cute but looked so young. Maybe that was because she couldn't get

Mason out of her head. He was a real man, not some boy fresh out of college. Or high school, which this guy might be.

She nodded anyway because hey—free drink. Taylor had taught her to never turn down a free drink. The bartender set down another cocktail, and Malia tapped her on the shoulder. Lucy turned away from the boy to chat with her friend.

"They're about to do the fireworks! Come on, we need to get a spot at the railing."

Lucy laughed as Malia grabbed her hand and almost dragged her to the railing, the boy forgotten but not the drink she'd snatched off the counter. They just reached it in time for the fireworks to start.

She sipped her drink and watched as the lights blurred and spun. One after the other, the lights danced and made her dizzy.

When the fireworks ended, everything was still spinning, so she leaned over to tell Malia, "Going to the bathroom. Be right back."

Malia nodded and continued talking to some cutie on her other side. Her brain was too fuzzy, but she wasn't so drunk that she couldn't handle going to the bathroom on her own.

As she walked, she questioned the validity of that statement. It was becoming harder and harder to walk straight. Everything kept dipping and swaying.

She pushed through the open hallway past the stairs to the ladies bathroom and stepped inside. She hit the stall and lurched into it, shutting the door behind her. She pulled her phone out of her pocket after she sat down and checked her messages. There were none.

This was bullshit. She called him, but it went to voicemail. She didn't bother leaving one as she knew she wasn't alone in the bathroom. She slipped her phone back into her pocket and finished doing her business, but when she stood and wiggled her underwear up, she hit the door.

It swung open, and she landed hard on the floor of the bathroom. The room spun, and Malia and the waiter from earlier looked down at her.

At least, she thought it was Malia. She was pretty fuzzy and moving too much to tell. Lucy's eyes felt heavy.

Malia's arms were crossed. "Took her long enough. Come on, Reggie."

He looked down at her, not even offering a hand as Lucy struggled onto her knees and swayed. "Bridal style or over the shoulder?"

Malia snorted. "I don't give a fuck. Let's just get her out of here."

At her words, Lucy's heart raced, and she looked up too fast. She tried to scramble away, as she asked, "What are you talking about?"

The two Malia's rubbed their temples and sighed, "You've had a bit too much to drink, Lucy, so I'm taking you back to my place."

Lucy slipped again and kicked the waiter away. "But Mason—"

"Oh, I've taken care of Mason, darling. Don't worry." Malia's voice was fainter, as if coming through a tunnel. What did she mean by that? Had she taken care of him like in the movies, as in killed him?

She began to panic. Her breathing grew erratic as she backed up into the corner, trying to kick at the waiter. The more she hyperventilated, the more she worried about the inevitable outcome.

Sure enough, everything went black.

Chapter Twenty-Eight

Mason groaned and held his head. This was the worst headache he'd ever had. He looked around, but everything was dark. He could see light coming from under a closed door to his right.

Panic raced up his spine. He felt around, realizing he was in a closet. Coats were above his head. He felt his pockets. His real phone and wallet were missing, but the phone in his boot was still there.

He listened outside the door. He could still faintly hear music overhead and voices, but it was soft and muted. Perhaps he was in the basement where the kitchens and staff were located? Did Hawaii even have basements?

He shook his head and pulled the phone out. He opened it and checked Malia's apps and messages.

Meet me at the Penthouse.
I have a surprise toy for you.

I've warned you not to interfere.

You'll like this one, I promise.

Then there was a picture of Lucy asleep in the back of a car. The contact was saved as Boss, and Mason had assumed it was the CEO of the corporation she worked for. This was the first message that indicated something more was going on though.

Mason's heart stopped. It felt like his veins turned to ice. No other messages came through. He opened the secure app and called his contact.

When she answered, he whispered swiftly and efficiently. "They have Lucy in the back of a car. You have to get her out now."

"Give me a few minutes to pull it all up on the computer. I'm not at the office right now—"

"I don't give a fuck who's at the office or where you are. Just get Lucy out of there. I swear to God—"

"Stand down, sir. We will protect civilians, don't worry. What about you?"

Mason rubbed his head. "I'm locked in a coat closet. I think I'm still in the bar somewhere. You should be able to track this phone, right?"

The woman snorted. "Yeah, stand by for extraction."

"And Lucy?"

"Working on it," she said before hanging up.

He held his head in his hands and breathed deeply. With his eyes closed, he felt like the room spun but couldn't be sure. Flashbacks of Amanda ran through his head, and he felt rage welling inside.

Now that he'd called it in, he had to bust out of here. He breathed, trying to maintain his heart rate and calm himself. There was no way he could punch his way out, but maybe the idiots were dumb enough to leave it unlocked.

He tested the handle on the closet. He grinned when it turned. It wasn't locked, but when he pushed, nothing happened.

He pushed against it harder, trying to get it to budge. He looked under the door into the sliver of light but couldn't see much from this angle. It just made him dizzier. Something was blocking the door though, that was for certain.

He closed his eyes and waited for the team to arrive. The longer he waited, the more helpless he felt. He had to fix this, but his hands were tied.

Well, figuratively, not literally at least.

He ran his hand through his hair and winced in pain. Someone must've hit him on the back of the head. His hand came away wet and sticky. He knelt and searched the pockets of the coats in the closet.

He pressed a kerchief to his head and kept refreshing Malia's apps to see where they were and if any other messages were sent.

His heart raced to see another from Lee.

Where the fuck did you go?

Back to the Penthouse to take care of some business. Do you still have him?

Passed out in the closet, yeah.

Good. Boss just arrived. GTG show a bitch a good time.

Lee's laughing emoji made Mason see red. He was going to kill someone tonight. A cold calm went through him, and he remembered the app to listen into her phone.

He pulled up the app and clicked around until he found what he was looking for. He turned the sound down so no one guarding the door would hear. Then he held it to his head.

"Lucy, wakey wakey," Malia said in a sing song voice. Groaning came faintly through, and he strained to hear.

"What? Where am I?" Lucy's words were slurred and groggy, but Mason's stomach twisted in nerves. He was both relieved she was alive and scared of what was to come next.

"You passed out at the bar, so I brought you back to my place. Don't worry. You're perfectly safe. I just have some questions for you, honey." Mason felt nauseous at Malia's overly sweet tone. Dread filled his stomach and made his hands shake.

Lucy groaned. "No questions. Too tired. Talk in the morning."

A rustling sounded through the phone, then Lucy gasped, "Ow, stop, that hurts."

"You're not going to get her to talk that way," Malia said flatly. What way? What were they doing to her? God, help her.

A deep voice replied. "You brought her here against my wishes. You stay out of this and let me do what needs to be done."

"I slipped her some drugs. All we have to do is ask, and she'll spill whatever secrets she's hiding," Malia said.

Lucy whimpered as he replied, "She'll tell us everything anyway. What's your name, girl?"

"Lucy."

"And your husband? When did you get married?"

Mason winced. If they'd given her some sort of truth drug to make her talk, this was about to go sideways.

"Mason. Wedding in December."

"Very good. Now why are you here?"

"To have lots of sex and write my book," she said sluggishly, then whimpered again.

The man laughed and a thud sounded through the phone. Lucy gasped and cried out in surprise and pain.

"This is pointless. She knows nothing," he said faintly.

"Lucy, sweetie, why was Mason following me yesterday?" Malia asked. Mason's entire body froze. Oh no, she *had* seen him.

Lucy groaned. "I don't know."

"Hm, what was Mason doing yesterday when he wasn't with you?"

Lucy whimpered again and gasped, "He was watching someone."

"Why?"

"To gather evidence, maybe? Ow, let go," Lucy cried. Mason bit his knuckle to keep from moving.

"And who is Mason gathering evidence for?"

"The FBI."

Mason's blood turned to ice in his veins and goosebumps crossed his skin.

The man cursed, and Malia's voice rose. "See? I told you I wasn't being paranoid."

"Fuck. Okay, where is this Mason now? Is he secured?" There was no response, but Malia must have nodded or something because he continued. "Okay, let's take them on a little fishing excursion tomorrow morning. Make it look like an accident."

Lucy cried, "What? Does that mean kill us?" Her voice became shrill and panicked at the end.

"Fuck, she's passed out again." Malia said with a sigh.

Mason winced, and his chest hurt. His heart raced so fast he was afraid it would explode, and his fingers itched to take action. He couldn't protect her from here, but now he didn't just have the FBI looking for him but this dirtbag too. They were going to send some guys to get him, if Lee wasn't already on his way.

A loud commotion echoed through the phone and outside the door where he was locked inside. Pops rang outside his door, but the pops through the phone made his blood run cold.

Flashbacks of last summer made him freeze in terror. Images of Amanda merged with Lucy, making his hands shake so bad he almost dropped the phone.

Then Lucy screamed, rattling his ear on the phone and snapping him out of his paralyzing fear.

Shouting outside his door had him jumping up, his head swimming with the sudden movement. He flattened himself against one wall and reluctantly exited from the app to slip the phone into his boot again.

Whatever was going on outside, now was the time to make a move and go find Lucy.

He shoved at the door, no longer afraid to break it down with all the noise outside. He turned the handle and slammed into it. It budged a few inches but didn't open all the way.

A desk and boxes were blocking even the view of the closet door. If the FBI was out there, they wouldn't be able to find him. But if it wasn't the FBI...

He didn't fucking care. Something was going on where Lucy was, and he had to get to her.

He took a deep breath and slammed his shoulder into the door again, pushing off the opposite wall with his feet. He turned into a leg press against it, and the door shifted a few more inches. Adrenaline flooded his system and made him dizzy.

"Novak?" a woman's voice rang out among the shouts, and relief coursed through him.

"Who's asking?" he answered.

"Over here, boys. That Texas drawl has to be him," she said. Boxes began to move, and Mason stood up, holding the wall and glimpsing the police uniforms and FBI badges on civilian clothes.

It took entirely too long for them to move everything, but when he finally busted through the door, he felt like he could breathe for the first time all night.

His vision swam as he found his contact, the same one who'd given him the binder.

"Lucy? Did you get Lucy?" he asked, finding the woman's gaze.

She nodded and frowned. "They're securing the site now. Come with me, and we'll find the details while the EMT crews look at that head."

Mason nodded, feeling the room spin and his head throb. He'd already forgotten about it in his worry for Lucy. He clenched his jaw and followed her, stumbling over his feet and fighting the urge to run out, take someone's keys, and go to the hotel he'd been watching. He had to get to Lucy and make sure she was safe.

Chapter Twenty-Nine

The paramedics patched him up, and the feds took his statement. His eyesight would spin, and he'd lose precious minutes closing his eyes and getting a handle on the vertigo.

They found his phone and wallet, then packed up the ambulance to head to the hospital. He argued until they said that's where Lucy was.

Details were minimal. He insisted on walking into the hospital on his own two feet, but refused to let them admit him until he was with Lucy. They threatened him with a sedative, and he just crossed his arms and glared at them, repeating, "Take me to Lucy."

Finally, they escorted him to another floor. An officer leaned against the wall outside her door, but he straightened when they approached.

The nurse in front of him huffed, "This is her husband." Mason didn't argue with her because married or not, Lucy belonged with him. The officer nodded and relaxed as they went inside.

She lay against the white sheets, too pale even for her.

Her arm was wrapped in gauze, but she seemed asleep. His heart had been racing for what seemed like hours but at the sight of her, it slowed and calmed.

He frowned and opened his mouth to ask the nurse for an update, but she beat him to it.

"She was grazed on the arm, nothing too serious. Just caught in the crossfire. The drugs in her system were more concerning. We've pumped everything out and pushed fluids, so that will help. She'll come to within a few hours. Now, if you'll let us check you in—"

He pulled up the chair next to Lucy and clenched his jaw. "Sure, as long as you can do it right here."

He didn't take his eyes off Lucy the entire time they asked questions. The lack of consciousness made him frustrated, and the nurse grew frustrated that he couldn't answer the medical history questions about Lucy. Eventually he called Helen and Pops to get the answers to the nurse's questions.

The phone rang. It felt like he was back in high school, calling to tell his Pops about some trouble he or Will had gotten in. It had always been better for him to find out straight from the horses' mouth than from the small-town rumor mill.

"Hello?"

Mason rubbed his temple and closed his eyes. "Thank God you're awake. Is Helen there?"

"Yeah, she's right here. Just a second. What's going on?" Rustling in the background lulled him, then Helen said hello.

Pops said, "You're on speaker, son. Y'all alright?"

"Mason? What time is it there? It's barely morning here."

Mason looked at the clock in the room and shifted on the seat. "One am. We're in the hospital."

His grandpa's rough voice barked at him. "What do you mean, you're in the hospital? What's happened?"

Mason raked a hand down his face and explained the situation.

"She was drugged and shot in the arm, but it's just a graze. She's going to be ok. The nurses have some questions that I can't answer. Can you help?"

"Of course, dear. Let me talk to the nurse."

Mason handed the phone over and only half listened as the nurse asked questions and typed them into the computer in the corner. His chest was still tight, and his stomach was tense and knotted as he replayed every step of the night, every step where he'd failed to protect her.

She never would've been in this situation if it weren't for him. It was all his fault. The nurse handed the phone back to him, and he took it absently.

"Mason? You call me the second she wakes up, you hear?" Helen's voice was sharp and brooked no argument.

"Yes, ma'am."

"Also, don't you let her out of your sight today." Mrs. Helen's voice came through the speaker, surprising him.

"Yes, ma'am." He hadn't planned on leaving her side for the rest of their trip at a minimum. Now that his cover had been blown, there was nothing that would keep him from Lucy.

"Mason? I'm serious. She's a big girl and stubborn, but don't let her out of your sight, preferably for a few days. She takes a while to process things, and she'll need someone there when she does. Promise me, Mason, please."

"I promise." He couldn't deny Helen any more than he could deny Lucy. Guilt ate at him as she lay deathly still on the bed. At least this was different than last year with Amanda. She hadn't even made it to the hospital.

He shivered at the cold seeping into his bones.

"Here's your grandfather." Helen's words brought him back to the present. More rustling and then his grandpa asked, "What happened, son?"

Mason felt tears threaten as the nurse left the room. He closed his eyes tightly and choked them back. "The person I was tailing caught on, and it all went to shit."

He clinically told him the highlights of the past two days, similar to the statement he gave the agent in the ambulance. Somehow Malia had figured out he was tailing her yesterday. Or rather two days ago now.

He should have paid more attention. He shouldn't have gotten so close to her. Not been in the same sandwich shop. Not sat at her table at the gala, not that he'd realized she'd sit at that table. That had been a pure accident.

And he'd had no idea Lucy was meeting her for lunch. He should have asked Lucy about her plans for the day. He should have known.

"Shoulda, woulda, coulda's will kill you, son. You have to let it go. What's done is done. Everyone's alright, and that's all that matters."

Mason sighed. "Yeah, but it's not always going to end in everyone being alright. It wasn't alright when I messed up last year."

"Lucy's not Amanda," Pops said softly.

Mason squeezed his eyes closed, and tears dripped down his cheeks. Swiftly, he wiped them away, growling, "I'll call y'all when she wakes up."

"No matter what time, day or night. Love you, son."

"Love you too, Pops." Mason felt his throat begin to

close as emotions threatened him once more. He hung up and pressed the heels of his hands into his eyes.

It took deep breaths and several long minutes before he regained control of himself enough to lean back. Now he was left with nothing but the beeping of the machines and his guilt. His head pounded, and the IV itched in the back of his hand.

The room became too bright, and he opened the bathroom door and turned on the light, then turned off the main room's light, rolling the IV stand with him. He settled back into the chair and waited, self-recrimination his only companion.

If he'd taken more care with his schedule, this could've been avoided. Why had he tried to juggle surveillance and hanging out with Lucy at the same time? It had been a recipe for disaster.

Lucy was lucky she'd only been nicked. He knew just how dangerous these situations could be. He shouldn't have let her in the same room as Malia much less eaten several meals with her.

Mason leaned back in a chair and kicked his boots off. He propped his socked feet on the edge of her bed, closed his eyes, and sighed as memories tugged him under.

It seemed like minutes or possibly hours passed when a soft moan echoed over the beeping of the machines.

Mason's eyes jerked open, and his heart pounded. His feet thumped to the floor as he remembered where he was, eyes going to Lucy.

She tugged her blanket up, a frown of pain on her face. He stood and grabbed her left hand gently, holding her still.

"You're awake. Don't move. You'll jar your arm and break open the wound. Let me cover you. Is this better? Are you cold? I can get another blanket." His voice was growly and low from sleep.

She frowned, her big, green eyes looking up at him so trustingly. "Thanks. I'm just so cold. What happened? Why am I here?"

He rubbed his temple with his other hand and went to the closet to dig for another blanket. "What's the last thing you remember?" He draped the blanket around her, tucking it in so it'd hold in her body heat better.

His head pounded, but he couldn't stop staring at her. He had to make sure she was really awake and recovering.

She leaned her head back against the pillows as she closed her eyes. "Fireworks, I think. You missed them."

He cleared his throat, but she didn't open her eyes. "I know, sunshine, I'm so sorry. I wanted to be there with you, but I was knocked out and locked in a closet."

She hummed, and her eyes blinked open sleepily. "Are you okay?"

He smiled, his eyes misting up. She had such a big heart, to think about others when she was the one in the hospital bed. He nodded, unable to speak around the knot in his throat.

"Break what open?"

He frowned, his mind fuzzy from lack of sleep. "What?"

"You said don't move because I'll break my arm open. What's wrong with it? It hurts like hell."

He nodded, feeling a stab of pain in his chest. "You were shot."

She jerked on the bed and started to breathe shallowly, so he stood and squeezed her hand, holding her still. He brushed the hair out of her eyes soothingly, crooning to her to breathe. Her ponytail holder was missing, and her hair was tangled around her on the pillow, yet somehow, she looked as beautiful as ever, if still pale.

He whispered, "Sh, don't move. It's okay. It didn't hit anything major. Just a scratch, really. You didn't even need stitches."

"Oh my God, I was shot. Oh my God. Mason, I—I can't breathe. Hold me, please—" Her voice broke and his heart right along with it. He couldn't stay away from her if he wanted to.

He crawled onto the bed with her on the non-injured side, shifting so both of their IVs were untangled, which took some finagling. They both shifted until her head was lying on his chest, and he had an arm under her head. He held her tight, some of the tension in his shoulders finally easing.

"Breathe with me, sunshine. That's it." He forced his breathing to regulate and soon hers evened out.

"Don't leave me," she whispered against his chest. He kissed the top of her head and closed his eyes hard against the emotions that threatened to choke him.

"Sh, just breathe, Luce. I'm not going anywhere." The low words lulled her back to sleep, and he soon felt her relax in his arms.

He kissed her head and whispered, "I swore no one else would ever get caught in the crossfire again. When you were kidnapped, I felt so helpless, locked in that closet. Unable to reach you. Unable to save you. You shouldn't have been anywhere near Malia and that mess, either. It's all my fault and I—"

His voice cracked, and he held her closer, tears once more tracking down his face. He ignored them. Perhaps this was the key to keeping her safe. Just hold her tight and never let go.

Chapter Thirty

Lucy's head hurt, and she was cold as she blinked awake. Disoriented, she realized she was still in the hospital room. Through the dim light, she saw Mason whispering in the corner with a woman.

She tugged the blanket up, and pain shot across her shoulder. She winced and looked at her left arm. A square bandage covered about an inch of her upper bicep. She shifted, testing her movement.

She gasped, and Mason spun around at the sound. In a blink of the eye, he was by her side, touching her hand.

The woman stopped at the foot of the bed and met Lucy's gaze with a smile. She was Asian, dressed in professional, nondescript pants and shirt with a surf shop logo on it.

"Ah, you're awake. Fantastic. How are you feeling?"

Lucy rolled her shoulders and struggled to sit up until Mason helped. His hands were gentle as he leaned her forward and adjusted the pillows, then handed her the remote to control the bed.

She pushed the button to sit up more and smiled tightly. Her mind was clearer, less foggy, but her headache lingered like a dull roar in the back of her head. It was nothing compared to the pain in her arm. But all she said was, "Fine, thank you. I have a headache and am sore, but fine. Can I help you? Are you with the FBI?"

Lucy looked from the woman to a frowning Mason, his arms now crossed and his face thunderous.

The woman sat in the chair Mason had vacated on her left. "Yes, I'm Mason's FBI contact. I have some questions for you about last night. We need your statement too."

Lucy nodded slowly and answered what she could. The woman's frown kept getting deeper and deeper.

"Look, I'm sorry, but I remember little beyond the fireworks. Just a fancy car, a guy pulling my hair and throwing me on a white leather couch, Malia..." she frowned, her mind foggy and thoughts swirly. "Malia was there, wasn't she?"

She looked to Mason who nodded, his gaze zeroed on the window to her left, his jaw set.

The woman stopped typing on her tablet and closed it with a tight smile. "Yes, she was dating Lee and working as the assistant for the CEO of Seaway Breezology, a biotech company. We've been tracking Lee's work with the international drug trade."

Mason growled, "I was tailing Malia to see if she had any dirt on Lee or could implicate him."

The woman nodded. "Right, but they had been so careful to keep the CEO out of it that we didn't even realize he was involved until last night."

Mason grabbed her right hand from where it lay by the remote and laced their fingers together. "He was the one at the penthouse with Malia."

Lucy nodded as understanding slowly clicked in her sluggish brain. "He was the one in the suit who hurt me."

Mason's hand squeezed hers, but he didn't seem to realize he'd tensed at her words. He just nodded curtly as the woman continued.

"Within a few hours of your rescues, we hit a few other targets in the islands—the main warehouse, the laboratory, things like that. It might not be enough to convict the CEO; he might plead plausible deniability. But if you two testify, we can at least implicate more and get all three on kidnapping and attempted murder."

Lucy's head swam, and she felt cold as ice again. "Oh—okay. What about Malia, Lee, and those involved last night?"

The woman nodded. "We got all of them. They'll be in jail for a long time, thanks to you."

She bit her lip. "So I'm safe? There's nothing else on these islands that will try to kill me?"

Mason touched her cheek, and she looked at him. "I'm not letting you out of my sight, so they'd have to go through me first."

The woman cleared her throat awkwardly. "Um, that won't be necessary. We got them all. You're safe. You don't have to commit now, but do think about testifying."

Lucy nodded and breathed a sigh of relief.

Mason asked, "Are you hungry? Let's get you some lunch. They said if you can keep food down, you can be discharged tonight."

The woman smiled and headed for the door, her tablet tucked under her arm. "I'll stop at the nurse's station and have them bring a tray. I'll be in touch."

Lucy shifted, the twinge in her arm making her frown. "How did I get shot?"

He rounded the bed and took the chair again. "When the FBI knocked down the door, you got caught in the crossfire."

Lucy's brows furrowed as she processed his words and tried to remember. Then there was a flurry of activity as lunch was delivered. Mason was sweet, opening her juice and making sure it was all within reach of her right hand.

After she ate, Mason called their grandparents. Lucy winced as Helen had threatened to head to Hawaii to take care of her. Ray had said she was already packed and had a ticket booked on the next flight, but Lucy told them both to stay.

She didn't want more hovering. She just wanted to forget the whole thing and enjoy her vacation. The emotional exhaustion hit her after they hung up, so she fell asleep. It was almost sunset when they were discharged from the hospital.

She frowned at how unsteady she was just standing and moving into the cab in her dirty sun dress from yesterday. She laid her head on his shoulder on the ride back to the resort, but neither of them talked. He just held her hand and stroked his thumb back and forth.

Mason reached for her elbow to help her walk to the golf carts at the resort, and she held back tears. He was being so sweet and taking care of her, but how much of it was him developing feelings for her and how much of it was guilt?

She knew firsthand how guilt could lead to this kind of behavior. Her dad had done it with her mom all the time. She'd witnessed countless times when he'd mess up, then come groveling back and be sweet and thoughtful. It never lasted, though.

They rode back to the room, and she was bone tired to

the point of exhaustion tears. She squeezed her eyes closed. She just wanted to relax and write her fucking book, maybe have more great sex. Was that too much to ask for a vacation?

She wrapped her arms around herself as they walked from the golf cart to their door. This was why she'd never tried to date before. Stupid shit like this happened. She always stumbled into some kind of trouble. Isn't this why she'd stayed holed up in their apartment for six years of college? As much as Taylor would let her anyway.

Inevitably, Taylor had dragged her out into society several times a year to parties. She probably needed to call her.

Lucy walked into their room and looked around, still so cold and needing a hot shower. She opened a drawer as Mason shut the door.

"I feel icky. I'm going to shower."

Mason nodded, hovering as if he thought she was going to fall over or something. "Do you want me to draw you a bubble bath in the jacuzzi tub? You're not really supposed to get your shoulder wet until the scrape closes over, which will take a few days."

Lucy felt her frustration mounting, but there was nothing she could do about it. She'd have to adjust her plans for the next few days to stay out of the ocean and waterfalls.

She nodded as she pulled her phone out of her purse—thank God they'd found it in the rescue—and plugged it into the wall.

The water turned on, and Lucy stepped into the bathroom to brush her teeth. Mason slid by her on his way to the bedroom. She finished up, then started to shut the bathroom door as Mason stepped up to it.

She frowned and looked down. "Can you give me a few minutes? I need to be alone."

He frowned but nodded. "Okay, but I'm going to check on you every so often. The drugs might still be in your system, and you seem unsteady on your feet."

She snorted and turned around with a flush of her cheeks. "I'm not going to fall asleep in the tub, Mason. Don't worry. But can you unzip my dress? With my shoulder, I can't really reach it."

The nurse had helped her dress earlier, but Mason's fingers on her back felt better. When he finished, she held the dress up and shut the door in his haunted face. She took off her underwear with shaking hands, too tired to figure out why he'd looked like that.

She stepped into the hot, bubbling water. It was the perfect temperature, and she sank her stiff body into it, leaned her head back, and sighed. Her body was fine, everything was fine. She told herself this was the last time something like this would happen. She'd had a good safe stretch during college.

Then there was the drug bust incident in December, and now this. Before college, life had been a shit show too. She really didn't want to go through another shitty phase of life, especially now that she was alone. Mom was gone, she'd moved out and lived alone. She was so very alone…

Memories of the past overwhelmed her, and the tears fell. Mason knocked and poked his head inside.

"You alright—oh." He frowned and stepped inside at the sight of her tears.

She sank into the water, quickly dunking herself before popping back up with a gasp. He sat on the edge of the tub and leaned against the wall with a frown.

The bubbles covered her body in the water, for which

she was thankful. She still didn't feel quite ready to be so open about being naked in front of him. He grabbed a towel and knelt beside the tub.

"You're not supposed to get your arm wet. Don't do that," he said, dabbing at her left arm with the towel. "The point of the bath was to not get your shoulder wet."

Something inside her snapped and the tears fell. She glared at him angrily. "I don't care. It's just a scratch. It'll be fine."

"The doctor said don't get it wet, so you better listen to her."

She scowled and splashed water at him. "Don't tell me what to do, Mason. I'll be fine. I'm a big girl."

His eyes flared as he knelt beside the tub and cupped her cheek. She froze at his touch, her body aching for him and remembering that she wasn't as alone as she thought.

He leaned close and growled, "I know you're a big girl, but you want to be a good girl too, don't you?"

She whimpered, feeling her body melt under his intense gaze and soft words. This fiercely protective man was struggling with his own emotions. Sure, most of that was guilt that she'd gotten hurt, but perhaps they could be more than just a vacation fling. He traced his hand down her neck and over her collarbone.

"Yes, master." Her whisper was barely heard over the jets in the tub.

His eyes flared at her words, and he traced his thumb over her lower lip. "That's better. Now what do you need? Water? Stiff drink? Ice cream? You name it, and I'll find it. I'll give you anything your heart desires," he said softly.

Her smile was wobbly as she rubbed her eyes. "Thanks, I appreciate it. Maybe just the shampoo and conditioner for now?"

He reached into the shower and sat them beside her. She grabbed the shampoo and began to wash her hair with one hand.

Then he batted her hand away and took over, lathering her hair. She moaned and closed her eyes, the feel of him massaging her scalp with repetitive strokes soothing her head and her soul. Physically, it was just the right amount of pressure. Emotionally, she needed to be taken care of like this.

"You're going to be alright," he said.

She sighed, and he gently tipped her head back. He used a cup to rinse her hair. She felt a tug on her hair, and she winced at the painful reminder of the man and the leather couch.

"I know. I just can't believe I was dumb enough to be drugged and kidnapped."

He rinsed her hair more, the movement methodical and relaxing. "Don't talk about yourself like that. You're not dumb. It wasn't your fault, little bird. It was mine. If it weren't for me, you wouldn't have even been in that situation."

She shook her head, squeezing her eyes tightly as water fell into them. "I still would have met her at the gala," she grumbled.

He wiped her face with the towel and resumed rinsing her hair. "But she wouldn't have suspected you of anything. She just would've been a random woman you met."

"Damn it, Mason, stop arguing with me. Let me wallow in my stupidity."

Silence stretched between them as tears rolled down her face. She buried her head in her hands and sobbed, drawing her knees up and curling into a ball in the tub.

He took the loofa and softly caressed her back in soothing circles. "Alright, sunshine, wallow away."

She cried into her knees, his hands stroking her bath until she was exhausted. He rinsed her back, and she hiccupped as she took the loofa from him. Frustrated with her own weakness, she scrubbed her body hard. The pain was good. It kept her grounded.

"Easy there, sunshine, you're alright. I won't leave you alone, and no one else will dare hurt you."

Tears tracked down her cheeks, but she ignored them as she splashed water over her to rinse off. "It's—it's not this. It's—it's not Malia," she hiccupped. He didn't say anything, sat on his haunches next to the tub, waiting on her hand and foot.

She leaned back and tipped her chin up, trying to keep the tears from falling, but the dam had broken. The more she tried to stop it, the more pressure increased on her chest until it exploded.

She choked out a sob. There was no point in keeping it in any longer. The pain of her childhood, the reminders of her dad, it all came to a head and spilled over.

Her chest hurt as she cried so hard, she shuddered a breath. Her heart raced, then she truly couldn't catch her breath and began to hyperventilate.

Damn it, the panic set in, making her angry at her own body. She knew what would happen if she continued on this path. She'd black out, and that couldn't happen in the tub. The more she worried about it happening, the more ragged her breathing became. She sat up straight and looked at him with puffy eyes.

Then everything faded.

Chapter Thirty-One

Lucy's body went slack, and she slid towards the water. He grabbed her uninjured arm and yanked her up before she sank under. Her head lolled to the side, her eyes closed and jaw slightly open.

He patted her cheek with his other hand and frowned. "Lucy? Lucy, wake up."

His heart raced as he pulled her out of the bath and grabbed the towel, his back screaming in pain. She started to slip, and he had to do some fancy juggling to keep her safe. Then he strode to the bedroom and laid her down.

He was just reaching for the phone to call for help when her lashes began to flutter. He leaned over her. "Lucy? Are you here?"

She took a deep breath and blinked wide, confusion on her face as she looked at him. "Where else would I be?"

He frowned. "You passed out. I'm not sure if it's a side effect of the drug or—"

She groaned and grabbed her head, then gasped at her nakedness. He tugged on the corner of the towel stuck under her, and she rolled and covered herself, curling into a ball on her side facing him, the covers a mess around her.

She took a few deep breaths and rubbed her nose with a finger. "It—it probably wasn't the drugs. Stupid, fucking panic attacks..." She shrugged.

He frowned and sat on the edge of the bed, his hand finding her ankle and just holding her tiny foot. He couldn't stop touching her, had to reassure himself she was here and well.

She'd been incredibly quiet about the whole ordeal in the hospital and on the way home. He'd expected more outbursts, but the smart-ass remarks in the tub meant she wasn't turning off her emotions like he'd feared. The struggle to process the trauma was real. It had taken him months to process Amanda.

She stared blankly ahead, her expression kind of lost. His chest tightened, and he stroked her foot. She jerked her foot, and her eyes sharpened as she glared at him. "Stop it," she grumbled.

He smiled at her ticklish behavior and tucked the knowledge aside for later. She shifted and sucked in a shuddering breath, making his heart ache to take away all her pain.

"Lucy?"

She looked up at him, as if he were a lifeline in the ocean. He wanted to protect her, keep her safe. Seeing her laying so pale on the hospital bed still haunted him.

"Hm?" she asked, looking at him through those thick lashes. Pink swept her cheeks, and he breathed a sigh of relief. Thank God, her color was coming back. When she'd blanked in the tub, she'd been as pale as she'd been in the hospital.

The blush on her cheeks was a good sign. It gave him

hope that this wouldn't be a life-altering experience for her, and she'd go back to her normal perky self eventually.

"You really should go to the doctor about the passing out panic attacks. That's not normal," he said.

She scowled and sat up slightly, adjusting her head on the pillow. "I told you. I've been doing this since middle school when my dad—"

Her eyes glistened as she trailed off, staring at nothing.

He reached forward and brushed the hair away from her face. "Your dad what?" he asked softly, hoping to draw her out as he settled on the pillows next to her and leaned on the headboard.

His chest hurt at the lost expression on her face. He knew that look from years of working with the Rangers. Trauma was trauma, no matter what happened, and her expression was one he'd seen countless times.

He went to the bathroom and grabbed her hairbrush, then returned to settled on the bed. "Come on, sunshine, let me brush your hair."

She slowly sat up, keeping the blankets and damp towel wrapped around her lush body. Slowly, he worked the brush through her hair.

"Tell me about your dad," he said softly.

She sighed and tilted her head back, eventually opening up under the methodical brushing. "He started doing drugs, but we didn't know it until he was fired from his job. It's why we left Crimson Creek. He bounced around from job to job after that. We lived in some apartments in bad neighborhoods closer to Fort Worth. Mom worked two jobs to make ends meet, but somehow dad always found money for drugs."

She went quiet for a while, and he just brushed the hair

away from her face over and over again, slowly. She shifted and took another deep breath.

"The drug bust back in December after graduation? I've been in a few of those before. Dad went to jail my freshman year of high school. After that, he was in and out of jail a lot, always for drugs but sometimes for other things."

Her voice became a whisper and slowed so he slowed his hands on her hair to match.

"My mom drank a lot to cope with all the stress. She'd get tipsy, and he'd be on something and acting out of his mind. They'd fight. He pushed her into the coffee table once. Broke her ribs."

Mason tensed as her voice trailed off. His body went cold, and he whispered, "Did he ever push you?"

She shifted as she shrugged. "Sometimes, but not as much as he did Mom. Last night when that man pulled my hair and threw me into the couch? That's nothing. I'm tough. I'm strong. I can handle it."

Her voice trailed off, and he eased her back onto the pillows. "You're one of the strongest women I know."

She stared at the ceiling, not agreeing with him or denying it, lost in her own memories. He laid down beside her, wrapping his arm around her waist and the fluffy blankets. She needed time to process, and he was going to be here through it all. He watched as sleep claimed her.

The conflicting emotions within him were overwhelming. He knew he had to protect her, but at the same time, his chest burned with anger towards her father, the powerful CEO, the world. Part of him wanted to lash out and hurt anyone who caused her pain, while another part struggled to maintain composure and think logically about how to navigate the volatile situation. It was a constant battle between his heart and his head, his humanity and his training.

He shook his head, trying to clear it, then eased off the bed. He pulled back the covers on the bed and eased them over her, towel and all, but when he turned to leave, her hand clamped down on his wrist.

"No. Don't leave, please. Just—just stay?"

She was still groggy, and the vulnerability in her voice tugged at his soul. He couldn't leave her even if he wanted to.

Her pleas rang in his head, and something twisted in his chest. He patted her hand on his wrist then lifted it to kiss her palm. "I'm just going to the bathroom, sunshine. I'll still be right here."

She nodded and hummed, her grip going slack once more. He turned and cleaned up, draining the water in the tub and brushing his teeth. It was barely dark, but he crawled under the covers next to her. He couldn't resist the call to be near her, touch her.

She sighed, tucking her body as close to him as possible. He ran a hand down his face again, moving the wet ends of her hair off him. It was going to be a long fucking night. He squeezed her tight and held on, afraid to let go, afraid she'd get hurt again. But most of all, afraid of how deeply he cared for this slip of a woman.

Chapter Thirty-Two

Mason awoke with a start, his heart racing. Something was wrong. What was it? It took a second to realize the problem.

Lucy's side of the bed was empty, her pillow cold. He scrambled to stand, holding his back and stretching the stiffness out of it. His phone was on the nightstand with a piece of paper under it.

You're adorable when you sleep. I banged around getting ready, but you didn't wake. The FBI agent called. They need me to fill out some paperwork. I'm going to meet her on Wakiki Beach. Text me when you wake up, sleepy head.
—Lucy

She'd left him. He was trying to protect her, and she'd left. He jerked on shorts, sneakers, and a plain t-shirt, brushed his teeth, and was out the door in minutes.

His heart raced as he jogged down to the main resort building and scanned his wristband. He jumped in their rental car, thankful for whatever agent had brought it back to their resort and left the keys in it, and headed to Wakiki, his leg bouncing.

Sure, she was an adult, but it was his job to protect her. He couldn't do that if she kept leaving him. This happened too often, leaving with just a note. And at the pineapple plantation, she'd ditched him in the maze for a laugh.

He'd need to talk to her about it today. It made his skin crawl with worry. He stopped at a stop light and pulled out his phone, thankful for the tracking app he'd placed on hers days ago. He pulled up the app to find her phone gps and found a parking spot nearby.

A flash of pink caught his eye across the street as he got out of the car.

Lucy. Her name was a prayer on his lips. She had an oversized bag and a floppy sun hat as she stepped out of the little cafe where he'd first met the agent. Seeing her eased some of the tension in his shoulders, and he breathed a sigh of relief.

He crossed his arms while waiting for the crosswalk sign to change, and his eyes followed her as she walked down the sidewalk. It was too loud to be heard, so he didn't even try to call for her.

She was a vision, a beacon of hope. Just being near her made him relax. The light changed, and he jogged across the street. She walked to the same corner, but was strolling idly, looking into windows.

A gangly teenager bumped into her from behind as Mason reached the other side of the street.

Lucy frowned and tugged on her bag, but the teenager wrenched it out of her hand and bounded away.

She yelled, "He has my bag!"

Mason's heart raced as the kid ran straight for him.

Dodging through tourists and never taking his eyes off the teen, he turned and clotheslined him.

The kid and the bag fell to the ground. Mason dropped and twisted him onto his stomach, pulling his hands behind his back.

"Mason?" Lucy asked as she stopped near them. A crowd formed a surprised circle around them.

Mason nodded to the contents of her bag strewn on the sidewalk. "Grab your stuff, then call the cops."

Lucy sidestepped around them and knelt, pulling her stuff back into her bag. She held it to her chest as someone helped her to her feet. Mason stood up, the boy's arms pulled tight behind his back, and saw a police officer.

The police officer waved the crowd away. "Nothing to see here, folks. Enjoy your morning. Now, what's happened?"

Lucy opened her mouth to explain but Mason beat her to it. He filled the officer in, and Lucy waved the bag as proof. A few bystanders corroborated the events. The police officer took their information, made the formal arrest, and marched the kid toward a tiny police vehicle.

Mason turned his head and pulled Lucy into his arms. She gasped at the hug, but he just pressed their bodies flush from knee to chest. For the first time that morning, he relaxed, nuzzling into her neck.

The words spilled from him into her ear. "What were you thinking? Did we not talk about your disappearing act?"

She leaned back to look at him, but he couldn't make out her expression behind her giant sunglasses. "Wha— what do you mean?"

Her hands clenched his shirt at the waist, and he tightened his grip on hers. He was practically vibrating with energy, shifting from foot to foot as the crowd surged around them. He looked around, placed a hand on her lower back, and hustled her to the line for a smoothie street vendor.

He forced himself to release her and rubbed his temples with a sigh, "I can't protect you if you keep disappearing."

She blushed and shook her head, a frown line marring her forehead. "I don't need protecting." Her voice was huffy, her nose and chin tilted up.

He groaned and linked their fingers, rubbing his thumb on the back of her hand. "Lucy, don't you get it? I was worried about you. You can't just run off like that."

His chest ached, but he couldn't hold these feelings in anymore. The worry threatened to consume him. The line moved, and he tugged her along, not releasing her hand. Somehow, he had to tell her how he felt without making her think he was chewing her out like her dad did when she was younger.

He pursed his lips. "It's my job to protect you, even if I'm not doing that great a job of it."

She frowned, and he wanted to see her eyes. "I think you're doing fine," she said softly.

He snorted and pulled her in for another hug, his breath a sigh. She pushed back on his chest and looked up at him.

He couldn't see her eyes, but her cheeks flushed as she rubbed his chest. "Mason? You are a great Ranger, a great friend, a great protector, a great master."

He smirked, and her lips tilted at the corners, his eyes locking on the movement and desire shooting through him as she continued.

"All's well that ends well, right? I'm alive, and relatively happy and healthy. That's all that matters right now. I didn't disappear. I left a note, which you found since you found me here."

He put his hand on top of hers and frowned, ignoring

the guilt of having tracked her phone without her knowledge. "Yeah."

His voice was gruff, and he ran a nervous hand through his hair. That cowlick fell down on his forehead, and she reached up to push it back with a smile. But he felt the weight of his words settle on his shoulders like a boulder. She was lucky to be alive.

Memories of Amanda lying in a pool of blood and Lucy in the hospital sent a pain of guilt through him, making his stomach churn. He couldn't let anything happen to her, but he couldn't develop a relationship with her either. If she would've died too, he never would've forgiven himself. As it was, he couldn't forgive himself for Amanda.

He had to step back before it was too late. He couldn't let her see how much he cared. She'd just called him a great friend, so he had to treat her as one. Just a friend. If he treated her as something more, it would make it that much harder to let her go when they returned from this little vacation.

He cleared his throat, stepping back and dropping his hand. "I mean, your grandmother would have my hide if something else happened to you."

She scowled and crossed her arms. "I'm not a child, Mason."

He put his hands on his hips and faced her, frustration at not being able to be with her forever making him mouth off. "I never said you were, but you sure are acting like one right now."

"I am not," she whispered furiously, leaning closer and fisting her hands at her sides.

He leaned forward too. "You certainly are. You've been kidnapped, shot, and now robbed since we've gotten here."

She waved her hand and scoffed. "Tis merely a flesh

wound. I'm not going to let it stop me from some more adventures."

He grinned and arched a brow. "Monty Python? Nice. We'll have to watch it sometime. Wait, don't distract me. If you think I'm going to let you run all over Honolulu on your own, you've got another thing coming."

She flipped her long ponytail over her shoulder and stared straight ahead in the line. "You don't have to worry about me. I was alone in college for six years. I know how to take care of myself. Besides, the ones I'd worry about are all locked up."

He snorted and crossed his arms, staring straight ahead and standing shoulder to shoulder with her. "And I know how to take care of you too, so let me do my job and keep you safe. We'll have a nice, relaxing rest of our vacation with no more danger. Got it?"

Her voice was sarcastic, and her nose wrinkled as she crossed her own arms and said, "Yes, master. Whatever you say, master."

Mason grinned despite himself. "That's more like it. Now how about a smoothie for my little bird?"

Somehow, he knew she was rolling her eyes behind those sunglasses, and it just made him grin wider. She opened her mouth to reply, but the person in front of them finished and the vendor interrupted.

"Yes, miss. What can I get for you today?"

Lucy stepped away from him and perused the sign before placing her order. He added his order as she dug out her wallet. He put his hand over hers and pushed it down softly, sliding his card into the machine.

She frowned up at him, then grabbed her smoothie and stomped away.

The vendor nodded as he took his card back. "Feisty one, isn't she?"

Mason smirked and grabbed his own smoothie. "You have no idea. Have a nice day."

"You too. Thank you, sir."

Mason caught her in a few strides, and they strode down to the water. The beach was already getting crowded, and he knew this wasn't part of her plan for the day.

Lucy stomped to the water and sank crisscross on the sand, watching the waves and letting them wash over her. She'd called Taylor and Nana Helen this morning to reassure them she was alright. She'd been on the phone with Taylor when the FBI lady had called her.

Mason had slept like a log, not even rolling over as she'd gotten ready. A stab of trepidation had shot through her at the thought of going out into Wakiki, but she refused to live in fear. The past few days had been chaotic and once-in-a-lifetime things.

Admittedly though, the robbery had her a little shaken up too. She drank her smoothie and breathed deeply to calm her nerves.

Mason sank to the sand beside her, not saying a word. They sat there until the sun became too hot.

"We need sunscreen," she murmured as she drank the last dregs of her smoothie.

He nodded. "Yep, it's almost time for the Hilo excursion that we won. Do you want to reschedule? It's been a traumatic few days."

She frowned and shook her head, sighing to realize she'd forgotten to check her phone calendar that morning.

"No, I don't want to give them that power over me. I want to keep adventuring and experiencing everything life has to give. If I don't, they win."

He nodded and sighed. "I was afraid you'd say that. Did you get my email with the itinerary?"

She bit her lip and nodded. He wasn't going to be happy about the changes she'd made to it two days ago while at the bookstore, but he'd picked boring things to do. She didn't want to fight with him anymore. Not right now.

Her phone vibrated, and she saw a text from Taylor.

Girl, did you survive the morning?
Are you dead???

She texted back.

What are you talking about?
I just talked to you a few hours ago.
Stop worrying about me. I'm definitely not dead.
Having the time of my life and about to go to Hilo for the afternoon.

How's the hunky Ranger and his dick treating you?

She'd told Taylor earlier about how he'd washed her hair and brushed it last night, which had left her friend squealing.

LOL His dick isn't doing shit.
Not since we came home from the hospital anyway.
He's overprotective today too which is annoying.
We're heading to some waterfalls today.

So happy for you and only a little jealous.

Try to relax and enjoy it, ok? And ride that dick.

Lucy snorted and grinned, drawing Mason's gaze as they stood up.

"What's going on?"

She shook her head and slipped her phone into her bag. "My roommate says hi."

"Tell her I said hi too."

She dusted sand off her butt. "I need to go back to the resort and change before we head to the excursion. We should still have time, right?"

He nodded, and she followed him back to their rental car. Half an hour later, they walked to the resort shuttle, Mason carrying her shoulder bag laden with sunscreen, water, and towels.

Chapter Thirty-Three

The resort shuttle dropped them off at the airport, and they took a helicopter to the other island.

Lucy alternated between pressing her face against the window for a better view and holding Mason's hand tight as her stomach lurched.

His voice was scratchy over the headset. "Never been in a helicopter before?"

She shook her head, but her grin was so wide her cheeks hurt. "No, but it's exhilarating. Oh look, is that Hilo?"

The pilot gave his tour guide spiel and flew over the island. She took probably a hundred pictures before they landed. A rental car was waiting for them, and soon they'd plugged in the gps, and Mason was driving them to the waterfall.

He didn't ask who was driving, but she didn't let it bother her. This was a vacation, and he was determined to take care of her. Besides, it gave her more time to sightsee and take pictures.

As they hiked to Rainbow Falls, she couldn't stop

looking around her. Everything sparkled with the morning sun, dew still shining like crystals on the plants. The dirt churned under their feet, and when she slipped, Mason steadied her.

They held hands the rest of the way, soothing the last of the nerves that itched under her skin. The nerves that made her worry about the state of her heart when she went back home.

The waterfall took her breath away and pulled her back into the present. She did a slow half circle to take in every sight, every ray of sun reflecting through the water.

"Wow, so this is why they call it Rainbow Falls. It's breathtaking."

He settled his hand on the base of her spine. "Not as breathtaking as you, sunshine."

She turned her head, finding him closer than she'd thought. Her lips tingled, and his blue eyes burned with passion. When their lips met, he gathered her into his arms. She felt off balance with her big bag behind her and him tipping her with the kiss.

But she wasn't worried. In his arms, she knew she was safe. Always.

He broke the kiss and cupped her face in his rough palm.

She still felt the world tilting when he released her and stepped back. She sat heavily on the nearest rock outcropping, sliding her bag to the ground. He stood with his hands in his pockets as he stared across to the waterfall.

The light filtered through the trees and fell onto his hair, the salt and pepper prominent in the light. He was rugged and fiercely loyal and protective. Was it any wonder she'd fallen in love with him?

She froze, realizing what she'd just thought, realizing

why this sense of dread had slowly crept up on her over the past week.

This was what she'd always been afraid of, the reason she'd always *wanted* to stay away from guys. She'd fall in love like her parents, but love didn't survive the hard times in life. Love ended in pain and loneliness.

The urge to get up and move hit again, and she swung her bag onto her shoulder and took off down the path with a glance to her watch. If she stayed still, she'd end up thinking and worrying and ruin the day. Or worse, professing her love and then things would be awkward when he didn't say it back.

She continued down the trail, trying to outrun her fear, trying to distract herself from the ache in her chest as they hiked. "We have half an hour to explore before we need to be back on the road for the next item on our itinerary."

He jogged up beside her and sighed. "Luce, can't we just take our time and enjoy it? Look around. It's gorgeous."

She nodded, slowing her feet with a frown. She pulled out her camera and hid behind the lens. "It is. I wish we had waterfalls like this in Texas."

He chuckled. "We have some, just not near the metroplex, and nowhere near this gorgeous. If you go up toward Oklahoma or down near Austin, there are some good ones."

"Have you been to any of them?"

They stopped at another viewpoint. He nodded and scrambled up and over a big rock as she walked around it. He paced a few feet on top before hopping down in front of her, shoving his hands in his pockets as he twisted his back here and there and held one side.

"I took Amanda to one near Austin for a weekend getaway. We stayed at a fancy place on the lake, ate like kings, and then hiked off the heavy meal."

He fell silent beside her, and she searched for a different topic. She hated that sad expression on his face, the way his shoulders fell when he talked about her.

"Maybe you can take me someday," she blurted. Her cheeks heated, but she didn't look away. He blinked as if not seeing the waterfall at all, then turned to face her.

The sad expression was gone, but in its place was a blank one. She didn't know how to interpret it. Damn him and his acting skills.

He shrugged, his face guarded. "Maybe. If the Texas Rangers retire me or stick me in a desk job to gather dust, I might as well move back to Crimson Creek and be a regular old police officer."

"But you don't want to do that, do you." It wasn't a question. She knew the answer, had heard it from him and Ray both.

"No, it's not what I want." His words speared her heart, making her stomach flip. Was he talking about the job or being with her?

For once, she wanted to take the easy way out and ignore it. She wouldn't ask for clarification. She would *not*. She might love him—God help her—but she still had her pride, damn it.

He continued, turning back to look at the waterfall. "I want to make the biggest impact and help the most amount of people. Crimson Creek is great, and the police department is in pretty good shape. The new sheriff is a good man, and he runs a tight ship."

"But?"

"But I feel like there's more out there for me. More people to save and help. I'm still useful. I can—"

His phone rang in his pocket, and he paused to get it.

She stopped and pulled her own out to take pictures, texting them to Taylor.

Her phone rang almost immediately. She glanced at Mason to see him still on the phone a few feet away, so she answered it.

"Hey, Tay, how's it going?"

"Oh my God, it's so good to hear your voice. I believe you now. You're not dead."

Lucy laughed and rubbed her forehead, setting her bag down and pulling out the water. "We talked this morning. Why are you worrying so much?"

"Oh, I don't know. It's not every day my best friend gets *kidnapped* by a drug king pin."

Lucy laughed at Taylor's dramatic, sarcastic tone. "It'll take more than that to keep me down. I'm doing great, Tay. Been taking it easy today, other than hiking to some waterfalls."

"Oh good, I'm glad. What else you have planned, babe?"

Lucy chatted about her plans as she walked to the end of the trail. "Oh, Tay, you'd love it here. Maybe we can come back together."

Lucy looked over to see Mason's raised brow. Hands in pockets, he must've finished his call.

"Looks like I gotta run. We're about to turn back. I wish you were here with me."

"Girl, same. Next time, we're going together. I want to get to know this new not-studying-all-the-time Lucy. I miss you."

Lucy smiled and dug her toe in the dirt. "I miss you too. Love you."

"Love you too. Bye bye."

"Bye bye." She hung up and tossed her phone back into the bag before offering him a water bottle.

"Who was on the phone?" Mason spat out, low and deep.

She tilted her head, looking at her watch. "That was Taylor. We're out of time here. Ready to head back?"

He took her bag and slung it over his shoulders. "What's the rush? Want to get back to the resort to talk to *Taylor*?"

She rolled her eyes at his tone of voice but stepped around him back down the path. "No, we have a tour to the lava flow in half an hour, and then have to be at the diving cave."

He placed his hand on her arm and spun her around. She tilted her head up to look at him, the sun through the trees preventing her from seeing his eyes.

"The hell we are. That's not the itinerary I forwarded you."

She shrugged, trying to tug out of his hands but not trying very hard. She liked the feel of him holding her tight. "Right, it's not. I called the lady the morning of the festival, and we changed it to something more fun. Surprise."

"What the fuck, Lucy? Lava flow? Cave diving? You're not supposed to get your shoulder wet."

She shrugged. "Yeah, I thought about that. But the wet suit will protect me, right? It's not like we're diving in bikinis."

He shook his head, his hands on his hips. "No, those are too dangerous. I had arranged for us to finish this waterfall tour, then go to the botanical gardens, and end with a trip to the farmers market."

She snorted. "Yeah, that was boring. We just did the botanical gardens earlier this week, remember?"

"That was a completely different island." His hands waved at his sides.

She stomped around him back down the trail. "Eh, once you've seen one, you've seen them all. Besides, I want to do things I won't be able to do back home. I need to step out of this shell and figure out what I can do, what my limits are."

"Going to a fucking volcano is your limit." He raced around her, walking backward to keep facing her.

She narrowed her eyes and placed her hands on her hips, stopping before he tripped. "It's not dangerous, Mason. They wouldn't have a tour for it if it was."

He leaned forward so they were almost nose to nose. "They do bungee jumping tours too but people still die on them. If everyone jumped off a bridge, would you too?"

She burst out laughing, placing a hand on his chest and pushing him slightly. He didn't budge, giant that he was, but she just grinned and shook her head.

"How'd you know I've always wanted to go bungee jumping? Not over land, though. Over water would be fun. I bet they have some cool ones on these islands. Oh, and zip lining!"

"Not today, they don't. Come on, let's finish the waterfall tour. There's another one just up the path that's supposed to be even more gorgeous than this one."

"Are you kidding me?" She jerked her hand out of his grasp and stepped back. So much for not fighting anymore. "We have this one day on Hilo, and you want to go to a botanical garden and farmers market? We can do that in Texas any weekend of the year."

"It's better than cramming so much into one day that you don't have time to enjoy it. Honolulu was way too busy. We could have spent all day at any of the places you dragged me to. We didn't even scratch the surface of the Cultural Center."

She backed up, still facing him. "Well, no one said you *had* to join me. That's on you. Same as today. You want to finish the waterfall tour? Be my guest."

He growled and prowled after her, forcing her to back up another step down the path. "Not without you. Knowing your luck, something will happen while I'm gone, and I won't be there to protect you."

She rolled her eyes. "Yeah, I've been fine on my own for twenty-three years. I could argue that I only got drugged, kidnapped, and robbed once I met you..."

"What the hell is that supposed to mean?"

The wounded look in his eyes took her breath away, and she tried to smooth it over. "Nothing. Just that you're great at your job."

He glared at her, his back going rigid. "Bullshit. If I was good at my job, you never would've gotten hurt. Amanda never would've died. And the FBI would've offered me the job."

He spun on his heel and strode down the path back to the parking lot. She gasped and raced to catch up with him. She put her hand on his back, and he jerked away.

"What about the FBI?" she asked.

He ground his teeth as he said, "They called and said they didn't want to offer me the job, that I was caught in just a few days and compromised the entire mission. They're not even sure they can close the international drug ring now because I blew the whole thing to smithereens."

Lucy giggled, and he stopped and glared, slamming his hands on his hips. "You're laughing?" he nearly shouted.

She wrinkled her nose and put her hands on his chest to

soothe him. "Not at you. The word. Smithereens. It's funny."

He pursed his lips, and his shoulders sank as the wind went out of his sails. He raked a hand through his hair. "I guess it is, but the FBI was my dream—"

She ran her hand across his chest, then up to his biceps. "I know it was, but you know what they say. When one door closes, another one opens."

He scowled, but leaned in and rested their foreheads together. He sighed, "It's a dumb saying."

She sighed, cupping his cheek. Guilt ate at her. "It's all my fault, Mason. I'm so sorry I got caught up with Malia. I didn't know she was your suspect."

He wrapped his arms around her, dipping his head to the crook of her neck. "It's my fault too. If I had told you at the art auction that she was the one I was gathering evidence on, then you would've stayed away from her. I didn't tell you she was dangerous, and it put you in harm's way."

She patted his back, then rubbed circles, soothing him like he'd done her last night. "I'm sorry the FBI is being a tool. I'm sorry I jeopardized your entire career."

He squeezed her tighter and sighed. "It's not your fault. I shouldn't have kept it all from you, especially after you met her."

She hugged him, breathing in the comforting scent. "We can't keep playing the blame game. It serves no purpose except to keep spinning our wheels. Come on, let's go have a fun day going on once in a lifetime adventure and ignore the FBI thing for now, okay? You'll just have to trust that it'll all work out."

He grabbed her hand and linked their fingers, turning to walk back down the trail. "I'm not sure how much fun I'll be today. I really don't want to worry about you getting hurt for all this crazy shit."

She squeezed his hand. "If you're with me, I won't get hurt. You're my hero."

He didn't reply other than a side eye glance. She wondered if she'd said too much.

Chapter Thirty-Four

Lucy leaned back in the bathtub. The bath salts were working their magic on her sore muscles. The day had been much more active than her normal, with over twenty thousand steps logged on her smart watch.

She didn't want to admit it but maybe Mason was right. She had over planned the day. Constantly worrying about missing the next event had her not really taking in all the sights and sounds that she'd wanted to. She'd gone from one extreme of never really getting out of her bubble at college to the other extreme of getting out too much to enjoy it fully. Eventually she'd find the happy medium.

Mason had dropped her off at the resort after she'd fallen asleep in the car on the way back from the airport. He'd given her strict instructions to jump in the hot tub or take a bath for her sore muscles, but to be careful with her shoulder.

He'd said he was going to meet his FBI contact again to discuss the phone call from earlier. She hadn't questioned him on it, even though it was already dark. She'd been too tired.

The phone rang again, and she turned off the jets to answer it.

"Hello?"

"Hello sweet pea, how're you feeling? Did I catch you at a bad time?" Nana Helen's voice was demanding, her teacher's voice that always got results.

She sighed and put it on speaker so she could get out of the now cold water. "Nope, just getting out of the tub. I'm sore all over, but good."

"Is Mason in there with you? Why did you answer the phone, child?"

Lucy chuckled. "No, he's not here. He's gone to talk to the FBI about the job. Did he tell you or Ray?"

She sighed, slipping on a robe and stepping through their room to the patio to sit on a lounger.

"No, tell us what?"

"Oh, well, I'll have him call Ray tomorrow. It's not looking good for the FBI job, though."

"Oh no, he must be so disappointed. I'll tell Ray to call him too. Other than his job, how's it going? Is there anything developing between you two?"

The stars above were brighter than anything in Texas and reflected on the water. She could see the faint outline of an island, and she gasped.

"What is it, dear?"

"It's lava! It's flowing into the ocean. Glowing orange and yellow, twisting like snakes down to the water. It's beautiful."

Helen chuckled. "I wish we could see it. Maybe next year we'll take a family vacation. Wouldn't that be nice?"

Lucy sighed and rubbed her forehead, thinking of what

next year would look like. Mason would be off saving the world, and she'd be safe in Crimson Creek. "Sure, Nana, but maybe I can get a room to myself next time?"

"Uh oh. That doesn't sound promising. What's going on?"

She swallowed past the knot in her throat and paused, thinking about how to answer. "Mason and I... agreed that this would just be a temporary fling. When we go back home, we're going our separate ways."

Helen paused before saying softly, "Flings rarely are just that. I bet he won't be able to let you go once y'all get home."

Lucy felt tears prick her eyes as she smiled and leaned her head back. "I doubt it. He really loves his job. Reminds me of dad before he was fired."

Helen's voice was softer now. "He's not your dad, sweet pea."

"I know he's not, but I've been thinking a lot about him and mom this week." She told Helen about throwing the seashell off the cliff, the significance of it. A few beats of silence passed before Helen replied.

"Your parents had one of the greatest, most tragic love stories I've ever seen in real life, but that was a completely different situation, Lucy, and you know it. That has nothing to do with you and Mason. Your mom and dad made their mistakes a long time ago, and there's nothing you could've done to change it."

Lucy wiped the corner of her eyes. "I know, but I can't handle being told what I can and cannot do. Mason decides everything. Like today, we went to Hilo, and he organized the excursions without even asking. Why can't we just have a conversation and do things we both enjoy?"

It was Nana's turn to pause, then she asked, "Lucy,

learning to communicate is one of the biggest parts of a relationship. It takes time to figure out."

"Nana, I don't have time. We leave in a few days, and then who knows when I'll see or talk to him again? I thought we were going somewhere real. It felt real. It felt like love."

"So lean into that, sweet pea. It's scary but it's so worth it," Helen said.

Lucy rubbed her forehead. "He's not over his girlfriend's death last summer. It's too soon. To him, this is just a vacation fling, a rebound maybe."

Helen sighed. "I can understand that. If he loved her as much as I loved your grandfather, it might take years for him to grieve and move on."

"Will he though? I can't compete with a dead woman, Nana. It's not fair to her memory or to him, and certainly not to me."

"That's true. You're the best in the world. It might take him time to see it, or he might get caught living in the past. If he does, he's not the man I thought he is. Maybe the bigger question is do you love him?"

Lucy's chest ached as the pressure increased. She sniffed and rolled her shoulders, trying to relieve the tension. "I don't know, Nana. I think so, but I'm so afraid of getting hurt."

"If you love him, just give him time, okay sweet pea?"

She sniffed and went back inside, laying on the cold and lonely bed. "I'll try, but I have to protect my heart, Nana. I won't be caught in a nightmare like Mom. She loved dad so much, and it killed her."

Lucy yawned and plugged her phone up. "I'm going to sleep now. Maui is tomorrow, and I'm going to go on a whale watching tour."

"Pack the motion sickness pills, just in case. Love you, sweetie."

"Love you too. Good night." Lucy pulled the covers up. She liked the breeze off the ocean and left the balcony door partially open. It wasn't that late, but she didn't know where Mason was. This was good, though. She didn't need to become addicted to sleeping in his arms.

She shivered, tossing and turning as she tried to go to sleep, tried to ignore the worry that he was working or in trouble somewhere.

Mason sat on the other balcony lounger in the dark and watched Lucy toss and turn. He hadn't meant to eavesdrop on her conversation with Helen, but when he'd walked to the door, he'd heard her soft voice. He'd changed course to walk around the side of the bungalow to their patio.

But her words had stopped him cold. All the hope he'd started to feel shriveled into a ball and died.

He frowned and looked up at the sky. She didn't want anything more than this vacation. Her mom had died from loving her dad. What had she said about it? Her mom had been trapped by her dad's drug addiction.

Did Lucy think he was trying to trap her? He knew she'd felt a little suffocated today, and they'd fought.

I won't be caught in a nightmare like Mom.

Her words haunted him. He didn't want to trap her or give her nightmares.

Maybe he should give her some breathing room. Tomorrow they'd go to Maui. He could give her independence back. She'd claimed he was trying to steal that before, hadn't she?

He sighed and gently lifted her to tuck the blankets around her. She murmured but didn't wake. When he finished changing and brushing his teeth, he tried to resist pulling her close.

When she curled into his side and sighed, his stomach twisted, and he wrapped his arms around her. He had to let her go when they returned to Texas, but he'd treasure these little moments forever.

The next day, Mason woke to an empty bed. Lucy was doing yoga on the patio, and he just laid there and watched. The way her muscles flexed, the way her curves jiggled.

He wanted to hold her close and never let go.

He frowned, throwing off the covers and stalking into the bathroom to get ready for the day. Last night, he'd decided to let her go, hadn't he? He had to stick to his guns.

At breakfast, he told Lucy he wasn't going on the whale watching tour.

She blinked those big, beautiful eyes and frowned. "You're not? But I thought—"

He shook his head and stabbed his fork a little too violently into the food. "I saw there's a charity fun run at the same time. I'd rather do that. Is that okay?"

She pursed her lips then took a drink of her juice. Finally, she nodded and took a deep breath. "Yeah, that's fine. I mean, we're both adults. We can do our own things. God knows we don't have to be in each other's hip pockets the whole trip. I didn't know you were a runner. What do you like about it?"

Mason shrugged, and they chatted about workouts and other hobbies. The entire morning, he was on edge. He definitely needed to release some tension and work out the thoughts that kept swirling in his head. Since she'd been kidnapped and shot, he'd been so filled with fear.

When they got to Maui, she took a cab to the whale watching tours, and he went to the town where the charity fun run was taking place. A starting line and a group of runners were already standing, stretching and waiting.

He wasn't in the best shape, his injury keeping him from some of his more strenuous workouts, but cardio was always helpful. He usually alternated between running and biking. Too bad he had left his headphones back in their room.

The race started, and he followed the crowd, neither pushing himself out front nor falling back. The air was still cool in the morning, but the sun was shining and sweat already beaded his brow. Soon, his head was steadily clearing as he thought of the future.

His stomach was still unsettled and had been all night. Simon's call yesterday had been a punch in the gut. It might've hurt worse than when he'd been shot in the back. It would've been tough, but really it was just one more way to prove himself. Now he didn't have the FBI waiting on him, he'd just continue with the Rangers.

They'd probably stick him in a desk job for the rest of this year, maybe the next two or three years too in an effort to push him out. Even before his injury, they were asking him to take on more administrative duties. He focused on his breathing as he ran, coming to terms with his lost dreams.

A motion to his left had him turning his head to look at the bay. A pod of whales jumped, causing massive splashes. His steps slowed as he watched.

Lucy's arrival in his life was like those whales. She brought ripples everywhere she went, and soon they turned into massive tsunami waves that threatened to drown him. He didn't know where he stood with her.

He knew where he wanted to stand. He wanted to be on

that boat tour with her. He'd wanted to do the lava tour with her yesterday too and had enjoyed the magical wonder on her face when they'd seen it.

The cave diving had been different. He'd been so worried about her getting her shoulder wet that he hadn't enjoyed it very much. Even though he'd been worried for her safety, he'd felt a certain calm at having her so close. Soon, they'd go their separate ways, and the idea of not seeing her every day gnawed at him.

It was only when he'd lost sight of her in the cave that his frustration had mounted, and his worry had threatened to drown him. Why did he have this overwhelming need to protect her, love her, and keep her safe?

He approached the finish line, no closer to solving the problems in his life than he'd been before. There was nothing to do but continue the path he was running. They had to go their separate ways in Texas. He might still be a Ranger, but that just meant he still had people to save. He could do that with the Rangers or the FBI; it didn't really matter.

By going back to work, he wouldn't trap Lucy into a relationship she didn't really want. That didn't mean that he had to ignore her for the rest of their trip though. They still had a few days left in paradise. He wouldn't be doing any more work for the FBI while he was here, so he might as well do what his heart wanted and spend every moment with Lucy.

He passed the finish line, his heart racing and chest aching. He panted and glanced around as the crowd dispersed now that the race was over. This was dumb. Why had he decided not to go whale watching with her?

He texted her.

What's the rest of your plans for today?
I'm done with my run.
Can we spend the rest of our time here together?

He walked around town for maybe half an hour before he got a reply.

The rest of our time in Maui?
Our flight back to Honolulu is in two hours, but sure.

He took a deep breath and typed, admitting a sliver of his feelings.

Not just today.
I want to spend the rest of our vacation together.

The three dots drove him crazy, and he bounced on his toes as he waited. He didn't want to trap her and would set her free when they got back, but he needed to soak up as much time with her as possible.

That sounds good to me.
We're heading back to shore now. Let me know where you're at, and I'll meet you.

He breathed a sigh of relief and walked to a little cafe on the edge of town that overlooked the ocean. He texted her his location and waited for her whale watching tour to end. The next few days would be everything she wanted. He wanted to make them perfect for her. Not just because he was trying to make up for getting her kidnapped, but because he wanted to see her happy, whether that was with him or not.

Chapter Thirty-Five

The last few days since the whale watching tour had been full of slower paced adventures, thanks to nightly conversations about what they each wanted to do the next day. They explored a few more places, both compromising a little. She'd joined him at the botanical gardens' cherry blossoms, and he'd braved a submarine tour around the island with her.

Lucy tried to keep their conversations lighthearted, ignoring the trauma and trying to move on. It was hard when he did such sweet things. He'd tucked flowers into her hair, held her hand almost everywhere they went, and asked about her book. He teased her about it, but also helped her talk through her plot problem as they explored.

Slowly, she got used to having him constantly at her side. They also spent a few days just lounging on the beach. It was Mason's idea, a compromise for a way to enjoy her vacation and still get something accomplished on her book. She worked on her tan while typing away on her tablet. She wasn't getting as much writing done as she'd like, but it was a vacation, after all, and she didn't obsess over it.

Finally, her shoulder scabbed over. She got cleared for swimming with just a few days left in their trip. Mason had insisted on taking her to the doctor to get the approval for water sports.

It was sweet that he'd insisted on the doctor's approval. She was in elementary or middle school the last time someone took such good care of her. He'd not touched her since the kidnapping though, except to hold her tight at night.

After they left the doctor, Mason asked, "So now that you're approved for water sports, what's your plan? I assume you have an itinerary ready to go?"

She grinned, a small thrill going down her spine. "You know me so well," she chuckled. "I want to go snorkeling or sky diving."

He'd snorted and turned the car back toward their resort. "You're kidding, right? Those are way too dangerous."

"They're perfectly safe. I'm more likely to get kidnapped than—oh wait, I've already done that."

He gave her the side eye, and she burst out laughing as he mumbled, "Not funny."

She definitely thought it was. They'd gone to the beach and had just walked, hand in hand, as they talked and people watched. They'd grabbed dinner at a food truck, then gone back to the resort, both of them falling asleep on the loungers as they watched the sunset.

That was yesterday. She'd thought after the doctor had declared her healed enough to get in the water that they would come back to the resort and hump like bunnies. Surely that was why he'd kept her at arms' length.

Their days had been incredibly relaxing, but she was getting sexually frustrated. Their time in paradise was expiring, and Lucy wanted to make each moment count. Although they didn't discuss the future, a bittersweet cloud hung over their happy bubble, knowing that they would still be going their separate ways at the end.

Lucy didn't want to think about how hard it'd be when they went back home, and she was all alone again.

She stretched, smiling at the memories of the past few days as the early morning light started to change. Energy flooded her like normal, making her legs itch. She needed to get up and do yoga, calm down and find her center, but Mason groaned and pulled her closer.

She smiled, relaxing against him. He'd slept with a hand on her all night every night, either holding her hand or wrapping his around her waist to spoon. Last night when they'd finally stumbled off the patio and pulled the covers up on the bed, he'd growled into her neck, "I'm not letting you go."

She'd smiled, a thrill going through her body and forming goosebumps. Getting her hopes up wasn't the smart thing to do, but she'd dreamed of them together back in Crimson Creek, living together in Ray's house and watching movies together.

She blinked the sleep away, rubbing her eyes and watching as the sky got lighter. She was content. For the first time in as long as she could remember, she didn't want to just jump up and get to work, rushing through to the next class, next assignment, next appointment, next task on her list.

She was perfectly happy to just lay there in his arms. The sun met the clouds as it climbed higher, blocking some of the rays. She sighed, knowing this relationship was just for the duration of this trip, despite what he'd said last night. They'd agreed in the beginning, and now that she'd gotten to know him, she knew he just wasn't ready to open his heart to another woman. His work was dangerous, and he was grieving.

And she... Well, you couldn't blame a girl for wishing they could have more. She frowned and turned in his arms, snuggling into his chest. She just needed to soak in all the boyfriend memories to tide her over. Eventually she'd move on and someone else would come around. There was no way anyone would ever measure up to him, though.

Groggily, he opened one eye and groaned, "Is it time to get up?"

She nodded, breathing in the smell of coconuts from whatever lotion he used. His arms tightened around her as he kissed her head and rolled the other way out of bed.

She sat up, the sheet pooling at her waist, and watched him walk to the bathroom in his boxers. When the water turned on, she threw back the covers and scrambled to join him. Maybe he would finally fuck her if she was standing in front of him naked.

He sucked in a deep breath when she stepped into the shower behind him, but he didn't say a word. He just stepped aside and helped her lather up, his hands roaming her body and cleaning every square inch.

They were both panting when his fingers dipped inside, and she propped a foot on the bench to give him better access. His kiss took her breath away, and he curled his fingers slightly. They'd had soft kisses since the kidnapping, but this one went down to her soul. It was like they were both holding their breath and savoring the connection that was so much more than physical.

His mouth grew hungry, sweeping his tongue inside and

making her knees weak from need. She rode his hand, gasping and breaking the kiss as her orgasm took her by surprise, convulsive waves gripping her as she tensed.

Her gaze met his as her pulsing slowed. His lips tipped up in the most panty melting smile she'd ever seen. His heated blue gaze held hers, bold and full of promises before he slid out and turned off the water.

He stepped out of the shower, leaving her feeling cold and bereft.

She trailed after him and stepped into the towel he held out for her. "What about you?"

He kissed her nose and lifted his eyebrows. "What about me?"

She frowned, confused because his cock was rock hard. She palmed it, making him freeze in his tracks. His eyes zeroed in on her like a hawk.

"Don't you want me anymore?" She hated how small her voice sounded, the vulnerability clear.

He pressed his palm on the door jamb of the bathroom, trapping her against it. Her core clenched, and she whimpered.

His eyes swept over her, his eyes heavy with desire. "I always want you, sunshine, but are you sure this is what you want?"

She felt heat spread on her cheeks as she nodded her head. "I'll always want you, Mason."

And not just physically. She stared at him, snapping her mouth closed and trying not to tell him just how much she wanted him as a permanent part of her life.

He cupped her face with his hands, and his eyes softened before he dipped his head and kissed her. His lips melted to hers like they were made for each other, and his tongue swirled inside, making her toes curl. Now that she'd had a taste of him, she wanted more. Craved him. Needed him to fill the empty void inside.

The fact she needed him so much but would be alone in two weeks terrified her.

She dropped the towel and wrapped her arms around him, pressing him closer, desperate to soak up as many memories as possible. He groaned, sinking deeper into the kiss.

He walked them to the bed, and the rub of their naked flesh against each other was delicious. He spun her around and pushed gently between her shoulder blades. "Hands on the bed." His voice sent a shiver down her spine, and she slapped her shaky hands on the comforter, toes digging into the plush carpet.

"Yes, master," she gasped. The words made his fingers squeeze into her ass and her core clench in anticipation. She'd say anything he wanted to get him to fuck her again. He teased her entrance with his cock, rubbing without entering no matter how much she wiggled against him.

"This is what you want, sunshine?"

She spread her thighs as his length pressed inside. She grunted, pushing back against him, yet still he denied her.

"Mason, please, I need you." She bit her lip, trying to keep her words from spilling out and scaring him off.

Instead, he filled her inch by delicious inch until he was hilt deep. He ran his hands over her ass, squeezing as he said, "God, Lucy, do you even know what you do to me, little bird?"

He withdrew, then plunged deep and slow. Over and over, he slammed in until her arms began to shake.

Had he gotten bigger? He felt like he was reaching to her throat, so deep as he rammed himself home, hard and primal against her. He rode her, grabbing her hair in his fist, and she met him thrust for thrust.

Her vision went white as he tugged on her hair. "Yes, pull my hair harder," she gasped, surprising herself.

The pace went wilder, and his spare hand reached around and pinched her nipple. Her entire body vibrated in response, and the tension that had built inside her exploded. Her body clenched around him, and her toes curled, but he kept thrusting, in and out, riding through her orgasm until he found his own.

His body tensed as he unleashed a torrential flood inside. She milked him, drawing out the wonderfully stuffed feeling. As the aftershocks slowed, she lost her grip and sank to the bed, turning onto her side to watch him reach for the towel on the floor.

He cleaned himself off, then handed it to her. She blushed and cleaned herself off as he turned back to the bathroom and his clean clothes. He smiled but it was tight with hidden meaning she couldn't decipher, and she sighed. The next few days would hopefully bring more sex just like that, return some of the closeness she'd felt before the kidnapping.

She got up and dressed, braiding her hair tight for their big hike.

Chapter Thirty-Six

An hour or so later, they had almost reached the top of Diamond Head. It was so humid she could practically see water in the air. Thank God she'd braided her hair.

She stopped at an overlook and pulled water out of her bag. Today, he had his own backpack. Her stomach growled, and he grinned.

"I have a surprise for you," he said, digging in his bag.

Her brows lifted but her lips turned down as he tugged her out of the way of other tourists. A pit of nerves settled in her stomach at the words. "Mason, I don't like surprises."

"You'll like this one, I promise."

He pulled out two wrapped paper packages and handed her one.

She unwrapped it and grinned, feeling part of the knot in her stomach dissolve. "A breakfast burrito?"

He nodded, grinning sheepishly as he unwrapped his. "Do you like it? I packed it up this morning when you went to the bathroom after breakfast."

She felt another brick fall from around her heart and

tears pooled in the corners of her eyes. "Mason, this is the sweetest thing. Thank you."

He shifted uncomfortably on the rock and ate his own burrito in silence. The rushing wind soothed her. It was so peaceful here. With him at her side, she felt like everything was right with the world.

"What happened with your first boyfriend?"

His question came out of nowhere, and she choked on her food. He handed her a bottle of water. After a few minutes, she could finally breathe normally and answer him.

"Back in high school?"

He nodded. "For such a small surprise like a burrito to make your voice go all soft like that, your ex had to have been a piece of work."

She snorted, "Yeah, he was that." She took another bite before continuing.

"We bounced around Fort Worth and Denton, but they were always big schools. I didn't really fit in and spent most of my time in the library. In middle school, we moved once a year for like four or five years, so I didn't get to make friends like everyone else. The other nerds and I usually had other things to do than worry about relationships."

She wadded up the burrito wrapped, and he put it back into his bag. "Then what happened?"

She shrugged and reapplied the sunscreen. "Mom died right before my senior year of high school, so I moved in with Nana. That was when I had my first date, my first time with a guy." She chuckled, and they started walking back up the never-ending stairs to the top of the crater.

"It was after prom. So cliche, right? Although looking back, I'm not even sure we had sex." Embarrassment filled her as she admitted the truth.

"What does that mean?" he asked.

"I don't think he even got it in, and it certainly didn't last long. I don't know. I might've been too tight."

He snorted and palmed her ass. Going up the stairs ahead of him, it was right in his face, and he didn't seem to mind. "You are pretty tight," he said with a squeeze.

She chuckled. "Why thank you, kind sir. What about your first time?"

He squeezed her ass once more before he let go and replied, "Back seat of an old truck. Took the girl home after a ball game."

She nodded. "That sounds just like you. Hopefully, your truck sex was better than mine."

He snorted. "Not likely. It was all of thirty seconds."

They laughed, their breath coming in short pants as they climbed higher.

Still, he kept the conversation going. "What about in college? You can't tell me the college guys weren't beating down your door."

She smiled, looking up to see how close they were to the top. "I mostly just kept to myself. Taylor had guys over, but not me."

He grabbed her hip, pulling her to a stop. He frowned, but she couldn't see his expression behind his sunglasses. "Wait, Taylor was your roommate?"

"Yeah, the one from December at the drug bust with the long black hair. She's the only one that kept me sane after losing my mom and moving again to college."

He chuckled and shook his head, raking a hand through his hair. "Yeah, I didn't get her name back in December. When she called on our Hilo hike? I thought she was a *guy* named Taylor."

Lucy laughed, a small thrill running down her spine.

Had he been jealous? Is that another reason he'd been so cranky, and they'd fought that day?

The air was humid, and his hair loved it, unlike hers. It was thick, and she reached out a hand to push it off his forehead.

"I can't wait to tell her that. She'll get a kick out of it. But no, she's definitely a girl. We roomed together all six years, which is unusual enough, but between my work and school schedule, and her own thing, we never really fought or had a rough time together. I don't have any siblings, but I like to think of her as a sister."

He kissed her softly. "I'm glad you had her, after losing your mom. My brother Will is still in the military. Barely see him now, but we were thick as thieves growing up."

Her heart ached for him. "It's hard being apart. You should make more of an effort to talk to him."

He scowled and linked their fingers as they climbed side by side now. "You don't even know how much I talk to him. Don't go telling me what to do."

She snorted and squeezed his hand. "But you can boss me around all you want?"

"Hey, I'm getting better, aren't I?" he asked.

She rolled her eyes even though he couldn't see her face as they walked up the stairs. "Yeah, you didn't talk me out of this massive hike. That's progress. Although, I'm kind of wishing you would've. This is exhausting."

He chuckled and squeezed her fingers back. "At least you didn't run a 5k a few days ago. I might try to slide down these stairs. Or just stay at the top. I can stay there overnight if I have to."

She laughed and shook her head. "We're almost there, then we can take a break."

After a few minutes of easy silence, he asked softly, "How did your mom die?"

She frowned, as she panted from exertion. "Heart attack the summer before my senior year. I was at work at the snow cone stand. The next thing I know, I was getting a phone call."

She shook her head as they crested the top. "I don't know who called it in. Dad might have been there, but we don't know for certain. I went to the hospital, but it was too late. Some of his stuff was gone when I got home. Haven't seen or heard from him since."

"I'm sorry, sunshine. I wish you didn't have to go through that."

The water shimmered for miles, settling some of her raw emotions. The wind blew gently of the salty air, and she let go of some of the bitterness and anger she still felt toward her dad. She nodded, smelling the coconut scent of him.

Mason pulled out two new bottles from his bag and handed her one. "Have you ever had coconut milk before?"

She shook her head. "Nope, where did you get it?"

"Last night when I talked with the FBI contact again. It's pretty good. I figure if we're going to go on all these adventures, we might as well try all the new things. Live in the moment and enjoy it and all that shit."

She chuckled and held her coconut drink up to clink against his. He'd not talked about the meeting last night or the one from a few days ago either, and she wasn't even sure if he'd talked to his grandpa about what they'd said while they were hiking in Hilo.

"To enjoying life," he said, holding his coconut milk up to hers. They clinked, and she repeated his words softly as thoughts of the future gnawed at her.

They drank in silence and caught their breath as the sun rose high above them.

"What's the latest with the FBI?" she eventually asked softly.

He shoved his hands in his pockets and frowned. "More of what Simon said on the phone. We went over the reports and talked about what I did wrong. Little things that I can do better, then we wrapped up some paperwork."

She put a hand on his back and stroked it in comfort. "I'm sorry, Mason."

He shrugged and twisted his lips. "Nothing I can do about it now. I'm thirty-five. I have two more years to prove myself to the FBI before I'll be ineligible due to age."

"Aren't there any other places you can apply to? CIA, Secret Service, that sort of thing?"

He tilted his head and stared at the water, the wind ruffling his hair. "When Amanda and I were fighting about it, I made sure all my applications were up to date. It's a waiting game, and I don't have a lot of time."

He went quiet at the mention of her name, and Lucy felt her stomach twist. To lose someone you loved was so hard, but to lose them in such a tragic way… She wanted to cry for him. She wanted to cry over the fact she was in love with a man who couldn't love her back. She wanted to cry a lot, since the kidnapping, but she told herself it was a trauma response.

She finished her drink in silence. They stayed up there until they ran out of snacks about an hour later, talking about her book, then he started packing up their trash and offered a hand to help her up.

"Ready for the next adventure?"

She arched a brow. "You really want to go to the geyser?

I feel like I'm your travel agent, just booking all these things. Is there anything else you'd like to do?"

He shook his head and slung his backpack on with a grin. "Just you, little bird."

She felt heat tinge her cheeks, but she felt a thrill at his words. She smiled, tracing her fingers up his arm. "Anytime you want it, hot shot. Maybe we can just go back to the resort for the afternoon? I mean, my legs are probably going to fall off by the time we get down to the bottom of the mountain."

He laughed, and the sound shot pure joy through her, making her smile. "Oh no you don't. You want the geyser, and geyser you'll get. I won't have you saying I held you back."

He was so sweet to think of what she wanted instead of just agreeing to the easy path full of sex. Not every guy would've made the same decision.

She linked their fingers as they walked back down the stairs. "You sure it's not too dangerous for little old me?"

"I'll give you a dangerous geyser when we get back to our room."

She burst out laughing, and he squeezed her hand with a grin.

He winked, his smile mischievous and making her heart skip a beat. "As for our excursion, I love a good adrenaline rush as much as the next guy. And if I'm with you, then I can keep you safe."

She beamed at him, bouncing on her feet as they walked down the mountain. "Got that right, but even if you weren't here, I'm tough, remember? I can handle it."

She felt her legs shake and burn with the effort of their climb, and all the while, her mind swirled with thoughts of her parents. The words had been her mantra growing up, but this time, she had to keep them in mind to prepare for them going their separate ways.

Chapter Thirty-Seven

Lucy's phone buzzed, and she stopped typing and picked it up. Her brows lifted to see a text from Mason.

I booked you a massage in half an hour.
You can call and reschedule if you're in the middle of a scene.
I also will have dinner ready in our room at seven o'clock sharp. If you're hungry, that is.
If you'd like to join me.

She looked at the time and her brows lifted. She'd been hanging out by the pool and writing for hours today. They'd decided that their last few days in Hawaii would have no excursions. They were both exhausted with Jello for legs from all their hikes anyway.

Mason had kissed her cheek and said he was going to run some errands. She grinned at his text like a lovesick fool. He had been doing errands for *her*, not for the FBI! Her heart felt like it would burst in bittersweet happiness. That massage would feel so good.

She bit her lip and thought of what to reply. In the end, she just sent a thumb's up emoji. She tried to finish writing her chapter, but her mind was now firmly on Mason.

She went to the massage deliberately turning her mind back to her book. It felt so good, she found all thoughts floating away on the soft sea breeze. When Lucy went back to the room, her mind was lazily trying to work out a plot problem in her book. She opened the door and gasped.

Rose petals were strewn all over the bed. On the table in the corner were two plates covered with domes, and a bottle of champagne sat in ice in the center.

Mason opened the balcony door and stepped inside. He was still dripping wet in his swim trunks, but his eyes were hesitant and wary.

She waved her hand at the room. "What's all this?"

He hunched his shoulders and looked down. Surely, he wasn't embarrassed by this show of—was it affection? Or something else?

"I'm sorry for harping on you this trip about being safe, passing out, and all the other things that had us arguing. I— wanted to do something to say thank you for a great vacation. I'm not sure I would've done half the things we've done if you weren't here with me, pushing me out of my comfort zone. I appreciate you."

Her heart stuttered, and she set her bag down by the door, stepping over to him. She cupped his cheeks and stared into his deep blue eyes.

"You don't know how much hearing that means to me," she said, tears pricking her eyes.

His brow furrowed, and he kissed her lightly on the lips, then leaned back. "You should be told things like that more." Her eyes widened in surprise. Did he mean he was going to say more nice things—or even better, keep talking with her or start an official relationship with her when they got back?"

He seemed to realize what she was thinking, because he abruptly stepped back and pulled out a chair, avoiding her eyes. "I hope room service is okay."

Slowly, she sat, still in her bikini and see through white cover up that she'd worn to the spa. He lifted the lid on the fish dinners, and she breathed in the spicy aroma.

"This smells delicious. I didn't realize how hungry I was. Thank you," she said, picking up her fork as he opened the champagne and poured.

"I hope it lives up to its reputation. It came highly recommended from the concierge."

"Is that who helped arrange all this? And the massage?"

He nodded and twirled his fork around the pasta. "Yes, he's a nice man."

They settled into silence as they both ate. She moaned as the sauce teased her taste buds. "Oh my God, make sure you tip that guy. This is so good."

His eyes darkened, and she felt her cheeks flush. She knew that look. It was his sexy time look.

"I'll do that. I'm glad you like the surprise. You'd said before that you didn't like surprises, but I took a shot."

She grinned and raised her glass to him. "I don't call you hot shot for nothing, you know. I'd say you hit a bullseye."

His shoulders relaxed as he smiled and took another bite. They were both dressed in their swimwear, which contrasted with the fancy, romantic dinner. Yet she didn't mind the view. Her eyes roved over his bare chest. She couldn't get over how muscled he was, how perfect for her, and not just the way their bodies fit together. Yet he wasn't hers, was he? He was still Amanda's.

He took another bite before saying, "Tomorrow's Valentine's Day. The concierge mentioned a masquerade ball tomorrow night at the Paradise restaurant."

Her lips twitched. "Mason, are you asking me to be your Valentine?"

He grinned. "Absolutely. Will you?"

Lucy's cheeks heated as a smile crept across her face. "Well, since you asked so nicely, I guess the answer is yes." She chuckled. This was her first Valentine to share with someone special, and there's no one else she'd rather share it with than the man she loved. She chewed and then asked, "We haven't tried that restaurant yet, have we?"

He shook his head. "No, because they have a dress requirement, and I didn't bring any collared shirts. I don't know if you brought anything suitable to wear, but if you'd like to go to the ball, we could go shopping tomorrow?"

Her lips quirked. "You *want* to go shopping? Willingly? Do you have a fever?"

He grinned and sipped his drink. "I had a massage today too, so maybe I'm feeling more relaxed than normal."

She laughed and shook her head. "How about we spend a lazy morning tomorrow at the resort morning? You can get another massage so you're nice and relaxed for shopping in the afternoon. How's your back feeling?"

He sighed and reached for it,stretching his muscles taut. "Good enough, but that might be a good idea. The massage today *was* amazing. How was yours?"

She nodded and smiled. "Perfect. Simply perfect."

He stared into her eyes. "Not as perfect as you."

Her heart tripped a beat, and she sucked in a deep breath. He nodded at her almost empty plate. "Are you almost done?"

She nodded. "Why? What do you have planned next?"

His smile widened as he stood up and filled their drinks. "I was thinking of sating another appetite after watching the sunset and holding my girl in my arms."

She stood, but her emotions kept her silent. Did he really mean she was his girl, or just for this trip? She smiled as he grabbed the glasses and led them to the patio, anticipation racing up her spine.

Chapter Thirty-Eight

Mason led her to the hot tub. The sun was just setting, and no one else was outside in the pool. He stepped into the hot tub with a sigh, turning to watch her take off her sheer cover dress. She pulled it up and over, then noticed his heated gaze travel down her body.

Nerves twisted her stomach. How did this man make her feel so special? The way he looked at her, she felt like the only woman in the world. She had all of his attention and desire. It was powerful, and she loved it. She loved him.

She swallowed past the lump in her throat, uncertainty making her stomach twist again. She couldn't tell him how she felt. Not until he was ready, not until he was past the pain of losing Amanda, not until he loved her too.

She could love him with actions while she still had him in Hawaii though.

Goosebumps broke out on her skin as she tossed her cover up aside and sank into the water opposite him. He handed her glass over, and she sipped. To their right, the sun sank into the water on the horizon. Birds chirped nearby, and a soft breeze teased the hair that had come loose from her braid.

Neither of them spoke, but after a few minutes of watching the sunset, he moved closer and took another drink. His hand settled on her thigh in the water, and she pretended not to notice.

Her heart ached for this man. She wanted him with a desire hotter than the sun. She drained the drink, just barely swallowing it all when his fingers traced the line of her bikini at the junction of her thighs.

She was lucky she didn't choke. She shifted slightly, opening her legs. His fingers slid inside and teased her folds. Heart racing, she leaned her head back and sighed, feeling her hips begin to float.

He shifted at her entrance, then he pushed two fingers inside, making her moan. He leaned closer and whispered in her ear, "God, you're so tight. I can't wait to wreck this pussy with my big cock."

She gasped and squeezed his finger. Her eyes flew open as he nuzzled her neck and need coursed through her. The sweet arranging of the massage and the candlelit dinner had her primed and ready; she didn't want foreplay. She moved to straddle him, dislodging his fingers.

He grabbed her ass as she ground down on him, holding his shoulders and gripping the back of his head as he sucked on her neck.

"Yes, Mason, please. Please, fuck me," she gasped.

Mason's hands let go of her ass, and he shifted to tug his shorts down. She pushed herself back and untied her bikini.

"Fuck," his voice released on an exhale, making it sound harsh. She ran her hands up his biceps as his eyes zeroed in on her breasts bobbing on the water.

"You're so fucking gorgeous, sunshine. These breasts are the perfect size for my hands."

He cupped her breasts and tweaked her nipples. She gasped and thrust her hips to him as she straddled him again, trapping his dick and pressing it against her clit. Her eyes fluttered closed as she rubbed herself on him.

"That's it, sunshine. Get off on that dick. Come all over it. Then I'm going to fuck you senseless."

She whimpered, feeling the need build faster than normal. The closer they got to leaving, the more her body craved him. His teeth raked her neck, and he twisted a nipple and gripped her ponytail. When he pulled her hair, she cried out with the crest of her orgasm, overcome by all of it at once. Pleasure rippled through her as she came, digging her nails into his back.

She moaned as he lifted her hips and thrust into her with one long, hard movement. Her orgasm peaked with him inside, and he held still as she clenched, gasping into her ear, "Fucking hell, Lucy, that's it. Come on that dick. Are you ready for me, little bird?"

She nodded with a whimper as he pulled out, then plunged deep. She screamed and threw her head back, then he did it again. She lost herself in the feel of him thrusting, filling her, stretching her. The tension built between her legs again until she quivered.

When he slid his hands around and pinched a nipple, she bucked, losing the rhythm and looking to him for guidance. His blue eyes were heavily lidded, but he leaned forward on the next thrust and captured her mouth.

He ravaged her with a savage kiss, his lips soft but his tongue twirling with hers, drawing her in until he could nip her lower lip. He deepened the kiss and pistoned harder, each thrust firm and wringing pleasure from every cell of her body.

A hand slid down her stomach and a thumb strummed her core, curling her toes as her orgasm hit like a tsunami. Stronger than the last, every nerve ending quivered, robbing her of her senses. White spots burst behind her eye lids, and he pinched her nipple as he thrust up one more time.

He groaned as he swelled within her, melting into her heat, pumping hot inside as he exploded, making her scream as her body milked him deeper.

His lips on her neck slowed to a tender dream as the aftershocks rippled through her body as gentle waves.

When she let her head fall to his shoulder, he wrapped his arms around her waist, holding her tight. The sun was long set, and her breathing was still ragged against his neck. He took a deep breath and kissed her cheek, holding her until her body went slack. Even when he slipped from her, still he held her.

His breathing was still labored when he asked, "Was the hair pulling okay?"

She nodded and sighed contentedly. "Yeah, I thought it'd trigger bad memories of that CEO pulling my hair and throwing me on the couch, but it didn't. It was a little of pain and a lot of pleasure."

He kissed the side of her head. "Good. Kind of hard to master your body if I'm afraid of triggering you, so I'm glad it didn't."

She giggled softly. "I think it's safe to say you've mastered it."

He squeezed her tighter, making her feel safe and protected. "Never. It'll take a lifetime to master you, little bird."

The silence stretched between them, heavy with things left unsaid.

Lucy buried her head in his shoulder, ignoring it as she yawned. She was already trying not to worry about the fact that they only had two more nights together. Was he thinking about their impending separation too?

He kissed the side of her head and said, "Come on, little bird. Let's hop to bed before we turn into prunes."

She let him lead her out of the hot tub and stood as he toweled her dry, rubbing his hands up and down her body. She closed her eyes and stood naked on the patio, not caring at all if anyone saw her, mostly because she was still thinking about only having two more nights together.

The next evening, Lucy put the finishing touches on her makeup and centered her face in the video chat window.

"How's it look now?"

Taylor squinted and then grinned. "I think that's perfect! The smokey eye looks great on you. Why did you never let me help with makeup before this?"

Lucy shrugged, backing away from where the phone was propped up and taking the robe off to get dressed. "There wasn't any reason to wear any before this."

"And you're wearing it for him? Damn, girl, you must *really* like him."

Lucy paused and frowned, letting the silence drag.

Taylor pounced and leaned closer into the video. "Lucy?" she asked slowly. Then she reared back and gasped. "Oh my God, you love him!"

Lucy spun around and patted her hair. "So what if I do? It doesn't matter anyway."

Taylor groaned. "Girl, what did I tell you? I knew this was going to happen. Luce, you have to protect yourself. Show him you don't need him."

Her heart lurched to hear her friend's words. She was afraid she did need him. Now that she'd had a taste of him, she wasn't sure how she'd survive going back to her lonely existence. She pulled up the dress and reached awkwardly around to zip it.

"It doesn't matter if I need him or not. We've agreed to go our separate ways when we get home, and that's that. Just let me enjoy my last night with him, okay?"

Taylor sighed and rubbed her forehead. "Fine.

Lucy turned to the mirror on the back of the door, and her eyes widened. "Damn, I should've gotten a bigger size."

Taylor laughed. "Let me see. Step back into the camera."

When she did, Taylor whistled. "Girl, you're busting out. Who knew you had boobs like that under all the colorful nerdy stuff you normally wear?"

"Hey, I'll have you know that I've slowly updated my wardrobe since graduation. It's much more tasteful. Remember when we went shopping for our graduation outfits and met the girl who worked at the store? She's been helping me."

Taylor leaned forward, propping her head on her pillow as she laid on her stomach on the bed. "I didn't know that. I really am missing way too much of your life. Can you believe that we've only hung out four times since December? That's not enough."

Lucy nodded. "Agreed. Let's do something weekly, starting when I get back. And I still think you should move in with me when you graduate in May."

"We'll see. Now, twirl around and let me see the back. What shoes are you wearing with it?"

She reached down and held up her silver heels.

Taylor gave a chef's kiss. "Perfect. You'll be the belle of the ball tonight. You'll knock him dead. Maybe after he sees you in this, he won't want to let you go."

Lucy paused, inspecting her reflection in the mirror.

"Lucy, it was a joke. Please don't tell me you're hoping he does exactly that."

She shrugged, then sat on the bed to put the shoes on. "Fine, I won't tell you."

Taylor groaned. "I had hoped you'd be the lucky one, the one who would never know the heartache of being dumped. I'm sorry, Lucy."

She picked up her phone and gave a sad smile. "I'd hoped so too, but it was bound to happen sooner or later. Just didn't know it would hurt this much. It's like there's a hole inside that only he can fill."

Taylor burst out laughing, and after a beat, so did Lucy. She tried to stop the tears but couldn't. When she finally stopped laughing, she had to grab a tissue and fix her makeup.

"Oh God, that's hilarious, Lucy. You're finally catching on to all the double entendre lingo. I'm so proud of you. Can't wait to hang with this fun new Lucy too. But for now, I'm gonna hop off here. You go slay him tonight, okay?"

"Will do. Thanks for the help, Tay. Love ya."

"Love you too. Later."

She hung up the phone and took another quick glance at her reflection. There really wasn't anything to say to Mason that hadn't already been said on the island, other than to declare her love. She definitely wasn't going to do that. It'd ruin everything, and she wasn't going to miss out on this magical night with him. She'd never been to a ball before much less with a hot older man whom she loved. Excitement coursed through her as she left their room.

Chapter Thirty-Nine

Mason sat at the bar of the resort, a whiskey in hand while he watched the door for Lucy. It was their last night in Hawaii, and it was more than a masquerade ball. There was going to be dinner, a show, and dancing.

Lucy had been thrilled this afternoon on their shopping trip. He'd followed her around, but she hadn't shown him what she'd picked out, mostly because she'd wanted the dress to be a surprise. He'd gotten another massage that morning and had bought a suit while out with her.

They hadn't touched or made out since last night though, and his skin itched to be near her. It'd been hours. He frowned, thinking of tomorrow when they'd catch their plane back to Texas. If he felt this out of sorts after just hours, what would it be like after a day, week, month?

He glanced at the doorway, and froze, drink halfway to his lips. His breath caught in his throat at the vision in pink lace. Damn, the surprise was worth it. He just soaked her in, trying to catch his breath and regulate his racing pulse.

A lighter color of lace draped her bodice like a second

skin, revealing a plunging neckline held up by one wide strap that wrapped around her neck. Bare shoulders made him want to sink his teeth into the tender exposed flesh.

She turned to talk to the hostess. He glimpsed her back, bare down to the base of her spine where the dress cupped her ass and made him salivate. The skirt flared just under her ass to fall in waves to the floor, the pink fading from cotton candy to a darker hue near the hem.

He smiled. She loved wearing pink, and he loved her in pink and out of it. Her hair was piled up in a fancy twist, her white mask tied behind her head. He adjusted his own navy-blue mask and then his matching tie.

Lucy smiled at him as he stood from the bar, drink in hand. He couldn't take his eyes off her. He tossed the last of his drink back, then strode through the crowd to her side.

Before he reached her, another guy stepped up and grabbed her hand, bending at the waist and kissing the back of it. She laughed and nodded, then went to dance. She held up her other hand to Mason and mouthed, "Be right back."

He stood frozen, his stomach in knots as he watched them from the edge of the dance floor. He sat back down at the bar, never taking his eyes off her.

If she married someone else, he'd have to watch her dance at her wedding with someone else. Watch her raise babies with someone else. Watch her smile at someone else the way she smiled at him.

Anger burned inside him, threatening to choke him. He didn't want to see her with anyone else. His stomach twisted, threating to bring the whiskey back up.

Damn her parents and their relationship. Her dad had trapped her mom, so maybe she wouldn't ever get married, in order to avoid the heartache. Either way, he would not force her into a relationship she didn't want and wasn't ready for. She deserved better than him and his up-in-the-air career.

That didn't mean he had to stand by tonight and watch her with some other jerk. Tonight, she was his.

He breathed deep, trying to get a handle on his rage, then strode through the dancers to tap on the man's shoulders.

"Care if I cut in?"

The man nodded and stepped aside, but Lucy crossed her arms and cocked a hip to one side, a teasing, coy smile on her lips. "Maybe I don't want to dance with you."

Mason narrowed his eyes and swept her into his arms. "Don't test me, little bird. Seeing you in this dress, dancing with some other man? You'll be lucky if I don't take you behind the building, flip up your skirt, spank your ass, and fuck you within an inch of your life."

She gasped, her head rearing back to look at him in surprise. Then she grinned. "Promises, promises."

Her teasing words and mischievous grin made some of the tension slip from his shoulders. He spun them about the dance floor. He leaned close to her ear, smelling oranges and the heady aroma that was just her.

"Are you wet at the idea of having sex where anyone can catch us?"

She shuttered a breath and bit her lip. "Maybe. Not sure that I'd be able to orgasm, though. I'd be too worried about being caught. I think that was part of my problem back in high school in that truck."

He growled and kissed the side of her neck. "Challenge accepted."

Just then the lights flickered, and someone walked onto the stage. He swung them to a standstill as the music stopped. The dancers went to find seats at the tables, so he escorted her to a small table in the corner along the wall.

It was darker in that corner, but he had a good view of the exits and the stage. He held the chair out for her. "Is this alright with you?"

She nodded, and a waitress came to take their order. He vaguely paid attention to the show. It was some sort of Hawaiian legend acted out on stage. They took their masks off to eat, and he was engrossed in watching Lucy's expression as she watched the show.

She was a soothing balm to his tortured soul. He hadn't been looking for her, yet here she was. Everything he'd ever wanted, everything he didn't know he needed.

The audience clapped but Mason could barely hear past the ringing in his ears. He loved Lucy. Everyone loved Lucy, but he loved her more than he ever thought possible.

Guilt speared him because he instantly compared this feeling to Amanda. He'd never felt like this with Amanda. Lucy made him feel alive, useful, protective, and cared for. With Amanda, he'd always had to fight for them.

It had been exhausting. With Lucy, it was too easy. They got along so well and had somehow learned to talk through their issues. He was more open with her than he'd ever been with Amanda, and maybe that was part of the problem.

His throat threatened to close as his eyes stung. The host went back on stage and said something else, then Lucy looked at him with her big, beautiful eyes and smiled softly.

"That was wonderful, don't you think? They're going to have more dancing now. Would you care to dance?"

He shook his head slowly, mesmerized by her. He moved his chair closer and caressed her upper back, causing his stomach to twist. Then he leaned in and met her lips, causing a shock wave to spread throughout his body. His hand cupped her neck and the other pulled her to him.

The kiss held promises of dark desires. It was long and leisurely because he didn't want this night to end. He didn't want to let her go, even when they returned home.

She gasped into his mouth, her hand settling on his cock. "Mason."

His name was like honey on her tongue. He nipped at her lips and pulled back, her eyes flashing in the twinkling lights of the party.

He cleared his throat. "About that challenge from earlier..."

She grinned even as her breath stuttered. "You—you're serious?"

He arched a brow. "I wouldn't have said it if I didn't intend to do it. I'm a man of my word, little bird."

Her lips tipped up at the corners as she said coyly, "You're no man. You're the master."

He grinned and kissed the corner of her lip. "That's right. Does my good little girl want to please the master?"

She nodded and bit her lip. His cock twitched in excitement, and he stood, taking her hand in his. She followed, and he pressed them flush together from thighs to chest.

"Then let's go, little bird."

He grabbed her hand and ushered her out the side door. They walked too slowly past another building and the lobby. The main pool area was shut down for the night, but soft lights illuminated it. To one side was the spa building.

They meandered around it, following the long path to their room. Moonlight illuminated Lucy's face, her mask hanging limp from her fingers.

He looked around, his heart racing. Then he led her off the path and around the side of the spa building.

Large hedges wrapped around it along with flower beds and exotic trees. They were cocooned between the shrubbery and the wall.

He pressed her against the wall with a kiss so deep he could feel it in his soul. Their lips met in a wet, hot slide, making him crave her wet, hot pussy. It was a brazen kiss that held nothing back. Wild with passion, they kissed like there was no tomorrow.

And there wasn't, not for them. They'd leave tomorrow.

The reminder made his kiss turn feral. He kissed his way down her neck and palmed her breasts. Her nipples beaded under the lace, and he played with them until she panted in his ear.

"Mason, please."

He growled, nipping at her neck. "That's it, little bird. Beg for me." He began to pull her dress up until it gathered between them. He stepped back as far as he could, with the bushes behind him.

His fingers trailed between her legs, and he placed his other hand flat on the wall by her head.

He growled, "Going commando, little bird? That's mighty bold of you. Might even say you're begging for it, without underwear on."

She gasped, her fingers digging into his biceps as he teased her clit. "You'd be right. I—I want you, Mason. Please fuck me."

He grinned and dipped a finger inside. "You're so wet for me, sunshine. I don't think I can fuck you just yet."

She cried out softly. "But—"

He bit her neck, making her shake in his arms. "Not until I've had a taste."

He took her hands and made her hold the bottom half of her dress. "Hold this, will you?"

The Ranger Gets His Girl

Then he sank to his knees in the dirt and buried his nose in her cunt. He breathed in the tangy aroma and licked up the seam. "Spread your legs for me, little bird. I'm hungry."

She gasped and spread her legs, lowering a little to almost a wall sit. His fingers found her opening and two slipped inside while he wrapped his lips around her little bud. Her hips jerked, then her hands found his head.

He groaned as his cock throbbed. She thrust into his mouth, and he sucked and licked until she was mewling in pleasure.

"Mason, please, I need to—I need to..." she trailed off as she jerked against him. He felt her pulsing heat around his fingers as she cried out. She quivered and her knees shook as she bore down on his hand and face.

He lapped up her juices, a sense of power and euphoria swarming over him. While her orgasm slowed, he undid his belt and pants with his free hand. He stood up and guided his cock into the throbbing wet heat of heaven.

She was too short, so he wrapped his hands around her ass and lifted. She gasped, her hands going to his shoulders as she balanced on his dick. Pressed against the wall, he slid out, then pounded into her. Over and over, he gave no quarter.

He was past the point of no return. Her damp heat stroked him, held him prisoner to her charms, her body, her love. He rammed himself home, his body hard, feral and primal against hers. She locked her legs around him, holding him captive.

Yet still he ached to go deeper.

"I want to stretch you with this cock. Take that dick, sunshine. Take me home."

She moaned and used her arms to gain leverage, riding

his cock as much as he was riding her. He lost himself in her wet warmth, and his balls tightened.

Tingles shot along his spine, and still he held back. "Come with me, Lucy. Come on my cock. I need your sunshine."

He couldn't hold it back anymore. His breath rumbled as he neared the edge of the cliff, then he stiffened and roared. His body jerked, every muscle tight as he poured himself into her with wave after wave.

She gasped in his ear as her pussy clamped down around him, clawed at his back and head to bring him closer, and squeezed her legs around his waist as he held her pressed against the wall.

Pure animal satisfaction flooded him as she pulsed around him, her body shaking as her orgasm crested. He swallowed her helpless cries with a kiss, drinking in the feel of her. He could kiss her forever. His tongue lazily danced with hers as they clung to one another, their bodies in sync as they came down from the high.

Her body went limp in his arms, but still he didn't want to let her go. She sighed into his mouth, and he broke the kiss to lean back. He could just make out her face in the soft moonlight. Half-lidded, her eyes closed and opened slowly.

She smiled a wobbly smile, and he felt like the luckiest man alive. When she looked at him like that, like he hung the moon... he wanted to be her hero. He wanted to give her everything he had.

Slowly, she released her legs from around him. He slipped from her but cupped his hand against her mound.

"Going commando means you'll have cum running down your legs."

She sighed and leaned back against the wall, holding the bottom of her dress up still. "That's not so bad."

He placed a palm by her head again and then brought his hand up to her mouth. "Or you can clean yourself up. Either way, it's a win win situation."

Her lips slowly tilted up in that sneaky smile he loved so much. "Why thank you for the desert, good sir."

She stuck her tongue out and licked his hand clean, her eyes staring at him the entire time. His cock twitched back to life, and he straightened to tuck himself back in.

He growled, "I hope you don't plan on sleeping tonight, because I have plans for you, little bird."

She grinned as he grabbed her hand and linked their fingers, walking quickly on shaky legs back to their room.

Chapter Forty

The flight back was a productive one for Lucy. She wrote on her tablet for almost the entire flight. Mason had switched his flight to be the same as hers, but he slept almost the entire way.

They were both exhausted from last night. The twinge between her legs felt good, like when you deep stretched in yoga and could feel the muscles burn for days. It was the best feeling, and she savored it, unsure when she'd next feel this way.

They began their descent, and Mason lifted his head and rubbed his eyes. She put her tray up and closed her tablet with a smile.

"Did you make good progress on the book?" he asked groggily.

She nodded and laid her head on his shoulder. He put his head on her head, kissing her hair with a sigh. Neither of them said anything else as the plane landed.

They walked hand in hand to baggage claim, still not talking. She wasn't sure if he was feeling as awkward as she was. The pressure on her chest had her breathing deep, long breaths.

He found her bag and rolled it to her, then turned back to find his own. Her phone dinged and she glanced at it as he came back.

"I'm parked in the garage, if you want a lift back to Crimson Creek?" he asked. His eyes were hooded, shuttered. She couldn't read his emotion as they wheeled their bags to the exit.

She shook her head. "Thanks, but Taylor's waiting outside. Do you need to go to Crimson Creek? I thought you had an apartment in the city now?"

He nodded as they went out the sliding glass doors. He put his sunglasses on. "I do. It's closer to the Ranger's office."

"Good luck with work. Don't let them stick you in a desk job if that's not what you want," she said, finding her own sunglasses. She needed to hide the tears in her eyes.

He walked with her down the sidewalk. "I won't. I'll fight for what I want."

She glanced at him and cleared her throat. That must mean he didn't really want her, huh? If he wasn't fighting for her, for them.

She wrinkled her nose and sniffed.

He asked, "You okay?"

She nodded and waved to Taylor, who was getting out of her car and popping the trunk. "Yeah, just these Texas allergies. They really hit hard when you've been away for a few weeks," she chuckled nervously, wiping at her nose.

He smiled at Taylor and nodded. "Taylor, nice to see you again."

Taylor glanced from one to the other with a wide smile. "Samesies. Here, let me take that."

Taylor took her wheeled bag and wrestled it into the trunk. Lucy looked up at Mason.

He reached up and held her chin between his finger and thumb before he leaned in softly and kissed her. It was a goodbye kiss that broke her heart. She choked on a sob, and his kiss turned savage as he crushed their bodies together.

He deepened the kiss, twirling his tongue with hers until she gasped. His mouth was merciless and hungry, and her body already ached for him.

He wrenched himself away, backing up two steps and leaving her bereft. They both panted heavily, then he took a deep breath and turned without a backward glance or another word. He walked down the sidewalk, then crossed the street to the parking garage.

Lucy lost sight of him. Only then did she turn back to Taylor's car and open the passenger door. She closed it and buckled up as Taylor pulled away from the curb.

"Damn girl, that was some kiss. No wonder you fell in love with him. Don't blame you *at all*," Taylor chuckled.

Lucy sniffed and turned to face the window. "Not now, Tay. Can we talk about something else? It's too raw."

Taylor tapped her manicured fingers against the steering wheel and bobbed her head. "Absolutely. So remember that professor from the class I dropped?"

She launched into a sordid story, but Lucy only half listened as tears streamed down her cheeks. Soon she had cried herself to sleep.

Lucy settled back into her new life in Crimson Creek with ease. She went back to work after the weekend, and everyone wanted to see all her pictures and hear all about her trip.

The problem was that a lot of her pictures involved Mason. She didn't want to talk about him or mention him. Not with small town gossips still getting to know her as the new girl in town.

After a week, she spent the night moving all the pictures with Mason into a special folder on her phone. It hurt too much to look at him, and she'd spent every night eating dinner alone and crying over his pictures.

She was cleaning up at the salon after a hectic few days of trying to get everyone's nails done before Spring Break when her cell phone rang.

Without looking, she answered it. "Hello?"

"Lucy?"

Her heart skipped a beat, and she dropped the broom. "Mason?" she gasped.

He cleared his throat and said, "Yeah, it's me. How are you doing?"

She picked up the broom and looked around wildly. The ladies still in the chair were staring at her.

She smiled at Katie, her boss, and said, "I'm going to take a break. I'll be right back."

Katie nodded, her brows arched as Lucy stepped outside and walked down the sidewalk. She knew Katie would ask for all the details when she got back, but she couldn't worry about that now.

"Fine. I'm fine. How are you?"

She stared at her hand, still holding the broom. Silently, she cursed herself and stomped back toward the salon, propping the broom up beside the door and continuing down the sidewalk.

"Good actually. I—I wanted to check in on you, make sure you're doing good."

"Yeah, I'm good."

He sighed, "That's good then."

There was a pause, then he chuckled, the sound sending a shiver up her spine. "Okay, this is awkward."

"Slightly. Is that the only reason you called? Get the awkwardness out of the way?" she asked breathlessly, pausing as she waited for his answer.

"No, it's not."

She paused again, staring into the bakery with blank eyes. "It's not?"

"No, we're friends, aren't we? Can't a guy just call his friend?"

She winced and sighed, but before she could answer he continued.

"Actually, I got some really great news and wanted to tell you first. The US Marshals called."

She frowned. "What do you mean, they called?"

His voice was higher, rushed with excitement. "They invited me to join them. I got the job!"

"Oh Mason, that's fantastic!" She felt a flood of relief at knowing she didn't kill his career in Hawaii. He sounded so excited, and that made her happier than she'd been since she'd come home.

"I know. I've been on desk duty with the Rangers, but this is almost as good as the FBI. I never dreamed the US Marshals would come calling, so I never even had it high on my list of possibilities."

"I'm so proud of you," she said softly. "It'll be a field position like you wanted?"

"Yeah, mostly protective details."

She snorted. "God, that's perfect for you."

He chuckled, "I know, right?" He paused, then his voice shifted deeper. "To be honest, you're the one person I couldn't wait to tell. Not even Pops knows yet. I'm calling him next, but I wanted to tell you about going to training before you found out from Pops or Helen."

"When do you leave? Where is it?"

"Tomorrow, out of state."

Her shoulders sank, her hopes at seeing him again dashed. "Oh, well, that's exciting. How long is the training?"

"Four and a half months. I won't have a lot of time to be on my phone, which is why I wanted to talk to you before I left. I—I just needed to hear your voice." His voice trailed off, and she rubbed her temple.

Was she supposed to read into his words? He'd just said they were friends, but then he wanted to hear her voice and she was the first person he called?

She bit her lip, "That's a long time to be gone from home, but yeah, it's good to hear your voice too."

She heard another voice in the background, then the phone muffled. When he came back, he said, "I need to finish cleaning up my apartment, but I'll try to make it to the Fourth of July at Pops and Helen's. I'm not sure when I'll be done with training though. We don't have an end date yet."

"Just take care of yourself, okay? Don't hurt your back or push it too hard trying to impress them," she said, worry for him making her words rushed. "Keep stretching it out."

He chuckled, and the sound echoed through her heart, warming her from the loneliness. "I'll try, but no promises. I gotta go pack now. Bye Lucy."

She hung up, her throat too choked with emotion to say anything. No sunshine or little bird. Just Lucy. They really were only friends now.

The bakery door opened, and Lucy looked up, tears rolling down her cheeks. A little curvy, dark-haired woman about her age frowned at her. "Are you alright?"

Lucy nodded and wiped her eyes, trying to remember the woman's name. "Yeah, I'm fine. Sorry, didn't mean to loiter."

The woman waved a hand, the pink polish matching a streak of pink in her otherwise black hair. "Don't worry about that. Do you want to come in for a pastry? We're closed, but I have some pretty decent leftovers from the day."

This was Maryanne, the bakery owner! They'd hung out at yoga night too, and she was a regular at the salon. Lucy shook her head and nodded to the salon down the street. "Thanks, but I need to get back to work."

Maryanne held the door wider. "Do you have a client waiting for you?"

Lucy paused and shook her head. Then Maryanne waved to the door. "Then come on in. I'll load you up with some treats to take back to Katie. Plus, you look like you could use a minute or two to pull yourself together."

Lucy winced and followed her inside. "I suppose you're right."

"What's got you crying on such a beautiful day?" Maryanne said as she headed into the back. She held that door open too and said, "Come on back here. It's just us."

Lucy followed her into the kitchen area. She pointed to a barstool next to a worktop with a large blob of dough in the center.

"Sit there while I fix you up a box of goodies, and you tell me all about it."

Lucy sat but picked at her nails. "What's to tell? Just man trouble. No big deal."

Maryanne snorted. "If it has you in tears, it must be a big deal."

Lucy sighed and put her hand on her chin. "Not really. I'm in love with a guy, but his girlfriend died last summer. It's too soon for him to let her go. He's still grieving, so I either have to wait or move on."

Maryanne set a to-go box down on the counter beside her, then circled the worktop to dig her hands into the dough.

She kneaded it and said, "That sucks. I was in love with my husband for years before he finally came around and saw the light." She laughed, and Lucy smiled.

They chatted for a few more minutes, then Lucy tried to pay.

"Oh, no need for that. These were just going to be tossed or go to the police station tomorrow."

Lucy frowned. "The police station?"

Maryanne nodded. "Yeah, my husband is the sheriff."

Lucy nodded, "Oh, okay. That makes sense. My grandma Helen married Ray, the old sheriff."

They chatted a few minutes more, then Lucy took the box back to work. She didn't realize it until she said it, but she did need to decide whether she was going to wait or move on.

She grabbed the broom and opened the door to the salon, juggling the box. Katie and her aunt Kat were alone now. They both owned the salon and worked there, although Katie also owned and operated the local bar.

The older Kat crossed her arms and sat in a clean chair. "So, who was on the phone, dear?"

Lucy smiled too brightly and held up the pastry box. "Just a friend. I ran into Maryanne. She sends her regards."

Kat grinned and held out her hand for the box, so Lucy

passed it over. Katie leaned against the counter and tilted her head. "Oh no you don't. You won't get away that easily. Spill the tea."

Lucy laughed and started to sweep again. "It was just an ex."

Could she even call Mason that? She wasn't sure that they'd ever decided what they were.

Katie frowned. "Do we need to go beat him up?"

Lucy chuckled, "No, it was a mutual break-up. He got a job promotion and was excited, so he called to tell me about it."

"Aw, that's kind of sweet that y'all are still friends," Kat said between bites of donut.

Lucy swept and thought about it. They were friends, but she wasn't sure that she could ever just hang out with him. She already dreaded the Fourth of July.

Chapter Forty-One

From spring break through the end of the school year, Lucy kept busy at work and in town. She made new friends at yoga on Thursdays, joined Helen and Ray's church, and went to Sunday dinners at their house. At nights, she worked on her book, diving in with a determination that helped take her mind off missing Mason.

At the end of May, she, Helen, and Ray loaded up and headed to Denton for Taylor's graduation. Taylor squealed as she found them in the crowd after the ceremony.

"Oh my God, I'm so glad you're here," she cried, tears streaming down her cheeks.

Lucy hugged her tight. "I wouldn't have missed this for the world. You're my sister from another mister, remember?"

They'd gotten together more often since she'd come back from Hawaii in February, but not as often as they both wanted.

Helen hugged Taylor next. "Congratulations, sweetheart. I'm so proud of you."

Taylor closed her eyes, soaking in the hug from the older woman. Lucy knew what this moment meant to her, so she stepped over to Ray.

He nudged her with his elbow. "How's your week going?"

She shrugged. "Alright, I suppose." She refused to ask about Mason. She hadn't asked at any of their Sunday afternoon dinners over the past few months. The pain had eased somewhat, but the loneliness hadn't. She assumed he was doing fine in Marshal school.

"How's the book coming along?"

She brightened. That was the one good thing that had come out of being on her own. She had plenty of time to write.

"It's almost done. I'm in the final chapters now."

Helen and Taylor turned toward her with watery tears. Ray grinned and put his thumbs in his belt loops. "Anyone hungry? Let's go celebrate."

Taylor nodded, and Lucy frowned. She looked more fragile than normal, less her peppy self. They went to dinner, and afterward, Lucy waved her grandparents goodbye from the parking lot.

She wrapped an arm around Taylor's waist and smiled. "So, are we going to hit up some frat party like my graduation back in December?"

Taylor wrinkled her nose and shook her head. "Not unless you really want to. I've stayed far away from frat parties, thank you very much. How about we go down to the Stockyards in Fort Worth? Some of my classmates are going to meet up at Billy Bob's in a few hours."

Lucy nodded. "Sounds like a great plan. Do you have anything I can wear?"

The Ranger Gets His Girl

Taylor laughed. "Of course I do. Let's go get ready to party it up."

Two hours later, they walked through the doors of the bar. Taylor found her other friends, and they grabbed a table and some drinks. The music was loud, and Lucy could hardly hear anything.

Taylor dragged her to the dance floor, and they laughed as they tried to keep up with the music. She was slightly tipsy when she motioned to Taylor that she needed a bathroom break.

She rounded the corner and stood in line in the little hallway between the men's and women's rooms. She was tapping away on her phone when boots stopped in front of her, and a man cleared his throat.

She glanced up, past wrinkled jeans and a pearl snap shirt, but his thick gray hair and gold-rimmed glasses showed familiar bright brown eyes. She blinked, then her brain caught up with what she was seeing.

"Dad?" she frowned.

He grinned and threw his arms wide, enveloping her in a hug that left her tense and uncomfortable. "Princess, you're here. Look at you, all grown up. Are you sure you're legal to be in here?" He laughed heartily and slapped his hands on his hips.

The other ladies in line stared at her, but she ignored them. "I'm twenty-three, Dad. I'll be twenty-four in a few months. Where have you been?"

She hadn't seen him in years, and his sudden appearance tonight left her reeling.

Her dad rubbed his jaw, and his eyes went cloudy in confusion. "Twenty-three? No, that can't be right. And what are you wearing? You need to cover yourself up."

She clenched her jaw, her spine straightening as anger

began to burn within her. "Where were you when Mom died?"

He looked back at her, focusing on her face once more. The bloodshot eyes, the dark circles under his eyes—it was all too familiar, the sign of his drug habit still present even after all these years.

He scratched his chin. "Eh? Oh, well, not sure what happened there. We were yelling at each other like always, then she got a terrible headache. She sat on the couch, and her eyes rolled back in her head. It was crazy."

Lucy's voice was barely audible over the music in the background. *Oh my God, he'd been there.* "Did you even call 911?"

He nodded nonchalantly, adjusting his crooked glasses as if it were a minor detail. "Of course. They came right away, so a neighbor might have called too. The hell if I know, I just know I barely had enough time to get all my stuff and get out. Didn't want them to find anything incriminating, you know."

She fisted her hands at her sides, but the woman behind her laid a soft hand on her forearm. "Don't. He's not worth the assault charges," she whispered.

Despite her short skirt and crop top, her body overheated at the new information. Rage filled her at his callous attitude and her body shook as her voice rose above the music. "You heartless bastard. You selfishly abandoned her to die while prioritizing your own possessions over her well-being."

He held his hands up, palms facing her. "Hey, I was protecting y'all from the cops finding drugs. You could've gotten in trouble."

Taking a deep breath, Lucy forced herself to keep her

arms by her sides as she continued to speak, seething with rage.

"Drugs that you brought into the apartment before leaving her to *die*. You didn't come back, didn't come to the hospital, didn't call me at school or work. I was barely seventeen, *Dad*, and I had to plan her funeral and do all of it myself. Then? I was left homeless."

He scoffed. "You weren't homeless. You moved in with your grandma, didn't you?"

The woman's hand fell as she gasped, and she whispered, "I changed my mind. It's totally worth it."

Lucy didn't hesitate but reared back and punched him in the face. The force reverberated up her arm, and she gasped at the pain.

Her dad fell back against the wall, his eyes blazing as he held his nose. "What the hell, Lucy? How dare you—"

Lucy pointed a finger at him, and her voice shook. "How dare I? How dare you, you jackass. I never want to see your face again. Find a different city to haunt. Go down south. I'm sure you can score better drugs down there anyway."

The woman wrapped an arm around her shoulders, drawing Lucy back into the group of women. The line for the bathroom had formed into a semi-circle of protection around Lucy as she stood, clenching her fists and staring daggers at the man she called dad.

He eyed the group of women, his eyes burning bright and narrow with rage. "We'll see about that."

He turned and walked out into the crowd still holding his nose. Lucy felt the adrenaline leave her body, and she sobbed. The woman drew her into a hug as she cried.

Somehow, Taylor found her, and the woman switched

places with her. "Oh my god, Lucy, did you really punch him?"

Lucy nodded and someone handed her a tissue. She wiped her nose, then Taylor took it and wiped under her eyes with a frown.

"I can't even imagine what you're feeling, Lucy."

Lucy hiccupped. "Mostly pain in my hand. I might have broken my pinky."

Taylor hugged her once more. "Well, come on then. Let's get out of here and go get an x-ray."

Taylor ushered her from the bar even as Lucy protested. "We don't need to get an x-ray. It's probably just the shock of it all. It'll be fine tomorrow."

She still didn't want anything to do with doctors, which her former roommate knew.

Taylor frowned as the lights of the street passed over her sharp features. "Bullshit. Better safe than sorry. You need your hands for work, Lucy. You have to take care of them."

Lucy groaned as she parked at urgent care. It was still hours later when the doctor came back into the room and put the x-ray onto the light on the wall as he talked.

"Well, the bad news is you definitely broke something. This small bone right here. We call it a boxer fracture. You'll need a splint, but it's a Velcro one. You'll be able to take it off to shower. Just try not to bend your fingers when you take it off. You'll need to wear it for a month and follow up with your primary care physician."

Taylor held her good hand and nodded. Lucy had never seen this serious side of her in all their six years together. She felt like she truly had a sister who cared. Tears pricked her eyes as the doctor shuffled through his papers.

"Now for the good news. You're pregnant."

Taylor's hand squeezed hers as she gasped. Lucy released her with a distracted, "Sorry. What was that?"

The doctor repeated, "You're pregnant. I'd say about three months or so based on the urine test, but that'll be something you want to follow up with your doctor about too."

Lucy frowned, her head swimming. "But I haven't been sick. Not really."

He shrugged. "Some people don't get sick. Some just think they've caught a cold or get a weekend stomach bug or eaten bad food. You need to follow up with your doctor."

Lucy's eyes widened. She had taken a day off in April for a stomach bug that had been going around. But practically everyone in town had had it. She started to breathe faster, thinking back to the trip to Hawaii.

Lucy's head was spinning as she panted. "But the birth control shot. Drinking tonight. Will that hurt the baby?"

She saw spots on the edge of her vision, and she leaned back on the bed, holding her head. She tried to control her breathing, but her heart was beating too fast. This couldn't be happening. What if she'd somehow hurt her baby?

Oh, dear god, she was going to have a baby. She felt like throwing up.

The doctor shrugged. "That's something to follow up—"

"With your doctor. We get it," Taylor said sarcastically.

Lucy looked at her and the room spun. "Taylor, I'm—"

The black spots on the edge of her vision closed in, then everything went black.

It was hours later before the urgent care physician was satisfied that nothing was wrong with her heart to cause the blackout. Taylor drove through the early hours of the night, and Lucy yawned but was wide awake.

"You feeling better?" Taylor asked, music playing softly in the background.

Lucy leaned her head back on the seat. "I guess. It's going to take a while to get used to the idea."

"Yeah, well, you have less time to get used to it than most, if you're already three months along."

The pressure on her chest made her rub at the spot, but nothing would ease it. There was so much to process. Mason. Her dad. *A baby.*

"Taylor, can you do me a favor?"

"Anything for you, babe."

"Don't tell anyone," Lucy said softly. "I need to tell Mason first, and I can't do that until I see him at some family function or another. He said he might come home for the Fourth of July, but he's not sure if he'll be done with training by then."

"What about Helen?"

Lucy rubbed her eyes. "Can't tell her either. Not until Mason knows. Swear you won't tell a soul."

"I swear, but if you think I'm going to let you do this alone, you better think again, sister," Taylor growled out. "Now that I graduated, I'm for sure moving to Crimson Creek."

"What about your job? You're so excited about the new job at the library in Denton."

Taylor hummed. "I'll work something out. I'll commute if I need to, but I'm going to be here with you every step of the way. You don't have to do this alone, babe."

Lucy felt the tears prick her eyes once more. "I—I'm so scared, Taylor. But I'm tough. I'm strong. I can handle it." Her life's mantra was on repeat in her head.

Taylor reached for her hand and squeezed it, reminding her of Mason. "That mantra has seen you through countless hours of studying and school, but I'm right here. We'll be strong and tough together, okay?"

Lucy nodded, her throat choking with emotion. "Taylor? I'm sorry about ruining your graduation night."

Taylor laughed as they pulled into Crimson Creek. "Hey, if something crazy didn't happen, I would've been a little worried. Which graduation after party earns top score, do you think? Mine or yours?"

Lucy giggled as Taylor pulled into the driveway of Ray's house. "Let's call it a draw. Will you stay the night? I don't want you driving so late."

Taylor turned the car off and said, "Uh huh, you sure that's the reason? It's okay to ask for help, Lucy."

Lucy shrugged and grabbed her purse and bag with her clothes from the graduation ceremony. "I know. It'll be nice to have company. Although I'll be going straight to bed."

Taylor chuckled as they walked up the sidewalk to the front porch. "Me too, girl. Me too."

Chapter Forty-Two

July

Mason stepped back into the office with a grin. He'd completed the US Marshal's training and had somehow been assigned to the Dallas office, just a few floors down from the joint FBI and Texas Rangers' office.

Simon walked by and saw him get off the elevator. He grinned and held his arms wide. "Novak, you're back! Great to see ya. How was training?"

Mason hugged him in the standard bro hug, slapping him on the back before releasing him. "It was good. Not too much stress on the back. Of course, I was the oldest one in the class, but I expected it."

Simon laughed and tapped some files in his hand. "Come, tell me all about it. I'm sorry the FBI decided not to bring you on."

Mason shrugged and followed him to his office. "It's fine. It all worked out in the end, didn't it?"

Simon nodded and sat behind his desk, tossing the file

The Ranger Gets His Girl

on top. "That it does. I'm glad the Marshal's listened when I hounded them to take you."

Mason felt his stomach twist, and he grinned. "That was you? Man, thank you seems like such a small thing. Let me take you out to dinner tonight."

Simon laughed and tapped the file. "I suppose we can eat. I'm casing a restaurant tonight actually."

Mason pursed his lips and arched a brow. "It's not the Henderson, is it? Because that's my first case for the Marshal's."

Simon's eyes narrowed, and he sat forward, suddenly all business. "It is. Caroline DelVeco?"

Mason nodded, running his hand through his hair with a sigh. "I had a feeling you or Johnson might have a file already on her. When I mentioned it to the new boss, he said to come feel y'all out."

"Who'd you get assigned to?"

"Sarmiento."

"Oh good. I like him."

"Me too," Mason said. He'd been in the office barely a week, so it'd been an adjustment, but they'd welcomed him with open arms. There'd even been a few good-natured ribbings over his age, since the cutoff to join the Marshals was thirty-five. He'd just barely made it.

They discussed his new office and coworkers, the differences between how the Marshals work and how the Rangers and FBI work. Then they circled back to Henderson's Pub and DelVeco.

"So, the drug ring that we've been busting up is like a hydra. We cut off the leg that was shipping through Hawaii, right?" Simon asked but didn't wait for an answer.

"While you were in training, we traced it back to the source in Colombia. Took it out, but another one with the same packaging and drug mixture popped up on our radar about a month or so ago in Guatemala."

Mason nodded and crossed his ankles, leaning back in the chair. Simon opened his laptop and typed while he talked.

"We think DelVeco is one of the cogs in the wheel. The drugs are coming into Dallas and funneling through her restaurant, or she's laundering money for the kingpin."

He spun the computer screen around and showed Mason some of the evidence they'd gathered so far.

Mason sat forward and frowned, "DelVelco reached out to the Marshals requesting protection if she gives information on a major crime organization. She hasn't given details yet. I'm supposed to make contact and see if it's a legitimate request or if she knows anything worth following up on, help with the application, and offer protection during the review process. Sounds legit, though."

Simon nodded. "She has a brother in prison. Not sure if that's connected or not."

Mason shrugged. "I guess we'll find out. What time do you want to go to Henderson's?"

They made plans for later that night, then Mason went to check in with Johnson. It was a good meeting with no hard feelings, which he'd been a little nervous about. He was heading downstairs to update Sarmiento on the plan when his phone rang.

He stopped on the landing of the staircase and answered.

"Hello."

"Hello, son. Are you busy?" Ray asked.

Mason grinned and shook his head, leaning against the wall. "Not really. I have a few minutes."

"Wanted to see if you'd come fishing with me this weekend. We missed you at the Fourth of July party. Helen wants us to have a fish fry with all our family and friends to celebrate your new job."

He frowned. "It's not that big a deal, Pops. She doesn't need to—"

"Oh, I know. But she insists. So, are you free or are you working this weekend?"

Mason rubbed his head and thought. It was only Tuesday. "I'm not sure, Pops, but I can try. I have my first case," he shifted from foot to foot excitedly. "I'm not sure what the hours will be or if I'll have the weekend off. Let me go feel out my boss and see how these things work. It's supposed to be a round the clock protection type thing."

"Ah, gotcha. Well, let me know when you find out. If you can't fish and could just show up for the party, that would be good enough for me."

He smiled and stretched his back. "I'll keep you updated, Pops. How's Lucy?"

He missed her like hell. She'd sent him a lot of the photos she'd taken in Hawaii, but he hadn't talked to her in months. The pictures helped. But every milestone in training, he'd wanted to call her and tell her about it.

Instead, he'd called Ray and inevitably guide the conversation around to her.

Ray chuckled. "She's still miffed that you weren't here for the Fourth of July party, but she's been upset a lot lately. Helen's daughter and son came to the Fourth, and Lucy unleashed a verbal whipping the likes I'd never heard. Didn't think she had it in her, honestly."

Mason grinned. "What'd she tear into them about?"

"Oh, missing the wedding and the holidays. Apparently, she's badgered them for months to get them to accept me being with their mama."

Mason felt a pang in his chest. "She can be pretty stubborn when she wants to be. It doesn't surprise me at all that she's want to convince them to her way of thinking. She got me to go on all those crazy adventures in Hawaii after all."

Ray chuckled. "True, but she sure doesn't like yelling. After she yelled at June and Rick, she burst into tears and ran into the house."

Mason frowned. "Tears? That doesn't sound like her."

"Eh, the sun might've gotten to her. It's been over a hundred and ten degrees every day this month."

Mason snorted. "I know. I've only been back in town for a week, but I'm already wishing I was back in the cooler east coast."

Ray chuckled. "You didn't miss this heat? Say it ain't so."

Mason laughed and leaned back against the wall again. "Don't worry, Pops. I missed Texas."

"Missed Texas or missed Lucy?" Pops asked.

Mason rubbed the back of his neck and tilted his head, stretching his tense shoulders. He tried to play it casual, but it was a long shot. "What do you mean?"

Ray snorted. "You ask about her every time we talk, son. She's been so lonely since she came back from Hawaii. I thought now that you're out of training and back in Texas, you could ask her out on a proper date."

Mason's heart leaped at the idea, and he desperately wanted to call her, see her, even just hear her voice. But back in Hawaii when she'd talked to Helen... she'd said she didn't want more. She was too scared about his job.

Mason banged his head gently against the wall and sighed. "It's not that simple, Pops. She doesn't want a relationship."

"Is that what she said?"

"I overheard her on the phone. Relationships are traps, and that's what killed her mom. I don't want her to resent me. Amanda resented me when I wouldn't get a safer job."

"Lucy's not Amanda," Pops said softly.

Mason frowned, his chest aching. "I know, I know. They're completely different. I can actually see a life with Lucy."

"Not if you don't tell her how you feel. You have to show your cards sometime, lay them all out on the table and tell her what you want. Then ask her point blank what *she* wants. She's going to move on if you don't get your butt in gear, son."

Mason's heart raced at the thought of her with another guy, and he straightened in the stairwell. "Is she dating someone else?"

"No," Pops said, making the knot in Mason's stomach release in relief. "But she will soon. Her college roommate moved into the house with her, and with two beautiful young ladies there, it's only a matter of time before the local cowboys are beating down the door."

Mason ran a hand through his hair, groaning as he pictured it. "Damn it. Alright, I'll tell her how I feel on Saturday after we're done fishing, *if* I can get off work. Thanks for talking about it, Pops. I've missed you."

Ray paused, then said, "I've missed you too, son. Will's going to be here this weekend too. It's been a long time since the three of us went fishing."

Mason swallowed past the lump in his throat. He'd missed his brother's return from deployment while he'd been gone in training. "It'll be good to see him. Let me go talk to my boss and work something out."

"Keep me updated. I love ya, son."

Mason sighed. "I love you too, Pops. Bye, now."

They hung up, and Mason continued down the stairs, thinking about family and his brother and—as always—his mind ended with thoughts of Lucy. He wondered if she'd let her hair grow out for the summer or if she liked Crimson Creek.

He ached to see her, to know that she was safe and well. She should be free and happy and healthy. At least he hadn't tried to make a long-distance relationship work. At least he hadn't trapped her in something she didn't want, like her father had done her mother. He tried to convince himself he'd made the right choice. It was a daily argument with himself.

Chapter Forty-Three

Later that night, Mason sat across from Simon in the dimly lit restaurant. He'd rolled up his pearl snap shirt sleeves and unbuttoned the first few buttons, but left it tucked into his pressed jeans.

The waiter brought their drinks, and Simon looked at his phone, texting with a small smile on his goofy face.

Mason lifted his glass and sipped, surreptitiously looked around, trying to spot anything out of the ordinary.

Simon put his phone down and looked at the menu. "Sorry about that. Melissa says hi by the way."

"How is she?" he asked politely. Simon talked about his wife and their teenagers. Mason listened with half an ear because the conversation made him think about Lucy.

The heaviness in his chest hadn't abated all day, not since his talk with Ray. He'd worked hard for five months to keep the hope at bay. He'd kept his head down at training and did a lot of soul searching.

But he'd been afraid to hope that Lucy wouldn't want to

try for a real relationship. He hadn't talked with her in months. What if what they had was only a holiday thing?

He thought back to the wedding and talking with her, after the frat party when he'd taken her home. It had always been so easy to talk with her, like coming home or putting on his favorite shirt.

"What's with that look on your face?" Simon asked, jarring him from his thoughts.

Mason sighed, "How do you and Melissa make it work? The long hours, the unpredictable schedule."

Simon's eyes glinted in the soft light and a smile spread across his lips. "Not going to lie. Some days are harder than others. Clear communication is important. I also trust her to handle just about anything life throws at her. She's so strong and independent, but you know that."

Simon chuckled, then added, "Are you thinking of settling down? Who's the lucky lady?"

Mason gave him a summary of how they'd met, of the wedding, the frat party, Christmas, and Hawaii. He finished the glass of wine and leaned back in his chair, crossing his arms.

"I'm just not sure this is the life she wants, you know?" he asked.

Simon nodded. "But if it is, it's so worth the risk, Mason. To be honest, I was afraid that what happened with Amanda would've turned you into a bachelor for life," Simon said quietly, frowning as he swirled his wine in the glass.

Mason nodded somberly, glancing around as the waiter arrived with their order. "Me too, me too, but Lucy is like a breath of fresh air."

Mason saw a tall, leggy brunette in a red blouse and black tight pencil skirt to her knees walk from table to table, laughing and smiling. The waiter filled their glasses of wine, then walked away as Mason dove into his pasta.

Simon nodded toward her and took a bite, looking down at his plate. "That's her, DelVeco."

Mason let his eyes slide from her and over the rest of the restaurant before he turned back to his plate and took another bite. It was delicious pasta but reminded him of the private dinner he'd had with Lucy in Hawaii. It had similar flavors and took him right back to that night.

He wished he could bring her to this place. For a pub, it had a soft, quiet atmosphere. It was more of an old-world place with leather booths that provided seclusion to most of the room. He couldn't even hear the voices from the booth behind him.

The woman stopped at the booth behind Simon and talked to those patrons. He could faintly make out her words as she smiled and then turned and lifted a hand. One of the waiters arrived as if by magic.

"Refills, Johnny, right away," she said before moving on to their table and smiling. "How are you two doing tonight?"

She had brown eyes to match her hair, but that was the only similarity with Lucy. This woman was dressed to the nines with bright red lipstick to match her shirt. Simon smiled and waved a bread stick.

"Delicious, simply delicious. This is homemade, isn't it?"

She beamed and nodded. "Yes, sir, my grandmother's recipe. I'm so glad you love it. It's one of my favorites. And how about you, sir?"

Mason lifted his wine glass and swirled it around as he sat back in his seat. "The wine pairing is great, but I was thinking it needed something less sweet. Maybe a 1978 Sarmiento Merlot? Do you have anything like that?"

Her eyes widened, and she looked from him to Simon and back again. Her smile fell a little, and she paled then nodded. "Yes, sir. I certainly do think I have a bottle of that in the back. Would you care to join me to sample a few merlots? Perhaps I can help you with a selection."

He nodded as she lifted a finger and turned slightly. The waiter appeared again, and she said brightly, "Don't clear their tables. We're going to the wine cellar to see if we have a specific brand. We'll be right back."

The waiter nodded, then moved to another table. Simon and Mason slid out of the booth and followed her through the restaurant. They went through the kitchen to a heavy oak door. She opened it and waved them inside, saying loudly, "The merlots are in the back on the right-hand side. I think I have just the thing."

She shut the door behind them and leaned against it with a sigh, seeming to wilt. "Oh, thank God, I was afraid I was going to have to disappear on my own."

Simon began feeling his way around the room, inspecting it for wires or cameras.

Mason frowned and faced DelVeco. "I'm Novak, and this is Peters with the FBI. Tell us what's going on."

It took several days to work out the details for DelVeco and process the application. Because Mason was new to the Marshals and had been out of town for months, both parties agreed that he needed to play a boyfriend role in order to protect her.

He was at the restaurant every night, flirting and fawning over her, but every time he caressed her hand or kissed her cheek, he felt nothing. There was no attraction whatsoever.

He knew he still loved Lucy, thought about her all day and dreamed of her every night, but the lack of attraction to Caroline still took him by surprise.

When Amanda had died, he'd not been attracted to anyone for months. Not until he'd seen Lucy at the wedding in December. It had been instant and all-consuming.

He still felt guilty about what happened with Amanda but thought about it less and less. Now that he'd had months to think, he realized he'd given up on love. After losing Amanda, he thought he'd not deserved love, that he wouldn't love again, but Lucy made him see he had so much more to give. Love might be worth the fight where Lucy was concerned.

Lucy was bright, fresh, and real. He wanted to date her for real and hoped to talk to her about it that weekend.

Logically he knew Caroline was an attractive woman. She was smart and sultry, and guys fawned over her every night. But she wasn't Lucy.

On Friday, his boss told him that he did need to work the weekend and watch Caroline. The application would be approved any day now as they were fast tracking it and others were collecting evidence to corroborate her sworn statements.

She'd named half a dozen individuals, both people who were bringing the drugs into the city and some who were to distribute.

So once again, he found himself at the restaurant bar, talking with the bartender and nursing a drink while he kept an eye on the patrons and Caroline. The bartender turned to help another customer, so he pulled out his phone.

Something was gnawing in the back of his brain about

the list of the guys Caroline had handed over. A sense of dread had settled in his stomach, but he wasn't sure why. He went back to the phone and kept digging. He scrolled through the profile of the guy who seemed so familiar.

John Gray was an alias. The fingerprints came back to a Seth McEntire. That name had set off the alarm bells in his head. He scrolled through the guy's criminal record, then saw it right there on his phone in big black letters.

Suddenly he froze, and his stomach knotted as he closed the phone. His spine tingled, and he glanced casually around the bar, running his hand through his hair. Nothing was out of the ordinary, but his mind was furiously connecting the dots.

His jaw clenched, and he stretched his back before opening the phone's app and hoping the screen would change.

The man was widowed with a daughter. Next of kin? Lucinda Gail McEntire.

He rubbed his temple as his stomach twisted. He took a deep breath, thinking of all the things Lucy had said about her dad.

Caroline wove her way through the crowd and stepped close to him, rubbing her hand on his back and brushing her breasts against his arm. He forced himself not to lean away as she invaded his private bubble, and he closed the phone once more.

He smiled tightly at her, as she wrapped her arm around him as she leaned in to whisper in his ear. "Hey, big guy. Heads up that one of the guy's on the list is due to arrive within the hour."

He stiffened slightly and frowned, wrapping an arm around her waist, and leaning in to nuzzle her ear. "Smile like you like it. Who is it?"

She turned her head slightly and giggled, her big eyes open wide as she glanced around and tipped her head more to the side so he could kiss her neck. She stiffened in his arms and whispered, "The guy on your phone when I walked up. Mr. Gray. Did you already know?"

Mason shook his head, scraping his five o'clock shadow along her skin. She smelled of vanilla, and it was nice, but it did nothing for him.

He missed the fresh scent of oranges, the natural feel of Lucy's body. He sighed, "No, I didn't know. Thanks, I'll let the boss know. We'll see if we can get a few more undercover guys in here. Don't worry. We'll protect you."

He asked her a few questions about why the man was coming tonight, but she just replied, "I don't know. He's not supposed to come until Monday when there's less of a crowd. That's why I'm so nervous."

He squeezed her in a side hug, then released her with a reassuring smile. "Don't worry. You're in good hands."

They worked out a plan on where the hostess should seat Gray, then he called his boss. He said in a loud voice for the benefit of any listening ears, "Hey man. Come on down to the Pub. I'm getting kind of lonely drinking by myself on a Friday night."

After more small talk and cajoling, with Sarmiento asking key questions on the other end of the line, Mason hung up. Back up was on the way, and they'd bring the surveillance equipment to live stream the microphone they'd hidden in a few booths around the restaurant.

He was to sit tight and keep an eye on things while protecting Caroline. But he could call Lucy and ask her about her dad.

He called before he could talk himself out of it or get too nervous.

"Hello?" she said breathlessly.

His heart skipped a beat and his throat closed to finally hear her voice. Why had he waited so long to call? He choked out, "Lucy, it's Mason."

She gasped. "Mason?"

He tossed his whiskey back and slammed it on the bar too hard. "Yeah, Mason. I have a question about your dad."

She paused, and he thought she might've hung up. He looked at the phone, saw it was still connected, and asked, "Hello?"

"I'm here. What do you want to ask?" Her voice was curt, and he frowned.

He frowned as nerves swarmed his stomach like a hornet's nest. "Your dad was dealing in Fort Worth when you were in high school, right? But you haven't seen or heard from him since your mom died, so you wouldn't know if he's still doing that, right?"

He rubbed his forehead and sighed.

She said, "I actually saw him in May."

Mason sucked in a breath, pain in his chest as fear gripped him. He hadn't known. What else had he missed in the past few months? "Why? How did that go? Did you find him and reach out or did he find you?"

The bartender refilled his drink as she answered.

"It was purely by accident, and it went as well as expected, I suppose. I ran into him at Billy Bob's after Taylor's graduation. I punched him in the face. Fractured my hand and had a splint for a month."

He sucked in a breath and looked at his own right hand. "Your thumb or a finger?" he asked. Why had he not talked to her at all in the past five months? He could've. His hours weren't regular, but he'd had at least one down evening a week.

The Ranger Gets His Girl

She'd broken a bone while he'd been gone, and he hadn't known anything about it.

"One of these little bones under the pinky, on the side of the palm."

He rubbed his forehead and sipped his drink. "I'm sorry I wasn't there, little bird. I wish I had been."

She gasped. "You—you do?"

He nodded even though she couldn't see him. "Of course I do. I want to be with you every day."

She paused, and he waited. Had he just made a fool of himself? He didn't want to ask her out over the phone, but he wanted her to know he'd been thinking of her.

She cleared her throat. "Is that all you wanted? To talk about my dad?"

He shifted on the bar stool and took a deep breath. "I was kind of hoping you'd be at the fish fry this weekend? I'd love to see you."

She paused again, longer. He heard soft music playing in the background, then she said, "I plan on it, yes. I was going to go fishing with Ray tomorrow, since you're probably working and won't make it."

His brows rose. "You fish?"

There were so many things he didn't know about her. He felt like he'd wasted so much time. He wanted to know everything about her.

"I used to go with my grandpa when I was really little. Ray took me a few times last summer, and we've gone a few times this summer already too," she said. Her voice was like a balm to his soul. It offered him hope.

Maybe he'd be able to talk her into a proper date tomorrow. One where she wasn't forced to accept because they were stuck rooming together in Hawaii.

The weight of his own inactions pressed on his chest,

and he cleared his throat. "I didn't know. Ray didn't say you'd be fishing too. He didn't tell me about your broken hand, either."

"Eh, I didn't tell either Ray or Nana about running into dad either. It was too raw and painful."

Mason's heart sank at her words. "I'm sorry for bringing it up tonight, but thanks for sharing, Lucy. It means a lot."

There was a long pause before she asked wearily, "Is there anything else you wanted, Mason?"

Just you.

But he couldn't say that, not over the phone. He wanted to see her face, see her expression, touch her, and show her how much he wanted to be with her.

He sighed as his coworker, Benson, walked in from the kitchen and caught his eye. He raised his glass and said, "Yeah, that's it for now. I want to talk to you tomorrow, Luce, so I hope to see you then?"

"Yeah, I'll be there," she said quietly. "Bye, Mason."

"Bye, little bird," he said, the pressure in his chest tightening. He hung up and walked to the kitchens, then to the office where they'd set up a mini-command center. It was time to set up the sting and see what dirt they could get on Seth.

Chapter Forty-Four

Taylor drove Lucy through traffic into the city. Lucy was too nervous to drive, and she needed the emotional support. Taylor glanced at her bouncing leg in the passenger seat and arched a brow.

"That was Mason on the phone," Lucy blurted.

Taylor nodded. "I heard. What'd he say?"

Lucy frowned and shrugged, picking at her nail. "He asked questions about Dad, then said he missed me and wants to talk tomorrow."

Taylor tapped in time with the music on the steering wheel. "That's good, right? Maybe you can finally tell him about the baby?"

Lucy nodded, nerves fluttering her stomach. "Something's wrong though. Why would my dad call and invite me to dinner on the same day that Mason calls to ask about my dad? Don't you think that's weird?"

Taylor tilted her head and cut through traffic to their exit. "Maybe a little, but maybe Mason was just using it as an excuse to call."

"Maybe," Lucy said, but heard the own hesitation in her voice.

"You don't have to do this, you know," Taylor said.

Lucy shifted nervously. "Meet with Dad? I kind of feel like I do. I never heard a word after I punched him in the face, and that was months ago. When he called, he said he'd spent the past few months getting himself straightened out. I need to see if it's real."

Taylor sighed, "I know how you feel, babe. Trust me, I know. My dad called from jail asking for bail again."

Lucy frowned. "But the last time you talked to him—"

"Was when he called from jail asking for bail. I know, I know. Why do we hope that they'll change, Luce? Why can't we just forget our deadbeat dads and let it go?"

Lucy shook her head as they pulled into the parking lot of the restaurant. "I don't know, Tay."

Taylor parked and turned the car off. "Are you going to tell him about the baby?"

Lucy frowned and shook her head. "Probably not. What's the point? If he's clean, that's great, but he'll still have to prove that this time it'll stick. That takes time. I've been down this road before, remember? In high school, he'd clean up for a few months, then be right back to it, then go to jail. I want to hope, but I'm afraid to."

Taylor patted her arm as they gathered their purses. "I know, but I'm here with you, babe. I'll be right here with you the whole time."

Lucy's smile was wobbly as emotions flooded her. She'd been emotional for months, and she was so tired of it already. She took a few deep breaths and opened her door. She adjusted her summer dress to hide her little baby bump and slung her purse over her shoulder.

"You can probably sit nearby and be fine. Maybe at the

bar or at a table beside us?" Lucy asked. Taylor nodded as they walked down the sidewalk to the front door.

The sun had set but the city lights of Dallas were lit up. This wasn't the best neighborhood, but it was decent enough, safe enough. It's funny how she'd become so concerned with safety since getting pregnant.

It reminded her of Mason, and she felt tears prick her eyes. He hadn't called since he'd finished training for the Marshals. She'd texted him a congratulations GIF when Ray had told her he was done and headed home last week. She'd hoped that that would open up the conversation.

But he hadn't replied until that call tonight. She was afraid to hope that her dad was clean, and she was afraid to hope that Mason would take a chance on her. She was tired of being so afraid.

She missed the fun Lucy, the one who would go on adventures and try parasailing and whale watching. Taylor opened the door to the restaurant, and they went inside. She smiled at the hostess and said, "I'm meeting someone, but I'm not sure—oh, there he is."

She pointed, and the hostess nodded, waving them to the dining section. Nerves jumped in her stomach, and she focused on her breathing. Taylor followed, talking quietly with the hostess.

Lucy sat with her back to the door, sliding into the booth in the back corner of the restaurant. Her dad wiped his hands on his napkin and smiled, holding both hands out.

"Princess, you made it."

She frowned and touched just the tips of his fingers, quickly pulling them back when he tried to close her hands in his.

"I did. How have you been?" she asked as the waiter arrived and turned her wine glass over.

Lucy shook her head and frowned. "No thanks. Just water, please."

Her dad guffawed, "I thought you were twenty-three now, but you're already turning it down? Good girl, better than your mom ever did, let me tell ya."

The hair on the back of her neck stood up, and her spine straightened. "Don't talk about Mama like that." Her voice was hard and cold, and for once her dad blinked and seemed to listen.

Then he smiled. It took her right back to her childhood before their lives fell apart. She softened and placed her order with the waiter. He walked away, and she reached for a breadstick.

She moaned. "God, this is delicious."

"Right? That's why I love this place. They have the best homemade pasta. Just wait."

She sipped her water nervously as silence descended between them. A brunette woman in red and black stopped at their table with a tight smile.

"Hello, Mr. Gray, what a pleasant surprise. Is there anything I can do for you?"

Her dad leaned back and smiled, but it wasn't the soft natural smile of her childhood. This one was practiced and made her skin crawl. It reminded her of a used car salesman.

He took the woman's hand and kissed the back of it, "Ah, Ms. DelVeco, I apologize for the short notice. I've just ordered my usual, though."

He released her hand and patted his slight beer gut. "Gotta fatten myself up before I head out-of-town tomorrow."

The woman nodded and clasped her hands in front of her. "I see, and when will you be returning?"

Seth waved his hand. "Oh, next week sometime, I think. Don't worry, I'll be back for my usual when I return." He winked at the brunette who blushed, nodded, and walked away.

Lucy frowned at the exchange and watched her walk away. "Is the food really that good?" she asked.

Her dad looked around the restaurant smugly. "That it is, princess. I don't suppose you'd like to spend some quality father-daughter time? You can join me this weekend on my business trip."

He put a hand on his heart, but his expression was the fake one he used to make with mom when he was setting her up for some trap or other.

Alarm bells went off in her mind, and she leaned back against the seat. "As much as I love to travel to sunny places, I'm not going anywhere with you."

"But princess, I just want to make things right. It'll be my way of apologizing for the last few years, and your way of apologizing for breaking my nose in May."

She snorted, her spine stiffening. "If you think I'm apologizing for *that*, think again."

His jaw clenched, then he smiled with too many teeth showing. "My trip tomorrow is just a short one down to Mexico for a few days. I have a house there. Please join me?"

Lucy tilted her head and frowned. "Do I want to take off to another country with my super unreliable long-lost father whom I haven't seen in years? Um, not just no, but hell no." She scoffed, but his eyes glinted in the light.

"I'm not long-lost. We saw each other just a few months ago, remember?" His voice was hard and tight, and it made her heart race in warning. It was the same voice he'd use before he and mom would get into a screaming and shoving match.

She nodded slowly, thinking of a way to keep him from losing it in the middle of the restaurant. "I do, yes."

She had to be careful. He was unstable and about to blow. She didn't know how he'd changed in the past few years, but she had to protect her baby. The table separating them made her feel somewhat safer, along with Taylor watching quietly from the bar.

Her phone buzzed as the waiter brought their food. She glanced at it, and her heart raced again to see a text from Mason.

Don't turn around. I'm in the restaurant with you.
We are trying to get your dad to talk about drug running.
There's a bug under the table to listen in.

Her ears burned, and her face flushed hot. Mason was here. Was this whole thing a set up? Was he using her to get her dad arrested? Fury, hurt, and pain warred within her, making her stomach hurt.

"Everything okay, princess?" he asked.

She nodded and took a deep breath. She had to get out of this dinner as quickly as possible. She tucked her phone into the hidden pocket of her sundress.

"Fine, Dad. Just a friend."

"The one who came in with you? She's the one who took you out of Billy Bob's, isn't she?"

Lucy's hand froze, then she continued to stir her pasta as she nodded. "Yes, my college roommate. She's amazing. We bonded over our moms dying and both having deadbeat drug addicts for dads."

She watched through her lashes as her dad's face

flushed. Damn it, why was she mouthing off? Growing up, she'd kept her mouth shut and her nose buried in a book. But now, years later, she couldn't keep silent anymore. Knowing Mason was nearby gave her courage to say what needed to be said.

"You watch it, princess. I'm not an addict."

She picked up a bread stick and snorted, throwing caution to the wind. "Yeah right. You were definitely on something at Billy Bob's, and now you're going to Mexico for a week? God, you're so obvious, Dad. You're running drugs, aren't you?"

She took a furious bite of her pasta, then moaned, but it was lost on her dad.

He leaned forward and narrowed his eyes. "Shut up. You're just like your mother, hounding me and not letting me just live my life. At least you're not a drunk like she was."

Lucy glared and pointed her breadstick at him. "At least I'm not selling drugs to kids off the street and corrupting the world like you are."

Dad slammed his fork down, making his glass wobble. "I'm not selling to kids. I'm selling to CEOs and businessmen with more money than you know what to do with. I have two houses in Mexico and one in Florida, but what do you have? Nothing. You're just some small-town nail tech with barely enough to scrape by."

She shrugged, fury flowing through her body like lava. "At least it's honest work, and I can look at myself in the mirror. You may deal to big wigs in penthouses, but those drugs trickle down to the streets, and you know it. You're a fucking bastard, a two-bit, low-level—"

His nostrils flared, and he stood abruptly. His glass tipped over, and Lucy jumped up to avoid the spill from hitting her dress. Seth grabbed her arm and dragged her through the door behind him into the kitchens.

"Ouch, let me go," she said, digging in her heels.

He hissed as he marched her past the stares of the kitchen staff. "Shut the fuck up or your sweet little roommate won't see the light of day."

Her blood went cold as she gasped. The surprise had her forgetting to resist. "Wh—what do you mean?"

"I mean that I'm not alone. I wasn't alone at Billy Bob's either, but you had that gaggle of girls. It wasn't worth the effort. But now? I've got a guy watching her right now. He's ready with a drug to slip into her drink that'll knock her out for good, if you don't come along."

"But why? Where are we going?" she asked, her voice raising in panic. Her heart raced. He pushed her out the back door into the dark alley where a car waited.

"You're a snot-nosed brat who never learned respect. I've thought long and hard since Billy Bob's on how to teach it to you. Got some guys in Mexico who'll let me do whatever I want, and you, princess, need to learn some manners."

He shoved her, and her hands landed on the hood of the car, jarring her body. "Are you crazy? Clearly your brain has been warped by too many drugs. You can't take me to Mexico."

"Watch me," he said as two big guys got out of the front seats of the car wearing suits. Her dad marched her past one, and the big guy turned and opened the back door for them. She put her hands on the top of the door and pushed hard.

"No, you can't do this."

"We're just going to have a good father-daughter trip.

That's all. And once you've learned some manners, I've got a Colombian friend who's looking for a new plaything."

His hand dug into her back, but she put a foot on the door frame. The big buys rounded the car, coming closer to her. Her heart rate was racing too fast, and her vision began to blur on the edges. No, not again. No, she couldn't—

"Lucy!" a voice shouted from down the alleyway. Pops rang out, and Lucy's eyes rolled back in her head. She dropped like dead weight to the ground, rolling onto her side as everything went black.

Chapter Forty-Five

Mason saw Lucy collapse, and it was his worst fears come to life. He and two other Marshals fired on the three thugs.

His boss rounded the corner behind him, weapon drawn and yelling directions. The thug that had been driving dove into the car as the other one fell to the ground. Seth ducked behind the open back door, and it blocked the shot.

Another coworker led the charge into the alleyway at Sarmiento's direction as the car's rear lights turned on. Oh God, Lucy was too close to the car. She might be caught by the back tire.

His heart skidded to a halt even as his feet ran toward her.

A coworker called out, "Gray, we have you surrounded. There's nowhere to escape."

Mason reached the back of the car just as it began to roll. He dove for Lucy, dragging her to the side of the alley as his two coworkers flanked the car, firing inside. He wedged Lucy between the wall and his body, his hands furiously raking along her head and chest.

"Dear God, Lucy, Lucy, are you alright? Are you shot? Lucy," he repeated as his heart raced and his hands shook.

Images of Amanda's lifeless body mingled with Lucy's warm one. He cradled her head, feeling the pain rip through him.

"Oh God, Amanda, please forgive me," he whispered, rocking her body in his arms as tears rolled down his cheeks.

She groaned, and his heart skipped a beat. It wasn't too late. He gently laid her back, cradling her head as he checked for gunshot wounds again.

Hope fluttered along with her eyes. Maybe she'd be alright, and he'd have a chance to beg her forgiveness. He needed her forgiveness for not protecting her tonight. For not talking to her for the past five months. For longing from a distance and not taking any fucking action to tell her how he felt before it was too late.

In the grand scheme of things, that was dumb. As she laid in his arms on the hot concrete, he saw that now. They could've worked on a long-distance relationship while he was in training. They could've talked on the phone and gotten to know each other even more.

He hoped and prayed it wasn't too late. His hands searched as her eyes fluttered.

No matter how hard he looked, he didn't feel any sticky blood or wet spots. Light from the car reflected off the alley, and her eyes opened all the way as she groaned.

She blinked up at him, and he could finally breathe. His lungs flooded with air as he gasped and rested his forehead on hers, "Oh thank God, I thought I'd lost you."

Relief swarmed through him, flooding him with joy as

if the dam around his heart had suddenly burst. He leaned back, tears rolling down his cheek as he held her head in his hand and caressed her cheek.

She smiled up at him, "Ha, you can't get rid of me that easily."

He choked back a half-sob, half-chuckle. "Fuck, Lucy, you scared the shit out of me."

She frowned and stiffened, struggling to sit up. He eased her to sit against the wall and glanced behind him. Sirens were faint but growing closer as his coworkers checked on the injured thug on the ground and cuffed the driver and Seth.

He glanced back at Lucy. She scrambled to her knees with a wince, then stumbled to her dad. He grabbed her around the shoulders, holding her back.

"How dare you," she screamed at the people around the car.

Seth sneered and spat on the ground. "Me? Damn it, Lucy, this is all your fault. If you would've just come to Mexico—"

"You fucking son of a bitch," Mason growled, his hands clenching on Lucy as he pulled her to his chest. Rage flowed through him, but he wouldn't let go of Lucy.

She was his anchor in the storm and kept him rooted to the spot.

Over her head, he stared at her father. "You've thrown away the best thing that's ever been in your rotten life. Take him away. Lucy, do you want to file a restraining order?"

He leaned back, cupping Lucy's cheeks and turning her head so that she wouldn't have to see him being dragged down the alley in handcuffs. She blinked up at him, her face blank with shock and confusion, anger and pain.

Shouting from the kitchen door drew their attention. He

looked over and saw Taylor punch one of his coworkers, then hook his leg and bring him down. She jumped over him and raced to Lucy, screaming, "Lucy! Lucy, are you alright? Is the—"

Lucy cut her off and stepped away from him, holding her hands up. "I'm fine. Everything's fine. I passed out, but that's it."

Taylor slammed into Lucy and spun her around in a fierce hug. They both laughed and cried, talking over one another. His coworker limped over, and Mason soothed his sore ego. When he had that sorted, he looked back to find Lucy and Taylor walking toward the ambulance.

Sarmiento called for him and crossed his arms. "So, I think you have something to tell me about your relationship with the victim?" he asked.

Mason ran a hand through his hair and told his boss every major incident they'd had so far, from the frat party to the CEO and Malia in Hawaii to everything she'd shared about her dad.

Sarmiento nodded and frowned. "You'll need to give a statement then too, but help collect evidence first. It looks like it might rain, and I want this all wrapped up first."

He nodded and got to work with the local police officers who had joined them. Apparently, the trunk was loaded with bricks of coke, Seth's 'usual order' having been filled while he was at dinner.

The driver was babbling about the deliveries and giving up everything in hopes he'd get a smaller sentence. One of Mason's coworkers elbowed him. "Help us load the coke into the truck. This car's been too shot up to drive out of here to evidence, so we'll have to have it towed."

Mason grunted and began carrying bricks from the trunk to the armored car the Marshals kept for just such an occasion. His coworker, Benson, walked with him, carrying bricks too.

"So, what's the deal with you and the victim?" he asked.

Mason sighed and growled, "Long story."

"What else do you want to do while we carry this shit?"

Mason lifted two more bricks to his shoulders and turned to walk back to the armored car. He frowned. How did he explain Lucy? Who exactly was she other than the woman he loved?

She wasn't his girlfriend or even his ex. They'd pretended to be married for a while, but he couldn't say that. He couldn't tell him that she was his cousin because she was only his cousin by marriage.

He pursed his lips and finally settled for, "I love her but haven't talked to her since I went to training in March. I called her earlier tonight, hoping to hit her up and see if she wanted to go out now that I'm back."

Benson laughed as they stacked their bricks inside. "Damn, I wish you luck, man. If my girl had been caught in something like this, I'd get the hell out of Dodge. Sounds like trouble."

Mason grinned and they went back for the last of the bricks. He didn't care how much trouble it was, Lucy was worth it. If he could only convince her...

He looked around, and Benson nodded to the ambulance. "Go on. I see that look on your face. It looks like the paramedics are done checking her and her friend over."

Mason breathed a sigh of relief as he jogged over to the ambulance.

Chapter Forty-Six

When Mason finally rounded the back of the ambulance, he found Lucy sitting inside on the gurney with a blanket around her shoulders.

Taylor sat beside her, their feet kicking in tandem as they talked in quiet voices. Taylor saw him standing at the back of the ambulance and hopped up. She asked the paramedic, "Are we free to head home? This is too much excitement for one night."

The paramedic nodded, but Benson appeared and said, "Not yet. We need to get both your statements. Novak, do you want to take the injured victim's statement? I'll take yours, miss, if you'll come with me? Also, I believe this is your purse and phone from the restaurant?"

Lucy nodded, and Benson put her things in the back of the ambulance. Benson winked at him as he turned away.

Taylor's eyes narrowed, and her hands went to her hips. She opened her mouth to argue with Benson, but Lucy's hand settled on her arm. Taylor looked down. They must've had one of those secret girl talks, because Taylor's shoulders slumped, then she nodded and hopped out of the ambulance.

Mason stepped inside and knelt in front of Lucy, taking her hand. She pulled her hand out of his and tucked it back inside the blanket, looking down and avoiding his gaze. The hurt and lost look on her face gutted him, and he ached to sweep her into his arms.

He hadn't seen her for over five months, and she was gorgeous as ever. When he'd realized it was her, he'd sat frozen to his seat in shock. By the time he'd processed, she was already sitting with her dad. He'd been so helpless, having already set up the microphones behind the picture frame at their booth.

Everyone had been in place from before Seth's arrival. He'd been there less than ten minutes when Lucy arrived, shocking him.

He caressed her cheek and cleared his throat, but Lucy shook her head and pulled back with a frown. "I can't believe you did this," she said softly, and a tear fell down her cheek.

He frowned. "What? I didn't do anything."

She wrinkled her nose and sniffed. "You used me. I don't know how you convinced him, but I should've suspected something was going on when he called out of the blue."

Mason shook his head. "I had no idea he was going to be here until about six, and I certainly had no idea you were coming too. I only realized he was your father tonight."

She rolled her eyes. "Oh please, you expect me to believe that?"

He touched her knees. "It's the truth. Why would I lie?"

She pushed his hands off, and he felt a stab of pain in his chest at the rejection. "You wanted to catch him in some horrible act and put him away. He's going away, isn't he?"

He nodded, "For a very long time."

Lucy nodded and wiped her nose. "Good, that's good. Maybe he'll finally get clean in there."

Her shoulders slumped, and he wanted to gather her in his arms and hold her. She suddenly looked even younger than twenty-three. She looked like a sad little kid with big watery eyes, like a bully had just destroyed her favorite toy.

His hands itched to punch the son of a bitch into a bloody pulp. He fisted them hard and focused on his job until he could process these swinging emotions of helplessness and rage.

"Lucy, we lost audio feed when he took you out the back door. What did he say? What happened?"

She sighed and closed her eyes, causing another tear to fall down her cheek. He brushed it away, and she flinched. His stomach knotted, and he dropped his hands to take out his phone.

He set it to record audio as she explained what her dad said.

"He threatened Taylor, said someone was going to drug her and kill her inside if I didn't go with him. He—he wanted me to go to Mexico where he was going to teach me some manners. I—I think he wanted me to apologize for breaking his nose at Billy Bob's back in May."

"But you didn't apologize, did you, little bird?" he asked softly, his stomach clenching.

She shook her head and closed her eyes. "Never. He left my mom to die, Mason, and left me to pick up all the pieces. He's lucky I only broke his nose."

He smiled, pride welling in him. "I'm so proud of you for standing up for yourself."

She sighed, and opened her eyes, staring over his shoulder blankly. "Me too."

"What happened after he said he was going to teach you some manners?"

Tears welled in her eyes, and she finally met his gaze. Her big, brown eyes shone with pain in the harsh light of the ambulance.

"He said he was going to give me to a guy in...um, somewhere, who was looking for a new plaything."

Mason's blood ran cold, and he sucked in a shocked breath. Seth was a piece of shit father and a shittier human. He swallowed hard and focused on the questions he was trained for.

"Was it Mexico? Florida? Colombia? Guatemala?"

"Colombia. He said he had a friend in Colombia," she frowned, then her face collapsed with a sob. "Why did he want to do that? Sell his own daughter? Didn't he ever love me?"

Sobs racked her body, and Mason stood and pulled her into a hug. Her body shook with tears, and he rubbed her back.

"If he loved me, he wouldn't have put me in this situation. He wouldn't have wanted to sell—sell me to some pervert. That's not love. I could see it in his eyes. He wanted to hurt me like he hurt Mama."

She choked on a sob, her breathing short and racking her body.

"Sh, it's okay. No one's going to hurt you ever again," he said soothingly.

She jerked her head back, and he dropped his hands. She wiped furiously at her eyes with the edge of the blanket. "That's right because I'm tough. I'm strong. I can handle it."

He smiled at her determined, fierce look. Then she

turned her eyes on him, anger shining through. "And I can handle it all on my own, but what I can't do alone is find out the truth of tonight."

He frowned. "What do you mean?"

She glared at him. "Think, Mason. There's no way it's a coincidence that my dad called me up out of the blue. There has to be an explanation, and I'm holding you personally responsible for finding out why. Are we done here? Is that enough of a statement?"

He sighed and shook his head. "What happened after he mentioned the Colombian?"

She scowled and tightened the blanket around her. "What do you think? They tried to force me into the car, and I panicked. I heard gunshots and passed out. Next thing I know, you're hovering over me like some kind of avenging angel."

He narrowed his eyes and frowned. "Why do you sound so angry about that?"

She shook her head and waved her arms, making the blanket shake. "Why do you think? I don't like being taken advantage of. I don't like being lied to. I don't—my own fucking father just tried to traffic me to Mexico, for fucks sake. Either I keep crying or I keep yelling and screaming. Those are my two options right now, so which would you rather have, hot shot?"

Mason chuckled at the nickname and turned the audio recording off on his phone.

"Oh, hell no, don't you go laughing at me, mister."

He quirked a brow. "Mister? I think you mean master, don't you?"

The paramedic's gaze shot to them, but Mason ignored him as Lucy jabbed a finger in his chest. "No, I don't. I mean mister. I'm furious, and part of it is because

I keep finding myself in these kinds of experiences *with you*."

She was getting worked up, and he didn't want her to pass out again. He had to diffuse the situation, so he teased her to draw her out from the fearful, lost little girl. "But I thought you loved excitement and adventure."

"Oh, fucking puhh-lease," she said, cocking a hip and jabbing him in the chest again.

"All I wanted was a nice graduation celebration with my bestie, then bam! FBI raid. Shots fired." She jabbed him in the chest at the end of each sentence.

"Then all I wanted was a nice, relaxing vacation to Hawaii, then bam! Drugged, kidnapped, shots fired again." She jabbed him with each of the last few words.

"And now here I was, trying to reconcile with my father, thinking he'd finally gotten his shit together, and bam! Attempted trafficking and—wouldn't ya know it—more shots fired. And here *you are*, right in the thick of it. Every. Single. Damn. Time."

His chest ached, and he crossed his arms to get her to stop poking him. "What's your point, sunshine?"

She narrowed her eyes at him and turned to the paramedic. "I'm done, right? You don't need me anymore?"

He nodded, his eyes wide as he stared between them. She turned and pushed her way past Mason, sitting on the back of the ambulance and then hopping to the ground. He jumped down, turning to grab her arm and help her.

She shook him off and tossed the blanket back into the ambulance. "My point, Novak, is that I'm fucking tired of being caught in the crossfire where your job is concerned."

He narrowed his eyes, "I never wanted you to be in the crossfire, but I can't—won't—change my job. I fucking love this job, and if you think—"

She waved her arms wide and screamed, "I'm not fucking Amanda."

People stopped and turned to stare at them, so he herded them to the other side of the ambulance facing the parking lot.

"I know you're not Amanda."

"Do you?" she asked shrilly. "Because I'm not so sure you do. I think you see me as a second chance, as a do-over. But I'm no one's second choice, Mason Novak."

"Damn right, you're not. You're my first choice," he said, crossing his arms again.

She waved hers wide. "No, I'm not. Don't you see? You haven't been able to let her go, which is why I didn't say anything about us starting something real back in February. You're still grieving her."

Mason's chest burned with an intensity that threatened to consume him. Each breath felt labored and heavy, as if he were drowning in molten lava. Despite his efforts to calm himself with deep breaths, the fiery waves continued to crash against him, threatening to knock him off his feet.

She rubbed her temples. "Mason, I can't keep fighting for your love while you're still haunted by her memory," she whispered, her voice barely audible over the roar of his inner turmoil.

He reached out for her, desperate for her touch to ground him, only to be met with rejection as she pulled away. In a fit of frustration, he shoved his hands into his pockets and spread his legs wide apart, trying to maintain some semblance of control over his emotions. If he couldn't touch her, he'd have to use words, and he was fucking shit at that. Still, he had to try.

"You're not competing with a ghost, Luce. There's no competition. Do you know how hard it was to see you go down like that? It about broke me. It was like Amanda all over again but even worse, more intense, and I was helpless to stop it or protect you."

She waved her hands wide as lightning rippled overhead. "It's not your job to protect me at all hours of the day, Mason, but it sure would be easier to do if you'd stop getting us into these situations."

His hands shook in his pockets. "I told you, I had nothing to do with any of this. It was all just a series of unfortunate events."

She gasped and reared back, startled. "Is that all I am? An unfortunate event in your life? A nice holiday fuck who might help you catch a bad guy or two by playing the damsel in distress? Fuck that, Mason, and fuck you."

She threw her hands in the air and stomped away, more lightning and now thunder booming.

Mason turned as a coworker called his name, spying the paramedic standing at the end of the ambulance, trying not to eavesdrop. Mason stepped toward the parking lot and frowned as the paramedic said, "No wait, she forgot her purse."

Mason turned and grabbed them. "Thanks, I'll see that she gets it." Then he leaned around the paramedic and yelled, "Benson, I'll be right back."

The paramedic looked into the parking lot as lightning flashed. "I don't think you should, man. She's pretty upset."

Mason waved him off and jogged to the parking lot. He saw her get into a little purple car, and Taylor drove away. Neither of them saw him waving, trying to get her to stop.

A lead weight settled in his chest, and a lump formed in his throat as he stood there. Rain began to fall, and his boss yelled to go secure evidence before the rain ruined anything.

What could he do to fix this? She was just so emotional.

Maybe if they both calmed down tonight, he could see her tomorrow and explain, somehow unfuck everything he'd done wrong tonight.

He stretched his neck and rolled his shoulders as he pulled out his phone. It rang for a long time before a groggy Ray answered.

"Pops, this is Mason. Sorry to wake you, but Lucy is on her way home now. Can you make sure she gets home safe and have Helen check on her in the morning?"

"What? What time is it, son? Why do we need to check on Lucy?"

Mason rubbed his eyes and sighed. "Her dad was involved in a sting operation tonight in Dallas, and Lucy met him for dinner, so she was caught up in it."

Ray groaned. "Don't tell me she got shot again."

Mason chuckled. "No, she's fine. Just in shock. Her friend, Taylor, is with her and driving them home."

A rustling on the other end came through, then Helen's soft voice said, "Mason? What happened with her dad?"

He gave a summary, then he said, "I tried to comfort her, but she ended up telling me to fuck off, pardon my language."

She sighed. "Well, I don't blame her. You need to pull your head out of your ass."

He frowned and pushed the rain off his hair. "Seriously?"

Helen was a stickler for the rules, so for her to swear something was very wrong.

"Well, you haven't even talked to her, have you? You just assumed you knew what was best and that was that. You've completely ignored her for five whole months. She's been worried sick about you and has no idea how you feel about her."

Mason sucked in a breath and the tone made him wince. He rubbed the sore spot on his chest. "How I feel about her..."

Helen sniffed and lifted her head high. "Do *you* even know how you feel about her?"

He scowled. "Of course I do. I plan to talk to her about it tomorrow."

Helen sighed. "I'm going to head to her house and make sure she's alright, but Mason? You better hope and pray that she listens tomorrow."

The line went dead, and he groaned. She was right. He shouldn't have just left her alone this whole time. Every time he'd called Ray to ask how she was, he should've just bit the bullet and point blank called her, asked her if she wanted to get together for real.

He had really fucked up. He pushed his hair back and leaned his head back, letting the rain hit. Shit, shit, shit.

"Novak, where are you?" Sarmiento called. Mason sighed and jogged back to the scene with her purse still in his hand.

Chapter Forty-Seven

Lucy cried herself to sleep that night. She grieved for her dad and all the missed events, the missed years of having a real father who'd show up and love her. She cried from shock and fear that something could've happened to her or her baby. She cried for Amanda, who must've been caught in a similar situation but hadn't survived.

She cried for the kidnapping nightmares triggered by the night's events. She woke up from a dream that Mason was holding her tight in a warm cocoon of his arms and cried when she realized he wasn't there.

When she woke up on Saturday, it was to a horrible headache all because the fucking tears wouldn't stop. Taylor pushed her bedroom door open and brought in a tray of food.

She smiled tightly. "Wakey wakey, eggs and bakey."

Lucy's brows furrowed. "Really?"

Taylor snorted. "Gotcha, didn't I? Helen dropped breakfast off. Apparently, Mason called them this morning to check on you."

Lucy groaned and pulled a pillow over her head. "I don't want to talk about him," she said.

Taylor chuckled and pulled the pillow off. Lucy leaned against the headboard, and Taylor put the tray across her lap. A knock on her bedroom door had her glancing up.

Helen stood in the door with freshly cut roses and a smile. "Hello, sweet pea. Are you up yet?"

Lucy's eyes teared again, and she wiped furiously at them with a laugh. "I'm up. Sorry, I'm not really presentable yet."

Helen waved to her food. "Is the food okay? I wasn't sure what your stomach was tolerating these days or if you were out of the morning sickness phase."

Lucy's hand froze with her fork half-way to her mouth. She met Taylor's surprised eyes, then looked at Helen. "You know?" she asked.

Helen smirked and sat in the corner reading chair, crossing her arms.

"Of course, dear. I'm old, not blind. I'm still a mother, you know."

Taylor chuckled and sat on the edge of the bed. "Nothing gets by you, does it, Helen?"

Helen smiled, pleased with herself. "Never. That's what made me such a great teacher and librarian."

"But how did you know? I was so careful," Lucy blurted. Her cheeks heated, and she looked down at her food, scarfing in another bite. She was famished.

"You've been having cravings for months. I'd stop by in the afternoons and find you taking a nap on the couch. You've always had boundless energy, even as a kid, so napping is definitely out of the ordinary. And let's not forget how you're suddenly not wanting to wear a bathing suit when we go fishing. Yet somehow you had no problem doing so last year."

Lucy winced even as she swiped a finger in the blueberry syrup leftover from her pancake. Taylor handed her a bottle of water, and she guzzled half of it before she came up for air.

Helen chuckled. "I see your appetite is back, so that's good news."

Lucy took a deep breath and nodded, putting a hand on her stomach with a frown. "I—I haven't had a chance to talk to Mason about it. Last night—was hard, but we didn't get a spare moment to talk about *this*."

She looked up and met her grandmother's clear brown eyes. "I'm sorry, Nana. I wanted to tell you so many times, but I felt like I needed to tell Mason first. Taylor only knows because she was there when I found out."

Taylor twisted her lips. "Girl please, you wouldn't have kept this from me in a million years. Don't even try to pretend otherwise."

Lucy giggled and nodded, handing her the now empty tray back. "Fine, you caught me."

Helen nodded and stood, taking the tray. "Let me, dear. Taylor, are you still going fishing with us today?"

Taylor shook her head. "No, I'm about to get ready for work. I've got the north branch library today."

Helen nodded and the two went out the door talking books and what was new in the library world. Since Helen had retired from teaching high school English, she'd started volunteering at the Crimson Creek library. She and Taylor had always gotten along.

Lucy pushed back the covers and grabbed clothes to take a shower. She had felt so drained last night that she hadn't wanted to move any more than she had to.

Yes, she'd get stinky, sweaty, and would swim in the river, but she needed to start the day fresh. Her stomach was settled from breakfast, but there was still a knot of fear and nerves.

She would see Mason today. She stepped out of the shower and looked at her body. Her baby bump was pretty obvious now, but she'd been able to hide it. Baggy tank tops and stretchy loose-fitting shorts had made that pretty easy.

She thought back to all she'd said to Mason and winced. She didn't like yelling and screaming, but it'd felt cathartic to finally get all that off her chest. She put her clothes on and brushed her hair, braiding it into one thick braid.

She grabbed her phone and went downstairs but paused when she saw a message from Mason from last night.

I hope you made it home safely.
I'm sorry about tonight. Can we talk tomorrow?
I'll be there in time for dinner, not sure about fishing yet.

She didn't reply, her stomach twisting in anticipation of seeing him. She'd missed him so much, but she didn't want to grasp at straws. She wanted to talk this out and get it all out in the open.

That morning, Mason pulled up to the boat launch and parked the truck. Caroline tucked her hair behind her ear and smiled nervously. "Are you sure this is a good idea?"

He gripped the steering wheel and nodded his head. "Until your application is approved and we can get you into the witness protection program, we have to keep this ruse up.

The Ranger Gets His Girl

What better way to do that than by having you meet my family? Don't worry though. I'll tell them the truth once you're safely away or maybe later today. It depends on a few things."

She bit her lip and nodded. His stomach clenched tight in nerves. He hated this idea, did not want to introduce her to his family as his girlfriend. It would either hurt Lucy and ruin any chance he might've had with her, or she wouldn't care, in which case it would hurt him.

It was a lose lose situation, but the boss said it was the best idea. He was new to the department, so who was he to argue?

His stomach was also nervous just at the thought of seeing and talking with Lucy again. Last night was stressful, but he hoped to sort it all out. He *had* to sort it all out. At the very least, he had to bare his soul, declare his love, and ask for her forgiveness.

He opened the driver's door and went around to open Caroline's, offering a hand as she climbed down. She wore short, silky blue shorts and a navy-blue tank top blouse with strappy sandals.

"Are you sure you're okay with floating the river and going fishing?" he asked again, eying her fancy clothes that screamed the Hamptons.

She smiled as they rounded the truck. "Of course. I grew up in the country. It's been a while, but I can handle a canoe. Do you need a hand getting it into the water?"

He shook his head and unhooked the tow straps from Pops trailer. "No, but can you grab my backpack and the little cooler from the truck?"

She nodded and went back to the truck while he unloaded the canoe. He was sweating by the time it was in the water. He offered her a hand and had her sit, checked that everything was secure, then he took his shirt off and tossed it in.

"Oh yeah, baby, take it off," she grinned, lowering her sunglasses to wiggle her eyebrows.

He laughed and shook his head. "Sorry, lady, the show's over. This ship has sailed." He pushed the canoe out into the water and held it steady to let her step inside. She didn't take her expensive sandals off but simply splashed into the water and gasped as she threw a leg over the side of the canoe. "Oh, that's cold."

When she was settled, he gingerly hopped in, the little boat rocking as he settled on the seat and grabbed the paddle.

He followed the familiar river as it wound to his grandpa's favorite spot. They rounded a bend and saw Ray already fishing, his canoe tied to a tree. Mason steered them next to it and hopped out.

He took the lead rope from Caroline and tied it to another tree, then turned to help her out of the canoe.

Ray finished reeling his pole and strode through the water to them. "Glad you could make it, son. Good to see you," he slapped a hand to Mason's shoulder and squeezed. Mason winced at the rough grip as Ray asked, "And hello, missy. Who might you be?"

Caroline held out a hand to shake and said, "Hi, I'm Caroline, Mason's girlfriend."

Ray's gaze swung to Mason, and his blue eyes narrowed. Before Mason could explain, Will came through the trees, shaking his leg. His hair was in a high and tight but was the same black as Mason's. He was a little leaner but had definitely bulked up while deployed.

Caroline gasped and lowered her sunglasses again. "Hot damn. Not one, but two? It's going to be a great day."

Mason didn't have time to say anything, as Will saw him and took off running straight at him. He braced himself as Will tackled him, and they splashed into the shallow water with a laugh.

"Mason! You made it!"

Mason grunted and hugged his brother back, shoving his head into the water and immediately jerking him back up as he sputtered and laughed. Will sat up and splashed him.

Mason punched him in the bicep, both of them slowly standing to their feet in the shallow water. "Damn, did you do nothing but work out while you were deployed? Holy shit, lay off the creatine, will ya?"

Will laughed, slapping him on the back in a tamer bro hug. "Me? What about you, Mr. Beefcake. That must've been one hell of a training program."

Mason wrapped an arm around his brother's shoulders and glanced at Caroline as she said, "Hello, I'm Caroline, Mason's girlfriend."

Will stepped forward and took Caroline's hand, bending at the waist and kissing the back of it. "Pleasure to meet you, miss. Too bad Mason saw you first. I'm Will."

Caroline quirked a brow and blushed, but Mason saw Ray cross his arms and frown. Mason ran a hand through his now wet hair and walked to where his grandfather stood with feet spread wide.

"What's going on, son?" Ray asked in that tone that brooked no argument, the one that said he knew you were full of shit and was just waiting for you to own up to it.

Mason sighed, "She's not my girlfriend. That's just our cover story. I'm protecting her until she can get into WITSEC, but I need to see Lucy today and couldn't leave Caroline behind. So, I brought her along."

Ray nodded and frowned. "They'll be here in an hour or so, I think. Helen was going to aim for mid-morning, definitely before lunch when it gets too hot."

Mason sighed. "Well, I guess we'll get to fishing then. Let me get Caroline settled first."

He grabbed their bags and cooler and took them to shore, finding a nice, flat spot away from the water. She was still chatting with Will, so he just sprayed sunscreen on and grabbed a pole.

He would wait for Lucy. He'd wait for her for as long it took. He let the line fly and thought of all the things he needed to say.

Chapter Forty-Eight

Lucy grabbed the picnic basket and hopped into Helen's car. She enjoyed the peace as they drove to the river where they were to meet Ray and Will.

They found the launching spot and parked. Last summer, Ray had bought Helen a fancy new canoe and painted *Pearl* on the side of it. It sat tied up in the water already.

She helped Helen load the picnic baskets into the canoe and had Helen get in first. Lucy untied them and hopped in. Together, they used their paddles to get off the sand bar and into the open river.

The current was lazy at the smallest part of the river, which is why the town had been named Crimson Creek. They paddled on the almost still water, and Lucy leaned her head back.

The sun felt good, and some of the tension and confusion within her melted. She wasn't sure what her talk with Mason would bring, but today was a good day. Her dad was safely behind bars, and she wouldn't have to worry about him showing up out of the blue anymore.

She hadn't even realized how much she worried about that until today. On some level, she'd always been nervous that he'd show up, rip her out of school, and force a new town, new friends, new everything on her again.

It might be another reason she hadn't dated in college. She'd been waiting for the other shoe to drop the whole time.

She and Helen rounded the bend in the river and saw two canoes on the shore at Ray's favorite, secluded fishing spot. They rowed gently over. Ray and Will stood in the shallows, casting down river.

Her eyes settled on the other two figures on the shore. Mason waded through the water from where a canoe was tied to a tree. Wearing only shorts, his muscles rippled in the sun.

Her breathing went ragged as she stared. She hadn't had much chance to get a good look at him last night. It had been a dark alley, then she'd been in shock.

He was fitter than he had in Hawaii, and he could've been an arm porn model then. Now he had clearly defined abs and appeared even bulkier.

As they floated closer and rounded the other canoe, Lucy frowned. The brunette from the restaurant last night lay sunbathing on a towel on the sand. She wore a red string bikini that showed more skin than she'd ever seen in real life. The woman was curvy in all the right places, and Lucy settled a hand on her stomach. She hunched her shoulders, self-conscious and glad she'd worn the baggy tank top and shorts over her bikini.

Mason walked toward the woman and handed over a bottle of water and sunscreen. The woman said something,

The Ranger Gets His Girl

then turned to offer him her back. Mason lathered her up, and Lucy gasped.

Who was this woman? What the hell was he doing?

They floated closer, and Mason finally saw them, even as his hands were on the other woman. They both had on sunglasses, but she knew that prickle of awareness that was his stare.

She turned her head and tilted her chin up as they ran aground on the sand. Her chest was tight at seeing him so familiar with another woman, but she was strong and tough.

She sat in the canoe while Helen got out first, then she stood and wobbled, grabbing the edge.

Suddenly, Mason's hands were on her elbow, and he helped her out. Her breath caught in her throat at his touch, and tears pricked her eyes. Once her feet were safely in the water, she froze as his hands slid down her arms in a gentle caress that gave her goosebumps.

She murmured, "Thanks."

Looking up at him, all the love that she'd held on to like a lifeline for all these months came crashing down around her. She was breathless as he took her fingers in his.

No, she couldn't do this yet. She stepped out of his hands, feeling the loss, but she couldn't get too used to his touch, not unless they turned this into something real. She couldn't let him touch her or she'd be lost. They had to talk first.

The cold water flowed around her knees, and she grabbed one of the picnic baskets.

Helen grabbed the other and said brightly, "Mason, you made it! We weren't sure you'd be able to get off work today. Can you secure the canoe? This is lovely, I'm so glad to see—oh, hello. Who might you be?" Helen frowned as the woman stepped toward them.

Lucy followed Helen to the sandy area where the woman now stood in the shallower water. The woman smiled nervously and waved to the basket.

"I'm Caroline, Mason's girlfriend. Can I take that for you? I'm sorry to have crashed your party today."

Lucy's vision swam, and she stumbled in the water. Mason's hand steadied her elbow, but she jerked it out of his grasp and waded as fast as she could to shore, water splashing up around her.

"No, Lucy, wait—" he said as he strode after her.

He was fucking dating. What the hell?

Helen looked at them and handed the basket to Caroline. "Well welcome, welcome. We didn't know Mason was dating."

Helen's tone was clearly one of disappointment, and Lucy winced. She hadn't known either. Why hadn't he said anything last night? Was *this* what he'd wanted to talk about?

She reached the shore and walked through the deep sand past Caroline's towel to a flat area. Mason's hand on her back made her lurch sideways and hiss, "Keep your hands off me, jackass."

He snatched the basket out of her hand and set it down. She turned to stomp toward the fishing gear in Ray's canoe, but he grabbed her wrist. She tugged hard, fighting him.

"Will you just stop and listen for a minute?" he grunted.

She pushed on his chest, trying not to curl her hand into it. Her body was already betraying her, wanting him, wanting to hold him, fuck him, and smack him on the side of the head.

Lucy clenched her jaw and hissed, "What could you possibly say that could help this situation?"

Caroline looked from one to the other, her forehead

wrinkled as she sat down the other basket. "Wait, what's going on? Who's she?" she asked Helen.

Mason opened his mouth to answer, but before he could, Lucy rounded on him and pointed her finger under his nose. "You didn't even tell her about me? Ugh," she glared and changed direction. Tears pricked her eyes as she stomped went back to the canoe, untying the rope.

Mason grabbed the edge of it. "I'll explain everything if you just give me a minute.

"You have a fucking girlfriend, Mason. There's nothing to explain," she said, throwing the rope into the canoe. She pushed it deeper into the water and called loudly, "I forgot something in the car. I'll be back soon."

She fell into the boat clumsily as it moved back toward the sharp drop off. She didn't care how ridiculous she looked. She needed to get away, take a breather, maybe just go home, and lay down. She didn't need this heartache, not coming off the chaos of last night.

Mason grabbed the canoe near the edge of the drop off and stood strong, not letting her move.

"She's not really my girlfriend, Lucy. It's a cover up, a role for work. In a week or so, Caroline will be joining the witness protection program, and our cover won't be needed anymore."

Lucy frowned, looking at Caroline on the shore and gripping the paddle tightly. "What do you mean?"

Mason growled, "I mean, we're not actually dating. I'm working, protecting her."

Lucy felt a stab of pain in her chest and inhaled sharply. "Protecting her like you protected me in Hawaii? Are you sleeping with her? God, Mason, you've been back in Texas less than two weeks and have already moved on. Nicely done, she seems lovely. Now let me go."

She dug the paddle into the water, trying to find the bottom to push off, but barely touched. The boat bobbed, and he held it tight, his biceps bulging.

He arched a brow. "Don't get smart with me, little bird. You're not hearing me. There's nothing between Caroline and me. I haven't so much as kissed her much less anything else."

"You haven't?" Her hopeful tone made her scowl. She didn't want to be hopeful. She needed to get away and protect her heart.

He shook his head. "Absolutely not. I'm not even attracted to her."

"You're not?" She felt like a parrot just repeating him.

He chuckled. "Nope. I only have eyes for you, Lucy."

She swiped furiously at her eyes once more, and Mason pulled the boat closer to shore, trying to ground it on the sand. She stayed seated, holding the paddle across her body protectively as she glared at him.

"I call bullshit on that. You were just putting sunscreen on her when I arrived."

"It's just a job. I'm telling you, sunshine, she's only here because of work. I'm working right now. I'm the new guy that hasn't been in town in five months. I'm the logical choice for a fake boyfriend slash bodyguard."

She splashed the water with the paddle, and he didn't even flinch. "How can you not be attracted to her?" Her voice was shrill and hurt, but she couldn't help it. She felt raw and vulnerable, like her heart was slowly being peeled open like an onion.

Mason leaned on the bow of the canoe, both hands on the edge and growled. "I'm not attracted to her because she's not you."

Lucy's lips pursed, and Mason released the canoe and

reached for her. She seized her opportunity, stabbing the paddle into the water and pushing the canoe back into the river.

Mason lunged for her. The water slowed him down, and he tripped. His hand caught the edge of the canoe, and Lucy screamed as it tipped over. Water went up her nose and made her choke.

She flailed her arms and couldn't see anything in the murky river. She found the bottom and pushed up. Hands caught her, and Mason hauled her to his chest as they broke above water.

She gasped and choked, blinking against the bright sun. Her sunglasses were gone downstream, but Mason stood them up and walked them back toward shore. She sobbed and held onto his arm with one hand while wiping her eyes with the other.

Great, now she was a drowned rat and had to finish this conversation. She took deep breaths, coughing to clear her throat.

Chapter Forty-Nine

Mason stumbled under their wet weight and pulled her into his lap in the shallows. His heart raced with adrenaline as he grumbled. "Damn it, Lucy."

He held her in his arms bridal style and crushed his lips to hers. All of his love burst like lava in his chest, but she stiffened in his embrace.

He froze, resisting the urge to sweep into her mouth and show her how much he'd missed her. He let her process the feel of their bodies pressed against each other, the feel of their lips as he pressed his mouth to hers.

Faintly, he heard Will say sarcastically, "Well, I guess you're not really his girlfriend, are you?"

Caroline giggled, but Mason didn't care. He was too busy trying to coax Lucy's lips open. He flicked his tongue across them, and she moaned, barely opening to his bleeding heart's need for her. He seized the moment and dove inside, swirling his tongue with hers in a dance as old as time.

He cradled her head with both hands. She had curves

for days and having her on his lap was heaven on earth. His dick twitched despite the cold water.

Still the kiss went on. His lips worked hers, begging for her forgiveness and telling her without words how he felt.

She jerked back, breaking the kiss. "Mason, what are you—"

"I missed you, Lucy, so fucking much," he said, resting his forehead on hers. She trembled in the cocoon of his arms.

"You did?" Her voice was shaky and tentative.

He nodded, eyes still closed as he just held her. "I did. I can't believe I didn't call you. I should have. I was just so afraid that you didn't want anything to do with me."

She leaned back and slapped him gently on the arm as she frowned. "How can you think that? Don't you know me at all?"

He kissed her mouth in small kisses. "I do, but when I overheard you say that your dad trapped your mom in a relationship and that wasn't what you wanted, I knew I had to let you go. The last few months have been torture, not because of the training but because I've been without you. Without your voice on the phone, your laugh, your mischievous look when you get an idea for an adventure. I want to experience life *with* you, not trap you."

She sobbed, but he kissed her deeper, trying to stem the tears. After last night, he didn't want to see her cry. They'd had enough tears to last a lifetime. When her breathing changed from tearful, he broke the kiss. She buried her face in his neck, her arms tight around his waist, but said nothing.

He was desperate to convince her, so he rushed on.

"I know your dad trapped your mom in an abusive marriage, and your mom tried to trap your dad financially."

She sighed, her breath tickling his neck and giving him goosebumps. "They made each other miserable, and it drove my mom into an early grave."

His arms squeezed tighter around her, and his chest ached. "I don't want to make you miserable, Lucy. I want to make you happy. If you'll give me a chance, I'll work every day to prove that won't be us. Is it possible? Did you miss me at all?"

She snorted. "I was miserable being apart from you these past few months."

He kissed the side of her head and then hugged her tight. "I'm so sorry, little bird. I should have called. Training made it easy to stay away from you."

She sniffed and grumbled, "Easier my ass."

He chuckled, caressing her head and rocking her gently on his lap. "Maybe that's the wrong word. Miserable would be more accurate. Every single day, I'd look at your pictures and remember the smell of your hair, the way you felt in my arms, talking with you as we walked on the beach or hiked. I've missed you more than I ever thought possible. I must've pulled up your number three or four times a day to call, then always chickened out."

Lucy sniffled and wiped her eyes. "I missed you too, but with your job—and I'm not saying give up your job like Amanda did. I'm saying where do you see this going? Do you want a relationship, and if so, how will that work with your career?"

She sat up and frowned at him, a worry line on her forehead.

His breath shuddered. This was his moment. He had to lay it all on the line. Show his cards. Shoot his shot.

He cupped her cheeks and peered into her eyes.

"I want to love you until the end of time. I want to wake

up with you every morning and cuddle you every night. I want to talk to you, see your face, hear your laugh, and make you happy all the days of my life. I feel like I've known you forever, even though I have so much more to learn. I love you so much, it's like I've always known you, like my soul recognizes yours. You're my heart, my whole world."

Tears poured down her cheeks, but she didn't look away as awe and fear warred on her face. "But your job is your everything—"

He peppered kisses on her face. "*You're* my everything, little bird. I'll find balance between the two somehow, but if push comes to shove, you take priority. Do you want me to quit the Marshals and join the Crimson Creek police force? Because I will, if that's what it takes to be with you."

"What? No, Mason, that's not what I'm saying at all. I'd never ask you to give up your dream job, your purpose."

He kissed her lips softly. "You're so selfless, Lucy. But all *I'm* asking is if you'll give me the time to see where this takes us. If you'll give us a real, fighting chance to make it. I never want to spend months apart from you again. I'd like to marry you someday, but if that's not something you want—"

She gasped and threw her arms around his neck, surprising him. He chuckled, a deep vulnerability making him say, "I'm not actually proposing now but just wanted to let you know where my head and heart are at about it. You'll know when I do, but I take it that's something you'd say yes to?"

Her words were muffled against his neck. "Yes, I'd like to get married someday, but I'm still worried about juggling your job. Long distance relationships don't work out. I might not have ever had a boyfriend, but even I know that."

He stroked the hair away from her face, but still she kept

her head buried. "That's what they say, but long distance might be what we need to get to know each other more. Maybe we need late night phone calls and video chats, real conversations to find out exactly what we are to each other."

She shook her head, a tear falling down his chest. He reached up and cradled her face in his hand, his other rubbing circles on her back. His chest ached to see her crying still. He desperately wanted to see her smile and happy and loved.

"Hey now, it's alright. There won't be that much long distance now that training is over. Sure, I'll have a crazy schedule, but I shouldn't ever be gone five months in a row again. The extent of long distance will probably only be a few days at a time. And only then if I need to spend a few days on protection duty or hunting a fugitive. Is that something you can live with? Just a few days without me?"

Lucy rubbed her temples and sighed. "Mason, I'm not Amanda."

He snorted. "Why are you so fixated on her? You're right. You're not Amanda and thank God for that. Amanda and I would've been yelling at each other by this point in the conversation. Contrary to this specific conversation, you and I have always been able to talk through things. You're different, and we work well together."

She finally looked at him, her brown eyes haunted. "Is that why you're here? Is that why you want to date me? Because we work well together?"

He shook his head. "No, not just that. Shit, I'm fucking this up, aren't I?"

Will called out. "Little bit, yeah."

Caroline giggled, and Ray grumbled, "Y'all are jumping around topics like they're hot potatoes."

Helen just sighed dramatically, but Mason didn't look

away from Lucy. He took a deep breath and exhaled slowly, trying to gather his thoughts and think rationally. It was hard to do when she was sitting on his lap, distracting him with her beauty and looking so adorable.

"Okay, let me just lay it all out, huh? Let's do this interrogation style with yes no answers. Ready?" She nodded, so he continued. "Amanda wanted me to have a different job, right?"

She narrowed her eyes cautiously and nodded. "Yes," she drew out the syllable.

He continued. "Do you think you can live with my job? The danger, the unpredictability?"

She rolled her eyes and said, "Yes, I'm proud of your hard work and your new job. You're my hero, Mason. Don't you see that? I would never ask you to give up your job. You love it so much and giving it up would make you miserable."

He nodded, sighing as a weight was lifted from his shoulders. He kissed her softly, treasuring her for seeing him for who he really was.

"It would slowly kill me, Lucy. It's part of the reason I was dreading being stuck behind a desk for the Rangers. I need to be out there helping people."

She placed her palm on his chest, and he sucked in a breath at the gentle touch. His hands caressed her back slowly, wrapping her up in the safety of his arms.

When she smiled, it was like the sun came out from behind a cloud on a rainy day. That smile gave him hope, and his heart raced.

She said, "Exactly why I admire you so much. If we are going to start dating, I need you to talk to me at least once a day, preferably more if you're gone. It's been a shit few months without talking with you. I think I could handle us being separated if we were still talking. Yes or no. Can you talk to me at least once a day?"

He placed his hand over hers on his chest. "Yes. See? This right here is good communication. Amanda and I never would've talked things out like this."

She narrowed her eyes and said, "I like this interrogation style. My turn to ask you some more questions. Amanda's only been gone for a year now. Are you sure you're ready to move on?"

Mason squeezed her hand and smiled softly. "Yes. Absolutely. What's it going to take for you to let Amanda go? She and I just weren't a good fit."

Lucy's eyes widened, and she sucked in a breath. *"Me* let her go? What about you? When are *you* going to let go of the guilt of her death?"

Mason paused for a moment, enjoying her attention, the sound of her voice.

Then her words penetrated his brain, and he said, "I think I started to let her go on that cliff in Hawaii. The pain and guilt have lessened over the past few months."

Lucy frowned. "I thought you loved her?"

He frowned. "I thought I did too. I had asked her to move in with me after all."

He saw the confusion and sadness on her face and kissed her softly.

"What I felt for Amanda is nothing like what I feel for you, Lucy. This is the real deal. I've never felt like this with anyone else. It's all consuming. I can't get you out of my head, my mind, my heart, my soul. And I don't want to get you out of there. I just want to be with you all day and night, see you smile and laugh and even just watch you work on your book."

Lucy put a hand on her chest and wiggled on his lap

with a frown, more tears dripping down her cheeks. "You—you can't just sweep into my life months later and *say* that."

He smiled, running his hands down her back and staring at her gorgeous eyes. He teased her. "That's not a yes no question, Lucy. Come on, play the game right."

She smirked, then bit her lip and glanced down nervously, hunching her shoulders in the cocoon of his arms. She looked back up, her expression fearful or hopeful, he wasn't sure.

"Mason, do you love me? You're saying all kinds of things, and I'm very emotional right now, and I just need to know if you love me."

Her words were rushed, and his heart broke at her uncertainty. He crushed his mouth to hers, trying to pour all his emotions into this one moment. He had to get through to her because he wasn't going anywhere.

Chapter Fifty

Mason cupped her cheeks and lifted her face as he pulled back from the kiss, a flood of warmth spreading through him as he said the words.

"Yes, I love you, little bird. You knocked the breath out of me when I saw you walk up that aisle in December. It was love at first sight, but every minute I spend with you, I fall a little deeper in love."

Her eyes misted with tears again, but she looked at him, definitely with hope shining in her eyes. If she could be brave and ask, then so could he. She was always encouraging him to go big and reach for the stars, even when she didn't intend to. She just inspired him every day to be a better person.

He wanted to be that for her. He took a deep breath and laid his heart bare. "Do you love me?"

"Yes, I—I love you, Mason." Her voice was so soft, but then she rushed on, stumbling over her words.

"I mean, how crazy is that? I haven't ever really had a real boyfriend before, so I have nothing to compare this to, this feeling inside when I'm with you or think about you. I—I love you. It wasn't part of the plan, but here we are."

He chuckled, kissing her softly before pulling back. Joy filled his chest, making him feel lighter than air. He grinned, peppering kisses across her lips. "Surprised you, didn't it?"

Her hands caressed his chest as she nodded, another tear falling down her cheek. His heart ached for her. He wanted to be closer to her, and he didn't think he'd ever get enough of her.

He hugged her tight, tucking her head into his neck like they both liked. "It surprised me too, sunshine. All I want to do is wrap you up in my arms and love you forever."

Now that they'd both said those three magical words, she came alive, talking a mile a minute. "I—I feel like that too. I'm going to worry about you running all over and fighting bad guys, but if we're going to make this relationship work, we need to communicate and let each other do our own thing. You're going to have to let me take risks and be myself too. I'm going to want to go on adventures and see and experience new things. Can you handle that?"

He nodded, kissing her again softly and delighted to see her animated and talking. "I'm willing to work on it. If I'm out of town for a few days at a time, I literally won't be able to step in and interfere with your life. I never want you to feel trapped or like you can't do what you need or want to do."

"I *want* you to be part of that life though. Help me make good decisions, maybe talk me out of doing stupid stuff that we both know will make me pass out or something."

She pulled back to look at him, and they both smiled, remembering the parasailing incident before she continued, "But I want to be an equal, sharing everything."

"That works for me. So, will you officially be my girlfriend and see where this relationship takes us?"

She smiled and nodded. "Yes, but under one condition."

His heart skipped a beat as he said, "Anything."

A grin spread across her cheeks, and the mischievous twinkle he loved shone in her eyes. "Stop bringing work home with you. Maybe if you keep work at work, I won't keep ending up in dangerous situations. As exhilarating as it is, it's also exhausting being shot at."

She chuckled, and he threw his head back and laughed, pulling her in for a hug. "Deal. I guess we'll see how long we can make it without being shot at before I propose, eh?"

She giggled, and he hugged her tighter, joy filling him at the sound. "That would be acceptable, yes."

He loved the way she talked, and it made him smile so wide, his face hurt. "I'm in this for the long haul, sunshine. I've never felt like this with anyone, and I won't let you get away."

Tears fell down her cheeks, and he wiped them away. She bit her lip and nodded, then licked her lips and said nervously, "I have one more yes no question for you. Do you want kids?"

He frowned and tilted his head, glancing over at Will. He wasn't even pretending to fish, just staring at them as the drama unfolded with a goofy grin on his face.

Mason smiled and nodded, looking back at Lucy. "I never really thought about it until we talked about our siblings in Hawaii—or rather how lonely you were without one. Having a brother is the best, so at least two kids someday. What about you? You didn't have any siblings to worry about, fight with, or protect during those crazy growing up years. Do you want kids?"

She nodded and scrambled back on his lap, pushing his

arms down. He leaned back on his palms in the water and stared at her as she sat like a queen on a throne.

"It's a good thing I do, because that ship is sailing now." He frowned at her words, but she took a deep breath and pulled her wet tank top tight.

He looked down, frowning as he tried to process. She had a little beer belly, and—his eyes widened, and he clenched his jaw. It took several attempts to swallow past the knot in his throat as his heart raced. He sat up, one hand hovering above her stomach before settling on her thigh, the other going to her back.

He choked out, "You—you're pregnant?"

She watched him warily and reached for his hand, placing it on her stomach and nodding. *"We're* pregnant."

He took a shuddering breath as his world tipped and spun. When the world righted itself, a sense of purpose, belonging, and hope for a better tomorrow made his chest tight. Then joy spread from his heart, making him too hot.

He laughed and threw his hands wide, falling back into the water.

"Mason!" she gasped, just before he went under. The water barely covered his face, but it was enough. Her hands rushed over his chest, trying to find a hand hold to pull him back up.

He sat back up, laughing and sputtering as he wiped a hand down his face. He shook his head, sending a spray of water around them. Lucy gasped as he tipped his head back and yelled at the top of his lungs, "We're having a baby!"

Birds in the trees flew off with a squawk. Caroline clapped, and Will let out a whoop of excitement. He said, "Hell yeah!"

"About damn time," Ray grumbled.

Mason tugged her into his arms again, and kissed her

with all the passion, hope, and love within him. She was part of everything good in this world, and he was utterly devoted to her and their baby.

Their baby.

His mind spun in time with their tongues as they kissed. He could scarcely believe it. He mentally recalculated the timing of his proposal.

He broke the kiss and asked in a rush, "Do you want to get married before the baby is born or after? I don't care either way, but you're mine, Lucy. Not just because of the baby, though. You were mine from the minute I first saw you. I just didn't know it."

She smiled and laughed as tears rolled down her cheeks. "Alright, hot shot, slow your roll. What happened to all that talk of getting to know each other and long-distance phone calls?"

The sound of her laughter made him feel buoyant in the water. He grinned and wrapped his arms around her. His hand hovered over her stomach, and he glanced at her.

She nodded, and he touched her. The skin was taught, and he couldn't believe the miracle. He sucked in a breath, "Last night, the baby—"

"Is fine. The paramedic listened, and the heartbeat was strong. He said to monitor for kicks, but she's been moving fine."

His heart stuttered and he looked up at her, his eyes wide and tearing up at the bright sun. He'd lost his glasses somewhere.

She shook her head. "No, I just call her a she. I don't know the sex. Taylor has the envelope hidden, but no one knows. I—I didn't want to look until I'd told you and—"

He kissed her softly, lazily sweeping his tongue inside. When they finally came up for air, he said, "Thank you. You are the best thing that's ever happened to me, Lucy. Thank you for keeping our baby safe. I promise not to bring work home ever again. Not even a potential WITSEC person like Caroline. It's not safe enough for the baby."

She giggled, and the sound made warmth spread in his chest. She leaned in closer to hover her lips against his. "Oh, *now* you want to be safe. I see how it is," she giggled again.

He grinned, barely brushing her lips with his. "What? I know how much you love adventure."

She laughed, and everything was right with the world.

Chapter Fifty-One

Lucy woke up as the vehicle pulled to a stop. She blinked and looked around. They were back at her house. She rubbed her eyes. "Sorry," she mumbled.

Mason chuckled from the driver's side. "Don't worry. I think you're entitled to a nap every day, right? Isn't that part of the pregnancy job description?"

She yawned and nodded as he opened the door and hopped down. She gathered her bag as he opened her door and offered a hand. After their fishing trip today, they'd gone back to Helen and Ray's for the fish fry.

Then Mason needed to drive Caroline home where another Marshal was going to take his shift overnight. It was dark now. Her stomach grumbled even though they'd called ahead to Caroline's restaurant and ordered to go boxes.

When Lucy had mentioned that she had only had a few bites of the food last night, Caroline had insisted on feeding them.

She'd said, "It's the least I can do, considering the stress I put on you today by introducing myself as his girlfriend.

That's not even mentioning the chaos of last night. You might not've been in that situation if it weren't for me running to the Marshals for a way out."

Lucy had smiled and had found Caroline to be as beautiful on the inside as she was on the outside. She had brought them both up to her apartment, and they'd all eaten dinner together with the other Marshal.

After, Lucy had shyly suggested they just go back to Mason's apartment, but he'd said, "I want to start as we intend to go on. In our house together. Do you think Ray will sell it to me for a decent price?"

Lucy had texted Taylor an update, and she was sleeping elsewhere tonight, seeing as she'd moved in to help with the pregnancy. Somewhere along the drive back to Crimson Creek, she'd fallen asleep. It was like all the tension between her shoulders from the past few months had suddenly dissipated, leaving her relaxed. Sleep had finally come easy.

Mason linked their fingers together as they walked to the front door. It reminded her of those long walks on the beach in Hawaii, and she leaned her head on his bicep.

She sighed, happier than she'd ever thought possible. Back in Hawaii, there'd been a cloud in the back of her mind the entire time. It had whispered to her that this wasn't real, it was only temporary.

Now it was gone. He'd mentioned marriage. Maybe theirs would be permanent like her grandparents had been. Theirs had been until death parted them. She'd hope and pray every day for that kind of marriage and try to ignore the example her parents had set.

He unlocked the door and then caught her off-guard when he swept her up in his arms. She squealed and locked her arms around his neck.

"Mason!"

He grinned and stepped through the doorway. "What? I told you I wanted to start as I intend to continue. Isn't it customary to carry a bride over the threshold?"

She laughed as he kicked the door shut behind them. "But we're not married yet."

He grinned and headed straight for the stairs. "In my heart, we already are. How does a shower sound? I think I'd like to wash off the river."

She sighed and leaned her head on his shoulder. "That sounds lovely."

He kicked in the door to her bedroom and walked straight to the bed. Gently, he set her on her feet. She smiled and turned her back to him, putting her hands on the side of the bed.

"Will you undo my zipper?"

He groaned, sliding his hands down her spine to her ass and then back up to find the zipper on the sun dress she'd put on at Helen's before the fish fry. His fingers were electric, sending shock waves through her body.

She was so wet for him already. She pressed her thighs together as fabric rustled behind her. The cool air hit her ass as he flipped her dress up.

He palmed her cheeks and gripped them, making her gasp. "Oh, how I've missed you, little bird. You have no idea."

She shuddered a breath, falling to her elbows on the side of the bed. "Tell me."

His hands paused, then he found the zipper and eased it down. Her dress pooled on the ground, leaving her in a pink polka dotted thong.

His finger ran down her spine slowly, inch by inch, making goosebumps spread on her flesh. "What do you want me to say, little bird?"

"Mason." His name was a plea on her lips, a prayer for more, a cry for completion. His breath tickled her ear, his body heat close but not close enough.

His voice was gravelly in the dim light of the room, the plug-in night light from the open bathroom door their only light.

"Do you want me to tell you how often I jerked off to your pictures? How I imagined your sweet lips wrapped around my dick?"

She moaned, her eyes closing as she swayed and spread her legs, pushing her ass back toward him.

"Or do you want me to tell you how I never want to be with anyone else ever again? I haven't so much as looked at another girl. You're like ambrosia. One taste wasn't enough to live on. I need to keep coming back for more."

He palmed her ass again, but his enveloping heat moved behind her. Then he kissed her ass. She gasped, squirming to get relief.

"Can I taste you, Lucy?" he asked, biting softly on her flesh.

She gasped, feeling her core clench. "You're the master. You tell me."

He chuckled, then he nudged her thighs wider. "Now there's a good little bird, such a good girl. If that's how you want to play this, then let's go. Put your knees on the bed."

His demand sent a thrill along her spine, and she pushed her ass back toward him, standing on her tiptoes. "But I want—"

He kissed one cheek, then the other, kneading her flesh softly.

"I thought I was the master?" he chuckled.

She moaned and eased one knee onto the bed, then the other. "Yes, master," she gasped.

His fingers dug into her ass, making her shake with need. "That's a good girl."

His finger dipped under the seam of her thong, and her breathing grew ragged. Her brain stuttered as she focused solely on his hands easing the thong down her hips to the floor. She crawled onto the edge of the bed on all fours and stuck her ass in the air. She spread her knees wide with her ankles hanging off the bed.

He groaned and ran his hands up the sides of her thighs. "God, do you know what you do to me, love? Seeing you spread out so open for me to do whatever I want?"

She felt a thrill at the new nickname. He loved her.

"Do it. Have your way with me."

His hands paused on her ass, "I want to worship you, but I'll only use my mouth."

"What? Why—I want to feel you inside me, Mason."

He chuckled, kissing her cheek again. "Is it safe for the baby?"

She gasped as he gripped her ass, spreading her cheeks wide. He was as sweet as honey, more addicting than sugar. And just like a bee, he had a stinger that could hurt or protect.

Or give her so much pleasure she saw stars.

She wiggled at him like a bird trying to catch the attention of a mate. "Trust me, all the books say it's fine. Maybe go slow at first since it's been a while?"

He trailed a finger down her crack, making her twitch. "Oh, I can definitely do that. Anything for you, my love."

She whimpered, both at the words and at his touch. He caressed her clit in a small, soft circle.

Her breath fractured, and she cried out, "God, yes."

"This is what you want, Luce?"

He started at the top and slid his finger down, circling it

again, over and over until she wanted to scream. Instead, she hit the bed with her fist. "Mason, please."

He chuckled, his hands massaging her ass and moving away from her clit. "Ah, there it is. Beg for me, sweetheart."

She whimpered. "Mason, please. Fuck me. Fuck me now."

He growled, "In a minute. But first, the feast of the gods."

She gasped as he spread her cheeks wide and licked her pussy from behind. Then his mouth found her clit, and she gave a surprised jerk before moaning. She buried her face in the bed as pleasure shot through her. Her toes curled as the pressure mounted.

She pushed her ass back, and his nose teased her entrance. She teetered on the brink, then fell over the cliff. With a shriek, her body shook as sensation ripped through her. It tore her apart like a hurricane. Heart pounding, body quivering, she saw white spots behind her closed eyelids.

Her entire body shuddered and clenched, jerking and shaking as she floated down from her climax.

His mouth released her, and she sank onto the bed, ass still in the air. "You liked that, little bird? Do you want more, or do you want the main course?"

The tip of his cock swirled around her wet opening, and she pushed back against him. "Give me your dick," she gasped.

She moved closer to the edge of the bed, wiggling and chasing his cock until he grabbed her hips and eased the tip in. She wiggled again, trying to thrust back on him.

He gripped her ass with his big hands and held her still. She jerked, trying to make him go deeper, but he held her too tight. She didn't move at all, and it made her clench and moan on him. "Oh, someone likes being helpless, do they?"

he asked, his voice deep as he rubbed her ass, spreading her cheeks.

She whimpered and arched her back. "Please. More."

He gripped her hips and eased himself in, too slowly, bringing him all the way to the hilt. They both groaned, his fingers on her hips biting into her flesh. She clenched around him, enjoying the feel of him, the stretch, the burn.

"God, I've missed you," she said.

He traced a finger up her spine, just holding her still as she clenched around him to get used to the sensation again. "I missed you too, love. Are you ready for more? I'm sorry, I'm not sure I can go slow. You feel so damn good," he groaned, sliding out slowly and plunging deep.

She mewled and jerked as he stilled again. She hit the bed. "Fuck me slow. Fuck me hard. Don't care. Just fuck me."

His fingers flexed on her hips, and he growled, "Thank God."

He slid slowly out and stilled at the entrance. She panted, her arms shaking in anticipation. His hand settled around her braid, gripping it tight and pulling her head back. Her back arched, and she cried out as he slammed back in.

Her heat captured him in a tidal wave of pleasure, and she surfed the bumpy ride, holding onto the sheets like a lifeline. Pleasure shot through her with every deep thrust, sizzling through every part of her until she was on the brink.

When they came, it was with the heat of the sun. Their bodies shuddered together, and she screamed her pleasure. Their souls fused in one hot, sticky release that bound them for all eternity.

He collapsed into a tangle of limbs, rolling them to the

side to spoon. She turned her head and met his wondrous gaze.

"I love you, Mason."

He reached for her hand, cupping her cheek, and she relished their connection, still present despite the physical aspect now being over.

His panting breath echoed hers. "I love you too, sunshine."

Her body relaxed, a sigh of contentment on her lips, and she realized this was all she'd ever wanted, a partner to ride the waves with.

He kissed her softly and said, "Come on. Let's wash off the river and sweat so we can go to bed. I can't wait to sleep with you in my arms again. I feel like I've not slept at all since we've been apart."

Her heart melted as he helped her from the bed and walked hand in hand to the bathroom. The bright lights blinded her, and the water turned on. Then he gathered her in his arms and just held her while they waited for it to warm.

He sighed. "I'm so glad we could finally talk today and work this out. I want to be close to you always."

She bit her lip and snuggled into his chest. "And you're happy about the baby?"

His arms squeezed her as he replied, "I'm thrilled. I'm not getting any younger, and my job isn't the best family life. I now know why you asked so many questions about my career earlier. Are you sure *you're* okay with it and how it might affect you and the baby, our family?"

She smiled and nodded, liking the sound of their family.

"I'm sure. I've always thought having a family was for everyone else, but not me. I never saw how I could move past this lonely little bubble I've lived in my whole life.

Having a family is a dream I never dared to dream. But with you? You make me think all dreams are possible."

He kissed the side of her head, then checked the water, and together, they stepped into the shower. "You anchor me, Luce. With the injury, I felt adrift at sea, unsure of where the tide would take me. I was so afraid of the Rangers kicking me to the curb. The Marshals are an entirely different company culture but such similar missions. I'm finally excited about work again, but it pales in comparison to how excited and happy I am to be with you."

She smiled and undid her braid while he lathered up. "I'm so glad you're happy, Mason."

His blue eyes pierced hers with a heavy look. "You keep me grounded in reality, give me something to look forward to that's not work. You remind me that there's more to life than work. With you, I have fun again. Go on adventures. See the world. Life seems brighter with you in it, and I never want to let you go."

His arms wrapped around, and they held each other. Finally, they switched places again. He washed the soap off while she scrubbed her hair.

"The baby is going to eat into your writing time," he said quietly.

She shrugged. "I know, although the last few months without you, I've made great progress. I'm running it through edits now."

His eyes widened. "Wait, you finished it?"

She shrugged shyly. "Just the first round."

He wrapped her in a hug and did a little naked dance in the shower. "That's amazing, little bird. I knew you could do it."

She giggled as he released her, only for his lips to cut off her laugh. She gasped at the power of it. Her toes curled as his body was branded to hers. He made her feel things she'd never felt before, and he was all hers forever. Almost.

Her breath lodged in her throat, and she deepened the kiss. She was hot but wasn't sure if her cheeks were flushed from being outside in the sun all day or from him or from the shower.

She was breathless at his love, his encouragement. She wrapped her arms around his shoulders, and her stomach leaped.

He gasped, breaking the kiss and jerking back. "What was that?"

She giggled. "The baby kicked. Here." She took his hand and placed it on the left side of her bump. It happened again, and the look of awe on his face brought tears to her eyes.

"That's—this is—oh Lucy, thank you. This is the best gift."

The tears rolled, and she ignored them. She rinsed her hair, but his hands didn't leave her stomach until the water turned cold. When they were snug in the bed, he spooned her again, his hand on their baby.

She smiled, feeling safe, warm, and loved, thankful that it was so vastly different to how she'd gone asleep just last night.

"I love you, sunshine," he murmured sleepily.

She smiled, her body relaxing as they both held a hand to her stomach. "I love you too, master."

Next in the Crimson Creek Series

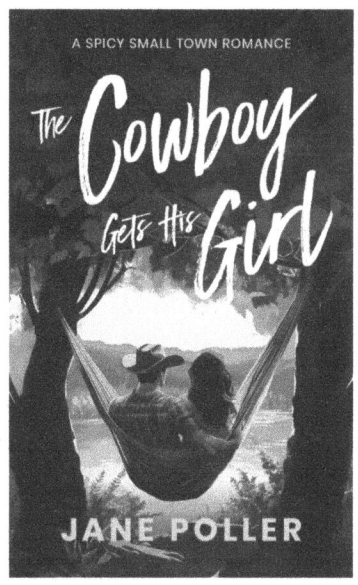

vinci-books.com/cowboy-gets-his-girl

She's a wildfire waiting to happen—and he's ready to get burned.

Librarian Taylor hides her wild heart beneath a sweet facade, but brooding cowboy Hunter sees right through it. He's sworn off local romance—but their age-gap attraction is irresistible. Can they tame each other's hearts, or will their passion burn out of control?

Turn the page for a free preview…

The Cowboy Gets His Girl: Chapter One

July

Hunter prowled the Electric Cowboy, sticking to the edges of the dance floor as he casually searched. He smiled at acquaintances as he passed, the music loud enough to make speaking difficult. That was fine by him. He wasn't much of a talker.

Actions were much better. Body language went a long way too. He'd spent the better part of fifteen years in and out of this little honky-tonk bar in Crimson Creek. He'd played drums in a band with his brothers, and their weekends were full, keeping them out of trouble in their early twenties.

Except someone had been missing. He looked around the dance floor, searching for his long-lost brother. Gunner and Landry had already gone home with their wives. His littlest brother, Parker, was dancing and laughing, grinding on some girl. But not Chase.

He walked past the bar and the mingling crowd to the

side room, pushing open the saloon doors. It was quieter here, but not by much. The crowd at one-thirty in the morning was mostly desperate drunks. He snorted. Or people like him, Parker, and Chase who had nothing to go home to.

As the oldest, it was his job to make sure everyone was taken care of. That included making sure his two bachelor brothers got home safely. Or at the very least, didn't drink and drive.

Couples were playing pool together, with one guy thrusting his hips into the ass of a woman bent over the pool table. Hunter knew her act. She liked to pretend to be an amateur pool player to get the guys to teach her, lean into her just like they were now. Then they'd end up in the parking lot or at the seedy motel on the outskirts of town.

He'd fallen for that trap a time or two in his youth. Different time, a different girl, but always the same result. *Nothing gold can stay.*

Several nodded and waved at him. To them, he was just a rough, quiet cowboy needing to escape a big family and a big ranch.

Maybe it was time to find a girlfriend. His family had long since stopped bugging him to bring a girl around. He hadn't dated in years, instead preferring to pick up a girl here once or twice a week.

Would a girlfriend help shake him out of this funk and get him back to normal? Two of his brothers were married with kids now, and sometimes he looked at them and wanted that acceptance and love. It wasn't quite outweighing the caution he'd felt since his last big breakup, though.

He wasn't sure there was a woman who could handle all of him. The itch was back, not that it ever really left. He needed to get outdoors and lose himself for days, but with their parents pushing him to take over more responsibility on the ranch, his ability to just disappear when he needed to get away was gone.

Plus, he had to help Chase.

He sighed and turned to walk through the back door to the fenced-in patio. Fire pits were burning even though it was a hot July night. This was where people were lounging at the outdoor bar and talking. All of them except Chase.

Chase leaned against the wall, arms crossed and feet wide apart, eyes wide, watchful, and wary. Tonight was his brother's first night at the Cowboy. It was a momentous occasion. Both of their married brothers and wives had come out to show their support too, but they'd long since left.

He stared at Chase as he walked. Hunter remembered that feeling of newness, the wide-eyed awe. The excitement of this place had first brought him here over a decade ago. It had been his home away from home, his oasis and sanctum. With all the expectations that came with being the eldest of five boys and running his parent's ranch, Hunter had needed the escape.

It'd been a long time since he'd felt anything like that. He'd gotten more and more depraved as time went on, but for almost a year now, he'd felt... lackluster about everything. Nothing changed, nothing made him feel alive anymore. It was just something he did, like checking the fences or washing dishes for Ma after Sunday dinner.

He was in a rut and didn't know how to get out of it.

Hunter joined Chase and leaned against the wall. Together, they gazed at the people around them.

It wasn't as loud out here, so he had no problem hearing

Chase as he said, "Hunter, I know you mean well, but can we go home now? It's too overwhelming."

Hunter sighed. "I know, but it was good for you to get out, Chase. The first six months, you were practically a recluse. You've been easing into life on the outside for the last year, right? You've been taking it slow and easy, but it's time to join the real world."

Chase shrugged. "I'm not like you, Hunter. I don't need to lose myself in a crowd. I just want to go home."

Hunter frowned but didn't say anything. He'd need to think about that. Did he love this place because he could lose himself for a while? He needed to mull that over.

Landry and Parker thrived with a crowd of people. That's why they were front and center in the band for all those years. They knew how to work the crowd. But Hunter preferred watching from the shadows, hanging back and observing.

Gunner was a chameleon. He could sit back and observe in the shadows, or he could step up to the mic and take charge like the sheriff he was. Chase was the closest to him, even after all the years away. He shook his head and smiled. Some things just never changed.

"You were in prison for fifteen years, Chase. So that's fifteen years plus the past year of freedom. I don't know how you kept your sanity all this time, but I'm glad you haven't changed too much."

Chase grimaced and shrugged. "I changed plenty. Prison makes you grow up quick." Chase's voice was gravelly and deep, hidden with things he'd not say yet. Hunter kept waiting for him to open up, but maybe his brother needed a softer touch. Lord knows his other brothers had gotten softer once they'd met and married their women.

Hunter smiled and shoved his hands into his pockets.

"Fair enough, but it's time to rejoin society and build a new life. Maybe even find a nice girl and take her home."

Chase snorted. "I'm not sure this is the right place to meet someone. It hasn't worked that great for you after all."

Hunter chuckled. With the way couples were cuddled up around the fire pits, he had to admit his brother was right.

His lips twisted in self-deprecation. "I guess you're right. Fine, let's head home."

Chase pushed off the wall, and Hunter led the way back inside, people-watching as they walked. It was much like watching the herd of horses on his parents' ranch.

Hunter's mind wandered, clinically noting Parker's moves on the dance floor and filing away tips he could offer later. His job as big bro never ended, even on his free nights.

He waved at Katie, the Electric Cowboy's owner. They'd grown up together. He'd even dated her way back when but had quickly realized they made better friends. Maybe that was why this was the one place where he'd been able to scratch the itch that was always under his skin.

He felt comfortable here. Safe and relaxed. Katie smiled and pointed to the dance floor with a lifted brow. Hunter glanced back as Parker stumbled on the edge of the crowd. He frowned and nodded at Katie, then caught Chase's eye and jerked his chin toward Parker.

Chase frowned and together they walked over to where he and a petite, curvy girl were drunkenly dancing together. Parker stumbled again, and Chase grabbed him, bumping into Parker's dance partner who was probably barely legal.

She spun on knee-high leather boots and jerked. Her sleeveless arms waved around in panic, and Hunter stepped in and caught her to his chest with a grunt.

The smell of strawberries rushed him. The feel of her

body flush against his seemed to stop time. His hands slid around her back in a hungry hello. Instinct made her clutch his biceps. Her back arched into him, pressing them closer as she gasped. The feel of her, the sound out of her mouth, the look of surprise... it all made the itch under his skin roar into a full-fledged need of hot desire.

Her head shot up, and she stared at him with bright green eyes. Her mouth was still open in surprise, and the ruby red lipstick made her plump and kissable lips beg for his attention. He pictured those red satin lips encircling his dick, and her dark green eyes looking up at him with just this look.

Her eyes widened in surprise. Her long black hair tickled his hands on her back. His hands tightened with the need to wrap her high, sleek ponytail in his fist.

Her features were sharp, but her face was round. It wasn't beautiful in the classical sense but arrested his attention in its uniqueness. Her button nose was a little too wide, but it matched her wide mouth.

Chase nudged him in the back and almost had to yell to be heard over the music. "Come on, man. Let's get him home. He's practically falling asleep."

"Take him outside. Let me get her sorted out."

Hunter shifted, his cock now painfully hard, and glanced down at the little woman in his arms. His heart was pounding in time to the music as he finally registered what he was seeing and feeling.

Shock made his fingers curl on her lower back.

Her strapless red dress had pulled down to her stomach when she tripped into his arms. And she was braless.

Her breasts were probably bigger than his hands. They were round and full and pressed against his chest. His mouth watered, and he wondered what color her nipples were. It was too dark on the dance floor to tell, with how she was pressed against him.

What would she taste like? Strawberries and cream? Salty popcorn?

Oh god, where had that thought come from? He was a gentleman. He juggled her in his arms and jerked her dress up as she giggled. Disappointment slithered along his spine as he wasn't able to see her nipples, and he refused to take advantage and cop a feel.

Her arms seemed to tighten on his biceps, and her smile got impossibly wider.

"It's not even our first date yet, and you're already to first base, slugger. How long will it take you to hit it out of the park?" She laughed at her own joke.

His heart seemed to stall at the sound. It vibrated through him, sparking life and something else deep in his soul. He wanted this woman with such intensity that it scared him. He felt like he was on a very high cliff, staring into her green eyes that begged him to jump.

He took a deep breath and the smell of stale beer and body odor from the dancers around him brought him back to reality. He shook his head and grinned. "Not sure you're in any condition to make that decision, sugar tits."

She laughed again, and he spun them slowly toward the bar. Every step was painfully tight in his pants. Hunter kept a careful eye on her chest to make sure her dress stayed up.

You sure that's the reason you're staring, son?

Hunter felt a pang in his chest at the ever-present voice in his head.

"Condition, decision. You're a poet!" Her voice wasn't as slurred as he'd expected, but she was definitely leaning on him and unsteady on her feet.

He grunted, "Maybe." He slid his arm around her back to keep her upright.

She wrapped an arm around his waist to walk by his side, not even questioning him leading her toward the bar. "Are you really? Don't joke around about it, for fuck's sake."

He shrugged. "Maybe I am, maybe I'm not. You'll never know."

She scowled. "What kind of answer is that? A home-run would've been *yes, I'm a poet. Can I read some to you?*" She said the last in a faux deep, mocking voice. She was witty for being drunk.

He barked a laugh as they stopped in front of Katie at the bar. Her brows rose in surprise as she asked, "What can I get you?"

Hunter nodded at the girl he loosely held against the bar. He was afraid if he let go, she'd fall down. "She needs some water."

The girl frowned up at him, opened her mouth to say something, then seemed to think better of it. "You know, I think you're right."

Katie slid a tall glass over, and said, "Why don't you let Hunter take you home?"

Hunter rolled his eyes at Katie and sighed.

The girl almost inhaled the water as she chugged. When she set it down with a thunk, she wiped her mouth with the back of her hand. "Are you sure that's a good idea? What if he's a serial killer or something? No, I think I'd better call a cab."

Hunter snorted. "No cabs out here, sugar tits. Did you drive?"

She nodded, "Yeah, but I'm not going to drive. I might be tipsy, but I'm not stupid. Don't worry." She squinted at Katie and leaned over the bar a little.

Hunter held his breath, waiting for her breasts to pop out of her dress again. He both desperately craved it and dreaded the thought of everyone else seeing her like that.

"Psst. Is he a good guy? If he takes me home, is he going to take advantage of me?"

Hunter scowled down at the back of her head, but Katie just waved a hand and chuckled.

"He's fine. He's a pretty good guy. He might look it, but he's not the take-advantage type."

The girl looked up at him with a squint. He wondered what she saw, and he shifted self-consciously, then she almost bent double. His hands immediately went to her waist to steady her.

He swallowed, finding his crotch pressed against her ass. Before he could register it, she was straightening and holding up her phone. She waved it around and grinned at him.

"Ah ha! Here we go. I'm going to text my friend and tell her you're taking me home, and if you try any funny business, you'll find yourself on the wrong side of the US Marshals. I know a guy."

Hunter rolled his eyes but stood still as she held up her phone and took pictures of him.

Katie chuckled. "You don't have to worry, sugar. His brother is the sheriff and isn't afraid to beat him up if he crosses the line."

Hunter pursed his lips. "Like he could ever take me." Katie laughed, but he continued, looking down at the little pint-sized bombshell. "But she's right. I'll get you home safe, and that's it. Nothing to worry about."

She glanced at him through her thick lashes and nodded before looking back down at her phone. When she finished, she grabbed his arm and lifted her leg to slide the phone back inside her boot.

Katie wiped the counter. "Y'all be safe."

"Thanks, Katie. See you next time," he said as he slid a hand along the girl's back and navigated them to the door.

They pushed into the hot, humid air, and he led her through the parking lot. "What's your name?"

She held out a hand, and he had to let her go to shake. She swayed but remained upright. "I'm Taylor, and I'm new to town. What's your name again?"

He smiled and hovered around her as she walked, gently holding her elbow as they talked. "Hunter."

She glanced up at him and smiled. "Ooh, are you going to hunt me down and eat me?"

It was his turn to stumble, and she giggled. They reached the Jeep, and he growled, "I'd love nothing better, sugar tits."

The Cowboy Gets His Girl: Chapter Two

Hunter grinned as she giggled, and he spied Chase and Parker on the passenger side, leaning against the vehicle. He squeezed her hip where her dress flared, falling to mid-thigh. Under his hand, he couldn't feel any underwear either. He swallowed past the lump in his throat and reached into his pocket for the keys.

And to adjust yourself like some green boy outta high school.

Taylor nodded like a bobble head, then held a hand to her cheek to force her head to stop. "It's been too long for me, personally, but like you said... I'm in no condition to make that decision."

She giggled again, and Hunter gritted his teeth to unlock the Jeep. He was still painfully hard. Chase got Parker in the backseat while Hunter helped the mystery woman.

"Where do you live, Taylor?" he asked as he flipped his drivers' seat up so she could climb into the back.

She put her knees on the floorboard, and her ass was waving almost in his face. Her red dress rode up to show

The Ranger Gets His Girl

cheek. Her bare thighs were ripe for the plucking. He wanted to flip her dress up and bite her ass.

Would her skin turn pink or red if he bit into it? How much could she take? Was she a screamer or a moaner? Either way, she'd be yelling by the time he was done with her, loving every moment. Was she as much of a glutton for it as he was?

She wiggled, and the lower curve of her ass peeked out from the bottom of her dress. He sucked in a breath and muttered, "Fuck me."

She wavered, her boot caught on the door frame. His hands were suddenly on both her hips to steady her.

Yeah right.

"I got you," he growled and unhooked her foot to help her crawl onto the seat. When she flopped onto the seat, her dress twisted and both tits popped out again. "Fucking hell."

"You alright back there? Need a hand?" Chase asked.

His fingers yearned to touch her, his mouth to taste her. Raw, wild need slid through his veins. He watched them sway, her nipples pebbling. Damn the light from the Jeep; he still couldn't tell what color they were.

"No, I've got two hands. I can handle it." His voice was choked. He knew exactly how he wanted to handle her. Rough, fast, and hard for starters.

She looked down at her bare, perky breasts and giggled again as she reached to pull up the dress. She struggled and yanked too hard, showing the crease in her leg where her thigh met her—

"Dear Lord, woman, get yourself under control," he said too harshly.

Her head popped up, and she froze with raised

eyebrows. She looked like a deer in the headlights, and a pang of guilt at the harsh words speared through him.

She frowned and stilled, putting her hands in her lap. "Yes, sir."

He stared into her green eyes for a beat too long, neither of them backing down. She was quick to listen, and the ideas spun in his head, teasing him and tempting him like he hadn't felt in a few years.

He reached for her seatbelt and buckled her in, thankful that her dress covered her tits again. The entire time, she stared wide-eyed at him, watching and waiting.

His voice was low and gruff as he felt for the belt buckle. It clicked into place, and he slowly moved his hands down her bare thighs before letting them drop to his side.

His mind felt dazed, drunk on the essence of her. He had to focus.

He cleared his throat and deliberately gentled his voice. "Taylor, if I'm going to take you home, I need to know where you live."

She nodded slowly and frowned. "I—I don't know exactly."

His brow furrowed. "What the hell does that mean?"

She flinched and seemed to shrink into herself. Then her spine straightened, and she leaned forward and reached into her boot. She pulled out her phone again and fumbled with it. Then she turned it around and showed him.

"I just moved into these apartments. Do you know where it is?" Her voice was much more slurred now, and he nodded as he slid his seat back to its normal position and climbed in beside Chase.

Hunter looked in the rear-view mirror as he shut the door and started the Jeep. Parker was out cold and leaning against the window. Chase sat with arms crossed, but a small smirk played on his lips.

"Don't start," Hunter grumbled, glancing at the goddess in the backseat.

He backed up and drove toward town. *Bruno Mars* blared on the radio, automatically connecting to his phone, and he started tapping his thumbs on the steering wheel.

Suddenly, she started singing softly from the back seat, her words slurred but keeping up well. He turned it up at the chorus, and they all sang almost at the top of their lungs.

Even Chase got into it, for once seeming to relax and smile as they sang. When the next song came on, she sang softly, but by the fourth song, she was quiet.

He pulled up in front of the apartment complex and parked. When he opened the door and flipped up his seat, she was out like a light. He frowned and unzipped her boot to find her phone, key, and a tiny wallet. He rifled through it, but none of it said which apartment was hers.

"What's the problem?" Chase asked.

Hunter explained and then shook her knee. "Taylor? Wake up, sugar. I need you to tell me which apartment."

She didn't move, just sighed and leaned her head back. She looked so peaceful in sleep, but he knew she was a dirty girl underneath that innocent exterior. He could feel it in his bones, had seen it in her eyes.

Chase said, "Check her phone? Any saved locations?"

Hunter used her thumbprint to unlock the phone, then he went to her map and searched for home. He sighed. "Thank God, it worked. Apartment 203."

He zipped her boot back up and tucked her phone and wallet into his back pocket. Then he gripped her key and eyed her.

"You're going to have to throw her over your shoulder, you know," Chase said.

Hunter sighed and nodded. He couldn't get her out of the back seat any other way. "Just avert your gaze. I don't want you staring at more of her than necessary."

Chase chuckled, but Hunter ignored the stab of jealousy that made him grind his teeth together. He grabbed her arm and eased her onto his shoulder. Then he slowly backed up and juggled until she was securely slung over his shoulder like a sack of potatoes.

His arm wrapped around her thighs, but he was afraid to tug down on her dress. He wasn't even sure if her breasts were still confined on his back. Hunter walked up the stairs to her apartment and unlocked the door, dropping the key on a table. He flicked the light and looked around.

Boxes were along every wall, but there was no big furniture to speak of. He went through one of the open doors to the single bedroom and flipped another light. A mattress lay on the floor, the headboard and frame still leaning against the wall.

He knelt and laid her down as best he could. Her legs landed on either side of his knees. She moaned, and the sound went straight through him. The tent in his pants hadn't gone down since he'd met her.

Her hands flopped to the side and her breasts popped free once more. He was on all fours with this gorgeous woman under him. He couldn't resist another look. Dusky nipples pebbled at the air. They were a mix between rose pink and strawberries.

He needed a taste. His mouth watered, and his hands clenched into the bedsheets to keep from reaching for her. He had to leave before he did something fucking stupid.

He went to push up, but then her arms were around his neck, pulling him down.

"Stay," she whispered, her lips raking along his jaw. "Don't leave me."

Her voice was like a dagger to the soul, and he ached to give her everything she desired. He'd never had such a visceral reaction to a woman's soft pleading whisper.

He groaned and let her pull him flush with her plump body. Her hips rose to meet his, and she ground herself on his dick.

"Shit, no, Taylor—you're not, I can't—damn it." He groaned and reached to untangle her hands. "Go to sleep, sugar."

She squeezed and resisted him, pressing her lips to his. He froze. Her lips were soft and plump and tasted like strawberries. He fucking loved strawberries. The scent flooded his nostrils, making his mouth water more.

But he had to be strong, for both of them. He pressed his lips to hers, but refused to open his mouth and dive into everything she was offering.

He pulled back, jerking her hands free and stumbling to his feet. She was sprawled on the bed, her dress bunched around her waist and barely hiding her lady bits.

She should've looked like a hot mess, but all he saw was the most gorgeous woman who didn't give two fucks what anyone else thought. He was mesmerized.

He adjusted himself and walked to the bathroom door. He rifled through a box and found a bottle of pain pills, then went to the kitchen and found a bottle of water in the fridge.

When he went back to her bedroom, she had turned onto her stomach and had one leg hiked to the side. Her bare ass made his mouth water, the thong barely visible.

But her gorgeous face was relaxed in sleep, one hand near her cheek and the other behind her. It took all his willpower to set both bottles on the side table near her bed, pull her boots off, cover her with a blanket, and high tail it out of there.

He was practically sweating by the time he got back to the Jeep. Chase stared at him when he climbed into the driver's seat. "You survived?"

Hunter slammed his door. "Barely."

Chase laughed, and Hunter drove them home, not even bothering to take Parker to his own apartment. Hunter was fucking done.

Tits and ass haunted him as he drove, but it was a magical laugh and big green eyes that flooded his dreams that night.

The Cowboy Gets His Girl: Chapter Three

Taylor woke up with a headache that put all others to shame. The pounding in her head wouldn't quit, and her eyes were glued shut.

She groaned, but the pounding continued, now with a muffled voice added to it. She lifted her hands and rubbed her eyes. God, what time was it?

She blinked and forced them open. Oh yeah, she'd moved. This was her new apartment. She really needed to get the curtains up. Light streamed through the window and across her bed.

She sat up and held her head. The pounding faded but a faint voice came through her open bedroom doorway.

"Tay? Are you here? You better be here or so help me God, I'll—"

She rubbed her eyes again before squinting at the door. "I'm here, I'm here," she grumbled as she climbed to her knees and stood up on wobbly legs.

Her best friend Lucy walked through the door with her

baby boy on her hip. She gasped, her cheeks immediately turning pink as her jaw dropped.

"Taylor Anne Grimes, you're naked!" Lucy nearly shouted.

The noise made Taylor squint, and she looked down. Her dress was bunched around her waist and her boobs flopped as she stumbled out of her dress and to a box in the corner.

She pulled out clean clothes, turning her back to Lucy, and mumbled, "I wasn't, but I am now. Who let you in?"

"I have a key, remember?"

"I believe your key is for emergencies. What if I had a guy in here?" Taylor glanced over as she walked to the adjoining bathroom.

Lucy rolled her eyes and turned back into the living room. Lucy's voice floated to her through the open doors. "It wouldn't be the first time I'd have walked in on you and a guy."

Lucy's voice droned on, but Taylor tuned her out. She turned on the shower and brushed her hair out while she waited for it to heat.

Her head pounded, and she looked around the bathroom for her bottle of aspirin. When she didn't find it, she went back to her bedroom where she found it next to her bed with a bottle of water.

She frowned and popped the pills. She didn't put the water there, so how did it... She was mid-drink when she froze, remembering parts of last night.

Fuzzy memories flowed through her head. There were some guys. Or one guy? Brown hair, hazel laughing eyes, and strong arms. She definitely remembered strong arms carrying her up the stairs.

"It's almost lunchtime, and I didn't even know if you'd

made it home. The last thing I got was a text with a blurry picture of one of the Williams' boys. Did he bring you home? What the hell happened after Mason and I left the bar last night?"

Taylor shook her head and said over her shoulder, "I'll tell you after the shower. I feel so gross."

She shut the bathroom door behind her, not in a mood to listen to Lucy yet. She loved her like a sister, but after six years of rooming together, she needed a few minutes to herself. Thankfully Lucy was used to her walking around naked.

She quickly braided her hair, loosely because her head still hurt. Then she stepped into the shower and leaned her head against the cool tiles. There'd been lots of drinking and dancing. The songs had changed after Lucy had left. That's when it all went downhill.

Then that man had shown up and rescued her from herself. What had Lucy said? A Williams' boy? She lathered up and scrubbed away hard, trying to wash away memories of her past like Lady Macbeth.

A thought made her frantically give a quick inspection, then she sighed in relief.

She might have woken up naked, but she wasn't covered in anything other than sweat. Even better news was that she wasn't sore between her legs, so nothing had happened.

Thank God. She had just turned twenty-four and had moved to this little town to escape her bad habits back in Denton. It wouldn't have been a good start for her to wake up to—

She shut down the thoughts. That wasn't who she was anymore. Grown up, graduated, and no longer living near campus, she had her own apartment and lived by herself. She was strong and could do this adulting thing.

She turned off the water and put on a clean pair of black leggings and a crop top before brushing her teeth and finally opening the door to face her bestie.

Lucy was in the kitchen pulling items out of boxes and putting them in drawers. The baby was playing on a blanket in the still empty living room. She didn't have a TV or a couch or even a coffee table.

Their apartment in Denton had been furnished except for their mattresses. Most of these boxes held things Lucy had collected when she'd moved out last year after graduation. A few were Taylor's mom's stuff finally pulled out of storage.

Those boxes remained stacked neatly against the living room wall. Taylor would happily wait years before opening those, but Lucy thought it was time.

Lucy glanced over and arched her brows, her brown hair pulled up in a bun. "Are you feeling more human? I've made coffee."

Taylor made a beeline for the coffee pot, then sank onto the floor, leaning against the wall as Lucy continued busying herself putting things away.

"We're still going to the resale shops, right? You need furniture. Mason is coming home at lunch, so he'll provide all the muscle. We just have to go pick the stuff out and wait for him in Denton."

Taylor nodded slowly, popping her neck and stretching. Harry crawled over to her and smiled. Taylor held her coffee up safely out of reach and played with him with her other hand. He sat back on his haunches and clapped and babbled.

She smiled at this sweet, innocent, precious little kid. His big blue eyes tugged on her heart and made her feel less alone.

Lucy picked him up and set him down on his hands and knees facing the other way. Then he took off crawling toward an overturned box.

Taylor chuckled. "Does he ever get tired?"

"Yep, that's why we need to get going to Denton. We have to time our trip so he naps in the car. Otherwise, it'll be a nightmare shopping with him. Are you ready?"

"Let me finish this cup?" Taylor asked as she took another sip of her coffee.

Lucy unpacked another box of mismatched plates and nodded. "That's fine. Where's your phone, by the way?"

Taylor shrugged and finished her coffee, one eye on Harry and mind reliving the events of last night.

Lucy went into her bedroom and returned, sitting in front of her and leaning an elbow on one knee as she stared at Taylor. "I don't see your phone anywhere and have called over and over. You lost it again, didn't you?"

Taylor closed her eyes and leaned her head back against the wall. "Oh god, I—I had it in that guy's Jeep, right? Did I text you then?"

"Yeah, Hunter Williams. Thankfully, you sent me the pictures. Your texts were just a bunch of letters that made no sense. I think his brothers were in the pictures too. Here."

Lucy took her phone from her back pocket and handed it over. Taylor opened her eyes and scrolled up. Most of the images were a blurry mess, but the more she looked, the more her memories returned.

She pulled her knees up, setting the empty coffee mug on the floor and burying her head in her knees as she handed the phone back over. Tears pricked her eyes and her stomach hurt.

"Tay, what happened last night?" Lucy asked softly, her hand patting Taylor's knee.

What happened? The tears fell silently down her cheek. She choked out, "Nothing. They just played some of Mom and Dad's songs."

"Oh hun, I'm so sorry." Lucy shifted, and Taylor felt her arms envelop her in a side hug.

Taylor squeezed her eyes harder, hoping to stop the flow. Stupid emotions that wouldn't stop. It must be the stress of moving and the new job getting to her.

"Have you heard from him lately?"

Taylor shook her head. Her dad only called when he needed bail money, so not hearing from him was a good thing. She wished he was still the man she'd grown up with.

The music had shifted to early eighties last night after her friends had left. It had thrown her into a serious mood. Normally she would've just gone home and read to escape.

But the guy she'd been dancing with had distracted her with drinks and laughs. He'd been competing with another guy for her attention. She didn't remember either of their names.

After a while, she'd stumbled into the Jeep guy. Hunter. A hazy memory made her gasp and her head shot up, eyes wide.

"What?" Lucy asked as she dropped her arms.

Taylor opened and closed her mouth before saying, "The guy who brought me home. Hunter? Oh god, I can't believe I did that."

"Did what? Did you hit on him?"

Taylor rubbed her temples, hoping the pills would kick in soon. "There were some seriously cheesy pickup lines, but that's not the worst part."

Lucy raised her brow skeptically, and Taylor waved her hands wide. "My boobs popped out on the dance floor!"

Lucy barked out a surprised laugh, making Taylor groan. Lucy laughed and Harry crawled over to see what the fuss was about. Lucy picked him up and kissed him, still chuckling.

Taylor frowned. "It's not funny. I was dancing with this other guy and fell into Hunter, and my dress practically fell to my waist."

Lucy's eyes sparkled as her laughter picked up again. Harry crawled away to a tipped over box and pulled clothes out. Taylor stood and righted the box, putting the clothes back in and handing him a random t-shirt to play with.

"I tried telling you not to wear that dress, didn't I? But noooo, you always know what's best." Lucy laughed again and gathered the coffee cup from the floor, then asked, "Weren't you most likely to live in a nudist colony? Why is this a problem?"

Taylor held her head with both hands and leaned against the kitchen counter. "Not in a public place like that. At least in a nudist colony, everyone else is doing it too, you know? Oh god."

Lucy shrugged, setting the cup in the sink. "What did he do when you ran into him with boobs flopping everywhere?"

Taylor rubbed her temples. "He pulled my dress back up, got me some water, and we went to his Jeep. My boobs popped out again, and he might've yelled at me."

"Yelled at you?" Lucy asked, brow arched.

Taylor nodded. "Told me to cover up and called me *woman*."

"Ugh, I know how much you love being called that." Lucy wrinkled her nose, and Taylor glared.

"Exactly. After that it all gets fuzzy, but he obviously brought me home. I remember him carrying me up the stairs, slung over his shoulder. I'm sure my boobs popped out then too and probably my ass. He definitely got more than an eye full."

Lucy giggled and followed her into the bedroom. "Based on your state of undress when I came in, I'd say so. Did y'all fool around?"

Taylor picked up her boots and felt inside with a frown. She shook her head. "No, I don't think so. I don't remember anything after the stairs. I got dizzy and must have blacked out. Damn it, my phone and wallet were in my boot, but now I can't find either of them."

Lucy glanced behind her to check on Harry. "I've told you to be careful about getting drunk in strange places, Tay."

"I know, I know. It's dangerous, but I did ask your boss, Katie, if I'd be safe with him taking me home. That's progress, right?" Katie owned the bar, but also worked at the salon where Lucy did nails.

Lucy sighed. "Yeah, it's a step in the right direction. I just worry about you."

Taylor smiled and pulled on her sneakers. "I know, and I appreciate it and love you so much, you have no idea."

Lucy tilted her head. "Why do I hear a but in there?"

Taylor grinned. "No buts. I wouldn't have moved to your little town if I didn't love you and hate the idea of being apart from you. After spending all that time on the cruise last month for your wedding, I just had to be closer to you. I've missed you this past year and a half."

Lucy's face softened, and she leaned against the bedroom door frame. "I've missed you too, Tay."

Taylor nodded and glanced around before going back

into the living room. "Great. Now that that's settled, we need to track down my phone. Let me pull up the find my phone app."

She found her tablet on the kitchen counter and turned it on. Her brows rose as Lucy looked over her shoulders.

"It's in the middle of nowhere."

Lucy chuckled behind her. "Not nowhere. I think that's Hunter's ranch. Looks like we're taking a detour to see a cowboy about a missing phone."

Taylor groaned and set the tablet down. "I must have dropped it on the floorboard of his Jeep last night. Great. This is just great. I have to face him so soon after I was practically naked."

Lucy's face scrunched in confusion. "You've been naked around plenty of guys. It's not that bad."

"Not that bad? The man practically tucked me in like a child, Lucy!" Taylor said, stomping to the tiny entrance table and grabbing her key. At least that had made it home.

Lucy picked up Harry and grabbed the diaper bag. "You just said practically twice back-to-back. He's really gotten to you, hasn't he?"

Taylor scowled and jerked the door open. "Wouldn't you be mortified if a stranger saw you like that?"

Lucy walked through the door and said, "Definitely, but I'm not you, remember? You're the badass who had the entire college boys track team bowing to you when they'd run into you—on a dare."

Taylor blushed and locked the door. "That was one time," she murmured, but Lucy kept talking as she started down the stairs, squirming Harry in her arm.

"Hunter's a rancher, an outdoorsman and responsible eldest brother. Mason and Ray have actually fished with Hunter a lot. Mason likes their family, and all the Williams' brothers are good people. You've got nothing to worry about with him."

Taylor locked it behind her and followed Lucy down the stairs. "That's great for him, but that doesn't mean I want him to know what I look like naked."

Her heart sank to her stomach as they walked to Lucy's car.

Lucy laughed. "No, I mean that he's always working at the ranch. You're living and working in town. After you get your stuff back, you'll probably never run into him again."

Taylor breathed a sigh of relief as they walked. She was trying to start over and needed to make a good impression with the town. She couldn't go to the bar anymore, last night had been a last hurrah kind of thing. She couldn't go home with pillars of the community like these Williams' boys. She couldn't do dumb shit like she was still a college kid.

It was high time she started acting like the librarian the mayor had hired her to be. It was time to grow up. And it started with facing the tall, dark, and handsome stranger from last night.

Grab your copy…
vinci-books.com/cowboy-gets-his-girl

About the Author

Jane Poller always wanted to write romance. After years of back and forth, she finally took the plunge and never looked back. She still teaches online and homeschools her teenagers full-time. But with a commercial pilot and Army veteran for a hubby, she has a lot of free time in between his trips to write whatever stories the characters demand of her. She lives in Texas in a small town on four acres with her family of four, plus their two dogs. When she's not doing all the family things, she's reading in the hammock by the pond, writing in the treehouse, quilting and crafting, or arguing with her characters who refuse to do what she wants.

www.ingramcontent.com/pod-product-compliance
Ingram Content Group UK Ltd.
Pitfield, Milton Keynes, MK11 3LW, UK
UKHW040122190326
469155UK00004B/1298